The Pursuit

by

Nathan Wright

Nathan Wright

This is a work of fiction. All of the Characters, organizations and events portrayed in this novel are either products of the author's imagination or are used fictitiously.

ISBN: 9781702349659

The Pursuit

The sun was beginning to sink low in the western sky; the day had somehow gotten away from the solitary rider. It was probably another hour and a half before it would become too dark to safely travel and this could present a problem if a suitable campsite wasn't found soon. The trail the rider traveled was nothing more than a deer path but it at least allowed the horse to dodge the worst of the undergrowth. Another thing that slowed the journey was the habit of the horse to pick at anything that looked tasty, she was hungry.

From the saddle horn hung one empty canteen and a second held little more than a sip; it was starting to become worrisome. This part of the Dakotas always had a stream or two, here and there, but this had been an unseasonably dry October. The last water the rider and horse passed had been early that morning just after breaking camp and continuing west. What they had found then was little more than a mud hole that allowed the horse a small drink or two.

The man who rode the horse was someone who preferred silence; the silence of the trail. He had spent time in towns before and found the noise a distraction. He also found townsfolk to be rude and overbearing. Out here all he had to worry about was keeping at least one canteen full of water and a little grass to stake his horse in at night. The land always provided.

As he rode he thought of how the land really did provide and this was a good thing, he had exactly one dollar in his pocket, not counting a few coins that wouldn't add up to another. He needed to find a job for few weeks, maybe even a month, just enough to make some winter money. Things like tobacco and coffee didn't grow on trees, at least not the trees he was seeing now. His horse might like a taste of grain too, the poor girl had made do on weeds and scrub for the last week or two and she was hungry.

The rider was employed but that was a whole nother story. The pay he was due got delivered once a month, but it seemed as of late he wasn't anywhere close to the town where his money waited. The territory didn't mind if one of its own worked a side job or two, the number of miles a man might be required to cover made it nearly impossible to get his pay to him on a regular basis, part time work would see him through.

What he really needed was to hole up someplace where he could work off his keep, a place where his horse could winter in a stall out of the harsh winds and weather. He tried not to worry. Something would turn up, it always did.

Food wouldn't be a problem for at least another day, he still carried part of a deer flank and this would provide supper tonight and breakfast in the morning. As the rider thought about a place to stop for the night he suddenly heard the ratchet sound of a Winchester, the sound was that of a bullet being chambered.

"Hold it right there stranger and don't reach for that iron on your side." The voice came from a man that was well hidden beside the trail.

The Pursuit

The man on the horse slowly looked in the direction the voice came from. Whoever had spoken couldn't be seen. The noise he heard was definitely that of a Winchester and at such close range there was no way a shot would miss. The rider decided he had no choice but to cooperate.

"Alright, what do you want," he asked in a calm voice, a voice that hid his real feelings of distress.

"Toss your gun to the side and then step down off that horse."

The rider slowly pulled his gun from the holster and tossed it near the front of his horse. As he swung a leg over he finally saw the man with the Winchester. He was about ten yards to the right kneeling behind a deadfall with the rifle resting on a forked limb and pointed directly at the rider's chest. A shot from that range would find its mark.

"Alright mister, I'll do as you say. Just keep your finger off that trigger if you don't mind," the rider said.

"You're in no position to be telling anybody what to do. Now step over to that gully to your left and be quick about it. I ain't got all evening to be spending with the likes of you," the man with the Winchester said. These words told the rider all he needed to know, this man intended to kill him.

The gully wasn't more than twenty feet away and already the rider could see that it ran deep, although the water that had carved it had long ago ran dry. It was apparent now that the man with the Winchester intended to shoot the rider and let his body fall into the gully where it would be easily covered with a little dirt and brush. It wouldn't be the first time a murder had been committed in such a way. Murderers liked to make sure their victims were hidden but they rarely took the time to dig a grave, the gully would do the job nicely.

The rider knew he had to do something and he had to do it fast. As he walked toward the gully the man behind the deadfall stood and followed. As the rider walked toward what would surely be his grave he slowly put his right hand into his vest pocket and pulled out a two shot Derringer, his move was hidden by the distance and angle of his body.

"Stop right there and turn around," the man with the Winchester said.

As the rider turned he smoothly brought the Derringer to bear and fired one well-placed shot. The man with the Winchester saw the tiny gun at the same time he heard the shot. He felt a tug at his chest and looked down to see his own blood spreading across the front of his shirt. His grip weakened as he dropped the Winchester and fell to his knees.

The rider stepped closer and kicked the gun away. "Before you die friend, do you mind telling me your name?"

The man just sat there on his knees holding his chest.

"By the amount of blood you're losing I figure you got maybe a minute before you pass. If you want me to notify anyone then you better tell me your name and where you hail from," the rider said.

With a shaky voice the man slowly looked up and said, "My name is Gene Blair, I'm from Kansas." He then let a weak cough escape.

"You got a horse tied up around here Blair?" the rider asked as he scanned his surroundings.

"No, horse went lame a day or so back, had to shoot it."

This explained why the rider had been stopped. "So your horse went lame and you figured on killing me and taking mine. Is that what you had in mind Blair?"

"Sorry mister, I guess I didn't think things out very well did I? And if it's any consolation, I wasn't going to kill you."

The Pursuit

The rider figured the dying man was trying to soothe his own conscious by what he said. He continued to look over his surroundings as he asked, "You traveling alone Blair?"

"I am, been that way nearly all my life." Blair said this with another slight cough but he didn't seem to be getting any closer to death. The amount of blood the man was losing seemed to be less than what it first appeared.

The rider continued to look over his surroundings, something didn't feel right, something other than the fact that he had just prevented his own murder. The man he shot was still kneeling but didn't seem to be any worse than he had been minutes earlier. He would just have to wait and see; maybe the little Derringer hadn't hit anything vital after all.

"How bad do you think you're hurt Blair?"

Blair had held both hands to his chest after being shot and was afraid to look. He knew it hurt like hell and he was having a hard time breathing. "I reckon it's bad mister; I think you done killed me."

The rider walked over and sat on the same deadfall Blair had used to conceal his position. "I'll just wait here a while so as to be able to bury you when the time comes. I figure it's more than you were going to do for me."

The rider pulled out a small pouch and began making himself a smoke. As he sat he continued to look over his surroundings. This wasn't the time to be caught off guard; that had already been taken care of once today.

After the better part of an hour the rider began to wonder what his next move was going to be. The man he shot was still sitting on his knees and didn't seem to be anywhere near death. He hadn't said much, he just slowly rocked back and forth on his knees. This was starting to present a problem; if the man didn't die soon then the rider would be forced to spend the night here. He really needed to find water and he didn't want to do it in the morning, he was thirsty now and so was his horse.

The rider stood and walked to where the wounded man knelt. "Better slide out of that coat and unbutton your shirt and let's have a look at that wound. If you were going to die then I figure you would have already done it by now."

Blair slowly moved his hands away from his chest fully expecting his blood to shoot out the hole the tiny Derringer had made. To his surprise that wasn't what happened. It appeared his wound had stopped bleeding. It still hurt like hell and he was having trouble breathing but all in all he didn't feel like he was at death's door.

After he finally got his tattered coat off and his shirt unbuttoned he looked down to see just how bad he had been shot. To his surprise he could see the bullet. It was lodged just under the skin. There was quite a bit of blood and his entire chest had started to turn the color of black and blue. It appeared the bullet had hit a rib and was slightly to the right of the entrance hole it had made.

The rider pulled his Derringer from his pocket and looked it over. He knew what kind of damage the little gun could do at close range, what he was seeing wasn't it. "I must have had a weak bullet or you would be dead Blair. I've seen it before, not enough powder from the manufacturer."

Blair slowly, with gritted teeth, reached for his coat and this prompted the rider to quickly draw his Colt. "You wouldn't be reaching for a hideaway now would you Blair?"

"No mister, I just figured out why that little gun of yours didn't do the job it was intended for." Blair reached into an inside pocket and pulled out a little book, one of those dime novels. As he looked it over he saw it had a hole clean through it. "You done killed my book mister," he said as he reached the novel to the rider.

The rider looked it over and read the title, "The Taming of the West."

"That was a damn fine book until you put a hole in it," Blair said.

"Shut the hell up Blair, you know you intended on killing me and taking my horse," the rider said. Blair just hung his head.

"You got it wrong mister, I've never killed anyone in my life," Blair said.

As the rider looked over the book he figured Blair was going to stick with the story about not going to kill him. "I reckon if you ain't going to die then I need to get that bullet out," the rider said as he pulled a long thin knife from his belt. Blair saw the knife and tried to back away, the look in his eye was one of pure terror.

"I don't think the bullet is all that bad, let's just leave it be," Blair said. The closer the rider got with the thin knife the more nervous Blair became.

"Nope, lead will kill you in a day or two if I don't get it out. Now the best thing would be for you to have a stiff shot or two of whiskey to dull the pain but we ain't got any of that so we'll just make due."

"Wait mister, I got some whiskey. It's over there with my stuff past that big deadfall," Blair said.

This surprised the rider. "What do you have, a man on foot couldn't be packing much?"

"I had to leave my saddle when I shot my horse; it was a damn fine saddle too. I carried what I could in my saddle bags plus a bed roll. There is also a canvas sack over there, don't leave it," Blair said.

Nathan Wright

"Why was you only carrying a long gun Blair? Anybody this far out in the wilds should have a handgun."

Blair looked in the direction of the deadfall. "I had one but ran out of ammunition a week or so back. When I lost my horse I left it and my gun belt with the saddle. I figured if I was on foot I needed to lighten the load."

"Ran out of ammunition, you make it sound as if you have been shooting at something. That something wouldn't have been another rider would it Blair?"

"You get me that whiskey and then get this bullet out and I'll tell you the story mister. Say, you got a name?" Blair asked.

The rider stood and as he walked toward the deadfall he said, "Jake Stewart."

Blair heard the name and at once took on the look of surprise. When the rider came back he was carrying the pair of saddlebags, along with the bedroll and canvas sack.

"Did I hear you right mister? Did you say your name was Jake Stewart?"

"Not, was Jake Stewart, is Jake Stewart. I don't like being referred to in the past tense."

Blair mulled this over a second or two. "Sounds like you're an educated man. Would you be the same Jake Stewart as the lawman out of North Texas?"

Stewart sat Blair's belongings near where the injured man lay. "I reckon that would be me. I would reach you your stuff but before I do you mind if I have a look inside first?" Stewart said as he was opening the two saddlebags. He had no intention of letting Blair anywhere near his belongings until he made sure there wasn't a weapon hidden inside.

"Go right ahead. I can't believe I've been shot by the likes of you. It will surely make a good story someday now won't it?"

"What makes you think you'll live that long Blair?"

The Pursuit

"Cause I figure you only busted up some of my ribs. They should heal up just fine after a few weeks."

Stewart looked at Blair. "You were going to kill me and leave me for the coyotes. I still might return the favor."

Blair grunted and the effort made him grimace. "How long are you going to hold that grudge Stewart? Just because I was going to do something, but didn't, don't mean you should hold it against me. And I done told you I wasn't going to kill you."

After Stewart was satisfied there wasn't anything in the two saddlebags that could cause him harm he tossed them to Blair. "The bottle of whiskey looks damn near empty. You better be getting a drink or two so the effects will start to take hold before I start carving out that bullet."

Blair did as he was told but as he sipped he kept a curious eye on Stewart. He was wondering what the man would do when he looked inside the canvas sack.

"Before that whiskey takes hold I need to ask if you spotted any water between here and where you said you shot your horse," Stewart asked.

Blair took another small sip from the bottle and grimaced as it burned its way down his throat. "I did at that. About two hours walk due north is a water hole but no stream. It must be fed from down under. I filled my canteen there and continued walking. That was until I heard you and that horse of yours coming along. You can't miss it. There are six or eight healthy looking trees there, I don't know their type. Never was much good and identifying trees and such. You could make it there on that horse of yours in no time at all."

"If you filled your canteen at that water hole then where is it?" Stewart asked.

"Hanging on that deadfall where I tried to bushwhack you," Blair said.

The word 'bushwhack' was spoken by Blair as if it, or its consequences, meant little to the man. It made Stewart feel that it was something that Blair had done before and had no problem doing again.

Stewart walked back to the tree and sure enough hanging on a broken limb was a canteen, it was nearly full. He walked back to Blair and again pulled his knife. "You're about as ready as you're going to get so hold still while I pry out that bullet. If you try anything I promise to shove this knife all the way through your chest."

Before getting any closer he pulled his Colt and placed it out of reach. He didn't relish the thought of the man taking his gun while he focused on the bullet. Two minutes later and the bullet was removed.

"If you got a handkerchief then it might be wise to use it to stop the bleeding. You bleed out now then it will be a lot less trouble on me," Stewart said as he picked up his Colt and returned it to his well-used holster.

Blair did as told and before long the bleeding stopped. "You did that a lot rougher than you had to Stewart. It hurt like hell."

"You're damn lucky I don't mount up and leave your ass out here for the wolves and coyotes. Tell me one good reason why I shouldn't do that anyway?" Stewart said.

Blair decided to push his luck. "Because you're a lawman, don't that mean you took an oath or something to protect folks that are injured?"

Stewart almost laughed. "The oath I took said I would bring justice to those that needed it. You tried to kill me; the justice I want to dish out to the likes of you is a hanging."

Blair thought about what Stewart had just said. The whiskey was taking hold real good now and his inhibition about saying too much was greatly reduced. "I didn't break any laws today Marshal. Just because I thought about doing something ain't a crime and you know it."

It was the first time Blair had used the word *Marshal*. Stewart now knew the man had heard of him. He also knew Blair was right, thinking about a crime is not the same as committing one.

"How would you know anything about the law Blair, other than breaking it?"

Blair looked into the distance as he thought about his previous life, one as a counselor of law. "I know a thing or two Marshal, maybe more than most. Wasn't that long ago that I practiced the trade in a town where I was respected, a town where men would tip their hats to me as I walked by. I spent years trying to do what was right, not only right by me but right by others. I took an oath to uphold the law, same as you."

Stewart listened but had a hard time believing what the bushwhacker was telling him. "If you are what you say then what has brought you to your current profession of murdering men for their horses?"

"I've never hurt anyone in my life Marshal; you can believe me when I say that. I know how things look and can't say as I blame you for your opinion. A desperate man will do desperate things when he sees no other way out," Blair said. His voice had taken on the traits of a man who was either drunk, or if not, would soon be.

Finally Blair passed out, either from the whiskey or the pain, maybe both. When Stewart was sure he was unconscious he checked his wound, it had nearly quit bleeding. It was obvious that at least one rib was broken and maybe even two or three. The bullet hadn't done that much damage, other than the ribs. The entrance wound was little more than a neat hole and it was only deep enough for the bullet to be under the adjacent skin. Stewart figured he caused as much damage with his knife as the bullet itself. There was little doubt in the marshal's mind that the paperback book had saved the man's life.

Stewart sat back down on the deadfall and considered his situation. The most urgent thing at the moment was water for his horse. He decided to ride in the direction Blair had indicated and try to find the water hole. First though he picked up the man's Winchester and placed it in his scabbard, he already had a long gun there but they both still fit nicely. No way was he going to come back here knowing Blair had access to a weapon.

Blair had also said he owned a handgun but had discarded it, along with the belt and saddle, when he was forced to shoot his horse. His explanation for this was that he was out of ammunition for the Colt. Still though, Stewart had never heard of a man tossing a perfectly good Colt because he was out of bullets. After considering some of the things Blair said, he figured the man was out of his element and had made several mistakes in the process.

As soon as he checked on Blair again he mounted up and headed off at a good trot. He figured he wasn't more than two or three miles from water and felt confident his horse would find it. She had always had a good nose for water. If a stream was within a mile she knew it. Stewart had always found it strange that a horse could smell water.

After fifteen minutes his horse perked up and also picked up the pace. Minutes later he saw the trees Blair had described. The horse Stewart rode was three years old and he had owned her for nearly two. She was stout and at times feisty, her name was Sadie. If Sadie decided she was unhappy with something then she would reach around and try to nip Stewart on the leg, it had happened more than once.

"Whoa there Sadie, let's check things out before we go barging in like we own the place," Stewart said to his anxious horse as he tried to reign her in, the girl was thirsty.

Anytime there was limited water in an area then you could bet there would be other critters about making use of it. Anything from rattlers to wolves could be close by, and that ain't even counting danger of the two legged kind. Once Stewart was certain there wasn't any danger he stepped down and eased Sadie a little closer. He yanked his two canteens from the saddle horn and filled them before letting the horse drink. No need of getting horse slobbers mixed in with his water. Once finished with the canteens he let Sadie drink her fill. He wasn't happy about letting her overdrink but knew he needed to get away from the waterhole as quickly as possible. It wouldn't be the first time someone waited near scarce water in order to cause mischief.

As soon as Sadie had her fill Stewart headed back in the direction he came from although he didn't ride at first, he didn't want to be high in the saddle if someone was about with another Winchester. The scrub would do a nice job keeping him and his horse mostly hidden. Once he felt he had gone far enough he mounted up and headed back toward the unconscious drunk.

As he rode he wondered what he should do. It wasn't his job to nursemaid a man who had tried to kill him. As much as he wanted to ride on he knew the man would most likely die if he did. But if he stayed what more could he do. He wasn't a doctor and if Blair's injury worsened there wasn't much he could do.

As he got closer he decided to put that worry aside so he could focus, wouldn't be nice to get jumped again at the same spot by the same man, even if he was injured and drunk.

When Stewart got to the spot where he had left Blair he was glad to see the man still there. It looked like he might have rolled onto his side in his sleep. After tying Sadie in some rough looking sage he checked on the drunk, he was sleeping soundly but in his effort to roll onto his side he had gotten his wound to leaking a little. Not much but still it was blood he felt the man couldn't afford to waste.

With little to work with Stewart took the man's coat and balled it up. He placed it against the wound and then buttoned the man's shirt over the rolled up coat to keep it in place; it made a snug fit that should keep a little pressure where it was needed. Once finished he felt confident it would keep the wound from breaking open again or at least until the man woke and tried to move.

Now that Sadie was watered and both of his canteens were full he decided to have a better look around. Not a good idea to make camp if you didn't know the lay of the land. After walking a big circle he decided the spot where Blair had tried to bushwhack him was not such a bad spot to make camp after all. There was the big deadfall to use for wood. There was also the big gully that would serve to keep someone from coming from that direction, which would make one less direction he would need to worry about during the night.

It would be dark in minutes and with that in mind Stewart went about the task of gathering wood for a fire. Just as darkness settled in he had a small fire pit constructed out of loose rock and dirt he scrapped around with his boot. He brought Sadie a little closer and tied her to the deadfall. There was a little sage nearby and she immediately went to working on her supper. The poor horse deserved a little grain, maybe even some oats, but that was a worry for another day. He quickly stripped his gear off the horse and placed it on the fire side of the deadfall where the light would play on it if he needed anything during the night.

All Stewart had for his supper was the leftover deer flank. The weather was cold enough that he didn't worry about the meat spoiling; it would keep a couple more days before it would become unsafe to eat. That wouldn't be a problem now because he would be forced to share it with the man that had tried to kill him.

What would have made both supper and breakfast was now going to be only supper for the two men. Stewart needed to grab the skillet from his gear, easy enough to find now by the limited amount of light the campfire gave off. As he walked over to where Sadie was tied out he made sure to stay out of her reach. A few months back he made the mistake of getting to close late at night and she had clubbed him with her head and neck, the blow knocked him to the ground. All he could figure was that she thought he was going to put the saddle back on and she didn't like that thought at all. Now she eyed him suspiciously as he walked in her direction.

There was a small coffee pot in his meager belongings but he hadn't had any coffee to make in at least two weeks. Then he remembered the two saddlebags that belonged to Blair. When he went through the stuff earlier he saw a tied up pouch. It might be tobacco, but then again it might be coffee.

Stewart carried his skillet and coffee pot back to the fire and then grabbed Blair's saddlebags. Sure enough inside the first one he opened was the pouch and in it was coffee. It looked old, hell it looked like it had been in the pouch for months. He would just have to give it a try. Even bad coffee was a sight better than no coffee.

Stewart poured water from a canteen and soon the smell of coffee invaded the camp. As it brewed he put the deer meat in the skillet and sliced it into thin strips with his knife, the same knife he had used to operate on Blair. No matter, he had wiped it off on his boot and that should make it clean. Men on the range did things at times that would make city folk puke.

Stewart used the thin knife to turn the deer steaks from time to time. When they were about finished he used the last of his pepper to give the meat a civilized taste. As he watched his meal cook he thought about his predicament. He was broke and out of supplies. He was now forced to play nursemaid to a man that had tried to kill him earlier in the day. He wasn't exactly sure where he was and was off at least three or four days in the mental calendar he kept tabulated in his head. And Sadie needed a stall and a little grain to use for the winter that was heading their way fast. It's funny how a man out on the open range without a care in the world can pile up such a list of worries so fast.

When the meat had cooked sufficiently Stewart sat the skillet to the side of the fire and used his knife as a fork, careful not to stab his own tongue. He ate slowly knowing this was all he had and he wanted to enjoy it. When he felt he had eaten about half of what was in the skillet he put the knife back in its sheath and went to the deadfall to roll a smoke, using the makings he found in the second of Blair's saddlebags.

As he watched the fire light play against the darkness of night he noticed the canvas bag that he had carried over earlier from the deadfall. He had forgotten to inspect it when he went through the saddlebags. That could have been a fatal mistake, what if there was a gun inside.

The Pursuit

Stewart quickly grabbed the bag and headed back to the deadfall, he now noticed how heavy it was. When he carried it earlier in the day he hadn't noticed the weight. It was securely tied with a canvas strip of the same making as the bag. After finally getting the knot undone he opened the sack and peered inside.

In the bag was a bundle of money, hell there were several bundles of money. Stewart looked at the sleeping drunk and wondered how the man had come about such a stash.

Stewart carefully took out the bundles and placed them to the side, there were seven and each looked to have at least five hundred dollars. What was left looked to be a few coins. When he ran his hand back inside and pulled out a couple he could tell by the faint light from the fire that they were gold coins. Again he looked at the sleeping drunk.

During the next hour Stewart went about the task of counting how much the canvas bag held. When finished he counted thirty-one hundred and twenty eight dollars in cash and roughly another two thousand in gold coins. What the hell?

Stewart decided to hide the sack someplace where it couldn't be easily found. Ten steps out of camp he found another deadfall, smaller than the first, and slid the sack under a spot where it couldn't be seen unless you knew where to look.

He went back to his spot near the fire and sat back down. He finished his second smoke and flipped the butt into the fire. It was now a good two hours past dark and he decided to get a little sleep. He took the bedroll that belonged to Blair and covered the drunk up so he wouldn't freeze to death during the night.

Stewart placed his own bedroll near the deadfall but before stretching out he got his Winchester from the spot where it lay beside his saddle. He also grabbed the one Blair was going to use to shoot him with earlier.

After getting situated he decided to look over the long gun that belonged to the bushwhacker. It was newer than the one he owned and seemed to be in better shape. Apparently it hadn't seen much action in the bushwhacking business.

Stewart decided to unload the weapon, no need to have two loaded Winchesters when only one man was going to be doing any shooting. The gun was empty, not a single cartridge inhabited the gun. He looked at the drunk. Blair was telling the truth, he wasn't going to shoot anybody because he didn't have any ammunition.

Now this puzzled Stewart. What did Blair intend to do with an empty Winchester? As he thought about it he believed he figured it out, Blair was going to push him into the ravine and then ride off on Sadie. As deep as the ravine was it would have taken some time to climb back out, the sides weren't that steep, but steep enough to make climbing difficult. The side was also sloped enough that it was doubtful if he would have been injured during the fall.

Stewart made one more check on Blair and decided he was so drunk he doubted he would wake during the night. Knowing the man probably hadn't intended to kill him earlier might make it easier to get a little sleep, but not much. Stewart would make sure to keep one eye open during the night, if such a thing were even possible.

Raymond Ellsworth poked the dying embers with a stick and decided the fire was past hope. He decided to start with some small twigs and after striking a match to get a little smoke going he would gather another handful of wood, it seemed to be everywhere. Apparently there hadn't been any wildfires in these parts lately or everything would have been burned up. Once the fire was going he sat his coffee pot near the edge and waited for it to brew, he needed his coffee.

There were four other men in camp, all still sound asleep. It was a good hour before first light and this was the usual time Raymond woke. He was an early riser and had protested the night before when the men made him travel well into the night. If you rise early then you turn in early, it was what Raymond had practiced his whole life.

Raymond wasn't the leader of this bunch, far from it. He had hired on because winter was on the way and his grubstake amounted to little more than twenty dollars. This job promised to pay two hundred and that would see him through till spring when work would be more plentiful.

The four men he traveled with were of a rough sort that in a way made Raymond a little nervous. They talked of men they had killed and banks they had robbed. Maybe it was true and maybe it wasn't, just tall tales meant to amuse. But there was something about the stories that led Raymond to believe that not all of it was a lie. Hell, if only ten percent of the stories were real then the four had done enough to get them the rope in more than one town.

It wasn't long before one of the four stirred, his name was Brimley and he was the meanest of the bunch, and also the leader. Brimley must have been born without a first name because all anyone ever called him was Brimley.

Brimley was a mean sort in the best of times and just plain bad during the rest. He had once tried to shoot an old burro just because he wanted to see how far the animal would travel before it dropped dead. Brimley had lifted a Colt off a man he had back shot and wanted to make sure the damn thing worked, that was when he shot at the old man's burro. The old man was Mexican and went to his grave cursing Brimley in a tongue he didn't understand. Brimley was originally from Chicago and didn't like hot weather where the Spanish language was more freely spoken.

The burro marched out of sight without the slightest bit of trouble. Apparently after the old Mexican had been shot the burro was pretty well spooked so when Brimley picked up the old Colt the burro was ready to call it quits and head out to greener pastures. It marched off into the sunset; apparently the bright autumn sun had interfered with Brimley's aim. After checking later there wasn't the slightest evidence of blood, he had missed.

"If any of you ever tell that I shot and missed something as big as a damn donkey then I promise to kill you," he told the four. They believed him.

Brimley slung the blanket to the side and tried to stand. He had drunk himself to sleep the night before and his legs knew what he wanted them to do but they were reluctant to obey. After getting part way up his knees buckled and he fell back to the ground. He looked at Raymond who was kneeling by the fire.

"You got coffee going Raymond?" he asked with a slur in his speech.

"It'll be another minute or two boss."

"Bring me a cup, even if it's cold."

Raymond took his canteen, the same one he had filled the coffee pot with and poured a tin cup halfway to the top with cold water. He then finished it off with the coffee that was now ready. He didn't like Brimley and made sure the first cup the man got was weak and cold. After all, he asked for it that way.

The Pursuit

"Here you go boss. I doubt it's hot but it will at least get you started," Raymond said as he tried to suppress a laugh. He realized he was playing with fire here but couldn't resist the chance to do something against Brimley.

Brimley tipped the cup up and took a cautious sip. When he finally figured it was cold he drank the weak brew all in one go. When he was finished he lowered the cup and wiped his mouth on the back of a dirty shirt sleeve.

"That's damn good coffee Raymond, bring me another," he said.

This nearly made Raymond mad because the last thing he wanted was for Brimley to enjoy the coffee. He would make sure the next cup was scalding hot. When Brimley got his second cup he mistakenly thought it would be warm at best and decided to drink the whole thing at once, which he did. When finished he lowered the cup and reached it back to Raymond. Brimley then fell back on his blankets and went back to sleep, he was still drunk.

Raymond went back to the fire wondering what kind of shape Brimley's mouth was going to be in after drinking coffee what was damn near boiling.

At a little past first light Raymond had two skillets going. One had beans and bacon, mixed together of course, and the other had skillet bread. Sometimes he wondered if the four kept him around only because he was always up early and knew how to cook. If it helped him get his two-hundred dollars then so be it. He only took this job because there just wasn't anything else to be had this late in the season, and he had looked damn near everywhere.

The other three smelled the food and soon were up trying to find a plate. As the four ate they talked of the events of the last few days. Today should lead them to the conclusion of what had turned into a five week hunt. The man they were after had lost his horse the previous day; they had tracked him until it was so dark they were afraid of riding right off the edge of a cliff.

As the men finished their breakfast they heard Brimley start to stir. This time he was a little more sober and had no trouble finding his way into a standing position. He must have noticed something wrong because after finally getting situated on his feet he ran a hand up to his face. He gingerly ran his fingers over his lips and then his teeth. Raymond made sure not to get caught looking.

"What in hell happened to me last evening? Did I get rattlesnake bit during the night?" Brimley asked as he came to the fire. His words were slurred like they were being formed by a man who had a tongue twice as thick as normal. Apparently he didn't even remember waking earlier and drinking the scalding coffee.

Raymond and the other three men looked at their boss and were astonished at the look of his face; Raymond expected it but had to look astonished just like the other three.

Brimley's lips were swollen and blistered. Even his chin looked blistered where the hot coffee must have run around the edges of the cup. As the men looked Brimley stuck out his tongue, or at least he tried to. It looked the same as the lips, swollen and blistered. Raymond felt a bit of relief that the man didn't know what happened because if he did he would probably shoot him.

Simpson Lang stepped closer to his boss and tried to get a better look. "Looks like if you were bit then it must have been on your tongue, damn thing is swollen nearly double."

The Pursuit

Brimley grabbed a canteen and slowly tried to take a sip, water just poured down the sides of his chin. "I can't feel anything, you see any bite marks?"

Again Lang stepped closer and looked his boss over. "Don't see any marks boss; I think you'll be fine in a day or two. If it was a rattler then there would be some marks. I think you just got stung by a scorpion, it won't kill you but the symptoms might last a day or two."

This seemed to satisfy Brimley. He knew scorpions frequented these parts and he had also been stung before. It hurts like hell but wasn't usually fatal. If it was a fatal bite then he would already be dead he figured.

Raymond offered his boss a plate of beans and bacon but he refused. "I can't eat nothing with my mouth in such a shape. Maybe if we stop around noon I'll try then," Brimley mumbled.

Now Raymond thought he would push his luck, "You want some coffee then boss? It's gonna be a long day."

"No coffee either," Brimley said as best as he could.

"Let's saddle up and finish this job, the sooner it's over the sooner we get paid," Brimley said.

"We going to try and bring him back alive boss?" Lang asked.

"No, that would be nearly a thousand miles to tote the bastard. Too many law between here and there. We find out where he's hid the stuff and then we bury him."

"What if he don't want to talk?" Lang asked.

"Oh he'll talk; a man in enough pain will tell you anything you want to know. It'll go a lot easier on him if he gives up the goat early. If he don't then I'll start by carving off a toe or a finger here and there. He'll talk, you can count on it," Brimley told the four.

Nathan Wright

By thirty minutes after sunup the five riders were mounted up. It had taken a little longer due to the shape Brimley was in. The trail they were following could be identified by a blind man. Blair either hadn't tried to hide his tracks or didn't know how. Brimley knew the man was an attorney and held men of that profession in low regard.

"Won't be long now boys, he's afoot and scared," Brimley said.

Stewart finally had to wake Blair up. Dark was fading into daylight fast and he wanted to get on the trail. Blair was extremely sore from the busted ribs but didn't refuse what was left of the previous day's deer meat. Stewart hadn't woke the sleeping drunk the night before, he just left what little supper he was going to share with the man in the skillet close to the fire. He also figured Blair needed his rest.

Stewart packed up the camp as Blair chewed his breakfast. Finally when everything was ready he looked at Blair and asked, "How do you feel this morning, them ribs going to keep you from walking?"

Blair was now afraid he was going to be left here all alone without any transportation. "Oh I can walk Marshal, you just point the way and I'll follow you. When I get tired though do you plan on doubling up on that horse of yours?"

"No, you walk and if you can't keep up then we'll stop. I still can't trust you and don't want to be that close to a man that was going to kill me yesterday," Stewart said. He wanted to see if Blair knew he was out of ammunition. If he didn't know the gun was empty then he really did intend on killing him and burying his body in that ravine.

The Pursuit

"I can walk Stewart and like I said I wasn't going to kill you. If you don't believe me then have a look at my gun, it ain't loaded and for that matter I don't have a single cartridge to my name."

Stewart figured that answered his suspicions. Blair hadn't planned on killing him, only stealing his horse. Stewart untied Sadie and mounted up.

"Which way we heading Stewart?"

After a moment's thought Stewart turned Sadie in the same direction he had been heading the day before, that was until Blair tried to bushwhack him. "We'll be heading due west. Town about three days ride from here."

As rider and walker started out it quickly became apparent the pace would be slow, real slow. Blair grimaced with each step and nearly fell a time or two. Stewart hoped the man would grow accustomed to the pain soon and could make better time.

"Tell me Blair about the money you got in the sack I got tied here behind my saddle."

Blair looked at the horse and said, "I wish I'd never seen that damn money Stewart. I feel like I've been chased half way across the world because of it."

Stewart suddenly turned in the saddle. "What are you talking about Blair? Are men following you?"

After a minute Blair finally answered, "I would reckon so. I was out of options when my horse went lame, that's when you showed up on that big horse of yours and I guess I wasn't thinking when I tried to knock you in that ravine and take your ride."

While Blair talked Stewart stood in the stirrups and looked in every direction fully expecting to see mounted riders hot on their trail. "Why didn't you tell me this earlier Blair? If they were chasing you yesterday don't you think they will be chasing you today? I for one don't want to be caught off guard; you done took care of that yesterday. And another thing Blair, we had a fire going just about all night. If the men that are after you saw that fire then we might have both been killed during the night you dumb bastard."

"Sorry Stewart. I should have said something sooner but you got to remember I was shot yesterday."

"Yeah, you were shot yesterday and if what you say is true you might get shot again today. How close do you figure your pursuers are?"

"They're real close Stewart, maybe a day, maybe less."

Stewart continued to scan his surroundings but for the moment their back trail looked clear. As he scanned the lay of the land he saw some low bluffs in the general distance they were heading that were dotted with scrub and a few stunted trees here and there. It was apparent the ground around these parts was mostly rock and shale, very little dirt and nearly nothing that resembled topsoil.

"If they're as close as you say they are then we'll head for that bluff, shouldn't take more than five or six hours. You feel up to it?" Stewart asked full well knowing the answer would be no.

"I can make it Marshal. After we get that far what do you intend to do? We can't very well hole up a day or two without water or food."

"If we make it that far then we'll rest until it's good and dark. At the slow pace we're making we can travel at night without fear of dropping off a canyon wall. We hole up during the day and travel at night. We are going to get real thirsty before we make it to any size town though."

The Pursuit

As the two men traveled Stewart kept a good watch on his back trail and at around three in the afternoon he spotted what he thought was dust rising a couple of miles back. It had to be riders.

Stewart had given up the saddle hours ago. The trip was proving too much for Blair. As Blair rode and tried to not fall out of the saddle Stewart held the reins of Sadie, it seemed to be the fastest. Where Blair had drug his feet and stumbled he now rode and this allowed the marshal to walk the horse at a brisk pace. All he could think of now was making it to the bluffs before they were overtaken.

As they got closer he could tell it would be a defensible spot. He would have the high ground and anyone trying to climb up would be seen way before they got there. The only problem was going to be water; he had two full canteens and a little in a third. He figured on giving Sadie all of one canteen. He would pour it in his skillet and let her drink. It wouldn't fill the horse by any means but it would allow her a small measure of relief.

Brimley and his four gun hounds had traveled no more than fifteen minutes when they picked up the trail of their quarry. As the sun rose Brimley was becoming more and more agitated, his mouth and lips continued to give him trouble and the midday heat was starting to take its toll. About one in the afternoon he came to a decision.

"Let's stop for a spell, I need to think," he told the four.

The men didn't start a fire, it would signal anyone for miles around where they were. The four that could eat, ate some hardtack and jerky, no coffee, just water from canteens they had filled at the same water hole Stewart had used the night before. If they only knew how close they were to their prey they would have pushed on. Again Brimley refused food, his mouth and tongue looked as if they were swollen nearly double. Raymond wondered at what point the swelling would interfere with the man's breathing.

As the men sat and chewed on their tough meal, Brimley came to a conclusion. "Lang, you and me are going to head over to Elk Bend. You three can handle Blair when you catch up with him. Try to bring him to me alive if you can. I want to have the pleasure of making him talk." Brimley also didn't want Blair to share the secret of where he had hidden the money to anyone but him.

Raymond looked at the other two that were to stay. Ballard Weiss and Brian Newsome were two of the sorriest excuses for human beings he had ever seen. Neither man had seen a bar of soap in years, or a razor for that matter. Raymond would swear they had vermin nesting in their shoulder length hair and shaggy beards. It was one reason he never put down his bedroll too close to the two, he wouldn't even let the two tend to his horse if he could keep from it.

The two filthy bastards looked at Brimley. "Now what do you want to do that for boss? We damn near got Blair caught and you want to head off in a different direction."

Brimley had been gingerly rubbing his chin and probing his mouth to see if his injuries had gotten any worse. If they weren't worse then they sure felt it. The pain was nearly more than he could stand.

"They got an old sawbones there. Maybe he can see if I was stung by a scorpion or if it really was a rattlesnake bite. The pain is something awful. Hell, if I had me a bottle of rotgut then I could make it. We ain't had us no whiskey in over a week and now I regret not bringing more. I figure you three can catch up

The Pursuit

with that Blair feller and then bring him to Elk Bend. I can get the information out of him and after we ride out of town we'll find us a secluded spot and put him in the ground," Brimley said with pain evident in every word.

Raymond knew exactly what was wrong with the man but wasn't about to say what it was. Brimley would kill him for sure if he knew. The situation was now maybe slightly better. If Brimley rode off with Lang that would only leave the two filth brothers, as Raymond liked to think of the two. Raymond wasn't afraid of these two, hell he could take a bar of soap and chase them all over the Dakotas.

What he didn't like about this new plan was the fact that with only three men after Blair he might be forced to use his gun to kill the man if things went south instead of as planned. Raymond had killed a couple of men before and never gave it a second thought. Now though, if he was forced to kill Blair before they were able to extract any information, he was afraid the men that sent them after Blair might hold him responsible and then he would be hunted down, same as Blair. Raymond would worry about that when the time came. Right now he wanted to be shed of the homicidal Brimley.

"Sounds good boss, the three of us will bring old Blair to you, shouldn't take long now before we catch up with the low down law preacher." The phrase *law preacher* was something the men had heard from the organization that had hired them. It was meant as an insult, and it truly was.

Brimley walked over to where his horse was tied and mounted up. "See you three in Elk Bend in a couple of days. I've changed my mind on you three trying to not kill Blair. As of now my orders are that not a hair on his head is to be touched until I get my hands on him. If you three manage to kill him then the very thing we were paid to find will be lost forever.

That would be bad news for the three of you; you understand what I'm telling you?"

Raymond and the other two shook their heads vigorously. They each knew if they let Blair get killed then they would be hunted down and killed themselves, that wasn't going to happen.

Brimley and Lang headed for Elk Bend while Raymond Ellsworth and the two filth brothers headed out after Blair. The three knew Brimley must have been in a lot of pain for him to head off in a different direction now that he was so close to his prey. Then something happened that told Raymond his day was going to turn our far different than what he had originally hoped.

"You know Raymond, you giving that scalding coffee to Brimley this morning was a pretty mean thing to do," Newsome said.

Raymond rode on acting like what Newsome said wasn't really that important. Hell, it was Raymond's word against Newsome's if it came right down to it.

"Yeah, I thought so too. I thought the pot had been sitting pretty close to the fire and after Brimley drank that second cup and never said a thing about it I just figured it wasn't hot at all. When I saw what happened later though, I knew what you had done," Ballard said.

Raymond rode on not saying a word. He realized if both the filth brothers knew what he had done he was probably in a pretty bad fix.

"I don't know what you two are talking about," Raymond said.

"Well, you can act like you don't know but we both know and unless you go along with our little plan then as soon as we capture Blair and make our way to Elk Bend then we're telling the boss what you done. What do you think old Brimley will do when he finds out all his suffering was caused by you Raymond? The both of us know, he won't doubt what we tell him," Ballard said.

Raymond knew he was in a bad way and decided to hear the two out. "What kind of plan are you two talking about?"

"Well, we hung back a ways while we were traveling this morning so no one could hear us talk. We figured that once you help us capture Blair then you can just disappear. That way your share of the money can be divvied up between the four of us. You think that's fair Newsome?" Ballard asked.

"I think that's real fair Ballard. What do you think Raymond?" Newsome asked.

Now Raymond's share was two-hundred dollars and that wasn't a lot of money in the big scheme of things. But that wasn't what these two had in mind at all. Raymond figured they would get the information from Blair and then kill him. They could ride on in to Elk Bend and tell Brimley that Raymond had managed to find out where the money was hidden and then double-crossed everyone. He was the only one now that knew where the money was.

After Brimley rode off to inform his employers that Raymond was their man then a new search would be mounted. The two filth brothers could then find the money and disappear. Even if Raymond managed to survive these two he would still be hunted for the rest of his days by the men that had contracted Brimley for the original job. All he could do now was agree and when the time was right try to make his escape.

"I reckon you two got yourself a deal. We find Blair and then you two take him to Brimley without me. I'll head on south and try to find a little work that way," Raymond said.

The two filth brothers bought it for the time being. Raymond didn't like being blackmailed and would even the score when these two were least expecting it. The three rode on paying careful attention to the trail.

Not more than twenty minutes after they split up with Brimley and Lang, they came to the spot where Blair had tried to bushwhack Stewart. They saw the spot where the fire had been made and also saw where a horse had been tied out. They had noticed horse tracks and footprints earlier at the water hole and just figured it was a solitary rider using the only water for miles. Now they suspected something else.

"Looks like someone got shot over here, got some blood," Ballard said.

With a little more looking they figured that a man had been shot and the man who shot him must have been the man on the horse. The tracks they saw indicated it was Blair who had been shot, once you follow a pair of boots long enough you can tell a lot.

"They pulled out first thing this morning. Looks like Blair is still afoot," Newsome said.

After following the tracks a ways Newsome identified that it was Blair on foot and he had been injured somehow, probably the one that had been shot. There was a speck or two of blood here and there coming from the man on foot. Newsome was a good tracker and could figure out things that most men would pass over.

"We better catch up with him quick before that new feller finds out where the money is hidden," Ballard said with a tone that indicated he was worried their treasure was about to be stolen right out from under their feet.

"We can't pick up the pace Ballard. These tracks indicate there is now a horse and rider with Blair. We don't know who

The Pursuit

this new feller is and I for one don't want to get shot from long range by a Winchester. We proceed at a safe pace. Blair is afoot and apparently injured, he can't make very good time now can he?" Newsome said.

With a little thought Ballard had to agree, if they went too fast they could stumble into an ambush. With the amount of money at stake anything was possible. "Alright Newsome, you're the tracker. We go at the pace you set and hope they don't get away."

Stewart and Blair made it to the bluff at a little after four in the evening. It took about an hour longer than the marshal had planned; walking wore on a man, especially a man that was keeping a close watch on his back trail.

There was a narrow gully on the south side of the bluff and it seemed to be the easiest route to travel if you were trying to make it to the top. There was a little loose gravel in the center but the footing was firm enough for the two men and Sadie to climb. The big horse could damn near climb a tree if she wasn't troubled with a rider in the saddle.

"We'll get to the top and scan from there to see if your pursuers have found our trail," Stewart said. He knew a blind man could follow the trail they had left behind in their attempt to get here before their tormentors.

"When we get up there can we rest a spell? I don't feel so good," Blair said.

The marshal knew the man had to be spent. He had lost some blood the day before, not a lot but any would take away a body's energy. "Yeah, we'll rest, and after it gets good and dark we head out again."

Blair didn't say anything else as the two began climbing the shallow depression. The bluff wasn't high but it was at least taller than the surrounding land. Twenty minutes after they started they were at the top. There was a stand of fir trees not more than twenty feet from where the two exited the gully. It was the kind of trees that could stand up to a harsh winter with winds and snow.

Sadie was led to where some winter sage swayed in the breeze and she immediately went to chomping on what she felt looked the tastiest. Blair managed to make it to where the trees would offer some shade, he found a spot where the rock was covered with moss and laid down, within minutes he was asleep.

Without a spyglass all Stewart could do was cup a hand over his eyes and look off into the distance. He scanned a portion and then walked a few feet to look again. Within fifteen minutes he had walked all the way around the bluff. Again he thought he spotted dust in the distance but couldn't tell if it was from horses or buffalo. The vast herds of years past had been decimated but there were still a few around, the big animals could survive in some of the harsher regions and this area seemed to be just that, harsh.

Stewart looked over the gully they had traveled up and discovered it wasn't a gully at all. It appeared the rock face had separated and spread apart from the main bluff making a break about ten feet wide that ran from the base all the way to the top. Over the hundreds, or even thousands of years, the break had filled with rubble making a trail from bottom to top. When he walked around the top he spotted a place or two where a man might make the trip up but it wasn't ideal and definitely not where a horse could travel. It looked like the break was the only way up, or down, for Sadie. It wouldn't be good for them to be caught up here; a man with a Winchester could keep them there until they died of thirst.

Stewart went to the trees and sat down but not before grabbing a canteen. He offered it to Blair first who took a pull and then reached it back. Blair had been sound asleep but Stewart knew he needed a little water after his climb up the break. The man was doing better than one would expect, especially with broken ribs.

"You spot anyone Stewart?" Blair asked.

"I think so, maybe a couple of hours behind us. Can't be sure of it though until they get closer, by the time they get here we will be long gone."

Since the two men had time to talk Stewart wanted to know the story about Blair and his pursuers. "Why are those men chasing you Blair? You kill somebody when you took the money?"

Blair had been lying flat on his back but now eased up onto one elbow. It was apparent the rest had put a little life back into him.

"No Marshal, nothing like that. I was an attorney back in Chicago some years back. My job was to review land titles and prepare deeds for right of way easements for a few of the railroads that have been pushing west for several years now. I lived in the city and worked hard. I saved every penny I could and spent very little. I have means of my own; the money in that sack, and the rest that I have hidden, isn't mine. It also doesn't belong to the men that are chasing me."

"If it's not yours then who does it belong to?" Stewart asked.

"Most of it belongs to several landowners in the territory; there are others in the adjoining states who are owed some of the proceeds but mostly folks from the Dakotas," Blair said.

"How many people are you talking about Blair?"

"Nearly five-hundred are due this money, each to receive different amounts. Some as small as a few hundred; the largest is around ten-thousand," Blair said.

"I counted what you had in that canvas bag last night while you were sleeping, it's nowhere near the amount you just described," Stewart said.

"You're right Marshal; the total comes to over a hundred and fifty thousand dollars. The bulk of it is hidden and I'm the only one who knows where it is."

Stewart eyed the man and wondered how much of what he just said was true. He was starting to believe Blair wasn't the outlaw he first had him figured for but the jury was still out on that. "If something happens to you then will the money turn up someplace, someplace safe like a bank?"

Blair eyed Stewart with suspicion. "Maybe Marshal, if something happens to me then the money might be lost forever. I have it hidden and it is hidden well. You could take a hundred men and search for a hundred years and you couldn't find it."

Stewart stood and went back to the spot where he thought he saw movement from before. He could now make out three horses and riders. They were heading toward the bluff and they seemed to be in a hurry.

"We got trouble Blair. Three riders heading this way fast, they'll be at the base of the bluff before we can make it down," Stewart said.

Blair eased to his feet and made his way to where the marshal crouched. Neither man stood for fear of being sky lined. "What do we do now Marshal? If they know we're here then they can wait us out. They can keep us here until we die of thirst."

The Pursuit

"I'm not so sure, if we can't go after water then neither can they. They might send a man but that would only leave two and our numbers would then be even. And don't forget, we got the high ground," the marshal said.

The three riders had followed the trail without the least bit of trouble. It was daylight and the tracks were fresh, still one man on horseback and the other on foot. When they spotted the bluff and the direction the tracks were heading they were able to increase their pace, they knew where their quarry was heading.

"There she is Ballard. A break that runs from bottom to top and their tracks are heading straight for it," Newsome said.

All three men scanned the bluff and wondered if there was someone up there pointing a Winchester at them. It was at least a mile and they knew a shot from that distance had a good chance of hitting nothing. When the range fell to five-hundred yards they would need to use more caution. Even at the shorter distance the shot would need to be an extremely lucky one.

"What do you plan on doing now Ballard, we can't rush their position? They could pick us off one by one," Newsome said.

"You got that right Newsome, but we can't wait them out either, they've probably got more water than we do," Ballard guessed.

Up until now Raymond hadn't said what he thought. He wanted the two filth brothers to charge the bluff and get their asses shot up but didn't dare say it.

"What do you say there Raymond? Surely you got an idea on how to flush old Blair off that bluff," Newsome said.

"Well, I really don't have a plan other than going up there with a white flag and telling them what they already know, surrender or die of thirst," Raymond told the two.

Ballard looked at Newsome and said, "You know that just might work."

Raymond couldn't believe what he had just heard; these two dumbasses thought he was serious about the white flag.

"Alright then it's settled, someone has got to go up there and convince them two to surrender. We will guarantee safe passage if Blair tells us where the money is hidden," Ballard said.

"Now all we got to figure out is who goes up there holding the white flag?" Newsome said. Both men looked at Raymond.

"You think I want to go up there. What if they decide they don't like the looks of a white flag or what if they don't know what a white flag means? They will shoot me for sure. I was only kidding when I said that anyway," Raymond told the two fools.

"Maybe he's got a point there Ballard and anyways, what if he goes up there and finds out where the money is and then gets away? No sir, sending Raymond is a bad idea," Newsome said.

Ballard thought about it and knew Newsome was right. "Alright then, it's up to either me or you."

Newsome threw both hands up in mock surrender, "You can just count me out. I ain't going up there holding no white flag."

"Alright then, I'll go Newsome. You just make sure you cover me with a Winchester and make sure no one gets off that rock besides me," Ballard said.

Raymond suddenly thought this was working out pretty well. The number of tormentors he was going to contend with had just been reduced by half. Once Ballard was on his way up the break he would deal with Newsome.

No more than fifteen minutes after Raymond come up with the worst plan in the history of plans, Ballard had rigged a short pole with a dirty white handkerchief tied to the end. He took off his gun belt but before he laid it on the ground he pulled the gun and slid in in the back of his waistband. If he got close enough he would kill the stranger and then get the information he wanted from Blair. If things worked out he might just kill Newsome and Raymond too and keep all the money for himself. The thought made him smile.

"Alright Ballard, you head on up and make sure you wave that flag for all you're worth. I'll stay here and keep a watch on things," Newsome said.

Raymond watched as Ballard entered the break and disappeared from sight. Once he was sure the man was far enough away he stepped behind Newsome and clobbered him with his Colt. Once he was sure the stinky bastard was out cold he went to his horse and got some rope. Ten minutes after Ballard started up the break Newsome was bound and gagged. As Raymond was finishing up with the last of the knots the stinky bastard came to. He couldn't move and he couldn't scream for help.

Ballard might have been out of sight when Raymond clubbed Newsome but from their lofty perch both Blair and Stewart saw what was happening. One man had started up the break while another had either knocked out or killed the third man. This was turning out to be an interesting predicament.

"What do you reckon that one feller has in mind, the one that tied up that other man down there?" Blair asked.

"I can't say for sure but it looks like the three don't agree on everything. We take care of the one that's on his way up here now and then we'll worry about the other two," Stewart said.

The marshal walked over to where Sadie stood and retrieved the other Winchester. He pulled a box of shells from a saddlebag and walked back to where Blair waited. "Here's your gun back, only this time you have ammunition. Take this box and load her up."

Blair reached for the gun and the box of ammunition. "You trust me Marshal after what happened yesterday?"

Stewart looked back over the edge of the bluff as he said, "I figure I can almost trust you Blair. At the moment I'm the only thing keeping you from meeting your death at the hands of those men down there. I might be asking for that gun back after the trouble has passed, are you alright with that?"

"I am, and you can have the gun back any time you want. Until then I plan on helping keep us both alive," Blair said as he opened the box of ammunition. "One more question, how do we intend to handle that man coming up the break carrying the white flag?"

"I've been giving that some thought and don't really have an answer yet. Maybe we'll just wait here and see how things play out. He should be here in another minute or two," Stewart said.

As Ballard climbed up the break a plan began to take shape in the back of his mind. If he could convince these two that all he wanted was the information of where the money was hidden; after that he and the two others at the base of the bluff would ride out. The two men could watch the three go and know it was safe.

The Pursuit

Yeah that was it, he would tell his story just like that. Once he had the information he would wait for the right moment and pull his hideaway and kill the two where they stood. When he got back to the bottom of the break he would jump Newsome and Raymond and shoot both before they knew what happened. Ballard was quite proud of himself; he had come up with a foolproof plan that would make himself rich.

"Can you see him yet Marshal?" Blair whispered.

"Not yet but he's close, I hear him clawing his way up the rubble. I don't remember it being that hard on you or me, not to mention Sadie. It sounds like a buffalo coming up the break."

"I hear him Marshal and you're right, he's making way more noise than he needs to."

The two men waited, both had fully loaded Winchesters and both guns were pointed where the break emptied out onto the top of the bluff.

"Hello the top, I got me a white flag and want to talk a spell. Do you hear me?" Ballard asked.

"We hear you mister. Why are you following me and my friend here, we neither one know you?" Stewart said.

"Well, I reckon you don't know me mister but you know why we are following you. You tell me what I need to know and I'll ride out of here, along with the ten men I got with me down at the bottom of the break."

Now Blair was within earshot of his tormentors and couldn't resist the chance to say how he felt. "Why you lying sack of you know what. What I know is not to be shared with the likes of you. Why you ain't nothing but a low down good for nothing," Blair said as he looked at Stewart and winked.

It was all the marshal could do to keep from laughing. "You probably scared him to death with all that mean talk Blair." After a moment Stewart continued, "That was the mildest chewing out I've heard in my entire life. Please don't speak again until I say it's alright for you to do so."

Blair thought the marshal had actually paid him a compliment and smiled. It was the harshest language the man had ever used.

It was apparent the little speech Blair had given had left Ballard a bit bewildered. "I don't know about any of that mister. I just want to know where the money is hidden and then me and my men will ride out. I'm going to stand up now and I ain't armed so don't shoot." Ballard hoped this would lull the two men into dropping their guard. He was a backward sort who thought people would believe what he said.

When Ballard stood up he wasn't more than fifteen feet away. No sooner had he came into view than Stewart hit him squarely between the eyes with a fist sized rock. There was a sickening thud as the man went down faster than he had stood.

Blair looked at the marshal with what could only be described as astonishment. "That was the luckiest throw I've ever seen in my life Marshal. When did you think of that?"

"Oh I don't know, I just figured if the opportunity presented itself then I would take advantage of it. You keep him covered while grab some rope and tie his hands and feet."

Five minutes after Ballard had been struck by the rock he was gagged and hogtied. The marshal thought he would live, although in his eagerness to hit the man he might have tossed the rock a little harder than he needed to. It wasn't anything Stewart was going to lose any sleep over because in the process of tying the man up he discovered the hideaway.

The Pursuit

"Looks like he planned on using this on me and you," Stewart said as he held up the gun. "Here you go, I just found you a Colt to replace the one you threw away a couple of days back, and this one has bullets," he said as he tossed the gun to Blair.

The marshal stripped off the gun belt and searched the man from head to toe. "Damn if this ain't the smelliest son of a buck as I've ever been around. I've seen hogs that had a more pleasant odor."

Blair had been keeping his eye on the break as the marshal tied and searched Ballard. "I can smell him all the way over here Marshal. After he's tied you mind dragging him over by the tree line?"

"That might be considered a bit mean, Sadie is over there and I'm pretty sure she wouldn't like the smell any better than we do."

Blair looked back at the big horse, "You might be right about that Marshal. Why don't you drag him that way anyhow, Sadie can stand it better than we can. My eyes are starting to water."

After Ballard was far enough away, and the two men could breathe again, Blair asked, "So what do we do now? Them two down there have still got us in a bad spot."

"I say we let them know we have their man all tied up and see what they think of that." With that the marshal stood and looked over the edge.

"Can you hear me down there?" Stewart shouted.

Raymond heard the man and wondered what had happened to Ballard. "I can hear you," he shouted back.

"I've got your man up here. He's knocked out and tied up," Stewart said and then waited to see what would happen.

What did happen surprised both himself and Blair. The man stood and walked into the open. He tossed his gun to the ground and held up his hands.

"Damn Marshal, all you got to do is speak and everyone within earshot starts surrendering," Blair said.

"Shut up Blair and keep an eye on that stinking bastard over there." Blair did as he was told.

"Marshal, if I might speak, how do you intend to handle this now? We just can't start climbing down through that break, we'd both be sitting ducks."

Stewart thought a second and then told Blair, "You're right about that. The only way to do this is for him to walk up here so we can tie him up. First though, I want him to drag that man he clubbed with his gun out into the open where we can keep an eye on him."

"That's good thinking Marshal, but if he don't agree what do you intend to do?"

"I'll just let you talk real mean to him like you did to the one we got tied up over there," the marshal said with a laugh.

"Stop that Marshal, I'll have you know that more than once in court I've had witnesses to start crying when they saw me get mad."

"Is that right? It was probably the laughter that brought them to tears. Now I need you to keep a real close eye on that man over there while I talk to his friend down below."

The marshal shouted directions to the man at the base of the bluff and to his surprise he did as he was told. He pulled the man out into the open and then started climbing up the break. Twenty minutes later he was standing face to face with Marshal Jake Stewart.

The Pursuit

"Now you stand real still mister and put your hands behind your back. Blair, make sure you keep that Winchester pointed at his head while I secure his hands."

"It would be my pleasure Marshal," Blair said as he pointed the gun where he was told.

After he was tied, good and tight, he was sat down beside stinky and told to start talking. Blair kept his Winchester pointed at the third man down below, just in case.

"My name is Raymond Ellsworth. I hired on with this bunch about five or six weeks ago. I was promised grub along the way and two-hundred dollars cash once the job was finished. They told me I was part of a posse, said we were working for the law. After a few days I started to suspect this bunch was trouble and I had unwittingly hired on and was right in the middle of it. Thought about just riding out but figured that would probably get me killed. "

Blair looked back at the two men and nodded at the marshal. "Go ahead Marshal, ask him what he was supposed to do with me once the job was finished."

"You heard him Ellsworth, what were your intentions?"

"I was only told we were after an outlaw by the name of Gene Blair. They said he had robbed some folks out of a lot of money and was on the run. We were to capture him and bring him back so he could be questioned. That was the story up until yesterday. That was when they said he was to be killed after they made him talk. It ain't what I signed on for Marshal; you've got to believe me."

Stewart thought about this and it did kind of make sense. Why else would Ellsworth knock out the third man when they finally had Blair right where they wanted him? Why would he give up so easily when all he had to do was get on his horse and ride away?

Nathan Wright

"Is there a reason why you didn't ride out of here when both of your friends were tied up?" Stewart asked.

"There is Marshal. I felt I needed to warn you. If you ride into town with Blair and these other two then there are some men in that town that will kill you on sight. I could have ridden out but thought you should know the odds you're facing."

"What town are you talking about?" Blair asked.

"Elk Bend, it's the closest by at least three or four days. With prisoners I figured you couldn't take them all the way to Rapid City."

This man Ellsworth was making a lot of sense. Everything he was saying was pretty much the way things were going to play out. "What kind of work did you do before you hired on with this bunch Ellsworth?" Stewart asked.

"I've done a little bit of everything Marshal. Never been on the wrong side of the law and wouldn't be now if these varmints hadn't misled' me. When you get to Elk Bend you can send a wire to Rapid City and check me out, a judge there by the name of Thurman Preston will vouch for me. I've done a lot of work around that town and even went out on a posse or two with a marshal up there, his name is Pete Savage."

Stewart knew both Judge Preston and Pete Savage and it went a long way that this man knew them too. "What will Savage and Preston say about you Ellsworth?"

"They'll tell you exactly what I'm telling you now. I ain't never been in no trouble before, never."

Blair started laughing, "First time I've ever witnessed a sentence that had a quadruple negative in it. Where did you learn how to talk Ellsworth?"

"Learned it like everybody else Mister, from my maw and paw. And I ain't never heard of no quad, whatever you said, negative before never."

The Pursuit

"There it is again, a quadruple negative," Blair bellowed until he nearly lost his breath with laughter, that was until the pain from his broken ribs straightened him out.

After Blair regained his senses he figured the man was probably being truthful but didn't know how the marshal felt. "Now what do we do Marshal? We need to be getting off this rock before nightfall. I don't envy walking down that break after dark."

"I reckon we can tie that stinky feller on the back of Sadie. Going downhill won't be much trouble for her as long as we do it before dark. You can stay here Blair and keep your Winchester trained on the man tied at the base of the bluff. If he starts to move before we get down there then shoot him. The last thing I want is to come out of the break and see a Winchester pointed at me," Stewart said.

"You don't need to worry about Newsome Marshal, I knocked him out and have him tied up nice and tight," Ellsworth said.

"Keep the gun trained on him anyway Blair. I ain't ready to trust Ellsworth yet. For all we know the man down there might not be hurt, or even tied up. He's just waiting for us to come out of the break so he can blast us," Stewart said.

Ellsworth rubbed his chin, "That's the smart thing to do Marshal. I can see where I wouldn't be someone you could trust."

With that said the marshal and Ellsworth went about tying Ballard on the back of Sadie. The big horse protested at first, it was apparent she didn't like having something so smelly tied to her back. Once Ballard was secure the marshal re-tied Ellsworth, but only his hands and these were tied in front this time. Stewart knew the man might fall on his way down the

49

break and if he did at least he could put his hands out to keep from landing on his face.

Stewart guessed they had about thirty minutes before dark, this should allow enough time for him to get Sadie and Raymond off the bluff. Once there Blair could hurry on his way but would no doubt be traveling part of the way in total darkness.

"Raymond, I'm counting on you to lead Sadie down the break. If you spook her or cause her to get hurt I can guarantee I'll bury your body out here after I shoot you, do we understand each other?" Stewart asked. Raymond indicated he did and made a promise to himself that he would get the horse safely off the bluff.

Once at the bottom of the hill the marshal checked on the other man. He was out cold and tied tight. "Alright Raymond, take the gags off your two friends but don't wake them up. I wouldn't want either to suffocate in their sleep."

Once Stewart had all three men where he could keep a close eye on them he signaled for Blair to make his way down the break. It was a good thirty minutes past dark when he made it to where Stewart stood guard.

Blair looked like he had stumbled a time or two in the darkness; his pants were torn at both knees and both hands looked bloody. "Looks like you had a rough time of it," Stewart said.

Blair flopped down on the ground; his breathing was heavy and labored. The broken ribs were causing him some pain. "I had to more or less feel my way down Marshal. I fell a few times but never got hurt much, other than my knees and my palms."

Raymond had been watching and listening. "Marshal, our horses are tied up a couple hundred feet back that way. In one of the filth brother's saddlebags is a bottle of whiskey. It might be a good idea to give Blair a sip or two. Don't let him get drunk though, just enough to dull the senses and ease his pain."

Blair stood and looked in the direction of where the horses were. "I'll check on that Marshal. You want me to bring the three in?"

It was apparent the mention of whiskey had given Blair his second wind. "You bring them in; I'll stay here and guard the prisoners."

Before leaving Blair turned back to Raymond. "Are the horses easy to handle are will they be skittish?"

"You might consider bringing them in one at a time. The one with the bottle is the big gray; walk beside her and not in front. She has a habit of blowing her nose on a man's back anytime she can," Raymond said.

Blair looked at the marshal and said, "I guess now me and you both have us a horse," and then he walked off into the darkness.

The marshal knew neither he nor Blair had any supplies and wondered what might be on the three horses, other than a bottle of whiskey.

"What have the three of you got on them horses other than that bottle?"

Raymond looked at the marshal. "Maybe three days grub, some coffee and a little tobacco, both the smoking and the chewing kind."

This was good news, the marshal and Blair hadn't eaten much in the last twenty-four hours, just a little bit of deer meat. At least now they could have some supper. It was another reason not to wake the two unconscious men, let them go hungry.

Nathan Wright

It wasn't long before Blair came out of the trees leading a horse, a gray horse. The marshal let Blair sit and watch the prisoners while he tied the horse and stripped the saddle and gear from her back. Once finished he dug out the bottle and reached it to Blair.

"Go easy on that stuff, you got two more horses to lead into camp," Stewart said. He wondered how Sadie would react toward the new horses, she could be mean at times.

By midnight all four horses were staked out and a fire was going. Stewart made sure to use his own coffee pot and skillet. He wasn't about to take a chance on using anything that belonged to the two filth brothers. He heard Raymond refer to the two using that name and now the name stuck. It was bad enough having to eat the grub the two men carried but at least it would be fried up using Stewart's own skillet.

Raymond said he did most of the cooking and made sure to keep everything wrapped in grocer's paper before it was put back in the men's saddlebags. Still though, if it weren't for the amount of hunger both men were suffering they would have just as soon waited until they made town in a day or two.

The marshal let Blair and Raymond sleep while he stood watch. About four in the morning he woke Blair and asked if he felt he could manage guard duty for an hour or two. All three prisoners were tied up tight and shouldn't pose a problem. Blair indicated he was feeling a little better; he could handle his portion of the guard duty.

At daylight the marshal woke and immediately went for his gun thinking one of the three had gotten free. He must have been dreaming because all three prisoners were sound asleep, so was Blair. He figured with the broken ribs and all, he might have been expecting too much from the man. They were a good two days ride from anywhere and it looked like the marshal

was going to need to stay awake the entire time, it couldn't be done.

"Wake up Blair," the marshal said as he kicked the man's boot.

Blair came awake and raised the Winchester. Stewart had expected this and immediately grabbed the gun.

"You wouldn't shoot me would you Blair?"

Blair rubbed his eyes and looked at the marshal, "I guess I dozed off Marshal."

"You did at that. You feel any better this morning?"

"Actually I do, a little supper and a little rest has me feeling alive again. Sorry about falling asleep."

"We never got our throats cut last night so I guess it worked out. We need to start heading toward a town pretty soon. Didn't Raymond say last night that he did most of the cooking for that bunch?"

Blair looked at the three men; the one named Raymond was awake and looking at them. "How long have you been awake?" he asked.

"Since right before you fell back asleep. I knew both of you were asleep and figured I better stay awake in case the two filth brothers came to and tried to get out of their ropes."

This sent a chill down the marshal's spine. Raymond was still handtied to the front and could have walked right over and relieved Blair of his gun, but he didn't. He had the perfect opportunity to kill both men and make his escape.

Stewart pulled his knife and walked over to where Raymond sat, he reached down and cut the rope off the man's wrists, "As of now you're a free man Ellsworth. And you are going to earn your keep by doing the cooking and helping with the guard duty." After he said that the marshal walked over and added some wood to the dying fire.

"Are you sure you want to do that Marshal? Twenty-four hours ago he was trying to kill me," Blair said with a shaky voice.

"I'm sure Blair. If he was going to kill us then you gave him the perfect opportunity when you fell asleep on guard duty. And he said he wasn't trying to kill you, he was only trying to apprehend you. One more thing Blair, I had to make the decision to trust you yesterday after you tried to bushwhack me, and so far I haven't regretted it, other than you falling asleep when you shouldn't have. Now I'm tired and hungry so shut the hell up."

Blair looked at Raymond Ellsworth, "I guess I can trust you too. The marshal is a mite grouchy this morning ain't he?"

Ellsworth stood and stretched. He was stiff and his wrists hurt from the ropes. "He is a mite at that. I'm not one to complain though because I figure there will be plenty of time for that later. We still got to make it to town and deal with Brimley."

Ellsworth went to the fire and began breakfast. Coffee was the first thing he fixed but was cautious to warn Blair and Stewart not to get scalded. He told them the story of how he had nearly killed Brimley with the hot coffee the previous morning and it went a long way in convincing the two which side he was on.

"That was good thinking on your part Ellsworth. At least it got us to where we are now," Blair said.

The three men ate and sipped coffee in silence. All three were wondering how the next few days were going to play out. Stewart was wondering how he had gotten himself in this predicament. From traveling alone to having to put his trust in two men he had just met and both, he recently thought, had meant him harm, funny how life deals out cards.

The Pursuit

"We better try to wake them two and untie their hands for a spell. They might need to relieve themselves before we hit the trail. Ellsworth, I'll hold a Winchester on both while you try to wake them. When they are awake you can untie their hands but keep their feet tied tight. They can make it to their feet and hobble around as best as they can, once they're ready you can retie their hands, in front this time so they can hang on to a saddle," Stewart said.

"Sounds good to me Marshal, but we are one horse short, how are we going to handle that?" Ellsworth asked.

"Of the two prisoners, which one has the stoutest horse?"

Ellsworth though a minute as he looked at the horses, "That would be the tan looking critter over there. It belongs to Ballard and I do believe it can travel for days without stopping. Why do you ask?"

"I believe you said the other man is named Newsome, the one you knocked out after Ballard started up the break. Newsome and Ballard can double up. I figure if that horse belongs to Ballard then it ought to be used to the smell by now," Stewart said.

"We going to offer the two any grub before we leave?" Blair asked.

"None, we got a ways to go and we need the two to be weak from hunger. That should help keep them tame for a while. If they behave today we'll give them half portions for supper tonight. If they complain any or try to get out of line then we let them starve until they get locked up," Stewart said.

Both Ellsworth and Blair listened and both agreed it was the best thing to do. A poorly fed man is less apt to think straight or cause trouble. He won't have the energy.

Ellsworth stood and walked to where the two men slept. He kicked both men's boots and stood back. Newsome opened his eyes and tried to sit up, he couldn't. Ballard looked the worse of the two and had to be kicked a couple more times before he showed any sign of life. He too tried to sit up.

"You two roll over onto your stomachs so I can untie them hands. Don't either of you try anything because the marshal over there has a Winchester pointed at you," Ellsworth demanded.

"Is that you Raymond? Did we get captured or something, if we did then why is my hands tied, and yours ain't?" Newsome asked as soon as the cobwebs started to part.

"Yeah we got captured Newsome, now let me get them ropes off your wrists."

Ballard finally managed to open his eyes. His face was a mess from where the rock had caught him. It must have hit his forehead and the bridge of his nose. Both eyes were black and swollen, he looked like death. "Did we capture Blair?" he asked.

Raymond finished untying Newsome and then did the same for Ballard. "You two got exactly five minutes before those ropes go back on, use the time anyway you want," Raymond told the two.

Thirty minutes later and the five men were ready to move out. Newsome and Ballard both rode Ballard's horse. Blair rode the gray he first brought in the night before, it had belonged to Newsome. Raymond's horse was a light brown sorrel of average build. Not the fastest or stoutest looking of horses, but it was a horse.

Blair still complained about his ribs and could barely make it into the saddle. He would need a few weeks rest before he felt anywhere near normal. A derringer might be small but it packs a punch.

As Blair and Raymond got the two men retied and mounted on Ballard's horse Stewart gathered up the three men's guns. All three owned Colts but they looked to be nearly worn out and not very well cared for. There was also one Winchester, one Sharps, and a Greener, which looked to be sawed off. The Greener belonged to Ballard who Raymond suspected liked to see the damage the gun would cause at close range.

"Here you go Ellsworth," Stewart said as he tossed the Greener to him. "You got the two shells in the chamber and if you continue to impress me then I might give you two more. Now keep that gun pointed at Ballard and Newsome and if either one as much as sneezes you blow them both into the hereafter," the marshal said. Ellsworth looked at the two and grinned, nothing would suit him more.

"You think that's a good idea Marshal, giving Ellsworth a shotgun?" Blair asked.

"Not really, but for lack of a better one that is the idea we are stuck with."

"But Marshal what if he turns that gun on us?"

"He won't, no way is he going to team back up with Ballard and Newsome. Them two will kill him outright if they get the chance. I believe Ellsworth might come in handy. I'm only one man and you are in pretty bad shape. If we don't trust somebody then we'll never make it to Elk Bend."

Blair's eyes grew wide. "You don't intend on going to Elk Bend after what Ellsworth told you are you Marshal?"

"I do, it's the closest town by at least three days. We need to get shed of Ballard and Newsome as soon as possible. We run the risk of getting killed the longer we keep them with us," the marshal said.

"I won't argue that Marshal. I don't like traveling with them two and I'm talking more about the smell than the getting killed part. If we ride with them two stinky bastards a couple of days then getting killed might be a relief."

The five men rode in silence. The two filth brothers were in front, followed closely by Ellsworth. Blair and Stewart brought up the rear at a distance of fifty feet or so. The marshal might have given Ellsworth a shotgun but that didn't mean he trusted him a hundred percent, maybe in a day or two.

About noon Ballard started complaining about food, or the lack of it. No one answered him, after a few minutes he figured he wasn't getting anything to eat until nightfall and grew quiet again.

"Ellsworth, fall back a little so we can talk," Stewart said.

As soon as the horses were side by side the marshal asked, "How well do you know these parts?"

"Not very well Marshal, a man by the name of Lang was the tracker for the outfit. He's the one that headed into Elk Bend with Brimley. From what I gathered though, it was maybe three days at the most and it's pretty much due north. I believe it's not a big place but it ain't that small either. Brimley kept talking about hitting the saloons and gambling houses after we captured old Blair there." Ellsworth looked at Blair and gave him a wink. Blair shot him the bird.

"Do they have a jail or did anyone say?"

"I believe they do Marshal. Brimley has some paper out on him but he didn't think an out of the way place like Elk Bend would be that up to date. The day before I gave him the scalding coffee he got pretty drunk, that's when his tongue got loose and I found out what kind of crowd I had fallen in with."

"If they got a jail then they have a sheriff. We'll go there first and get these two locked up. After that I'll figure out what to do about this man named Brimley. We'll check on Lang too, might be papers on him as well," Stewart said.

"Since you mentioned papers, I would bet those two up there have a bounty on their heads as well. I don't know that for sure but by some of the things they've talked about they have done some pretty bad deeds in their day," Ellsworth said.

The men traveled until nearly dark before they found a spot where water was close. The horses needed it bad but were forced to cool a minute before they were allowed to drink.

That night and the next were uneventful, partly due to the starvation rations Newsome and Ballard were on. The men used their time at night to sleep; hungry men need lots of sleep. About noon on the third day the five were within sight of the town of Elk Bend.

Sitting on a rise about two miles out the group of riders looked the town over. It was of fair size with a main street and a few lesser side streets. It was crowded up against a hill by a wide slow moving river, a river that wouldn't make a good sized creek if it were all gathered in one spot.

Smoke rose from several chimneys and foot traffic could be seen on the boardwalks. There were riders on horses and wagons being pulled by teams. What was most unusual about the town was a steam powered sawmill located about a mile down river, put there no doubt so it's runoff wouldn't pollute the stream which supplied water for the folks of Elk Bend.

The mill looked to be a busy place with men about and draft horses hitched in pairs pulling logs to the blades and others being used to pull funny looking wagons containing what must be railroad crossties from the other end of the mill to a holding yard where the ties were neatly stacked.

"Looks like this is a busy place Marshal, you reckon there is a railroad somewhere around here that would need all those crossties?" Ellsworth asked.

"Not that I'm aware of. Closest depot I know of is at Langley or the one at Fort Clemons. That's a good two days ride from here. No way would they be cutting timber here and then transporting it that far," Stewart said.

"How are we going to go about getting into town unnoticed?" Blair asked.

Stewart sat his horse as he looked the town over and thought. There was a wooden bridge that spanned the shallow stream that looked about the size used for wagons. The other side of the bridge connected to a road that led directly to the main street. There was one wagon going across and another on the other side waiting to go across in the opposite direction.

"I guess we take our two prisoners across that bridge and head them to the jail. If the sheriff ain't around then I'll swear out the warrants myself. I guess since I was the one who arrested them it's only fair that I do the warrants. We travel the same way as we're used to, Ballard and Newsome first and Ellsworth next. Me and Blair will bring up the rear. If those two try to make a run for it Ellsworth then unload that Greener on em," the marshal said.

"What do we plan to do after we get them locked up?" Blair asked.

Stewart looked at the man, "How about we worry about that after these two are safely behind bars." With that the five men moved out.

The river was slow moving and clear. In a couple of the deep pools trout could be seen. Blair looked at the fish and wondered if an eating establishment in town served it on the menu. He really hoped so, trout was tasty and he was tired of trail food.

"Say Marshal, do you have any money?" Blair asked.

"Yes I do, I got one dollar. Why do you ask?"

"I was just thinking, maybe we could hole up here a day or two and let my ribs heal. And while we're here we grab us a decent meal or two."

"That sounds real good Blair but you know that dollar I mentioned won't last forever."

"I know that Marshal, so what do we do if we're broke?"

Stewart looked at Blair and then pointed at the canvas bag tied on the back of Sadie.

"Oh no Marshal, that belongs to the folks that were swindled," Blair said with a hint of self-righteousness.

"No problem Blair, we'll just use the dollar," Stewart said with a smirk. If what Blair said about the money was true then the marshal knew it couldn't be used for food. But where did that leave them, hungry and homeless?

The main street of Elk Bend was hard packed crushed stone that looked like it had been placed there by the town, it made for a dry street. The businesses on either side looked prosperous and seemed to be doing a brisk business. There were at least two general stores and even a hardware. Down toward the far end were several saloons and right in the middle was a building that had a sign hanging over the door, Sheriff's Office, it read.

"Looks like we found what we were hunting for Marshal," Blair said.

The five men rode up out front; there was a hitch rail that looked like it got some pretty good use. The edges of the top rail were worn smooth. Stewart stepped down from Sadie and tied her to the rail.

"Blair, you stay on your horse until Ellsworth gets the filth brothers off that horse they're riding." It was the first time the term had been used around the two and at the moment the marshal didn't care. It appeared Ballard and Newsome didn't care either, neither commented on the remark.

Once everyone was dismounted the marshal opened the door and pointed, "Alright, step inside so we can figure out the accommodations."

Ballard and Newsome did as they were told. As soon as the two cleared the door they both broke into wide grins. Sitting at the desk and wearing a sheriff's badge was none other than Brimley. His face and tongue had done a lot of healing in the last three days.

When Brimley saw the two he never made a move, he never even cracked a smile. If he was glad to see them he wasn't showing it.

Blair and Stewart didn't know the man sitting at the desk but Ellsworth did. As soon as he saw the man he raised the Greener and pointed it at Brimley's head.

"Brimley, how did you get that sheriff's badge? You must have stolen it," Ellsworth said as he held the Greener on him. Brimley still didn't look surprised; he just sat there with the slyest of smiles starting to come across his face.

Stewart, not knowing what Brimley looked like, had first assumed the man was really the sheriff. He now drew his Colt as he faced the man. Blair also held the worn out gun the marshal had given him a few days back. The three had Brimley covered twelve ways to sundown, that was until they head the distinct sound of a Colt being cocked behind them.

"Hold it right there boys."

Ellsworth immediately recognized the voice, it was Simpson Lang.

The Pursuit

Brimley jumped to his feet and pulled his own gun. Sixty seconds later Stewart, Blair, and Ellsworth, were disarmed and marched to the back where they were placed in a cell, all three in a single cell."

"Well Ellsworth, it looks like you done changed sides on me. I reckon I can deal with that," Brimley said as he looked at Blair. He had a description of the man he had been searching for and the description fit Blair pretty well.

"You must be Blair, me and you are gonna have us a little talk later and I can tell you right now, you ain't gonna like it. Who is this other feller?" Brimley asked as he looked at Stewart.

"That's a marshal; he's the one that helped Blair here make it to town. We wouldn't have got caught if it hadn't have been for Ellsworth there. He backstabbed us in order to get his hands on the money," Ballard said.

"That's right boss, we had the situation under control until Ellsworth started working for himself. Untie us and I'll teach him a lesson he won't soon forget," Newsome said.

Both Ballard and Newsome held out their hands so Brimley could cut off the ropes. As Brimley finished locking the cell door he turned and pointed his gun at the two.

"I reckon you two ain't much needed anymore. I got Blair and as far as I'm concerned you two ain't no different than Ellsworth, the three of you are the same as one."

Ballard was momentarily speechless but found the words soon enough, "You're kidding boss, right?"

"Unlock that other door Lang so these two can get tucked away nice and cozy like. Not the cell beside this one, leave an empty space between. I wouldn't want anyone to reach through the bars and strangle somebody," Brimley said as he looked back at Blair.

Nathan Wright

"I'm going to let the three of you simmer for the night. First thing in the morning I'll figure out what to do with you. Right now me and Lang are going for some supper, we are civilized folk now."

As Brimley walked past the cell that held Newsome and Ballard he looked at the two, "I found papers on you two, said dead or alive. You two are the only ones that know me and the next time you use the name Brimley then I'll make sure dead is how I get paid the bounty. My name is Sheriff Brooks and this here is Deputy Little."

Brimley, or Sheriff Brooks as he was now calling himself, looked at the other three men, "You three hear that, same goes for you." with that the new Brooks and Little slammed the door and were gone.

"Let's go to that saloon we ate at last night Deputy. I took a shine to the little lady that served us our food. Boy she was a looker, the kind that makes a man want to take up city life," Brimley said.

Lang thought the hot coffee had scalded more than Brimley's mouth and tongue; it must have cooked his brain as well. The waitress he was referring to was as homely as sin and two days past cold. "Sounds good to me Boss and you're right, I think that little lady would have ran off and married you if you had the nerve to even half ask her."

Brimley looked at Lang and smiled, "You really think so?"

Lang almost laughed as he said, "I would bet money on it boss."

"When we finish up with supper I want you to take those four horses to the livery and tell the hostler they belong to me. Tell him to sell the four along with the saddles and gear and I'll be over to collect. And remind him who the new law is in this

64

The Pursuit

town now. I expect him to give me the money and then it's his problem to make the sale and collect his pay."

"Don't you want to go through their gear first boss in case there might be anything of value?"

"Not really, but you did touch on something important. Take their guns to the general store and see what they will pay you for them. You can do that as soon as you get the horses and saddles priced at the livery. This is working out pretty good Lang, hiding out here as the new sheriff is the best idea I've had in a while."

Lang wasn't about to argue with Brimley. The two men could spend the winter masquerading as the new sheriff and deputy for the town of Elk Bend. It would sure beat being holed up in some dugout out in the big nowhere. Hot food and warm blankets, not to mention a roof was about as good as it gets he thought.

"What about Blair and the money boss? You plan on moving on after we find it?"

"I don't think so. Just think of it Lang, we will be rich and no one will know. We could lay low here for a year or two and when I'm sure the coast is clear we can head out, might go as far away as California where no one will know us. I doubt anyone knows us now, them dodgers the sheriff had were some of the worst drawings I've ever seen. He did us a big favor when he tried to arrest us. Now he's feed for the wolves outside of town and we're the ones running this place," Brimley said.

It was true that Brimley and Lang had killed the old man not less than two hours after they arrived in town. The first place the two went was to an old sawbones to see what could

65

be done about Brimley's injuries from the scalding coffee. No one in town recognized the two until the sheriff spotted them in a saloon after their doctor's visit.

It seemed Brimley and the sheriff, a man by the name of Walter Bledsoe, had shared a bank robbery about fourteen or fifteen years back. Brimley had since stayed with his lawbreaking ways but Bledsoe had taken the straight and narrow. He had been in Elk Bend for the last seven or eight years and the folks liked him so much that they just kept him on.

The last year for Bledsoe hadn't been the most pleasant one for the old man. He was nearly sixty years old and the years hadn't gone lightly on him. The wear and tear of those years all showed on his face, that and twenty more. The last couple of years had seen a cancer take up residence with old Bledsoe, he was dying.

He'd been told by old Doc Sattler that the cancer was there to stay, no way to treat it or to cut it out for that matter. The last time he went to see the doc he was told, "You got one month, maybe two Sheriff, but if I was you I'd be taking care of my personal affairs sooner, rather than later."

Bledsoe hated to hang it up, he wanted another ten years but as it looked he wouldn't get another ten days. He had come to accept the news and was determined to spend what few days he had left doing no more than he had to. He was going to walk the streets and say hello to everyone he met in a town that had treated him with kindness. As he talked to folks around town he tried to hide the pain he was in, sometimes it was a little and then at others it would just about make him pass out.

That was what he was doing when he saw two men coming out of the doctor's office three days back. He stood and

The Pursuit

watched as the two walked down the street and entered the Big Whiskey, a saloon that offered the usual spirits, along with food and gambling.

Bledsoe went to the sheriff's office and started going through his dodgers. He didn't need to look far; he had ink on a man by the name of Brimley. As he sat and looked at the dodger his memory came back to him. The man that he robbed the bank with all those years ago was none other than Ed Brimley.

The face on the dodger was the same man but whoever had made the drawing wasn't very good with the charcoal. If Bledsoe hadn't known the man so well back then there was a better than average chance he wouldn't recognize him now. The more he looked at the face the more he knew that Brimley was in Elk Bend. It might be the crowning achievement of his life as a sheriff if he arrested the killer.

The dodger said, *500 Dollar Reward*, under that it read, *Dead or Alive*. The five-hundred dollars would buy Bledsoe a good coffin with enough left over to purchase a stone marker. The thought of his funeral now made him smile whereas before it was nearly unbearable.

The sheriff got up and checked his Colt; it was old but had barely been used. He put on his hat and started for the door when it swung open and in walked Brimley, along with the other man from the doctor's office. Brimley was holding a gun.

"Well if it ain't my old partner, hello Bledsoe, how you been?"

Bledsoe was thinking about going for his gun. Brimley could figure what the sheriff was about to do and said, "I wouldn't do that Sheriff. You behave yourself and no harm will come to you."

"Thought I recognized you Ed, who you got with you there?" the sheriff asked in a calm voice, calmer than he really felt.

"This is Lang, Simpson Lang, you and him don't know each other. I thought I recognized you Bledsoe when you was looking in the saloon at me and Lang. You was doing a real good job of staying hidden but you forgot about the mirror behind the bar. I saw you right off and decided to come over here and get re-acquainted."

Bledsoe knew he wasn't going to outdraw these two so he would just see where the conversation was heading. "What can I do for you Ed? I was just on my out for some supper and maybe you two could join me, that is after you both put those guns away."

"That is mighty neighborly of you Walter. First though, I wanted to make sure I didn't get arrested for something you and me did a few years back, namely that bank robbery. If that little crime has ran out of time then we can be friends again," Brimley said.

"If you are worried about the heist we pulled then you can stop worrying right now. The statute on that ran out almost two years ago. You could go to any judge and confess and there ain't a thing he could do about it. The time done ran out."

Brimley seemed relieved when he heard this. "I reckon there are no hard feelings about me walking in here holding a gun on you then. But before I put it away I want to see all the wanted posters you got. Let's just say I've become a cautious man in my older days."

Bledsoe realized he had left all the posters on top of his desk. Brimley and Lang both looked, the sheriff knew he was in a bad way.

The Pursuit

"Tell you what Walter; I believe you came in here after you left the saloon to see if my handsome face was decorating some of that paper over there. Lang, how about you going over and having a look while I stay here and talk to my old friend," Brimley said as he held the gun on Bledsoe.

The poster with Brimley's face wasn't in the stack of papers, it was right on top. No sooner had Lang made it to the desk than he held up the poster. "Looks like whoever does the wanted posters needs to take a lesson or two about drawing. It's you boss but damn if you ain't ugly."

"Just shut up and bring me the poster. Then I want you to go through the rest and see if you recognize anyone else," Brimley said.

Lang went to the sheriff's desk and pulled out the chair; if he was going to sift through a bunch of papers then he might as well get comfortable. Brimley had the sheriff take a seat on the long bench that sat against the opposite wall. He thought he and his old bank robbing buddy might catch up on old times.

"Say Walter, it is okay if I still call you Walter, or would you rather I refer to you as Mister Bledsoe or Sheriff?" Brimley asked.

Walter Bledsoe had nothing to say to Brimley, if he had his druthers he would put a bullet right between the man's eyes and after that arrest his corpse for belonging to such a bastard.

"Well, since you don't have an opinion on the matter I guess I'll just call you Walter, just like the good old days. Anyway, I was wondering why there ain't a big pot of coffee on the stove over there; it would be right neighborly of you. Is there anything you would like to ask me Walter, I mean it's been all them years and I'm sure you got questions?"

Nathan Wright

Walter looked up at Brimley and a question did come to mind. "What in hell happened to your face Brimley? I mean, don't get me wrong because it is an improvement."

Brimley bristled at the question, he drew back and struck Walter on the jaw, he might have struck him a little too hard. The sheriff fell off the wooden bench, as he fell to the floor his head struck the stone wall of the jail. His body fell in such a way that the majority of the sheriff's skinny frame only added to the impact. His neck twisted on impact and he lay still. The man's neck had been broken.

In that second while the brain still has the ability to think right before death consumes it, Sheriff Walter Bledsoe could see a field of clover and in the distance his long dead wife waved at him. Death for the sheriff was a release from his days of pain and suffering, and it was better than he could have ever dreamed.

Brimley just stood there looking at the sheriff as he rubbed his knuckles. "Wake up Walter; I didn't hit you that hard. Wake up damn you." Walter didn't wake up, nor would he ever.

"Lang, come over here and see what's wrong with him. Be careful though, he might be setting a trap."

Lang looked up from the wanted posters; he had tried to ignore what Brimley had done but now was forced to see it first-hand. He stood and walked around the desk and over to where the lawman lay. He reached down and felt the man's neck to see if he could feel his heart beating, it wasn't. He also knew by the angle of the head compared to the position of the body that the man's neck was broken.

"He's dead Brimley. Just how hard did you hit him anyway?" Lang asked.

"Not hard enough to kill him. He must have done it when his head hit the floor. You keep looking at them dodgers and see if there's any more ink on me. If there is then wad it up and toss it in the stove. Better check for one on you too," Brimley said.

Brimley sat down on the same wooden bench the sheriff had used and looked at the man now lying at his feet. He didn't hit him that hard he kept telling himself. He must have hit the floor and that's what done it, yeah that was it. In all his life Brimley had justified the laws he had broken by blaming someone else. He was now blaming his old friend because he hit the floor wrong.

Minutes later Lang sat holding two dodgers. "They put out ink on both of us boss. You think this town has a deputy that might have seen these and would recognize us?"

Brimley thought a minute. "I wouldn't think so. That drawing of me is so bad I doubt if anyone would put the two together. You on the other hand look a lot like the drawing they did of you. As far as a town deputy there ain't one. I asked the doc while he was looking over my burns and he said the man that used to be deputy pulled up stakes and headed south a few weeks back, said he couldn't stand another winter in Elk Bend."

"That's good. I'll just slide these two posters into the fire. What are we going to do now?" Lang asked.

Brimley got up and locked the door and then went to the sheriff's desk and sat down. He was quiet for the longest time, Lang knew he was thinking. The man was evil and had evil thoughts so when it came time for a plan he made sure he thought out all the possibilities.

"Bring me that badge off of old Walter's shirt. It'll be dark in a couple of hours. We'll load him out the back door onto your horse. We'll tie him up in some burlap first to make it look like he ain't nothing more than a sack of supplies. Hell as skinny as he is he'll be a light looking load of supplies if anybody sees us. We'll take him out into the wilderness and leave him for the wolves and bears. By morning there won't be anything left," Brimley said.

And that is exactly what the two did. Just after dark Lang brought the two horses around back while Brimley rolled Bledsoe's body up in two blankets he took off a couple of bunks in the jail.

After using a little rope the body looked little more than a rolled up rug, or maybe a hundred pound sack of mule feed. Brimley rode his own horse as he led Lang's horse carrying the body to the edge of the timber line and looked around. It was dark, so dark he couldn't make out anything in the timber. In the distance he heard the howl of a wolf, or was it a coyote? He could never really tell the difference.

Lang, who had followed on foot, caught up and stood there catching his breath.

"Can you see anything Lang? I don't want to go trotting into that wilderness, its pitch black."

Lang looked but for the life of him his vision couldn't penetrate but a few feet. "Let's untie him and drag the body in a little ways. If he is found in a day or two there will be signs of wolves, I'm sure of it."

"That's good thinking. Help me get him off your horse."

Two hours after dark and the body of Walter Bledsoe was hidden in the dense brush that blanketed the edge of the forest. The two men used some dead branches and fallen leaves to completely cover the body. When they got back to the sheriff's office they went in through the front door fully expecting to find someone there asking questions. The place was empty and looked no different than when they had left.

"We pulled it off boss. If anyone finds the sheriff they won't know what happened, no one saw a thing. Now what do we do?

The Pursuit

We can't just stay in this jail, someone is going to come in sooner or later and want to see the sheriff about something," Lang said.

Again Brimley sat and pondered his next move. Finally he looked up from his thoughts and said, "You write pretty good don't you Lang?"

"I reckon I can do about as well as the next person. Why do you ask?"

"I was thinking. How about you writing a statement and pretend you are Sheriff Bledsoe? In it you say how you been hankering for a warmer climate and decided to head on down south and in doing so you officially appoint one Earl Brooks as the new sheriff, that's me, and one Sam Little, that's you, as the new deputy to take effect immediately."

"That's good thinking Brimley, real good. While I figure on the words I'll use you see if you can find something in here with the dead sheriff's signature on it. With a little practice I can disguise my writing to look like his. It might not fool everyone but it will fool most," Lang said.

"Get to writing; I'll look for a signed paper in that cabinet over there, it looks like one of them filing cabinets they have at the courthouse," Brimley said.

Thirty minutes after he started Lang had a signed document lying on Sheriff Bledsoe's desk. He had practiced a few times and when he felt he had the writing down pat he wadded up the practice sheets and tossed them in the fire. He then produced a document that didn't look that bad. Bledsoe wasn't the neatest when it came to penmanship so one sheet of chicken scratch didn't look that much different from the next. Lang and Brimley signed below the fake signature of the now deceased former sheriff. Of course, they signed as Earl Brooks and Sam Little.

Brimley stood back and admired the document that now gave him a new name and a new life. With the ink Lang found in the stack of dodgers he was glad to be someone else himself.

"First thing in the morning we'll go around town and explain that the previous sheriff left town and headed south," Brimley said.

"What about his horse, won't they know his horse is still in town?" Lang asked.

"They won't, the sheriff sold his horse a few weeks ago. The doc told me that. He also said Bledsoe was sick and didn't think he had long to live. Amazing what an old country doctor will share with a man who wants to make conversation. I guess when an educated man like that old doc finds another smart man like myself it just makes him want to talk," Brimley said.

Lang jumped to his feet and tended the fire. It was the only way he could keep from laughing out loud at what Brimley had just said about himself.

"Anyway, I got it all figured out. Bledsoe told us an old friend of his was in town and about to pull out heading south. Said he invited Bledsoe to go along and he agreed. He just gathered up a little of his stuff and then hopped on that wagon out of town. How does that sound for a story?" Brimley asked.

Lang stood there thinking about what he had heard. "You know, this whole thing is just about crazy enough to work. All we got to do is convince a few folks that we are the new law in town and if they got a problem with that then too bad. Bledsoe done made us the law around here, that document I wrote out proves it," Lang said.

Both men locked the door and headed to the cells in the back to catch a little sleep. Bledsoe kept a clean jail and plenty of coffee stocked on a shelf above the stove. Brimley and Lang slept like babies that night.

The Pursuit

True to their word they were both out bright and early the next morning informing anyone they met about what had happened. Most folks seemed to understand that the old sheriff was a sick man and didn't blame him for heading to warmer climates. He deserved to spend his last days any way he wanted.

"See there Deputy Little, when I figure out a plan I figure out a good one. Even if the folks back in Chicago send anyone else this way looking for Blair, or even us, we will be well disguised as the new law of Elk Bend," Brimley said.

"Speaking of Blair, what do you plan on doing when Raymond, Ballard, and Newsome, show up with him?" Lang asked.

"Oh, I got a plan on how to get the information we need. Once he tells us where the money is hidden you can go out there to the spot and see if he told the truth. If he did then we won't need him around anymore. We get rid of him and the money is ours."

Wilbur Westbrook looked out over the town of Chicago from his seventh floor office in the newly built Home Insurance Building, a nine story steel frame building with a masonry and stone exterior dubbed the world's first skyscraper. The building had been completed in 1884 and commanded a scenic view of the surrounding streets and other, lesser buildings.

Wilbur always liked to watch the residents of the city as they ran here and there in what looked, not that much different than, ants scurrying about. He had been one of the ants not that long ago. Now he lived a life that in his younger days he could only dream of.

Nathan Wright

He lived in a fancy section of Chicago on the north side which was in view of the waterfront but not close enough to be troubled by the booming industry the area represented. Living on the north side suited Wilbur, it was a place where people with money treated him as an equal. His wealth might not have been the old money that earned a man a higher level of respect but it was money all the same. If his money didn't earn him the respect he had always craved then at least the appearance of it would.

Wilbur Westbrook was a powerfully built man. As a boy of fourteen he had gotten a job on the docks as most young men of that era did. The work was hard and the hours long but it built resilience in the young man, along with muscle. It was a good thing, a stout man could survive whereas a lesser man might not; the docks were a dangerous place. You learned fast how to stay away from the ever present trouble that infested the area, and it wasn't just the other dockworkers you had to worry about.

The Chicago Police Department hired some of the city's worst, out of favors to political cronies, and sent them to the dock precincts. These notorious men weren't trained as policemen, they were just given a gun and a club and appointed a district to do as they saw fit.

They patrolled in pairs and skimmed money from the workers and small businesses in their watch area. This had resulted in Wilbur, along with every other dock worker, getting their two week pay skimmed on a regular basis. The police weren't standing there when the money was paid to the workers; it had already been taken out by the payroll clerk who then gave it to the officers that were charged with the watch where Wilbur worked.

The Pursuit

After two years Wilbur Westbrook had managed to save nearly five hundred dollars and it was all in a bank not more than three blocks from where he worked. One reason to pick a bank so close to his job was to keep from being robbed in between where he got his money and where he deposited it.

Wilbur figured he would have had at least twice that much if it weren't for the crooked cops. He lived in a cheap apartment he shared with two other dockworkers, this was part of the reason he had managed to save as much as he had.

Money was tight even for those fortunate enough to have a job. Working every hour they could was the only way the three could afford a roof over their heads, they got a place cheap and split the rent three ways.

Wilbur didn't just live in a cheap rundown apartment, he ate cheap too. Some of the food he ate was prepared in the apartment, some he bought on the street from vendors he found to be tolerably clean and reasonably priced.

The two men, or boys it should be said because they were the same age as Wilbur, complained and growled every day about the cut the crooked cops were taking from their pay. These two hadn't saved a dime due to drinking and cards. Neither were that good at cards and when they drank, which they always did, they managed to lose all the money they had on them. Wilbur was the more frugal of the three and usually had to help feed the two the last two or three days before each payday.

More than once Wilbur had to pony up the extra cash for rent when the two fell short. He didn't like it but what could he do? The landlord wouldn't just evict the two that came up short every month, he would evict them and Wilbur too.

One night when all three were sitting around the wooden pallet with four legs the boys had built for their table, a plan was hatched. In the two hours they talked before turning in for the night it was decided that something had to be done about the two cops.

"What are you saying Eli, are you talking about murder?" Wilbur asked. Eli Dobbs was Wilbur's oldest friend.

"Damn right and it won't be murder, it will be payback because they have been murdering us a little at a time when they skim our money. The three of us are starving."

The third boy that rented the apartment was a wild eyed Irishman by the name of Patrick O'Malley. Everyone called him by the initials his name represented, Pom.

"I think we would be doing the dockworkers a favor by getting rid of those two," Pom said. "Not a man would hold it against us if we took matters into our own hands."

The three concluded their discussion by agreeing to talk it over some more the next night. If you work the docks you went to bed early. Anyone that couldn't do the work was promptly fired, his position was then just as promptly filled by the hundreds of men standing idly by who were waiting to hire into your old position.

The next night the discussion resumed, "We don't have any guns and if we did the noise would alert anyone within a mile. We fire a gun then there's no escaping, someone will identify us," Eli said.

"We don't have guns, we don't use guns. We take maybe a three foot section of pipe and do the job. We bludgeon them until they stop breathing and then leave the bodies where they lay. We hammer them good and it'll be a warning to the next cops that get put down here and think about stealing from the workers," Pom said.

"What about that payroll clerk? He has to be just as crooked as the cops or this wouldn't be happening," Eli said.

The Pursuit

Wilbur didn't like the way the talk was heading now. "We don't touch the clerk. He has a family and none of us can say for sure he is skimming anything. It might just be the cops. We don't touch the clerk unless we find out later that he was in on it."

The three sat quietly for a few minutes. The only noise was the empty growls of their stomachs. Tomorrow was payday but today they were broke. Eli and Pom didn't have a penny to their names and there was no way Wilbur was sharing the information about his little bank account. He would just let his stomach complain, the same as his two friends.

"We do the job tomorrow night as the two are leaving from their meeting with the payroll clerk," Wilbur said.

Pom and Eli looked at each other. Finally, after a minute of silence, Pom said, "That will mean they have the money with them. Not just our money but all the money for the other workers that they steal from every two weeks."

Eli listened and then a smile came over his face. "If we get back all the money from a two week payroll then we can give back what is owed to the other workers."

Wilbur hit Eli with the back of his hand, it wasn't a brutal blow by any means but it did get the attention of the two.

"We do that and they'll find our bodies in the river. Everyone will know we killed the two cops; what do you think other crooked cops do to someone that has harmed one of their own? They murder them; I know this from some of the stuff I hear at the docks. We tell no one, do you both understand what I'm telling you?" Wilbur said.

Both boys nodded in agreement. Eli was still rubbing his forehead when he asked, "So what do we do with the extra money?"

"We keep it, split it three ways but we can't spend any of it. We show any extra coin around the docks then we implicate ourselves. We still wear the same worn out clothes and eat the same rotten food and once every two weeks we do without lunch, same as now. No one can find out what we did, do each of you understand?" Wilbur asked.

Again the two nodded their heads in agreement. It was beginning to be a given that Wilbur was the one with the brains, he could figure out the plans and he could do it while the other two were still trying to get their heads in gear. He was also starting to be the leader of the three in other ways, what he said, the others always agreed with.

What the three boys, or men as they should be referred to because they were each now sixteen years old and had the muscled physiques of men twice their age, didn't know was that the two cops didn't just pick up the cash that was skimmed from workers in their precinct, they also picked up for the other eight cops that had workers at the docks in their precincts as well. And some of the other precincts had double the number of men on the payroll as the one where Wilbur and his two friends worked.

The next day the three worked their ten hour shifts loading and unloading freight and anticipated their retribution on the cops that were living off their hard, backbreaking work.

At the pay line, men were lined up from inside the office all the way out the door and halfway down the block. It was like this every other week as the dock workers waited to get just enough money to last twelve or thirteen days, never enough to last the fourteen that would get them to their next payday.

Eli got his pay first and waited on the sidewalk outside for Pom and Wilbur. Once all three got their money they hurried to the spot where they would hopefully even the score. None of

The Pursuit

the three stopped as they walked through the alley in order not to draw attention to themselves. They wanted to see the spot one last time in daylight to again familiarize themselves with the layout.

The alley was good, there was little light and it actually had three ways out thanks to an abandoned warehouse that the three had scouted out the previous night. It had a boarded up doorway that went into the alley about a third of the way down from the closest street to the docks. They had broken away the barricade and fixed it back so it would collapse inward with very little effort. Once inside the warehouse they would put the barricade back in its casings and then push a pair of steel racks against it to make it impossible to move unless you did it from inside the warehouse. They could then pick and choose which of the many doors and windows at the opposite end of the building to use for their escape.

The three decided it would be best if they split up after the deed was done, in that way maybe if one did get captured it would be better than all three. There was little worry about this because at that time of night very few people wandered the streets in this part of the city, it was just too dangerous. The three weren't worried about running into a thief on their way back, they were powerful and fast and if they couldn't fight their way out of trouble then surely they could outrun it.

Pom was against splitting up after the murders and robbery; he rightly surmised that there was strength in numbers. Again Wilbur had it figured out.

"If someone says they saw three men running away from the block where the crime was committed then it won't take long before they figure out that the three of us live in the same crappy apartment, are seen on the same filthy streets from time to time, and all work at the docks. We split up and get back to the apartment as fast as we can. We also split up the money so if any of us get caught then at least all won't be lost. We get back and then count it but it don't stay in the apartment."

"If we don't keep the money in our apartment then where do we keep it?" Eli asked.

"I got a spot, it's dirty, it's nasty, and the smell will make you puke your guts out. It's at the cattle yards, you know where they kill the cows that get brought in on the train cars and then saw up the meat. I worked there a few months before I got the job at the docks. There's a place where the pipes run into the river. At that spot there is a shed that houses all the output piping, a fairly good sized building made of masonry and brick. Inside there's a bunch of left over crating, most of it is broken and rotted. We put the money in three or four different spots and cover it with more crating. That building never gets any traffic, no one can stand the smell," Wilbur said.

"If it's so bad then how do you know about it?" Pom asked.

"One of the discharge pipes got clogged while I worked at the packing plant. Me being the new man, they sent me down there with a shovel, no one else wanted to go, I didn't either but they said I go clean out the pipe or I go home. So I went."

Eli and Pom liked the plan but Eli had one more question, "What if the pipe gets clogged again and they send someone else down?"

"Not a problem, right after I cleaned it out they spent a little money and opened the pipes directly into the river. Stuff falls a good twenty feet to the water below. Before they had it going through a series of pipes that let it out at near water level and it was these turns in the pipe that would always get clogged. Then you had to go down there and unbolt the cleanout at the top of each turn and dip it out with a shovel.

The Pursuit

Now there's no turns and it never gets clogged. One of the fellows I worked with down there told me that a few months back."

It was a good plan, or at least it was as far as how to escape and where to hide the money. The one thing left to figure out was also the hardest part of the heist.

"So then it's settled, everything except how we take care of the cops," Pom said.

"Are you sure we have to do away with the two, can't we just get the money and leave them there alive?" Eli said.

"No other way Eli and I thought we already agreed on this yesterday," Pom said.

"But what if they have families?" Eli wanted to know.

"Neither are married Eli, both used to be but I think their wives either died or ran off. I done a little checking around this morning. Others at the dock hate them as much as we do and know every little piece of dirt there is to know about them. I couldn't be too specific, or ask too many questions, but I gather they are hated about as much in their private lives as they are as cops.

"They both spend their money, or should I say our money, at the gambling houses downtown, not to mention the houses of ill repute. Think of that, we don't have enough money to eat the last day or two before payday and them two are playing the cards and the ladies," Wilbur said. His voice had gotten animated near the end, thinking of the two cops brought out an anger he tried to keep hidden.

"So how do we do it?" Pom asked.

Wilbur explained his plan of how to deal with the two cops as they travelled the alleyway they had used after every visit to the payroll clerk. These two were so predictable that they had used that alleyway for the last two months and probably a lot longer than that. When Wilbur began to put this little plan together in his mind a few months back he had staked out the two crooked cops as they left the office and each time they left they had used the same alley. It might have been because it was so dark and deserted. Rats like the darkness.

Wilbur went over the plan and then went over it again. The two cops would be armed with night sticks and Colt revolvers. The versions the police department used were not the shiny nickel plated weapons most men preferred. These were nearly black with black grips so they wouldn't reflect any light. They were some of the best guns Colt produced and the dark finish was unique to Chicago. A few had found their way out west but if you saw an unfinished Colt you could just about bet where it came from.

As luck would have it the night of the robbery was cold and rainy. The darkness prevailed, not only in the unlit side streets of Chicago, but also in the minds of the three soon to be murderers. Each had to remind himself that these cops had stolen from them and it had to stop. They knew if either of the three had been caught stealing they would have stood a good chance of being shot themselves. Cops in that time and era were notorious for shooting first and laughing about it later. Some even carried an extra gun to plant on someone they killed under suspicious circumstances to make the dirty deed look like self-defense.

At a little after ten that night the three were ready. They wore dark clothes and had gone as far as to blacken their faces with chimney soot. They wore dark hats pulled low to help keep the light rain from washing away the soot.

As the time neared all three men became anxious. What if the two cops used a different alleyway this night? What if there were three, this had never happened before but a stressed mind will imagine what the eyes can't see. What if they were spotted before they had time to spring their trap? There were as many ways for the plan to fail as there were stars in the sky, although this night there were none.

Finally the time came and the three tensed even more, if that were possible. Five minutes went by and then ten. The thought began to take shape that the two cops must have used another alley on this night and not the one they had used every previous night for at least two months.

Just when the three were ready to call off their plans, voices could be heard at the end of the alley. It was the end the two cops would be using if it really was the cops they expected. The three grew deathly quiet as the sounds grew closer. Standing perfectly still they could each hear their own hearts pounding in their chests.

As the voices grew close the three knew it was the two they wanted. They talked loud as they approached, probably too loud but for two men that had side arms they were confident they could handle anything. After all, nothing had happened in this alley before.

There was a stack of old crates about halfway down the alley on the left hand side. It choked the alley down by nearly half but still left about eight feet from the edge of the crates to the opposite wall.

As the two cops passed by there was a spark of light as someone leaning against the wall lit a cigarette. "What the hell?" one of the officers said in a startled voice.

"What are you doing there hiding in the dark like that? It's a good way to get yourself shot," the second officer said.

Pom had been elected to be the one to stand and light the cigarette as the two cops walked past. It was planned to get them to turn their backs to the stack of crates. They had been stacked by the three in a way that left a section near the end that would conceal two men, men who held three foot steel one inch diameter pipes.

As soon as the match was struck and the two cops faced Pom to give him a good dressing down for startling them, Eli and Wilbur made their move. At about the same time both jumped from cover and struck the two cops viciously, by the sounds it was obvious both suffered cracked skulls and probably this first assault was fatal.

Both men went down in a heap, neither made a sound other than that of their bodies striking the base of the alleyway. It had been devised by Wilbur to quickly grab the small cases the two would be carrying to prevent any blood from getting on them. No sooner had the two collapsed from the initial assault than Eli and Wilbur delivered a vicious attack that would have killed the men five times over. Wilbur especially, he struck the fallen man in front of him repeatedly. Even after Eli finished Wilbur continued to strike until he was stopped by Pom.

"We have finished it Wilbur, it's time to get out of here," he whispered. With that Wilbur and Eli dropped the two pipes beside the bodies.

Wilbur looked at the two and then went down a short distance to where the opening was they would use for their escape. When he was almost there he turned and went back to where the bodies lay. Eli and Pom thought he was going back to mutilate the bodies some more but when Wilbur got to where they lay he reached down and removed their guns and the two small ammunition pouches they had clipped to their belts. Once he had the weapons he hurried back to where his friends stood.

The Pursuit

The three then pushed the barrier open and once inside they looked both ways down either side of the alley, no one was there, no one had heard the vicious assault. Satisfied there were no witnesses the three replaced the barrier and then pushed the two heavy steel racks in place.

Ten minutes after the match had been struck and the attack started, the three exited the upper end of the warehouse. They all wore loose fitting jackets and inside each was a paper bag filled with money. The two cases the cops used to carry the money were loaded with rocks and tossed into the waterway. They would sink in twenty feet of murky water, not to be seen again.

Eli went left at a casual pace staying in the shadows. His path home had been planned by Wilbur and he had already traced it earlier that day. He knew all the possible escape routes he could take if he was followed.

Pom went right; his path would take longer and would also allow for the darkest streets and alleys. Again the path had been planned by Wilbur and rehearsed earlier.

Wilbur waited for his two accomplices to make it out of sight before he stepped out of the warehouse. He also went right but before he would take a left turn he would go three blocks farther down the street than Pom. His was the longest path of any and this was by design. He wanted to be in the shadows to watch and listen if an alarm was sounded and people started running in the direction of the attack.

As the three slowly made their way home they kept a close eye out for any more cops that might stop them and ask unwanted questions. The bags of cash each man carried was well concealed in their coats but they could still be searched if they were stopped. Pom and Eli knew if they were detained they would look nervous and guilty of something, there was no way to hide the kind of fear and anxiety both men carried.

Wilbur on the other hand was cool and confident. His plan had so far gone off without a hitch. Each of the three carried a fourteen inch steel wrench to deal with anyone that might try to interfere with them on their journey back to the apartment. As Wilbur walked he began to wonder about Eli and Pom. He had great confidence in the two but this was the first time either had broken the law and that might make for mistakes.

An hour after he set off Wilbur climbed the ramshackle stairs to the rundown apartment. As he unlocked the door he wondered what he would find inside, his two friends or a room full of cops. He found neither; he entered and then closed the door behind him.

After closing the door he sat down at the rough table the three men used and waited. Five minutes went by and then he noticed something just outside the window on the fire escape. It was Pom and Eli. Both had stepped outside onto the small landing when they heard someone climbing the stairs.

"You two can get in here any time you feel like it," Wilbur said. He had known both were there from the start, it was part of the plan. He just let them stay there a few minutes so they could listen for anything unusual on the street below. The ragged curtains parted and Eli and Pom stepped inside, each wearing big smiles. Once inside Pom closed and locked the window, the curtains were pulled and all three sat at the table.

"We did it Wilbur, we really did it," Pom said.

"You two have any trouble on the way here?" Wilbur asked.

"Not me, had an old drunk stand up in front of my path but he was so wobbly all I had to do was step around him and come on home. I was afraid if I hit him he would make a scene and draw attention so I just walked past him. He asked me for a nickel but I didn't slow down or speak. A few seconds after I passed him he fell back against the building and slid down the wall," Eli said.

"Me neither, I just walked here like I owned the whole town," Pom said.

The two sounded tough and confident but Wilbur suspected both were carrying a bad case of the nerves. "I took a few extra streets getting here. Had to sidestep a couple of cops that were standing under a street lamp of all places. The first thing I did after leaving the warehouse was to stash the two guns and ammunition. I got em hid real good and they are there for when we ever need em. Bring the other two bags in here and let's get a count. Something tells me we got a little more than we planned on," Wilbur said.

The three men opened the bags one at a time and separated the cash. It was in every denomination from ones to hundreds. The real surprise was the two five-hundred dollar bills that were in the third bag. Five-hundred and thousand dollar bills were rare and usually never made it to the street. It was the first time any of the three had ever seen a five-hundred dollar bill, Wilbur had seen a fifty once but that was it.

It took nearly an hour to separate the money into denominational stacks. The final count came up to seven-thousand, seven-hundred, and seventy-two dollars. As the three counted Wilbur was the one keeping the running total. When he finally told the two how much they had neither spoke but both sported big smiles.

"That's ten times more than we thought Wilbur. How do you figure that much money was in the two bags the cops had, it don't make sense," Pom said.

Nathan Wright

Wilbur began to look worried, it was the first time his friends had seen him look this way concerning the robbery. During the planning stage they both thought he had ice water for blood, he never had any doubts about what they were going to do. Now he looked both troubled and deep in thought.

Finally Wilbur looked up at the two. "We must have gotten the take that the rest of the cops on the waterfront get. I figured it up in my head. If each of us was losing about six dollars and fifty cents every two weeks then with the number of men that work from this precinct of dockworkers would have been about six-hundred dollars. The way I figure it this represents the money stolen from roughly twelve-hundred men every two weeks. That would be our dock and five or six others."

The three looked at the pile of cash and wondered now what to do with it. They couldn't just hide it at the cattle yards and leave it there forever. At some point they would want to use it, after all isn't that what money is for?

"We need to get this to the waterfront and get it hidden. This is evidence and the longer it's here the more chance we take. We split it up evenly and put it back in the three bags. We split up and meet at the brick piping building I told you about. we need to hurry, the longer we wait the more chance the two bodies will be found and then anyone on the street will be subject for a stop and search," Wilbur said.

Fifteen minutes later and all three were on their way to the waterfront. An hour and a half after that all three were back at the apartment.

Both Pom and Eli had argued as they were repacking the money to keep out twenty dollars apiece to use for a little extra food but Wilbur wouldn't hear of it. "We do anything out of the ordinary and we're caught. We don't touch the money until things calm down a bit."

"And how long do you think that will be," Pom asked.

"A month, maybe six months, but we don't touch the money or go anywhere near it," Wilbur said.

"But we are hungry at the end of every pay period. It'll be hard to not think of the money when our stomachs are growling," Eli added.

"Your stomachs won't be growling, we, the three of us, just got a six dollar and fifty cent raise," Wilbur said.

By the looks Wilbur got from his friends neither had thought about the extra money. "Do we agree then? We don't use the money, we don't talk about the money, and we don't act any different than we have been. If we do then expect twenty or more mad as hell cops to come tearing through that door and don't expect to get arrested. They'll kill us before they take us in."

The three never slept much that night, or at least what was left of it. When they started out the next morning at six-thirty they walked the same route to work they had used for months. This route did take them past one end of the alley where they had killed the policeman the previous night. None of the three dared to look down that alley.

Once at the entrance to the docks Eli finally got the nerve to whisper, "Did you see that, no one was at the alley. No police, no noise, no nothing."

Wilbur scanned the surrounding area, workers were making their way through the fence and heading to their work. "The bodies haven't been found yet. It won't be long though. Those two were probably supposed to check in this morning and when they don't a search will be conducted. Before the midday meal all hell will break loose around here."

The three never said another word, they just split up and headed to their work stations. Each would be wondering what would happen when the two bodies were found. It wasn't every day that two of Chicago's finest got clubbed to death in a deserted alley.

The minutes felt like hours as the three worked and sweated in the cold morning air. Each was alert to any excitement that might indicate the bodies had been found. It had been agreed to meet by the entrance and use one of the benches positioned there to share their lunches, one apple and two slices of bread with the thinnest of layers of sticky blueberry jam smeared in between. As hard as the three worked they needed at least twice that much food but times were what they were.

From the benches they could see up the street to where the alley emptied out on the side near the docks. Still there was no excitement, nothing to indicate that a terrible crime had been committed there.

With the noonday meal over the three went back to their jobs, refreshed from the food but distressed by the lack of attention the alley was getting. It was as if it would be better to get it over with than to put it off. Someone find the bodies and start the search.

At six that evening the three left the docks and headed to spot a couple of blocks away where they could get a sliced roll and a little meat shoved inside for eight cents. It was cheap and it was good, something the three always ate the day after payday.

The old gentleman that sold the rolls was an Italian and his grasp of the English language hadn't caught up with the number of years he had been in Chicago. Wilbur suspected that since he was Italian he went home every night to others that spoke his native tongue and not English. He sold his food from a cart that he pushed by hand, a bright red cart. The old Italian probably made a good living selling his rolls because there was always someone there telling him what they wanted.

As the three stood there waiting to buy their roll Wilbur noticed the happenings around them. People walked here and there but no one seemed to be gathering to talk about anything. If the truth were known many would be in crowds of five or six talking about the terrible murders of two outstanding policemen. None of this was happening.

Not more than twenty feet away was an old lady selling the evening newspaper. She was no different than the hundred other times Wilbur had seen her. He wanted desperately to go over and reach her a nickel for a paper but he couldn't. He had never bought a paper from her and to do so now might bring attention to himself. He realized he was being overly paranoid but if he and his friends were to get away with what they had done then this was the caution they would be forced to use.

The three got their rolls and walked to a small dirty park where even dirtier benches were placed. As they sat and ate none spoke. Each was dealing with their own demons. The lack of excitement over the murders was almost as bad as if everyone in the city were running to and fro screaming their heads off about it.

"It's getting late, we don't want to stay on the street any longer than we usually do. We go to the apartment and play some checkers. Maybe I'll let you two win for a change," Wilbur said to the two.

"Maybe tonight is the night one of us wins for a change," Eli said.

Wilbur was glad to hear it, the two were starting to settle down a bit. He suspected though when the police began knocking on doors and questioning people on the street about the murders then the nerves, as he liked to call them, would be back.

The night was uneventful, all three left for the docks at the same time the next morning as they always did. Again they walked the same route as before but this time there was a difference. A wagon pulled by a single horse was sitting at the entranceway to the alley. Policemen were everywhere it seemed, but looked to be more in curiosity mode than trying to solve a double murder. They didn't look excited or angry. Wilbur figured this must be normal.

As the three got closer it was noticed that the wagon was from the office of the coroner for the City of Chicago. No hiding the fact now, the bodies had been discovered.

"You three there, stop and have a word," a policeman wearing everyday clothes said.

Wilbur had already told his friends to let him do the talking and for them not to speak unless directly asked a question. "Yes Officer, what can I do for you?" he said in a steady calm voice.

As the officer got closer he said, "Detective, not officer. Did any of you three see anything unusual around here in the last day or so?"

Wilbur scratched his chin as if to be thinking before answering, "Well yes Detective. Three men came across this very street night before last and wanted me to follow them to where they said they had a bottle of Scotch Whiskey hidden. Said they was in a sharing mood and thought they would share their generosity with me."

The detective's eyes brightened, maybe this was a lead. "Well did you go with the three?"

The Pursuit

"Oh no, you see I work at the dock and day before last was payday. Them three, I suspect, knew that and wanted to get me in an alley and take me of my pay. Probably would have knocked me out or killed me in the bargain I believe," Wilbur said.

The detective looked around as if he was thinking of his next question. "You say there were three of them, what did they look like?"

Again Wilbur's hand went to his chin as if he was thinking. "They weren't dressed like the usual folks around here, not like dockworkers at all. They were dressed more like dandies, you know, suspenders and pin stripped shirts. Two of the three wore bowler hats and the third was bareheaded. And when I say bareheaded I mean bareheaded, the man didn't have a hair on his head."

"When they spoke was there anything unusual about their speech, you know, did they talk like they were from this neighborhood?" the detective asked.

"Well, only one spoke and he sounded Irish. He had a heavy Irish accent if you know what I mean?" Wilbur said. He knew the two they killed were Irish and he also knew that most of the officers and firefighters in the City of Chicago were Irish. It might create confusion if the detective thought the killers were of the same nationality as most of the city's officers.

The detective wrote down everything in a little notebook he carried. When he finished he looked at Wilbur. "Is there anything else you can tell me about the three?"

"That is about all I remember. It was dark, as it always is after I stand in the pay line to get my two weeks' worth. I wish I could tell you more Detective, but that's all I remember. We need to be going now," Wilbur said as he turned and briskly walked away. He wanted to get far away before the detective asked him his name, which he was sure he would.

As the detective raised a hand to try and summon the three back he was interrupted by another officer and by the time he turned back they were gone. He had managed to allow someone that had given him the most information he had gotten all morning to leave and he had failed to ask his name or where he might be found if more information was needed.

Once the three were around a corner they sprinted down that street and ducked into the first alley they came to. They were in a hurry to take the longest route possible in case they were followed.

"Alright now, we head back to the docks but we use the waterway down under the pier. And for the next few days we leave that way as well. No way do we want to run into that detective again. Also it might be a good idea if we don't travel together anymore. He'll be looking for three of us, if anyone asked we didn't see a thing. If the same detective spots me and tries to ask any questions I'll tell him I've never spoken to him in my life. He'll think he has the wrong man and that will be that. He will never find the eyewitness and hopefully he and his other Irish thugs will search for the three I described," Wilbur said.

And that was that, after a few weeks the murders became secondhand news and before long the city's other problems took the spotlight, as they always did.

Wilbur and his two friends worked another six months at the docks and then promptly quit. The money was used to rent a small storefront and soon the three were loansharking and running illegal whiskey. As each year went by the operation was expanded and the money rolled in.

The Pursuit

As Wilbur Westbrook stood looking over the city he thought about these things that had happened all those years ago. His two friends were still with him and he saw each once a week to discuss different aspects of their operation.

The operation that was making Westbrook the most money at the moment was his deed and title work for some of the eighteen railroads that called Chicago home. It wasn't the legally charged fees he was charging the roads, although they were substantial, it was the acquisition of the land they required for their westward expansions that was bringing in money in ever larger amounts.

Westbrook felt his status was now elevated to the point that he required his first name not be used when anyone conversed with him. He now asked, even demanded, that he be referred to as Westbrook or Mr. Westbrook. He considered his given name to be hokey and old fashioned.

Westbrook was waiting for Eli and Pom to bring him the news he needed from the Dakota Territory. One of the men there who Westbrook had once trusted almost as much as Pom and Eli was now on the run and for good reason. If he was caught he was to be killed, that was after he gave up the information he and only he had.

There was a knock at the door and an elegantly dressed woman stepped in. "Your two partners are here Mr. Westbrook."

"Show them in please."

Moments later Pom entered the plush office followed by Eli. Both went directly to the well-stocked bar that occupied a corner of the office. It was a testament to the two men's long relationship with Westbrook that they were allowed to help themselves.

Westbrook walked from the window and took his seat behind the finely appointed desk that dominated that side of the room.

"I presume the news from Rapid City is favorable Gentlemen?" Westbrook asked.

As the two men finished pouring bourbon into cut crystal glasses they turned and walked to the plush wingback chairs that faced the desk.

After getting seated Pom spoke, "The news isn't what we expected. The man Blair is still on the loose but his whereabouts are known and an attempt is now being made to apprehend him." Once finished he took a sip of bourbon. What would have made any other man wince never affected Pom in the least; he had been a bourbon drinker for years.

Eli now spoke, "That was two weeks ago, we haven't had any more news since then. The last we heard two weeks ago was that Blair would be apprehended within forty-eight hours and we would be getting a wire verifying that. The wire hasn't arrived."

Westbrook looked at the two and knew they had more information. "Continue," was all he said.

"When the expected capture and follow up wire, confirming all was taken care of, didn't arrive, we did a little checking around. As you know we have a few men in the Dakota Territory of our own. They are the ones who found this Brimley and Lang for us. They were advertised as two of the best trackers and bounty hunters in that part of the territory," Pom said.

Westbrook suspected that things had taken a turn for the worse. "What did your contacts say?"

The Pursuit

"Apparently, Brimley and Lang have gone out on their own. We believe they have apprehended Blair and are now in possession of the information we need," Eli said.

Westbrook stood and returned to the window, "As you know, it's not about the money. Blair knows where the hundred and fifty thousand is hidden and I would have liked to have retrieved it but if we don't I assume it's just the price of doing business in that part of the country. No gentlemen, the problem is the information itself. If the railroads found out how we go about acquiring the land they need for their expansions then we will lose all our contracts with them. Again, that isn't the worst of the problem. If they find out, then both of you, and myself included, will be going to jail for a very long time. If they find out about some of the deaths attributed to this venture then we could be hung." Westbrook said that last part with a little drama added to the word 'hung.'

Eli and Pom continued to sip their drinks as they wondered what Westbrook would have them do. Finally Westbrook returned to his desk and looked at his old friends.

"Both of you will head to the Dakota Territory on the next train. It shouldn't take more than four days to get there. Once there I want you to put together a posse, not the law dog kind, the vigilante kind. Have our contact out there gather all the men they think will be needed and have them ready by the time you two arrive," Westbrook said.

Eli and Pom relished the chance to head west. Both were good with guns and accepted the challenge as it was presented to them.

As the two got up to leave Westbrook added, "I expect daily telegrams on this. Take your code books so no one will know what you're sending. All we need is for some nosey telegraph operator to start sharing our messages with the local law."

Upon checking it was learned the next train heading west left Chicago at five the following morning. Both Eli and Pom quickly secured berths on Pullmans and then hurried to their respective homes to pack. Both relished the opportunity to use the expensive handmade Colt Revolvers each had locked up at their homes in safes. Both men were regulars at a shooting range on the outskirts of Chicago and felt they were good with guns, which they were.

The sound the cell door made when Ballard and Newsome were locked up was one of total defeat for the two. Only a couple of days earlier both had planned to share in a fortune once they made Blair talk and found out where the money was hidden. Now they were both at the mercy of the homicidal Brimley.

None of this was lost on Blair, Stewart, or Ellsworth. The three men would never have expected Brimley and Lang to get the drop on them the way they had. And now to find out that the two had somehow managed to get themselves named the town's sheriff and deputy, it was beyond belief.

"I guess in the morning I'll probably see my last sunrise," Blair said philosophically.

Stewart and Ellsworth knew what he was talking about. He, and only he, knew where the money was hidden. Once they recovered the money then Blair would be killed, it was a good bet that the other four men in the jail would also be killed to silence any witnesses.

"How long will it take someone to go and get the money once you tell them where it is Blair?" Stewart asked.

The Pursuit

Blair thought a minute before saying, "From here I reckon maybe a day, might be a little less than that."

"Well then you're safe for two days at least, no way would they harm you until someone rides out there and finds out whether you were telling the truth or not. Truthful or not they would still need to ride back to town. Two days, and then it's over."

"What are we going to do Marshal? I figure Brimley and Lang are holding all the cards. Surely there is something we can do," Ellsworth said.

About that time Ballard and Newsome decided to cause a little trouble of their own. "Hey Ellsworth, I bet you ain't feeling so good about your chances now that you're locked up over there with Blair," Ballard said,

Stewart figured he didn't want to listen to the two dumbasses for the next two days and decided to try and talk some sense into the pair. "Ballard, you and Newsome listen up before Brimley gets back from his supper.

"Shut the hell up Marshal. The way I see it you are in the same boat as me and Newsome here, so don't be trying to act like the law no more because you ain't," Ballard said.

"Alright, I guess I can't argue with your logic, but I need to fill you two in on a thing or two. Would you two be willing to listen?" Stewart said.

Ballard and Newsome whispered amongst themselves for a while before looking back at Stewart. "Alright Marshal, you got yourself a deal but first what is that word logic you mentioned? Neither me nor Newsome here know what you're talking about," Ballard said. As bad as things were looking it was still all Stewart could do to keep from laughing.

"Don't worry about that little word right now, we got other things to discuss. Now the way I see it, you two are in the same shape as the three of us. Now the only way any of us stands a chance of walking out of here alive is if we all work together. Are you two with me so far?"

"Go on Marshal, let's hear what else you have to say," Newsome said.

"Alright then, if you two hear something me and these other two locked up with me work out, I don't want you to go blabbing it to Brimley or Lang. I don't have a plan yet but if one presents itself I would like to know that you two are on our side. Can you do that, can you promise to keep your mouths shut?"

Again the two whispered to themselves until finally Ballard looked at the marshal and said, "We agree Marshal. If somehow an opportunity comes up for either you three, or me and Newsome here to escape, then we promise to include you three and, I reckon you will include us."

Something about the way the two looked at the marshal made him think he might have just heard a big bold faced lie. At least maybe the two would keep their mouths shut and not taunt Stewart and his cellmates for the next day or two.

Brimley and Lang finished their suppers at the Big Whiskey and were about to leave when a stranger, hell in this town everybody was strangers, walked in and asked the bartender a question. The bartender was shaking his head up and down as he pointed at the table where Brimley and Lang sat.

Brimley watched as the man turned and headed his way. When the man made it to their table he asked, "Would you be the man who claims to have been appointed the new sheriff of Elk Bend?"

The Pursuit

Brimley looked the man over. He was of average build but past average in age, he must have been about seventy if not a day or two older. And he wasn't wearing a gun. "I'm Sheriff Brooks and this is Deputy Little, what can we do for you?" Brimley might have asked what he could do for the man but he had no intention of doing anything.

"Well Sheriff, my name is Clarence Fields and I run the General Store across the street. Anyway, I always close up for an hour at noon and go home for lunch. When I got back I found the back door to the storage room kicked open. I ain't figured out what they took yet, I just came here looking for you."

Well wasn't this some kind of hello? When Brimley had killed Sheriff Bledsoe and taken over his job he really hadn't considered the fact that someone might expect him to actually do any sheriff work.

"Tell you what Mister Clarence Fields, how about you go back to your store and see if anything was taken. If nothing is gone then no crime has been committed. If something is gone then make a list and bring it to the sheriff's office, then I'll know how to proceed. Just look me up over there after you get your list made, I'll be there after I pay for mine and the deputy's suppers here," Brimley said through black smiling teeth. He also never had any intention of paying for the suppers. He would do what he wanted and take what he wanted from this town, after all, he was the man wearing the badge.

Fields turned and headed out the front door. He was disappointed in the way the town's new sheriff had spoken to him. It was as if robbing a general store wasn't a crime at all.

"Well Lang, me and you got stuff that needs to be getting done. Let's both of us head on back over to the jail."

As the two stood to leave the ugly waitress came from the kitchen and as she walked by she smiled at Brimley. Her teeth were nearly as black and nasty as his were, she even had a front tooth missing. The smile was all it took for Brimley to retake his seat.

"Tell you what Lang, head on back to the jail and check on our prisoners. If everything's alright then you can take the horses to the livery and see how much the hostler over there is willing to pay. After that me and you will take their guns to that Clarence Fields feller and see how much he is willing to pay us for them as well. Me and you keep arresting people and selling off their horse and guns is starting to make me wish I had become a sheriff a long time ago."

Lang noticed Brimley undressing the waitress with his eyes. The thought nearly made him lose his supper. "Alright boss, don't do anything I wouldn't do." If he did anything at all with the woman it was more than Lang would do.

As Brimley motioned for the missing tooth waitress Lang went out the front door and headed for the jail. He was anxious to get the horses to the livery and the guns to the general store. It had been a long day and he wanted some sleep.

When he entered the sheriff's office he fully expected to find another of the town's residents inside needing help with a sheriff matter. To his pleasant surprise the front room was empty.

As soon as he made it through the sheriff's office he opened the sturdy door to the cells in the back and stepped in. When he turned to look at the prisoners the first thing he saw was a Derringer pointed right at his nose, it was held by Stewart.

The Pursuit

"Don't say a word Lang and don't reach for your gun. Ease over here next to this cell and do it quick or you're going to be missing a good portion of your head," Stewart said.

Lang thought about trying to draw on the marshal but knew what kind of damage a Derringer could do. They might be small but they used a large caliber shell that would make a decent size hole, beginning at his face and ending at the back of his skull. He did as he was told.

When Lang took the three steps to the cell Stewart occupied, Ellsworth reached through the bars and relieved him of his keys. Stewart reached through and took the man's Colt out of its holster while Ellsworth unlocked the door. After a quick search it was determined the Colt was the only gun Lang possessed. The town's new sheriff and deputy had failed to search the five men earlier when they put them in the cells. Stewart figured the little Derringer had now got him out of a tight spot twice in the last few days.

"Alright, put Lang in that cell and lock him up," Stewart told Ellsworth. As he said this he reached the Derringer to Blair. Now there were two men armed.

"Let's get out front and get the rest of our guns before Brimley shows up," Stewart said.

Ten minutes after Lang walked into the cell room Stewart and his men were armed to the teeth. Again Blair was in charge of the Greener, he also had the old worn-out Colt. He stood in the cell room and begged for any of the three prisoners to whisper a word, not a man made a sound.

Ellsworth now had a Colt holstered at his side along with a Winchester. Stewart had his trusted Colt and Winchester and was itching to face down Brimley. He marched back to the cell area and confronted Lang.

"Where is he?" was all the marshal said.

"Across the street at the Big Whiskey, he's over there talking to a waitress."

As Stewart turned to leave Ballard said, "Turn us loose Marshal, we had a deal."

Stewart took the Winchester and rammed it through the bars of the cell hard enough to knock Ballard to the floor. "The only deal me and you had was for you to keep quiet while I worked out our escape. When you spoke just now you broke our deal by talking. After I get Brimley captured I might just march in that cell and beat the living hell out of both of you." With that Stewart stomped out of the cell area but before leaving he told Blair to lock the main door and after that to keep that Greener pointed at the prisoners.

"It would truly be my pleasure," Blair said.

Stewart and Ellsworth stepped from the sheriff's office and headed across the street. The Big Whiskey was well lit by the look of things. When the two men stepped to the batwings and peered inside they didn't spot Brimley at first. The saloon was smoky and doing a brisk business.

There was another room past the saloon and it appeared men and women in that room were seated at tables and eating. After clearing the first room, the saloon portion of the Big Whiskey, Stewart and Ellsworth walked into the dining section. There, sitting against a wall was Brimley and he had his arms around someone in the chair right beside his, Stewart assumed it was a woman but could have passed for a man.

"Stay here Ellsworth and keep a lookout. Make sure no one in here tries to interfere," Stewart said. Ellsworth took up a spot where he could cover the marshal.

Stewart headed for the table where Brimley sat. He must have been preoccupied with the woman sitting with him because he didn't see the marshal until he was nearly at the table. When he saw Stewart he was frozen in fear. This was the last person on Earth he expected to see in the Big Whiskey tonight. He didn't go for his gun, he couldn't even speak. Suddenly the marshal saw the floor get wet beneath Brimley's chair. The town's self-appointed sheriff must have had a weak bladder.

"Stand up Brimley and face me like a man," Stewart demanded.

The woman sitting in the chair beside Brimley quickly stood and headed back toward the kitchen but not before winking at Stewart. Ellsworth saw this and tried not to laugh.

Finally Brimley found his tongue, "I left you locked up in my jail. How did you escape?" And then Brimley added, "Did you kill Lang?"

"Lang is locked up with Ballard and Newsome. Now get your soaking wet ass up and march over to the jail. I have a good notion to put all four of you in the same cell overnight and see how many of you are still alive in the morning."

Brimley pushed his chair back from the table and stood. It was then that he noticed how wet the front of his trousers were. Stewart reached over and took the man's Colt before it got wet and then marched Brimley to the jail. As he dripped his way past Ellsworth his former gang member laughed out loud. Stewart almost laughed himself.

Once at the jail the marshal had calmed considerably. He didn't put Brimley in with Ballard and Newsome; he knew the two would kill the man for sure. He locked him in the cell with Lang who protested that he didn't want to be locked up with a man who had just wet his pants.

"Shut the hell up Lang, he'll dry out soon enough," Blair told him.

Stewart looked at Blair. "I couldn't have said it better myself.

Once everyone was locked away nice and tight the newly freed Stewart, Blair, and Ellsworth, went back out front and made a pot of coffee.

"Marshal, don't you think we better get that sack of money off my horse out there, that's assuming the money is still there?" Blair said.

"Tell you what, how about you and Ellsworth stripping our gear and then taking them down to the livery, I saw it at the edge of town as we rode in. I imagine Sadie is tired of standing out there tied to that hitch rail," Stewart said. "Just bring the gear in here, saddles and all.

"Going to the livery might not work Marshal without money," Ellsworth said.

Stewart stood and went back to the cell area. "Lang, I want you to reach me every cent you got on you through the bars and don't say a word while you're doing it."

Lang did as he was told and in all he reached a hundred and twelve dollars to the marshal. "Brimley, I want you to take what money you got and toss it out here on the floor. I'll have it scrubbed after it dries so it doesn't smell so bad," Stewart told him.

Stewart went back out front. "Here's half the money I took from Lang. Take all four horses to the livery. Have them brushed and fed. And make sure Sadie gets corn or oats to eat. Hell, give her both. After that go to that eating place across the street, not the Big Whiskey, the other one, whatever its name is, and have them fix a bunch of grub and bring it to the jail. The three of us are going to hole up here till morning. We'll be well fed and rested by then."

The Pursuit

It wasn't long until Blair and Ellsworth were back. "The hostler was glad to hear Brimley and Lang are locked up. He said he and most of the town knew Sheriff Bledsoe didn't leave town in the middle of the night. Said a few of the men went out looking and it didn't take more than an hour to find the sheriff's body. They didn't even bury him Stewart, just covered him with some tree limbs and left him for the wolves. They said they brought the body back to the undertaker and he is making arrangements to have him buried properly," Ellsworth said.

"The way I see it, Lang and Brimley are guilty of murder, probably more than this one too. What do we do now Marshal?" Blair asked.

"Well, we can't stay here. I don't believe Elk Bend has a telegraph. When we rode in I never spotted a wire anywhere. We'll need to get to a town and try to get some information. Right now we're working blind, you might say."

"I agree with the marshal. Those four we got locked up back there are working for some powerful people. If they find out that Brimley and his gun hounds have failed then they'll send more men to finish the job they started. Even staying in Elk Bend might be dangerous, we don't know who we can trust," Ellsworth said.

Stewart and Blair knew what Ellsworth said was true. If powerful people were behind the attempted kidnapping and murder of Blair, and that job wasn't finished, then those responsible would send someone else to take the place of Brimley, someone more capable. Since Stewart and Ellsworth were now involved it was most likely they would be targeted too.

"Alright, we spend the night here in the sheriff's office. The building is solidly built and we can rest peaceful because of it. All of us have had a rough few days. In the morning we'll spend what money we got over at the general store and get enough to see us through to Rapid City. They got a telegraph there but the best thing they got is Judge Preston and Marshal Savage. We make it there and we'll have us some help."

"What about them criminals we got locked up in the back Marshal, did you forget about them?" Blair asked.

"No I didn't. When we go for our horses in the morning I'll talk to that livery man. He'll know who in town he can trust. Them four are now the property of Elk Bend as far as we're concerned," Stewart said.

Even though they were in a jail Stewart decided that one man should stay awake during the night. The three took shifts but still managed to get rested by the next morning. About an hour after first light Blair and Ellsworth were sent to the same restaurant to see if they would bring food to the jail for not only themselves but also for the four prisoners. The prisoner food wasn't to be anything special though, just rough grub.

After the visit to order the food they were told to head over to the general store and give the man what money was left and order it up in trail food. They needed enough for a week but if there wasn't enough money to just prepare whatever it would buy.

The four prisoners ate like refugees when the food was slid under the bars to them. The man from the livery had rounded up five men he trusted and made sure they were all armed. There would be two men at the jail at all hours. The rest of the townsfolk, after hearing what had happened to their beloved sheriff, agreed to have him buried in the church cemetery and a stone marker prepared, all of it to be paid for by the town of Elk Bend. The money Brimley had on him was to be used to offset the price of feeding the prisoners until other arrangements could be made.

The Pursuit

Stewart took Lang's horse from the livery to use as a pack horse and headed for the general store. Clarence Fields was so glad Stewart had arrested Brimley and Lang that he refused to take any money for their food. He gave it all back and told them they had done a great service for the town by bringing Sheriff Bledsoe's murderers to justice.

When the pack horse was loaded Stewart could tell that Fields was a generous man. He had been told they needed enough supplies for a week and it looked to be that, and more.

After Stewart was sure the prisoners were guarded properly and the town would be patrolled for the next few weeks he and his two companions set out for Rapid City. Before riding out he assured Fields that once he made it to Rapid City arrangement would be made to have the four prisoners brought there to stand trial for the murder of Sheriff Bledsoe.

As the three men rode out of town they felt they were home free, in the back of their minds they knew it was a long trip and if they ran into any trouble there wouldn't be anyone around to lend a hand.

About an hour after leaving Elk Bend Stewart told the two riders to pull up so he could share a bit of information he had gotten just before leaving the jail that morning.

"While you two were loading the supplies on the horses this morning I went back in and had me a little talk with Brimley and Lang. During the night I kept trying to figure out why those two came to end up in Elk Bend. I know the story Brimley told you and the other two, but something about that story just wouldn't hold water," Stewart said as he stopped Sadie and reached for his canteen.

"What was it you didn't believe Marshal?" Blair asked.

After Stewart took a long pull of water he recapped his canteen and hung the strap back around the saddle horn. "Ellsworth said the five were within an hour, maybe two, of catching up with Blair. I just kept thinking that a man who was within a couple of miles of capturing the man he was searching for wouldn't turn and head into town, I don't care how much pain he was in. It just didn't make any sense," Stewart said as he prompted his horse forward again.

The three rode a ways in silence, each man thinking as they went.

"You know Marshal, even that dumbass Ballard thought of that. He was the first to speak up that morning and ask Brimley why he was so intent on heading into town. We all knew he was in some pain but I didn't figure it was the kind of pain that would prompt him to give up on the hunt," Ellsworth added.

"That's right, we all seen him the day he and Lang got the drop on us. He looked bad but I've seen men hurt way worse and they still managed to see to the needs of the day. Look at Blair over there, he was shot and has two or three broken ribs and he has ridden every step we have. As a matter of fact it was Blair's injury, and his stubbornness to continue with things, that gave me the idea of talking to Brimley and Lang this morning," Stewart told the two.

Upon hearing this Blair sat a little taller in the saddle. He had always thought of himself to be a little less tough than other men. After hearing it the way the marshal explained it he now felt he was tougher than he had given himself credit for, and he was damn sure tougher than Brimley.

"So what did you find out Marshal?" Blair asked.

"The way I figure it, we got about a one in ten chance of making it to Rapid City alive. Brimley said he got a wire just before they tracked you to where the five split up. The wire said two men were on their way here to take over the hunt for Blair. The two men were to meet up with a dozen men that work for an outfit by the name of Baldwin Felts.

"When Brimley read that wire he never bothered to send a reply. He knew he and the four that rode with him would be killed as soon as the two got here and met up with the twelve toughs from Baldwin. I asked him how he knew this and his answer seemed sincere.

"He was given the name of a spot where the meeting would take place and he would be paid off. He knew the place, a box canyon twenty miles north of Rapid City. He got to thinking that if he was to be fired then why would they want to do it in such a remote spot? Just meet him at the train depot and pay him off. He knew why, he and the rest of his gang was being lured to such a place, to be killed," Stewart said.

The men rode on in silence for a while until Blair asked the most logical question. "If that's true, and I have no reason to believe otherwise, then shouldn't we be riding for Rapid City with all available speed?" It was a good question; Ellsworth had been wondering the same thing.

"I asked Brimley what town was he in when he sent and received the telegrams. He said it was Langley, the closest town to Elk Bend with wires. He said the message he got said the two men from Chicago were coming to Rapid City and were meeting up with the twelve Baldwin Felts men there, and then heading to a nearby town called Fort Clemons.

"Once the men all met up and made it to Fort Clemons they would be heading to that box canyon to settle up what money was owed to Brimley. After that the search would be in the hands of Baldwin Felts. That's when Brimley took off for anywhere he felt he could hide out and blend in for a while until the Baldwin Felts men gave up.

"He said he lost his nerve that morning and decided to leave it up to Ellsworth, Ballard, and Newsome. He knew about Elk Bend and he knew the sheriff there. He hatched the plan to take on a new identity and in the meantime hoped Ellsworth, Ballard, and Newsome, caught Blair. After he recovered the money he planned to kill all four and then wait it out," Stewart said.

"Well now that just beats all. Looks like Brimley had in mind to steal the money all along and somebody found out about it. Any way it worked out I was going to be dead," Blair said.

"So now what do we do Marshal? There are only three of us and from what you said we are up against fourteen trained gunmen. I ain't against a standup fight but those odds are the same as suicide. You gave us a one in ten chance, I think it's closer to zero," Ellsworth said in a grim tone.

"Thanks to Clarence Fields at the general store we got supplies for at least ten days. If we are going to fool our pursuers then we will need to use as many days as possible. We go to Rapid City using the most out of the way route we can think of. We stay in the ravines and timber when we can. Don't use any of the trails," the marshal told the two.

Both Blair and Ellsworth were quiet for a while as they thought over all that had just been said. It was obvious the two were thinking about their chances, and they didn't look good. By noon they figured they were a good twenty miles away from Elk Bend. It was time to rest the horses and maybe figure out a plan, something that might increase the odds to five to one instead of ten to one.

Water was still hard to find as the trio headed west. A small clear stream was found a little after one o'clock and it was decided to rest the horses there. No one had gone through the supplies Fields had given them and it was decided to see exactly what the men were going to be living off of for the next week or so.

There was a fifty pound sack of horse grain and this was already known by the three. The rest of the supplies were in empty flour sacks, the fancy kind that women picked out and dared their husbands to nick or tear. Once the flour was used by ranchers, or farmer's wives, they would be sewn into dresses and underwear by the women folk. Women had been known to wait for a new supply of flour to be delivered to a general store so they could pick out a pattern they liked. These sacks though would be lucky if they weren't used for bandages before this trip was over.

It looked like this wasn't Field's first time in packing out trail grub for an extended trip. The best thing found was a side of bacon wrapped in grocer's paper and wrapped tightly in burlap. The oddest thing they found was a dozen and a half of eggs in a sack filled with straw. Each of the men smiled when they discovered the eggs. The other pleasant surprise was a sack of biscuits, twenty four in all.

"These eggs will need to be used up in the next day or so, any longer than that and they stand a good chance of being broken or spoiled," Ellsworth said.

Blair and Stewart were told by Ellsworth that he did the cooking while he and his previous lawbreaker companions were traveling. He said that was for two reasons, "I'm a good cook and you saw them filth brothers. Would either of you eat anything them two touched?" Both Blair and Stewart indicated they wouldn't.

The men found some jerky and by the color it could only be beef. They sat and ate jerky and biscuits for lunch as they considered their plans.

"I say we head north for two days, dead north and that should put us far enough away from the route the Baldwin boys will be using, it might help keep us safe," Ellsworth said.

Blair agreed, "I like it, we head two days north and then turn west four of five days before turning back south toward Rapid City."

Stewart said nothing; he just chewed his jerky and looked off into the distance. He was a hard man to read at times which Blair and Ellsworth were starting to find out.

"Well, what do you say Marshal, what do you think of mine and Blair's plan?" Ellsworth asked.

"Not bad, but not good either. If I was those Baldwin boys, that is the same route I would take getting to Elk Bend. The reason is there ain't much in the way of trails on the northern route. There also ain't much in the way of other travelers. That is also where the box canyon is where Brimley said they were supposed to meet."

Ellsworth looked at Blair and neither man had another plan worth sharing. "So what do you recommend Marshal?" Ellsworth asked.

"Oh, part of your plan is good; the part about going north, the only thing wrong with it is two days north isn't enough. We need to go at least four days north."

"Four days north is nearly a hundred and thirty miles Marshal. That would put us near the Badlands," Ellsworth said, his voice nervous.

"That's right, but the way I plan to travel is this, we start early and we move hard. We travel till dark and the next day we do it again."

Again Ellsworth said, "The Badlands, you intend to go through the Badlands."

The Pursuit

"That's right, we ride into the Badlands and then we turn west. We do all the westward riding in the Badlands. After a few days of doing that we should be able to turn south and sweep completely around anyone looking for us," Stewart said.

Blair wasn't that familiar with the Dakota Territory and had only heard a few rumors about the Badlands. But what he had heard was enough for him to have reservations about going there. He would just as soon go straight to Rapid City and take his chances.

"What do you know about this place called The Badlands Marshal?" Blair asked.

After a few minutes Stewart looked at Blair and said, "It's rough country, not a lot of grass for the horses and not many trees to use for firewood, or shade for that matter. It's home to rattlesnakes and prairie dogs. The best thing about it though is a man can ride right by you; if you know where to sit your horse you won't be spotted. The terrain is broken with lots of places to hide at night. This time of year, and this far north, there should be water from snowmelt. You wait till you see it, it is truly beautiful country."

"You think the Baldwin men will go through that part of the territory," Blair asked.

"They might, but I doubt it. They will try to get to Elk Bend to take care of Brimley and the others first. Once they find out Blair wasn't caught they'll turn their attention back to us," Stewart said.

"What about the townsfolk? You think they'll be alright, we done rode off and left them there alone with four pretty bad men," Ellsworth said.

Ellsworth didn't know it but his worry for the folks of Elk Bend had just proven to the marshal that he wasn't an outlaw, or a killer. Outlaws and killers wouldn't give a damn about the inhabitants of Elk Bend.

"They'll be alright. I doubt that detective agency would be the type to shoot up townsfolk. That wouldn't look good on a fancy outfit like that. No, I figure the two men from Chicago will have papers that will require the four prisoners be released to their custody. Once they ride out of town then they can dispose of them any way they like. Whoever is behind all this is a force to be reckoned with, and they won't stop until they get what they want," Stewart said.

Eli Dobbs and Patrick O'Malley stepped off the train onto the depot in Rapid City at about the same time Blair and Stewart were climbing the bluff to evade Ellsworth, Newsome, and Ballard. The two men from Chicago were met by a man named Dorian Matus. Matus was the lead detective for Baldwin Felts in the territory and he would be in charge of the hunt for Blair. He was also to make sure that a man by the name of Brimley and his crew were hunted down and silenced. That wouldn't be a problem for Matus; he was experienced with such things.

Eli and Pom each stuck out a hand and shook. "I presume you have a plan for us Matus?" Eli asked.

"I do, in the days since I received the telegram from Mr. Westbrook I have been able to trace the whereabouts of Brimley and Blair up to and including Thursday of last week. A dispatch rider that does the circuit with the territorial courts in the area was in a small town last Thursday and came about some interesting information. There seems to have been a change of sheriff in that little town, the place is called Elk Bend. The new sheriff fits the description of the man known as

The Pursuit

Brimley. The dispatch rider knew I would be in Rapid City so rather than mailing a letter he simply looked me up here.

"The dispatch rider had been on Westbrook's payroll for more than a year and he regularly sends information to Chicago in the form of letters, never the telegraph. It was a good thing he had the presence of mind to find me rather than sending the information by mail.

"The last information actually received from Brimley was from a town called Fort Clemons, it's the next to last town in that area with both rail and telegraph service. I feel the information is solid," Matus said.

"How many men do you have for the job Matus?" Eli asked.

"There are eleven besides me, all are trained as marksmen and each can handle himself in a fight. I assure you my men will get the job done," Matus said.

Eli and Pom smiled, they were sure Westbrook would be pleased if this matter could be wrapped up in the next few days.

"Let us get our gear from the train and then grab a meal. When do you want to leave?" Pom asked. It was evident both he and Eli were excited to be going on a hunt, a hunt not of game but of men.

Matus took out a pocket watch and after opening the face and checking the time he looked up at the sky as if he trusted his instincts more than he trusted his watch. "I wanted to start immediately but it will be dark in a couple of hours, we leave at first light."

"What arrangements have you made for our horses?" Eli asked.

"You have two fine mounts at the livery. My men also have their horses there. It's going to be a caravan of sorts, fourteen horses and riders, three more horses will be used as pack animals. They will come in handy if we lose a horse or two along the way. Seventeen horses for the next two weeks, in this kind of terrain, and at the pace I plan to keep, will almost guarantee we lose a couple," Matus said with a smile. It was as if he relished the possibility of killing his horses on this journey.

"Alright then, it's settled. We leave at first light. In the meantime I want to get checked into a hotel and get this rail dust off of me. I also look forward to a hot meal," Pom said.

Matus stood as the two men gathered their luggage. If these two were worried about a little road wear while riding in a plush Pullman and were anxious to get to a hotel and have a fine meal he wondered how they were going to hold up on the back of a horse for two weeks sleeping out in the open and eating trail grub. He almost laughed at the thought.

After the two received their luggage from the baggage car they headed for the boarding house that had been booked for their stay. Although they would be leaving in the morning their rooms were rented for a full two weeks. When Matus made the arrangements he thought about the two city boys from Chicago coming out west to play the part of cowboys. What Matus didn't know about Eli and Pom was the two were more dangerous than any of the Baldwin Felts men in his group. Eli and Pom had committed some of the most heinous crimes the City of Chicago had on the books and neither had ever been considered a suspect. The two were ruthless and well versed in the pugilistic arts.

After escorting the two city boys to their rooms and helping them with their luggage he excused himself and headed back down the stairs.

The Pursuit

"Wait Mr. Matus, Pom and I would like you to have dinner with us tonight so we can go over the information you have acquired a little more thoroughly," Eli said.

Matus stopped on the stairs and made a face before painting on a smile and turning back to his employers. "I would be delighted, shall I meet the two of you back here in, oh say in an hour?"

"That would be fine," Eli said as he turned and went into his room.

Matus continued down the stairs and as he exited the boarding house he had to keep reminding himself it was his job to babysit these two for the next two weeks, after all he was getting paid for it wasn't he.

After the hour was up Matus entered the foyer of the boarding house and waited for the two city boys to descend the stairs. As he stood he looked into the side room to see the two sitting there reading the evening paper. When they saw him they each got up and all three headed for the door.

As the men walked no one spoke. It was the custom of Eli and Pom to notice everything as they walked. It was a habit that had probably saved their lives more than once in Chicago. Here in a backwater town on the American frontier it was doubtful if anyone would know the two but old habits were hard to break.

Not knowing the town at all the two followed Matus and hoped he was taking them to a place where the food was good. They went down two streets and then took a side street; in the distance was a sign that read Rapid City Diner.

"Is a diner the best this town has to offer Matus?" Pom asked.

"The name is a bit misleading. I guess the man that owns the place figures the name diner is more appropriate than some of the fancy names restaurants get named back in Chicago," Matus said.

Eli and Pom were a few steps back as Matus lead the way inside; both men gave each other a look at what the Baldwin Felts man had just said. Each noted the contempt in the man's voice and wondered if he was going to be like this the entire trip.

Matus led them to a table in a back corner that looked to have been prepared for the three. "I took the liberty of arranging a table for our dinner. I hoped it would be something that would suit the two of you. I figured you two are more accustomed to linen table cloths and napkins than the bar of a saloon."

This was more than Eli could stand, before Matus could take his seat he stepped between the man and his chair, "Let's get something straight right now Matus, Pom and I have been in some pretty tight scraps in the past. Scraps that would make a man like you run to your mommy, so the next time you say something that either one of us feels is a put down I will personally whip your Baldwin Felts ass. I hope you understand me."

Matus looked at Pom, Pom gave him a wink and a nod and then said, "You know Detective, I've seen what Eli can do to a man, hell I've helped him do it, so if I were you I would watch what I say."

Matus was astonished that these two city boys would make such a threat to him. He was a detective that had been in his own share of tough spots and wasn't about to be talked down to or threatened. "I myself have been in a few situations where I felt I was out of my league; this isn't one of them, I can assure you. I have survived all of them and I expect to survive my dealings with the two of you. I am originally from New York and feel anyone from Chicago that thinks he is tough should try a night or two on the streets of that city." When finished Matus waited for what would happen next.

Nothing happened. Where Matus was wrong about Eli and Pom was that these two wouldn't do anything obvious, they would choose a time when no one was around and teach their adversaries what Chicago street justice was like. Matus would get his education, but not here.

"Well, I think we both understand each other now Matus. You will refrain from treating either Pom, or myself, in the manner in which you have done already or one of us will not survive our little journey. Do we understand each other?" Eli said.

Matus grunted and took his seat. He wanted to get this dinner over with so he could get away from these two pompous asses.

The conversation that was to fill the two men from Chicago in on the plans didn't take place. Eli and Pom felt no need to speak to the detective and Matus felt the same way, multiplied by two. After the meal was over Matus looked at Eli and asked, "Shall I pay for my own dinner or is it covered by your firm?"

"Oh, it is our treat Detective," Eli said.

Matus stood and dropped his napkin on the plate in front of his chair. "It was no treat at all. Be at the livery at daybreak in the morning or me and my men will leave without you." With that said the detective turned and walked away.

Eli and Pom just looked at each other. They each pulled an expensive cigar from a jacket pocket and lit up. Neither was concerned in the least at the way the detective had spoken to them.

Matus walked to the hotel where he and the other eleven Baldwin men were staying. There were six rooms rented, two men to a room. All eleven men were in one room playing poker. Matus walked in and told of the two assholes they would be traveling with. "I say the two have an unfortunate accident on this trip. It won't affect Baldwin Felt's relationship with the railroads in the least if the two ride out in the morning and never come back. These Chicago boys are getting a little too much business anyway and that information ain't coming from me either. Some of the higher ups are talking of easing the bastards out of all the railroad business and letting Baldwin handle the land acquisitions."

The other men in the room knew it wasn't any of their business but agreed with Matus. He was the boss and he didn't get that job because he was stupid or weak. He was one of the smartest and toughest field agents Baldwin Felts had. He had been approached by some of the higher ups at Baldwin about moving to the main office in New York to help run the ever expanding detective agency but had always declined. He liked the rough and tumble field work and more than one person felt he liked the occasional killing that was attributed to him. Matus was a dangerous man.

Matus was tired and decided to head to his room. The rest of the men were told to finish up the game and turn in soon, tomorrow was going to be an early day. Matus turned and left.

The second in command of the twelve was a man by the name of Elon Dietrich, a big New Yorker of German descent. He was as tough as Matus and relished the thought of eliminating the two Chicago boys in the next few days.

The report would explain how the two just weren't cut out for the rough and tumble ways of the west. They would both be buried in graves that would never be found and that would be that. If Matus said the two had to go then the other eleven agents would see that it happened.

The Pursuit

Thirty minutes later Dietrich told the men to finish their game, he was turning in. The big German walked to the next room and opened the door, lying on one on the two beds in the room was Matus, his eyes were open wide and his expression was that of suffering, his face was blue and he was clutching his throat. Dietrich raced to the bed and looked at his boss, it was evident the man was already dead.

Stepping back to the next room he summoned the other men. They all surrounded the building and searched the nearest streets. Nothing was found. A doctor was summoned to inspect the body for clues.

"This man has the look of someone that is choking," he said.

He looked in the throat. "Bring that kerosene lamp closer please," he said to Dietrich.

With the lamp held just right something could barely be seen wedged in the back of the dead man's throat. The doctor rummaged in his bag until he found a long thin pair of pliers. It was the same pliers he used to retrieve bullets from patients, both alive and dead. With steady hands he slowly reached inside and grasped a chunk of cooked beef. He slowly removed the beef and held it up to the light.

"Did this man have dinner in his room," he asked.

"No Doc, he ate dinner with a couple of men that just arrived in town," Dietrich said.

The doctor continued to look at the piece of beef as he shook his head.

"What do you see Doc," Dietrich asked.

"Well, it's not what I see; it's what I don't see. There are no bite marks on this beef. Anytime a man chews it will leave marks and there are none." The doctor looked at Dietrich. "Why would a man put a piece of meat of this size in his mouth and not chew it, it appears he just tried to swallow it whole." the doctor said.

Dietrich didn't speak at first, he was deep in thought. "Thanks Doc, can you have the coroner sent over immediately. The body needs to be prepared for a long trip back east."

After the doctor and the coroner left with the body the other Baldwin men came back into the room, they wanted to know what Dietrich was thinking.

"Was he murdered?" a man by the name of Jason Orwell asked.

"I can't say for sure but it looks that way. What I can't figure is he was only out of our sight for maybe thirty minutes, probably less. Another thing, Matus knew how to take care of himself. He was as good as they get in hand to hand fighting. We were right next door and never heard a thing," Dietrich said.

"Matus wasn't no pushover. He was as stout a man as there ever was. Why aren't there any defensive marks on the body? Why didn't he struggle and create some noise, we were right next door and would have heard it," another of the Baldwin men said.

"Who in this town did Matus know that would have wanted him dead?" Orwell asked.

Dietrich thought of the two Chicago men and also what Matus had said about them. But it couldn't have been the two Chicago men; they were here to do a job, same as the Baldwin men. But still, they were the only ones that had gotten on the wrong side of Matus.

"We proceed as planned. In the morning I want to observe the reaction of the two Chicago men when I tell them what happened here tonight. You men do the same. If we suspect they had anything to do with this then they won't live to see the sun go down. Are you all with me on this?" All the men agreed.

"One more thing, I want two men in the corridor during the night armed with handguns. If this could happen to a man the likes of Matus then it could happen to any of us. Two guards all night, we'll do it in shifts," Dietrich said.

It was doubtful if any of the men would sleep during the night. All were too disturbed that a man as fearsome as Dorian Matus could be killed in the span of thirty minutes while eleven Baldwin Felts agents were only one room away.

Dietrich spent the night trying to figure out how it had happened. He was anxious to get to the livery the next morning and see the reaction of the two Chicago men. It had to be them he kept telling himself. But if these two had managed to kill someone like Matus then they could kill any of the other Baldwin men if they chose.

But if it was the two from Chicago why would they have killed Matus anyway. He didn't know the two and surely they needed him to help find the fugitive Blair. Dietrich knew Matus had a way of talking down to people, could he have said something during dinner that had upset one, or both, of the Chicago men bad enough that they would come over here and kill him?

And if they did silently kill Matus then these were two men not to be trifled with. It might be best to do the job and be shed of both as quickly as possible.

The next morning the eleven remaining Baldwin Felts men packed up their belongings and deposited them in the one room that had been reserved for two more weeks. The gear they needed for the trip was all stored in five large trunks locked up nice and safe in a jail cell at the sheriff's office. The first rule of business for any new job was to find a safe place to store the trunks, and where safer than a jail. There were things in the trunk that were considered dangerous; Baldwin equipped their operatives better than the U.S Army.

Not a man of the eleven had said more than ten words that morning. Elon Dietrich was now the head of the group. He had spent the remainder of the night searching his mind for clues to the murder of Matus.

After turning in five of the six keys to the old gentleman that ran the hotel they all headed for the sheriff's office to retrieve their gear. The sheriff had told Matus and Dietrich someone was always at the jail and sure enough this morning there was a fire in the stove, the smell of hot coffee greeted the men as they entered the front room.

"Morning Deputy, we've come to get our gear," Dietrich said.

Deputy Cecil Spriggs had heard footsteps on the boardwalk out front and had instinctively put his hand on the worn Colt in his holster. He hadn't lived as long as he had by not using caution, especially at the hour of the morning when not many law abiding citizens prowled the streets.

"Everything is where you left it. Heard one of your men choked to death last night over at the hotel. I saw a man choke to death once, not a pretty sight," the deputy said.

Dietrich wasn't in the mood to talk about the death; he wasn't in the mood to talk to this western hick at all. "I'm not so sure about that Deputy, he died but I don't think it was something as simple as choking."

Cecil removed a large round steel ring from a peg on the wall that contained the keys for the cells in the back. "If he didn't choke to death then what are you saying? Are you suggesting that your boss was killed? If so then that would be a matter for the law here in Rapid City," Cecil said as he suspiciously eyed the man.

Again Dietrich wondered how long he was going to have to suffer this fool before he and his men could retrieve their gear. "Deputy, I doubt you, or anyone that works for the sheriff in this town, could find the man who killed my boss even if you carried a lantern and had an entire week to do it. If you don't mind I am in a hurry, can you open the door so we can get our gear?"

Cecil was nearly to the door that led to the cells in the back. When the man with the New York accent said what he did the deputy stopped and turned to the group of men that crowded the sheriff's office.

He eyeballed the group and figured he wasn't going to let such a statement slip by without a word of his own. "I reckon you fancy city boys and your fancy gear think you can traipse around out here and do as you please and say as you please. I reckon when one of your men comes running back here begging for help from me and the other men that keep this town safe then I'll have a good laugh. We'll come when we're called, even if it is for city boys the likes of you."

Cecil wasn't saying what he was saying just to hear his own words. It had happened a time or two, men from back east talking down to folks that lived in these parts. It had also happened that when one of them got in trouble it was up to the sheriff and his two deputies to come to the rescue. Cecil didn't figure a group as large and well-armed as the one he faced now would ever need his help but he said it anyway, it made him feel better.

"That's good to know deputy, me and my men here will sleep better knowing you will be here to lend a hand when the eleven of us get in trouble," Dietrich said with a sneer. Several of the other Baldwin men sniggered.

Cecil didn't like what the man just said, as a matter of fact there wasn't anything the man had said since walking in the door a few minutes ago that was even halfway neighborly. He figured the best thing to do was give these men their gear so they could go get their horses, that was if they could find the livery. The thought made him chuckle.

Dietrich and his men grabbed the trunks, two men to each, and headed toward the livery. Once there they separated and loaded their gear onto the pack horses. It took more than thirty minutes before everything was finally secured.

At the exact moment when Dietrich was about to say something spiteful about Pom and Eli the two walked in. He faced both and felt like drawing his gun and killing the two where they stood.

"About to send someone to wake you two up," he said.

"We were told to be here at a quarter of six and that is what we have done. Are we ready to head out?" Eli asked.

"Not until the two of you get your horses loaded. I said we would leave at a quarter of six, not start loading our gear at that time."

Pom looked at the hostler and asked, "The two horses we requested to be saddled and our gear stowed, are they ready?"

The old man looked at the crowd that seemed to fill his livery and said, "They are and as you requested they were ready before the Baldwin men got here this morning."

Dietrich heard this and almost exploded. He was ready to give the two city boys from Chicago a good drumming down about their mounts but it appeared they were one step ahead of him.

The Pursuit

Eli looked around and said, "Are you a man short this morning. I only count eleven and it seems the man missing is your boss Matus."

When Eli said this he wasn't smiling, Dietrich couldn't tell what the look represented. "Matus met with an unfortunate accident last night, he won't be joining us."

Eli and Pom both grabbed the reins of their horses and headed for the main door. Neither asked about the unfortunate accident or if it resulted in injury or death. As the two exited the livery Dietrich and the other men watched them go.

Ellsworth, Blair, and Stewart, formed a line with Stewart in front followed by Blair and Ellsworth who led the pack horse. It had been determined that none of the three would talk as they rode. With any number of men chasing them it was best to use the added sense of hearing to help avoid danger.

Each time water was found the horses were allowed to drink and the canteens re-filled. As the riders approached the badlands the terrain began to change. Trees grew sparse and grass for the horses even more so. At about an hour before dark Stewart had the other two prepare a camp.

As Blair grabbed a skillet and some scarce wood for a fire Stewart stopped him. "We won't be making a fire here Blair. The smoke could be seen for miles around. After we get our gear stored we take only enough as we might eat and head off a mile or so that way," he said as he pointed.

"Good idea Marshal. We can make a small fire there after its good and dark then we head back here to spend the night. We used to do something similar back in the war," Ellsworth said.

Nathan Wright

This surprised the marshal, "You were in the war, which side?"

Ellsworth smiled, "Both I guess. I started out for the North but was captured when Sherman and all of us was terrorizing Atlanta. They took me to some sort of prison and damn near starved me to death. I escaped and was promptly captured again. I told them I was from the south and had barely escaped capture by them damn yanks. They believed it and put me back to fighting but only this time I wasn't wearing blue, I was wearing gray."

"Didn't those stupid rebels recognize the uniform you were wearing when they recaptured you?" Blair asked.

"Wasn't wearing a uniform, the one I had managed to rot off of me while I was being held. When I escaped all I was wearing was nothing more than ragged pants one of the guards had managed to pilfer for me. He felt sorry for me and the rest of the prisoners I guess. He was from Tennessee and me being from Kentucky, well we held a kind of kinship. The North and the South was filled with boys from Kentucky so the way I talk would fit in with either side."

"How many men from the North did you kill while you were wearing the Gray?" Stewart asked suspiciously.

"Don't you worry about that Marshal. I was the only man in my unit that never drew any ammunition. The day the South surrendered I had exactly the same number of shells as I did the day they put that southern uniform on me and reached me a gun. I was in a few battles but never pulled the trigger a single time. It was late in the war and the South was purely beat. All I had to do was last it out, and I did," Ellsworth said.

"Well I don't know whether to call you a Johnny Reb or a Yank now. That has to be the most peculiar story I for one have ever heard," Blair said.

The Pursuit

"It's true, every word of it. As for what to call me I reckon just an American will work, after all, that's what we all are."

"We better get to moving. We take the pack horse with us in case a cougar or bear are about. I want to get our food cooked and get back here before it gets too late," Stewart said.

Blair had done enough traveling for one day and decided to protest. "Why don't we forget the fire and just eat here Marshal?"

"Because some of the grub that store clerk gave us needs to be eaten in the next day or two, we can't eat it raw and we can't let it spoil. Now let's get the move on, I don't like traveling after dark. It'll be dark in fifteen minutes and by that time we will be a good mile and a half from here. We'll build a small fire and cook up what we need."

"But how do we find our way back Marshal?" Blair asked.

"You don't need to worry about that. Sadie here will walk us back here with no trouble at all. She knows the story, we've done this several times in the last two years."

The marshal was right. It didn't take more than thirty minutes to skillet up half the eggs and three pieces of beef the store clerk had given them. Once finished Sadie led them back exactly the way they had traveled before.

"Alright Blair, I want you to stand the first watch. If you hear anything I don't want you to yell out. Just get the attention of either me or Ellsworth. One thing to look for is when the horses start to fidget. If they do then it's either an animal or a man, either one could be bad so make sure you stay on your toes and don't fall asleep, our lives depend on it," Stewart said.

The three watches went off without the least bit of trouble. Blair had even managed to stay awake during his turn, something that surprised the marshal.

The next morning the men quickly made a breakfast of beef jerky and biscuits. Thirty minutes after first light the three broke camp and headed due north. The going was getting easier as they approached the Badlands. What was beginning to be troubling was the lack of water. Since the previous day none of the men had spotted a trace of a stream. Even evidence of where water had once run in the small depressions looked to have been dry for months.

"We might need to change our plans if we don't spot water soon," Stewart said.

Blair and Ellsworth knew he was right. This wasn't country to go traveling in with only what you could carry in a canteen. Folks that traveled land like this usually had wagons and hauled water with them in barrels.

By three that evening it was decided that the three wouldn't head any farther north, they would turn west and back into land where timber grew and water ran. It was the only choice the three had.

It was decided to steer clear of their previous campsite in case someone had picked up on their trail, it was doubtful but it was also the smart thing to do.

That night the three made camp and again headed off to build a fire and cook up some grub before heading back for the night. This evening was going to be anything but uneventful. If the men enjoyed the way the previous evening went then this was going to be one for the books.

As they headed back Sadie slowed and then stopped. Stewart knew something was up; he knew Sadie and trusted her instincts. Stewart was in front followed by Blair with Ellsworth bringing up the rear. He also led the pack horse.

As the men sat and listened none of the three could hear anything that would indicate danger. Sadie did though, she smelled it first and then, standing still as she was, she begun to hear it. Stewart pulled his Colt and soon Blair and Ellsworth did the same.

The first sound that told of something being out there in the darkness was the breaking of a limb, or branch, and shortly after that another. There was a quarter moon tonight and the clouds had parted, enough light was about to at least let the men see into the shadows.

With a roar and a rush a brown bear charged the three. Sadie had finally figured out what the noise meant and when the bear charged she was ready to leave, she bolted.

Stewart re-holstered his gun and held on as Sadie charged into the darkness away from the terrifying sound. Blair and Ellsworth did the same knowing their horses would take a route directly opposite the bear. It was a good thing too because the three men weren't exactly sure where the bear was, the horses knew though.

After a few terrifying minutes Sadie came into the campsite where the men had stored some of their gear earlier. Once in camp Sadie stopped and listened. Seconds later Blair and Ellsworth made it there. The three men jumped down and retrieved their Winchesters. The horses were quickly tied to a nearby tree as the men prepared to defend themselves.

As they waited they could hear the bear running in the opposite direction from where they stood. It was snorting and moving off at a run, as they listened, it seemed the bear was chasing something. That was when Stewart noticed the pack horse was gone.

"Ellsworth, which way did the pack horse go when that bear broke from cover?" he asked.

"When the bear came out of the trees she jerked free and took off. I think the bear followed her."

135

Nathan Wright

When Ellsworth checked he found part of the lead he used still attached to the saddle horn. It was old and frayed and must have given way when the excited horse took off. Probably a good thing or he would have been torn from the saddle and the bear would have been on him in seconds.

The three began to breathe easier as the sounds of the snarling bear grew faint. "We better keep the horses close and stay alert tonight. That bear might decide to pay us another visit and if it does we can't afford to keep offering up horses," Stewart said.

The reminder of the night was uneventful, no more bears showed up. The bad news was the pack horse never came back either. The three hoped that once she calmed she would come ambling into camp to be near the other horses, it didn't happen.

The next morning they took inventory of what they had, it didn't look good. All that was left in the way of food was a little jerky and two biscuits. The sack of horse feed was there and the men still had all the canteens, but the food was gone. Even the coffee and tobacco that had been on the pack horse when she bolted was now only a fond memory.

"We'll head back in the direction of the attack and see if we can pick up the trail. With any luck that pack horse will find us or we might stumble on her," Stewart said.

No more than an hour later they did stumble on the pack horse, she was dead. Apparently, in her fear and subsequent mad dash to put some distance between her and the bear, she ran off a shallow cliff in the darkness. If the fall wasn't fatal then the chasing bear was.

It looked like the bear had fed on the carcass all night. It had also torn into the foodstuffs that were carried in the pack, nothing of use was left. Blair and Ellsworth stood guard while

The Pursuit

Stewart searched the area around the carcass for anything that hadn't been either eaten or contaminated by the bear, nothing of use could be found. Even the coffee and tobacco was ruined. It looked as if the bear had torn into the packages and sampled some and then promptly threw it back up. The sight was almost as disgusting as the body of the dead horse.

"By the looks of things that was one big bear. If it hadn't have been for the pack horse leading the big bastard in the opposite direction, away from us, then one of us could have been that bear's meal," Stewart said.

"Shouldn't bear be either in hibernation or heading for their den this time of year?" Blair asked.

"He probably was, or he might have been a bear without a territory to call his own. They do that sometimes; move until they find a place where no other male bears are about. This one was looking for a last meal before winter and it looks like he found it," Stewart said.

"Alright then, it looks like our plan has changed again. We're broke and all out supplies are gone. What do you think we ought to do now Marshal?" Ellsworth asked.

Stewart was still looking over the destruction the bear had caused when Ellsworth asked his question; the marshal was out of options.

Stewart looked at the horse Blair rode and saw the canvas sack of money, the same sack of money that had caused the three to be out here in the first place.

"Blair, I want to know where the rest of that money is hidden and I want to know right now. I don't plan to ride all over creation with killers chasing me without knowing what this is all about. Now you got two choices, the first is you tell me the story of how you got us into this mess and where the rest of the money is hidden so we can recover it and give it to the judge in Rapid City," the marshal said.

Blair looked at the marshal and said, "That was only one choice, you said there was two."

"There are two, I hoped to not need to go to the second one but here it is. Unless I know what's going on then as far as I see it no crime has been committed. If that's the case I can't spend any more time riding around out here in the middle of nowhere broke and hungry. We part ways, you go wherever you want and I head to Rapid City and pick up my next month's pay, which is probably sitting there right now in the bank."

It didn't take Blair long to decide which choice he liked best, "We go northwest for a day and a half, maybe two, as best as I can tell. The money is there in a bank and there might also be someone there that can help us."

"What's the name of the town Blair?"

"Sweetwater, the town is called Sweetwater," Blair said.

Stewart and Ellsworth just looked at each other. Both had heard of Sweetwater and both had heard different stories about the place.

"Sweetwater ain't more than a little mining operation, and that was a couple of years ago. I doubt anything is left there now," Stewart said.

"That ain't what I've heard Marshal. Sweetwater is booming, got all the miners in that area coming to Sweetwater to have their ore weighed and get paid. Everything from there goes north toward the railroad," Ellsworth said.

Blair had been to Sweetwater and knew both men were a little bit right and both were a little bit wrong. "Sweetwater is a town Ellsworth, you are right about that. It's mostly owned by a gentleman there by the name of Norman Fowler, most folks there call him Big Norman."

The Pursuit

Stewart looked at the horizon; dark clouds could be seen coming from the west, the kind of clouds that could mean only one thing this time of year, snow. "I've never been in that part of the territory before, can't say as I've even been close to that area. If you say a day and a half on horseback then you must be talking what, forty or fifty miles?"

Blair looked around; he had been in and around these parts for years scouting out routes for possible track expansion for some of the railroads he contracted with. He knew the land as well as anyone, not as well as some of the dwindling Indian population in these parts but he still knew it pretty well. "That's about right Marshal, day and a half if we don't have any more bear trouble. Two days at the most."

Stewart thought over his options, there weren't any. "Alright then, we head northwest to Sweetwater. You can fill us in on the story after we get there but I can guarantee you one thing Blair, when we get there we better plan on dipping into that sack of yours for some money, we're broke and as I see it me and Ellsworth here have been working for you now as bodyguards for at least the last four days. You can just call it a protection fee. All we need is money for food when we get there, we can still sleep on the outskirts of town, surely that's still free."

Blair agreed, he felt Stewart and Ellsworth were helping get the money back to its rightful owners and in doing so surely no one would begrudge them a little money for food. He was going to be hungry himself by the time they got to Sweetwater.

"Alright then, we better be moving, that weather to the west looks like it's going to beat us to town. We ride hard and bed down someplace where no one can find us. Tomorrow we do the same. The horses got grain and that's way more than we got. With any luck maybe the two days can be cut to a day and a half. Believe me, we are going to be hungry as hell by the time we make it to that town," Stewart said.

"What if we see us a rabbit or even a deer, can't we shoot it?" Blair asked.

"No we can't, you shoot a gun off around here and anyone within five miles will know where we are. And even if you do shoot something are you planning to eat it raw because we ain't starting a fire to cook it. The smoke could be seen for ten miles. We just ride and let our growling stomachs keep us company," Ellsworth said before the marshal could.

"Well, there ain't any reason to be hateful, I swear you two are grouchy as that old bear last night," Blair said.

Stewart looked at Blair, "That old bear ain't hateful now I bet, it has a full stomach."

The men rode the rest of the day only taking breaks to allow the horses to cool and drink when water was handy. That night they took turns keeping watch. One thing Blair learned was that a man with an empty stomach wasn't nearly as likely to doze off.

The next morning dawned cold and crisp. Stewart guessed it to be mid twenty's but not much colder than that. The sky had grown dark with big rolling clouds that looked to be so heavy with snow they might just fall out of the sky from the weight. It didn't take long to leave camp with no fire to contend with, and no breakfast for that matter.

"You know, I can do without a meal or two but damn if I don't miss my coffee every morning, a man shouldn't be denied his coffee you know," Ellsworth said. Blair started laughing.

Ellsworth looked over at the man, "Did I say something funny to you Blair?"

The Pursuit

"You did, you managed to start and finish your last sentence with 'You know.'"

Stewart now figured Blair had some sort of personality trait that allowed him to pick up on what men said and how they said it, either that or he was just a bastard. He remembered the mention of the quadruple negative from a few days back, whatever that was. Blair better be careful because this was the second time he had laughed at the way Ellsworth talked.

Later that day, just as snow began to fall, the outskirts of a town could be seen as the men headed up a long valley heavy with cottonwood and ponderosa pine. This was nearly as far north as trees of this variety could be found. Farther north was prairie lands and mostly scrub, not many trees.

"Looks like I was about right Stewart, we made it just shy of two days. Say, what do you make of that sound?" Blair asked.

All three men listened as they sat their horses. "Sounds like a stationary steam engine, maybe like one that's used at a sawmill," Ellsworth said.

The trail the men rode led out onto a road that was wide enough to be used by wagons. It was apparent from the wear and tear that this was a well-used road. As they traveled they soon came into view of a large wooden building where logs were being hued into crossties.

"I don't see a railroad anywhere Blair, this kind of reminds me of the sawmill over in Elk Bend. Why, it looks like crossties are being produced in the thousands, but where is the railroad?" Stewart said.

"Well Marshal, the truth of the matter is that a railroad is being built to service this area. It will go near the town of Elk Bend and run through this long valley here at Sweetwater and head on west. It's the reason I've been surveying and buying

141

property for my employer in this area for the last couple of years," Blair told the two.

The men rode right past the sawmill on their way into town. The mill was on the down river side of town and it was apparent why, the mill produced a lot of runoff which appeared to be sap from the bark of logs. There was a steady stream running from a pipe into the center of the river.

I wonder if that slurry is bad for fish," Ellsworth asked, more or less thinking out loud.

About a half mile past the mill was the first buildings of town, consisting of shacks and rundown houses that looked to be abandoned. "Those are some of the original dwellings for Sweetwater. As folks became a little more prosperous they started building more permanent structures in what is now the town," Blair said.

As the three approached the edge of town it became apparent that Sweetwater was a very prosperous town indeed. It looked to have two main streets connected by side streets. Again, as in Elk Bend, the town was crowded against the low hill by the river.

Toward the center of the main street closest to the river the buildings all had covered boardwalks and in a few places the boardwalks had been extended to the back street, the one closest to the mountain. Some of the streets had been covered with crushed stone; this, Blair said, was some of the rock from the mines located on the mountain.

"You keep referring to that as a mountain Blair. It's more like just a low hill if you ask me," Ellsworth said.

Blair chuckled, "Well, we need to call it something and mountain just seems to suit it better than hill. There are hills in places like Kentucky; I prefer not to use the term."

The Pursuit

"You got something against Kentucky Blair?" Ellsworth asked in a tone that was suddenly harsh.

Blair suddenly remembered the story of Ellsworth fighting for both the North and the South, and that he was originally from Kentucky. "Not at all, I have grown quite fond of bourbon and tobacco from Kentucky. The lady folk from that fine state are some of the prettiest I've seen too," Blair said in hopes of smoothing the feathers he may have ruffled.

Ellsworth gave Blair a sour look, "Nice try Blair, but I don't believe your sincerity. Just be careful in the future when you speak of Kentucky." Blair looked at the much larger Ellsworth and considered it good advice.

The street the men traveled was busy, at least the street adjacent to the small river. Not only were there men going in and out of the businesses but also it seemed the offices for the town of Sweetwater were located on this street. After looking around Stewart noticed he didn't see anything that resembled a courthouse.

"You indicated you have been here several times Blair. Does this town have anything like a courthouse and if so where is it?" Stewart asked.

"No courthouse Marshal. All the town's offices are located on Main Street. You can distinguish the city buildings from the others because they have their names etched into the glass of the entrance doors, while the businesses have hanging signs."

Stewart looked right and saw such a door, it read, 'Sweetwater Mayor.'

"Is there a sheriff in town, or at least a deputy?"

Blair looked at Stewart, "Not that I know of Marshal."

As the three men walked their horses down Main Street Stewart kept looking the town over. There were the usual saloons and eating establishments, all with the unique names that were so common in western towns.

There was the Thirsty Prospector Saloon, and the Steak and Goat Restaurant, and by the look of things that was only a small sampling of what the town had to offer.

"Well Blair, if there is no law in this town then what happens when someone starts trouble," Ellsworth asked.

"The man who runs the town allows each store or shop owner to deal with trouble as they see fit. As long as it's considered self-defense, or to protect property, then it's totally left up to the town's residents and shop-owners to deal with trouble. Not a man in town is ever more than five feet from a gun. You may not see a weapon in the saloons or stores but you can bet one is nearby."

"So, no sheriff and no deputies, would there be anything to resemble a town marshal?" Stewart asked.

In the west there were two types of marshals, the federal type that did the blessing of the territorial courts and had jurisdiction anywhere they cared to be. And then there was the town marshal which usually consisted of a man wearing a badge. His jurisdiction stopped at the boundaries of the town that had appointed him. The town marshal carried even less authority than a local sheriff.

"Nothing of the sort I believe Marshal. The man who built the town happens to be pretty good with a gun so if anything, or anyone, becomes more than the local business owners can handle he comes down and takes care of the matter himself," Blair said.

Stewart looked suspiciously at him before asking, "You say, comes down and takes care of the matter. Is this man supernatural or maybe some sort of spirit? You have aroused my curiosity."

The Pursuit

"No sort of thing Marshal. When I say, comes down, I only mean from his home, he lives there." Blair pointed behind the town, higher up on the mountain.

Stewart and Ellsworth turned and looked in the direction Blair was pointing. There, sitting on a bench of rock jutting out from the side of the mountain, was an elegant mansion. It hadn't made itself apparent to the two men due to the direction they had entered the town. The view it commanded was of the entire town and even part of the sawmill.

"My goodness Blair, such a house in this part of the country is rare, or should I say unheard of. You mentioned the man that inhabits such a place built this town. What did you mean by that?" Stewart asked.

"I mean it exactly as it sounded Marshal, the man that lives there built this town. About four or five years ago this was little more than an elk trail. As the story has been related to me, there weren't more than three or four families living here, they occupied some of those old abandoned houses we saw as we entered town. When Mister Fowler came here he designed the town and also laid out the foundations for the sawmill."

As Stewart and Ellsworth continued to scan the mountain, and the house that dominated it, Blair continued. "Word got out and soon folks from all over the north began to come into town searching for employment. It was said that a man could make a good living here if he was honest and could produce an honest day's labor."

"Are you saying that one man did all this, one man owns everything here?" Stewart asked.

"That's right, but Mister Fowler doesn't own the entire town. He decided a few years back that the town would be better served if a few of the more industrious of its citizens were allowed to start businesses of their own. You see that

145

leather goods shop down the street, it's owned by a man that worked hard and earned the trust of Mister Fowler. He was allowed to acquire a loan at the bank and start his own shop. There are several more such businesses in town but I'm not sure how many or which ones they are."

As Stewart listened something dawned on the marshal. "So, am I to suppose the hidden money is in this bank you mentioned?"

"It is, and it's even earning interest as we speak, I'm the type that never likes money to sit if it isn't making more money, hence the interest."

"Is there anything else you can tell me about this Fowler?" the marshal asked.

"Well, I already mentioned the sawmill. He has any number of contracts with the railroads back east. Two are pushing competing lines just north of here in an effort to service towns farther west."

"As far as I know there aren't any towns farther west, not of the size that would make a railroad profitable," Ellsworth said.

"Mister Fowler is a speculator. He convinced the two lines that the first one to get commercial service into the northern Dakota Territory would reap huge profits from the emerging timber and cattle businesses that would spring up once rail service was established. Fowler is a salesman, he played one railroad against the other and wouldn't you know it, both raced out here and started surveying. That's where me and a few others come in. We know the lay of the land and the best routes for the new lines."

"Sounds like this Fowler must have had either some financial help or a pretty thick bankroll of his own to have built this place in the span of four or five years Blair," Ellsworth said.

The Pursuit

"I suppose so, but I don't know which. I do know the town makes money, and lots of it. The timber for the railroads alone is worth a fortune. And it ain't just crossties either. Tracks ran through this country need several tunnels and lots of bridges and both take timber. And one more thing I might have forgot to mention, he has three silver mines on that mountain where the house is. Not near the house mind you, but close, maybe a mile on up stream."

"Well Blair, sounds like you know about all there is to know about this Fowler," Stewart said.

"I wish I could say I did but I would be lying. The information I have is directly related to the survey work and deed preparation I was contracted for. There is a mystery to the man. I can't put my finger on it but I wouldn't want to be in business against him, I believe when he sets his mind to something he gets it."

"So if this is such a thriving place then where does all the supplies and equipment come from? It sure doesn't come up through Rapid City or Langley," Stewart said.

"I wondered that at first myself and did some asking around. Apparently the terrain between here and Rapid City is pretty rugged and there ain't the first sign of a road. Northeast of here is a little town that sprang up about four years ago. One of the two railroads made it that far because they serviced more of the northern territory than their competition. That was the end of the easy track so the going has been a lot slower lately, to say the least.

"Sweetwater gets everything it needs from the depot up north. Two heavy wagons a day travel that twenty five mile road, two going north and two returning south. They always pass at a halfway trail house where the horses are switched out. Four horse teams only need to pull twelve or thirteen miles a day and then they get a full day's rest. The road between here and that railroad spur is constantly being improved and upgraded to make it easier on the teams of horses."

Ellsworth felt like being a smartass, "Let me guess, Fowler owns the road, the trail house, and the railroad spur at the depot. Would I be wrong in saying that?"

"No, you would be exactly right," Blair said.

Stewart had heard enough about this miracle worker. He walked over to Blair's horse and untied the opening of the canvas bag that contained the money, then pulled out two-hundred dollars cash.

"You can't do that Marshal, that money belongs to the folks that it was taken from," Blair said.

"You can bill me. We done talked about this Blair; we are broke and need food and a place to stay. Also Sadie has a loose shoe and maybe one of these other two horses might need some blacksmith work. Once we get out of this mess then Judge Preston down in Rapid City can figure out what to do about the two-hundred, until then just call it a loan."

Blair knew the marshal was right. Hell he was hungry himself and the only money the men had was in the canvas sack. "You're right Marshal. We'll use the money to resupply here and then try to make our way to Rapid City."

"Damn right we will Blair, but first I want to meet this Mister Fowler you speak so highly of. A lot of what you've told me has me wanting to ask a few questions," Stewart said.

At this Blair took on the look of someone that might have had his grave stepped on. "I really don't know how that could be arranged Marshal. The only time Mister Fowler comes off the mountain is if something happens in the town of

The Pursuit

Sweetwater that absolutely needs his attention. Other than that he never leaves the mansion."

"Well Blair, thanks for the history lesson. Now can you lead us to a livery and then a restaurant, my ass is missing what my mouth usually sends it," Ellsworth said with a chuckle.

"Very funny, not to mention disgusting. The livery is on the next street up and then back near the edge of town," Blair said.

Stewart and Ellsworth figured as much. No one wants a livery in the middle of town. Folks don't mind riding a horse but they really don't want one bedded down next to them.

As the three walked the horses toward the livery they never got the first glance from any of the townsfolk. No one looked their way and no one said howdy. Either this town was unfriendly or everyone was afraid of the way Stewart and his companions looked. After thinking about it the marshal figured the three needed to see a barber, and after that a bar of soap, or should it be the other way around? Another reason the townsfolk were acting skittish might have been because of the weather, the snow that had been just flakes most of the day was now getting harder. Folks were hurrying to finish their business and then head home.

The livery was a spiced up affair, the building looked nearly new. It wasn't so much big as it was long. The street and the mountain had it crowded in so the owner had decided to make up in length what he couldn't accomplish in width.

The name on top of the door read, 'Fowler Livery.'

"By the name Blair, I assume this isn't owned by any of the townsfolk?" Stewart said.

"I suppose that's the case Marshal but that could be deceiving. A few of the businesses were started by Mister Fowler and then sold outright as long as the name was allowed to stay the same. This might be just such a business."

There was a door that was wide and tall on hinges, this must have been the door for horses, or even a wagon. Stewart didn't want to open that door and let the cold blowing snow in unless it was the only door to the place. He stepped to the side and found what he wanted. A porch with a door and window. He stepped up and gave the door a healthy knock.

Wasn't more than ten seconds until the door opened and a man stuck his head out, "Well howdy stranger. What can I do for you," he asked.

"We got three horses that need a stall and some feed. One needs a shoe looked at if someone around here does that kind of work," Stewart said.

The man smiled and stepped outside. "Are they out front?"

"They are, all three tied to your hitch rail," Ellsworth said.

The man hurried to the front and looked the three over. "Snow looks to be getting harder. We better get them inside and then I'll have a look at that shoe." Five minutes later and all three horses were in stalls. A quick look at Sadie and sure enough she had nearly thrown a shoe. It was loose and rattled when the man tapped it.

"Good thing you got here when you did, I'll have this fixed in the morning if that's all right. I've done let the fire cool for the day. How long you intending on staying?" the hostler asked.

"Just long enough to rest up and get resupplied, maybe leave day after tomorrow," Stewart told the man.

"Let's see, three horses, two nights and a little blacksmithing thrown in to boot. You want me to check them other two?"

"I guess so. We got a ways to go and wouldn't want one to come off the rails," Stewart said.

The Pursuit

The man laughed, "Rails is a good way to put it. Tell you what, how about twenty dollars for the two nights in cash and we can settle up on the rails after I see what they need."

"Sounds fair," Stewart said as he pulled out a twenty and reached it to the man. "All we need is our saddlebags and rifles; you got a tack room for the saddles?"

"Sure do, I'll take care of that after you head out," the livery man said.

"Stewart grabbed his Winchester and saddlebags. He also took the canvas sack from the back of Blair's horse, careful to not jingle the coins in the bottom of the bag.

"If you're looking for a place to stay I recommend the Rest Haven. The rooms are clean and the rates are fair. There is also a barber on one side and an eatery on the other."

Stewart headed for the door followed by Blair and Ellsworth. "That's smart, put the three things a traveling man needs side by side," he said to no one in particular.

"You can see the town was laid out with some thought. I guess that can happen if all the shots are being called by only one man and that man has money," Stewart said. His tone wasn't one of admiration but more of contempt, he suspected something.

Ten minutes after leaving the livery the three men stepped into the lobby of the Rest Haven. They were greeted by a man wearing a suit. He looked to be the owner rather than just someone that worked there. Suits in the west weren't easy to come by and hardly something your everyday man would wear.

"You gentlemen looking for a room?" the man asked.

"Three rooms if you got em. I've been around these two about as much as I care to admit. What's the rate?" Stewart asked.

"Rooms are five dollars a night, which is a multi-room rate. One room at a time is six."

Stewart didn't care, it wasn't his money. "That will be fine, is the barber next door open late, me and these two trail bums need some cleaning up."

"Yes he is as a matter of fact. It seems most of his business comes at the later hours," the man said as he looked at the two men with Stewart.

"Why hello Mister Blair. It's good to see you, what's it been? Six weeks since you were in town?"

"That's about right, six weeks; maybe even seven or eight."

"Well I was told to let you know if you made it back to town to notify Mister Fowler. I believe he has some business to conduct with you."

Stewart looked at Blair to see what kind of reaction he had. It was a cross between surprise and shock.

"Well, I'll see if I can meet with him tomorrow. As late as it is me and my friends here need to see that barber and then maybe some supper," Blair said. Stewart thought he noticed a bit of a stutter.

Stewart paid and the three men signed the ledger. Stewart made sure to sign his name without adding the customary Marshal to the front of his signature. He had pocketed his badge before entering town and had also cautioned Blair and Ellsworth not to call him marshal while in town.

The three were each given a key and minutes later they deposited their saddle bags at the foot of their beds. Stewart wondered about the canvas bag of money and decided to take out all the cash and put it in his pocket. Not that he really worried about someone breaking into his room and taking it, no one in this town had looked twice and the three. It was as if they were invisible.

The Pursuit

They all met back at the foot of the stairs and agreed the barber could wait, they were starved. Out the front door and one door down was a saloon that had a sign that read, Whiskey and Food. The name of the saloon was the Thirsty Miner, appropriate.

As with establishments like this the front room was for the saloon and through a side door were any number of tables if you wanted food.

Stewart went in first followed by Blair. As was Ellsworth's custom he always laid back to see what he could see. Stewart thought it was smart, he could see the reaction of anyone that saw Blair and the marshal. If something was about to happen Ellsworth would have their backs. After Stewart and Blair were seated Ellsworth could enter knowing they had him covered. Ellsworth told the marshal he had always done this, he was by nature a cautious man. Stewart wondered why the man hadn't run for sheriff somewhere.

Once the three were seated they took in their surroundings. The restaurant looked to be doing a good business; probably the weather had driven some folks inside for the warmth and aroma. The room was large and well-lit by kerosene lamps that hung from specially built sconces attached to the walls. These were spaced about six feet apart and ran the entire length of the room. There was even a chandelier hanging from the center of the ceiling and this was adorned by five kerosene lamps as well. All the lamps were turned low but with the number of lights the room possessed it still made the place seem warm and cozy.

The tables were round and each was covered by a different color of checkered tablecloth. The coverings were identical in pattern but different in color and this gave the place a bright cheery look. In the center of each table was a small tray and on the tray was the ingredients you would add to coffee; sugar along with a small pitcher of what looked like either milk or cream.

"They must have some milk cows around here for there to be cream. I doubt this is brought in by wagon," Ellsworth said. After some thought he added, "It might be that new cream that comes in a can. I've heard about it but never had the chance to sample any."

It wasn't long before a lady came by wearing a cloth apron that was made of the same material that covered the tables. She reached each man a one page menu and then asked, "Would you gentlemen like some coffee while you figure out what you want to eat?"

"Coffee for the three of us, and you can bring the special for each of us, along with lots of bread and maybe some butter if you have it," Stewart said. The woman retrieved the menus and left.

"Now why did you do that Stewart, I wanted to see if this place served any trout? The farther north you go the more abundant the trout are and the tastier it gets," Ellsworth said.

"Because as hungry as we are I didn't think it would matter. The special is usually always ready and we can get our food faster."

As Stewart and Ellsworth talked Blair looked around the room, he seemed nervous. This wasn't apparent at first but the marshal did take notice after a few minutes and wondered what had the man so pre-occupied.

Stewart was right about the special because no more than ten minutes later the same woman came back carrying two plates. Another trip brought the third plate and on a separate tray sat three cups of coffee.

The Pursuit

Ellsworth anxiously looked and to his surprise the special was trout. "If the special is trout then they must be plentiful in the streams around here this time of year."

As the men ate and sipped coffee Blair continued to look around, he was taking in everyone in the room and took special notice of the door that led back to the saloon. Anytime anyone entered he was keen to see who it was and if he knew them, at least that's what the marshal figured.

Blair was so concerned with the other patrons that, even in his state of hunger he was only nibbling at his food. "Say Blair, if you don't like trout then slide that plate over here, I'm never a man to waste food like this," Ellsworth said.

Blair had eaten his potato and nibbled on some of the other food on his plate but hadn't touched the trout. He slid the plate toward Ellsworth and said, "Just take the fish and leave the sides."

Ellsworth did as told and then pushed the plate back. Blair noticed he was being watched by the marshal and decided to pay more attention to his food. He grabbed a roll, broke it in half, and then spread some butter. He finished all his sides and then had another roll. He decided he was hungry after all and didn't want to leave until he was satisfied.

Before Ellsworth and Stewart were finished Blair pushed his chair back and said, "I must have eaten too fast or maybe it's just too much food on an empty stomach. If you two don't mind I'm of a notion to head back to the hotel and lie down, these last few days have taken a toll on me. I believe these broken ribs have taken a lot out of me too. Maybe I'll just make use of the barber in the morning." And with that he turned and left.

There were two more rolls on the plate and Ellsworth decided he would grab another one. "I reckon Blair ain't up to the pace we've been traveling Stewart."

"You might be right. I had forgotten about his broken ribs until he mentioned it before he left. Maybe after a good night's rest and the trip to the barber in the morning he'll feel better."

Just as Stewart was about to reach for the last roll Ellsworth snatched it and said, "He ate pretty good, maybe a nights rest will put him back on track. You reckon we can eat here again in the morning? As tasty as the food was this evening I would surely like to try their breakfast."

Stewart noticed a man standing in the saloon that had looked his way more than once, but not trying to be too obvious about it. "Might be a good idea at that Ellsworth, if the breakfast is anywhere as good as this trout then we are in for a treat."

The lady came back by and asked if they wanted any dessert but both declined. As bad as Stewart wanted to see what the dessert was he also wanted to go inside the saloon to see if anything looked out of the ordinary. The man that had been eyeballing them had given one last look as he moved from the door and out of sight.

"How much we owe you ma'am?" Stewart asked the waitress.

"The total comes to five dollars and fifty cents," she told him.

Stewart reached into his pocket and pulled out a five and a one. "That was a fine meal, just keep the change." The lady took the money and smiled.

After she left Ellsworth said, "Five dollars and fifty cents. That's nearly two day's pay where I come from."

The Pursuit

"You're right. The twenty dollars for the two nights stay for our horses was a little pricy too, nearly double. And I still owe for any blacksmithing work he does."

Ellsworth thought a second and asked, "The only other money we've spent was at the hotel. I'm not that familiar with things to do with hotels but was five dollars a night per room about normal?"

"Not by a long shot, never paid more than three a night and that was in a place as good, if not better, than the ones we've got now. By the looks of things it would cost a lot for anyone to visit this town for more than a day or two."

Ellsworth was looking at the saloon as the marshal talked. "Say Stewart, have you noticed that man with the tan hat and green checkered shirt standing in the saloon watching us? He don't do it obvious like but he is keeping a close eye on us just the same."

"I did notice it and thought it was just my overactive imagination acting up, but now I'm not so sure. What do you say we go in there and have us a drink. Maybe we can figure out if this is something we need to be concerned about."

Stewart and Ellsworth stood and walked out into the bar area. It was a bit noisier there and the crowd seemed to have increased. Men were playing cards at three different tables in the back, off to the side, opposite the dining room, was a section that contained two billiard tables in an alcove of the saloon.

"Would you look at that, billiards. I've only seen one other table this far west and that is back in Rapid City. Always wanted to play that game but never had the money and when I had the money I never had the time. What do you say we play us a game Stewart?" As Ellsworth said this he wasn't looking at the two tables, he was scanning the room through the mirror behind the bar. Stewart was doing the same thing; they were both looking for the man wearing the green checkered shirt and the beat up tan Stetson.

"Let's have us a drink and see if he reappears Stewart."

"Not a bad idea, I think I could use a drink and after that we can head to the barber next door."

Stewart and Ellsworth had their drinks as they continued to scan the room but the man they were looking for must have left. "If he was looking for us then he must have skedaddled when he saw us head this way Stewart," Ellsworth said as he drained his glass.

There was a grandfather clock at the side of the room near the door that led into the restaurant, it was six-thirty. "We better be getting to that barber, I wouldn't want him to close before I get these whiskers tamed," Stewart said.

"How much for the two drinks," Stewart asked the bartender.

"Two bucks ought to cover it friend," the man said.

Stewart swallowed as he pulled out the money. As they left Ellsworth said, "Two bucks, when you could buy the whole damn bottle for four, what kind of town is this anyway?"

"I don't know but it would cost a man forty dollars a day to stay and eat in this town. Something just don't feel right. I don't make much more than forty dollars a month as a marshal."

"You reckon we got enough money to get a couple of barbering jobs and a little tub work Stewart?"

The marshal knew he had all the cash from the bag stuffed safely in his pocket but wondered how long that would last in a town as expensive as this.

The temperature had plummeted while the two ate their suppers. It was now back to around twenty-five degrees as best as the marshal could tell. Both men pulled up the collars on their coats as they took the few steps from the saloon to the barbershop. By the amount of light coming from the front window it was apparent the place was still open.

Ellsworth pushed the door open and looked inside. There were two chairs for cutting hair and both were occupied by what had to be the barbers. "You got time for a couple of shaves?" he asked one of the two men sitting in the chairs.

Both men jumped to their feet and as they did they both pulled the apron off the back of each chair and motioned for the two tall strangers to take a seat. "We got the time, the snow has everyone heading home early tonight I believe. Either that or they're next door sampling the beer and whiskey."

The word *night* was appropriate because this far north and this late in the year meant the last light of day was gone by a little after five-thirty. It was now going on seven o'clock.

As the two barbers put the aprons around Stewart and Ellsworth's necks one asked, "What will it be this evening?"

"Haircut and shave for me, is there also the use of a tub somewhere in town?" Stewart asked.

"In the back, we have a room where the tub is located and it will give you privacy. The water is changed after each bath and hot water added if that is what you want. The price is two fifty per bath. Five dollars total."

Ellsworth looked at Stewart and wondered how much it was going cost for all this. When the barber asked him Ellsworth said, "I'll have the same as that man's having, make sure I get new water," he said with a chuckle.

The two got haircuts and shaves and after that each took his turn in the tub. By the time they were finished both felt like new men and by the price they were charged they should have actually been new men.

"Five dollars apiece for that little bit of work, those two are making a fortune," Ellsworth said.

"Once we ever get back to Rapid City I doubt if Judge Preston is going to agree to reimburse Blair for the money we've spent in this town. I might need to pony it up out of my own pocket. If that happens it could take me three or four months to pay it all back."

"You know Stewart; I wouldn't say anything to the judge about it if I was you. The way I see it, Blair ain't been telling us the truth about the money anyway. Something about his story just doesn't add up. If the money is in the local bank here then why was he packing all that other cash and gold around with him? It would have been just as easy to leave it here with the rest of it. That sack must have weighed twenty pounds and that's a lot for a man to add to the load his horse already has to carry."

Ellsworth felt bad about the marshal having to pay for their own expenses and decided to say something about it. "If worse comes to worse and the judge don't reimburse you then I'll pay my fair share. You don't need to shoulder the whole load while we're in Sweetwater."

"Let's get back to the room and check on Blair. After that I plan on checking out how a mattress feels compared to sleeping on the ground," Stewart said.

The snow had continued to accumulate while the two were at the barber. It was a short sprint to the hotel and both were glad to be back inside. "If I had my clothes cleaned I would feel a lot better," Ellsworth said.

"Just be happy with the shave and haircut, I bet it would cost another twenty bucks to hire a washer woman."

The two headed up the stairs. The door leading to Blair's room was closed, when Ellsworth knocked there wasn't any reply. "We best leave him to his rest. After all, you did say you shot him a few days back."

"I only shot him because I thought he was going to shoot me first. I'm turning in, if you get up before me then knock on my door and we'll find us some breakfast," Stewart said.

When the marshal opened the door to his room he had his hand on the butt of his Colt. Once inside and sure no one was there he struck a match and lit the kerosene lamp by his bed. Everything looked as it had when he left earlier. Fifteen minutes later he was sound asleep.

The night was peaceful and by daylight the next morning the marshal was awake. When he looked out the window he saw that the storm had passed on sometime during the night but it did manage to leave behind a few inches of snow. This wasn't anything to worry about because in another few weeks a normal snow would be a foot or more. The sky had cleared and it promised to be a sunny day, although cold.

The marshal walked over and tapped on the door to Ellsworth's room and a minute later it swung open, the marshal was looking down the barrel of a Winchester. "Sorry Stewart, this town must be giving me the scares I guess. Every noise I heard last night made me jump."

"No hard feelings, I would have probably done the same thing. Did you hear anything out of Blair in the next room last night?"

Ellsworth stretched and yawned as he thought. "I must have been pretty tired, don't reckon I heard any noise last night."

"You just said every noise you heard made you jump, now which is it?"

"Every noise I heard in my dreams Stewart. Are you always this grouchy this time of day or do I just bring out the worst in you?"

"Get your boots on and make it fast, I want to try out the breakfast next door. How long before you're ready?"

Ellsworth looked at the marshal, "Two minutes and don't rush me."

"I'll go and wake Blair," Stewart said as he stepped away from the door.

He went down one door and knocked. A minute later and he knocked again, no answer, not even a sound.

Now the marshal began to wonder if maybe Blair had died during the night, after all he had been shot a few days back. Ellsworth came out of his room and stepped to Blair's door. "He already gone out for breakfast?" he asked.

"I doubt it, he would have needed me to go along to pay for his meal," Stewart said.

As the marshal wondered what to do Ellsworth pulled his room key and inserted it in the lock, it worked. Neither man knew what to expect so both pulled their guns. As Ellsworth eased the door open he asked if Blair was awake, still no answer.

When the door was fully open it was apparent the room was empty. The bed hadn't been slept in and none of Blair's belongings were there.

"You reckon we got the right room? I mean, the same key apparently fits every lock in the building," Ellsworth said.

Stewart looked at the door in comparison to his own room, "It's the right room alright. I thought he was acting a little strange at dinner last night. He cut out of there with no advance warning."

The Pursuit

"He started acting strange after the man here at the hotel said Fowler had been asking about him. But where could he go, he didn't have any money?"

Stewart turned and went back to his room. He pulled out a drawer in the chest and looked inside; the sack of money was gone. "He came in here after he left the restaurant and took what was left of the money in this canvas bag."

"You said that bag had roughly fifteen hundred dollars in it," Ellsworth said.

"It did but before we went to get something to eat last night I decided to take out all the paper money, I have it in my pocket."

Ellsworth was glad of that, "At least we have enough to not be arrested for vagrancy. But why would he take what was left and leave when he said there was all that money in the bank?"

Stewart thought about this and figured he needed to take a little walk to the bank and see what the business hours were. Stewart and Ellsworth pulled their collars high and their hats down low as they went out the front door of the hotel and headed in the general direction they thought the bank would be in.

Ten minutes later they were standing in front of the Sweetwater Savings and Loan. Both knew the bank wouldn't be open at such an early hour but that wasn't why they had made the trip. Right there, etched in the glass of the door, was the hours. They closed at seven the previous night.

"If I remember this right, didn't we leave the restaurant about six-thirty last evening?"

Ellsworth thought and then remembered the grandfather clock. "You're right, it was six-thirty when we went into the saloon for that drink."

"And Blair hurried out of there at least twenty minutes before we did."

Ellsworth looked at the door again. "Do you think he came here and cleaned out the money and then headed out of town?"

"Stewart started down the steps of the bank as he said, "I would bet anything on it. I believe he allowed me and you to escort him here so he could get the money and leave. He had men chasing him and he used us to ride shotgun, so to speak. The son of a bitch used us."

Stewart and Ellsworth headed toward the livery to check on their horses, livery men always stirred early. As the two rounded a corner they could see smoke coming out of a flue pipe at the livery. "You reckon that's his blacksmith furnace going this morning? He said he would be working on shoes."

"I certainly hope so, but what I'm really looking for is Blair's horse," Stewart said.

Again Stewart went to the side door as he had the previous night and knocked hard. A minute later the same man opened the door. "Good morning, come on in out of the cold and grab yourself a cup of coffee. I got a fresh pot over there on the stove and it should be just about ready.

The two were more than glad to come inside and both headed straight for the coffee. The two men probably figured at the prices they were being charged it wouldn't set the man back very much.

"I was just about to make a new shoe for that horse of yours mister, the one you call Sadie. I was going to check out all three this morning but your friend came in here about seven-thirty last evening and said he had some business to tend to and needed to leave. I got his horse ready, even put the saddle on for him. He seemed to be anxious to get away so I figure it must have been some pretty important business for a man to head out in the kind of weather we were having last night."

"We thought he had left sometime during the night but didn't know exactly when. We never saw him after supper. Did he say anything else about what the hurry was all about?" Stewart asked in a down to earth tone.

"Not really, he just said something had come up that required him to get where he was going in a hurry."

"Did he have anything with him when he left?" Ellsworth asked.

"Well, let's see. He had his saddlebags and one large bag that he made sure I fastened on real good. He said it had his papers and stuff in it. It felt pretty heavy to have been loaded with only papers though. The way it felt, and the hurry your friend was in, I figured he had just lightened the bank out of a bunch of cash and was trying to make his getaway," the man said and then laughed. If he only knew.

"When will you have the other two horses finished?" Stewart asked as he thought about the turn of events.

"Sometime this afternoon I reckon. You think you'll be leaving before tomorrow?"

"Probably not, but if we did I just wanted to know our horses would be ready to travel," Stewart said.

"Thanks mister, I guess we will be heading over to grab us some breakfast," Ellsworth said as he headed for the door.

After both men exited the livery and were back outside on the boardwalk Stewart said, "I figured as much. Blair has played me for a fool. He made sure he was at the bank at just before closing and then he rode out of here with the very money he said belonged to some folks that were swindled."

"I still believe the part about folks being swindled, but now I think Blair was the one that done the swindling," Ellsworth said.

"Well, I reckon walking around without any breakfast ain't going to get Blair back here. Let's eat while we figure out our next move. Are we still planning on going back to that same place as last night?"

Ellsworth couldn't think of a better idea so that's where the two headed. The saloon wasn't serving customers; after all it was only seven-thirty on a Friday morning. The door to the saloon was still unlocked so both men entered and headed to the back where food was hopefully being served. The saloon looked bigger now that it was empty and they could get a better look at the place. Chairs were neatly turned upside down and placed on the tops of tables. The barstools were all lined up neat as toy soldiers. Whoever managed this place and saw to its proper closing was doing a good job.

To their pleasant surprise the restaurant was doing a brisk business. "Now where do you suppose all these folks come from Stewart? We've been out and about for the last forty-five minutes and I didn't see a soul on the streets?"

Stewart was starting to wonder about that himself. They picked a table and headed toward it. Again the two men never got a stare or a nod as they each pulled out a chair and sat down. "This town is starting to give me the spooks Ellsworth. It's as if everything is being controlled. Even the movements of the town's residents seem to be as if in a play of some sort and me and you are the spectators, or maybe the audience."

Both men scanned the room with intense curiosity. Everyone was eating and carrying on conversation. Not loud or boisterous but reserved and quiet. Everyone seemed to be wearing the makings of a slight smile as they talked and ate.

The Pursuit

There were two or three women wearing the same type of apron as the lady was wearing the previous night.

"You know Stewart, if someone was to take out a small bell right now and ring it, and then everyone in this room would stand and face us and then bow, I wouldn't be that surprised. As a matter of fact I would probably stand and applaud."

What Ellsworth said seemed preposterous, but also very plausible. This town and its citizens weren't that much different than an orchestra, each had a part to play and they were doing an excellent job of it.

"May I offer you gentlemen some coffee this morning?" a young lady wearing a checkered apron asked.

Ellsworth and Stewart had been so deep in thought that she startled them. Both men snapped out of their trances and looked at the lady. Each was a bit embarrassed; each knew they had jumped when she appeared and spoke to them.

"Coffee would be nice and maybe some biscuits and gravy. What else would you recommend?" Stewart asked.

"Every Friday we have omelets stuffed with peppers and mushrooms. They are very good; some of these folks are here just for our omelets," the lady said as she motioned toward the other diners.

"That sounds fine, would you have any bacon? If you do I would like that as well," Stewart said.

The woman indicated they did and then headed back toward the kitchen.

"Do you think you could let me order for myself sometime Stewart? So far we have eaten here twice and I have yet to speak a word to the waitress."

"Sorry, I hoped you would keep an eye out for trouble while I ordered. We are vulnerable in this town and I can't figure out why."

"I understand, but next time how about you keeping an eye out and let me do the talking?"

Both men were talking in little more than whispers so as not to draw attention to themselves. As they waited Stewart thought he noticed something, so he asked Ellsworth if he noticed it also. "Has anyone got up from their table and left yet?"

Ellsworth looked around and for a moment he only noticed the other patrons. Just when Stewart thought he hadn't heard him he said, "You know you're right. We have been here fifteen minutes or so and I don't believe anyone else has come in and no one appears to have left. Now what are the chances of that?"

Shortly the waitress brought the coffee and after she left the two men continued to notice the happenings of the dining room but trying to not be too obvious about it. When the food finally arrived the two decided they were hungry and it was probably just their tired overworked imaginations causing them to see trouble everywhere they went.

The waitress hadn't exaggerated when she said folks came in on Fridays just for the omelets, they were delicious. "You ever remember getting an omelet, or even hearing the word, around these parts before Ellsworth?"

Ellsworth chewed his food and swallowed before answering. "Come to think of it I haven't. I don't know of a place even in Rapid City that makes anything close to being called an omelet. It's just scrambled eggs and if you want peppers and mushrooms stirred in then you just ask for it. Maybe these folks are just different."

The marshal continued to scan the room as he finished his breakfast. When the lady came back he asked how much he owed and braced himself for the answer.

"The Friday special is three fifty, I hope you enjoyed it?"

The Pursuit

Stewart was pleasantly surprised as he pulled out four ones and reached them to the lady.

"I'm sorry but its three fifty each," she said as she looked at the two men.

Ellsworth nearly choked on his last bite when she said this. Stewart grudgingly pulled out a five and added two of the ones, there would be no tip for this meal.

The waitress didn't seem the least perturbed at the lack of a tip and thanked the two men as she headed back toward the kitchen.

"Seven dollars for two plates of eggs with bacon and two cups of coffee. We better get our horses and get the hell out of Sweetwater Stewart before they start charging us for the air we breathe."

The marshal was putting the two left over dollars back in his pocket when he noticed something. "Hey Ellsworth, look over there by the door. I think that's our friend from last night."

Ellsworth looked in the direction of the saloon and sure enough there stood the man that was wearing the green checked shirt and tan Stetson the night before. "Well, I'm just going to go over there and have a little talk with that man," Ellsworth said as he started to get up.

"You won't have to, he's heading this way," Stewart told him.

The man weaved his way through the room but slowed as he approached the table. Today he wasn't wearing the lumberjack garb from the previous evening. He was dressed as any respectable business owner in a prosperous small town might dress. He was clean shaven and his clothes looked starched and pressed. He was also wearing a gun.

"Good morning gentlemen, may I have a word with you?"

Stewart took a foot and slid out a chair. "Be my guest but if you don't mind how about keeping both hands on top of the table where I can see em."

The man smiled and did as requested. "Is there a reason for the caution? I hope no one in Sweetwater has given you cause to believe we are unfriendly."

"The town has been friendly enough but the folks that live here seem a bit standoffish. Let's just say until I get to know someone, especially someone wearing a gun, I like to be cautious," Stewart said.

The man smiled as he looked at Ellsworth and stuck out a hand. "My name is Patterson Hartman."

Ellsworth shook as he said, "Raymond Ellsworth."

After that Hartman turned his attention back to the marshal. He stuck out his hand again and shook the marshal's hand. The marshal didn't offer his name.

Hartman released his grip and said, "I'm sorry, but I didn't get your name."

"Jake Stewart. Why were you in the saloon last evening keeping an eye on me and my friend here?"

"I must offer my apologies for that; I thought you might have been someone that I had known in years past. I looked in a couple of times but finally decided you weren't the same man. I am very sorry if I seemed rude. It was not my intention."

"You asked to speak to us, we are both listening," Stewart said.

"Yes, my employer would like to arrange lunch with the two of you, along with the third man you are traveling with. By the way what would his name be?"

"His name is Gene Blair. Me and my friend here might be able to meet with your boss if you can tell me what it's about and who he is," Stewart said.

The Pursuit

"His name is Norman Fowler but I'm afraid I'm not at liberty to say what he wants to talk to you about, it might be as simple as lunch and a friendly chat about nothing. Would this Gene Blair also be able to attend if the two of you agree?"

"Mister Blair won't be able to attend, but the two of us will see your boss," Stewart said. He assumed Norman Fowler was Hartman's boss, a man he wanted to ask a few questions.

The look on Hartman's face took on the look of worry. "Has Mister Blair gotten sick or been involved in an accident?"

Stewart found the question to be revealing. It implied injury or sickness, not the simplest solution that possibly the man had left town. It was as if the question implied Hartman expected Blair to meet with some sort of physical injury.

"No he's fine, but at the moment he isn't here and we might not find him before this lunch you mentioned," Stewart said in hopes the man believed him.

After a second for the news to sink in Hartman smiled and said, "The invitation still stands. If you can find Mister Blair then please let him know the invitation is extended to him as well."

"We'll let him know if we see him. Where do we go for this lunch?" Ellsworth asked. He hadn't spoken, other than to tell his name, and felt he needed to say something.

"There will be a buggy in front of your hotel at noon. The driver will be expecting three men, he will take you to the appointed location," Hartman said as he stood. "I will inform my boss, he will be expecting you," he said before turning and leaving the room.

After the man left Ellsworth looked at the marshal. "What do you make of that? I wonder if it's wise for us to go."

"Let's wait and see if the driver and his buggy actually shows up. I think Fowler really wanted to meet with Blair and not so much you and me. If that's the case then the two of us might not be getting that free lunch after all if we can't produce Gene Blair," Stewart said.

"Well, if it ain't free we shouldn't go anyway. Probably cost the two of us twenty dollars apiece."

Stewart laughed. "Let's go back over and check on that livery man. If this lunch is as unfriendly as I suspect it'll be then I want Sadie ready to travel if the need arises. To tell you the truth I've felt a little on edge knowing Sadie wasn't travel worthy. It's funny how a man feels like a prisoner if he don't have a horse."

The walk back to the livery was short, but cold. Once they entered they found the same man but this time he was working the anvil and hammer. The blacksmith and the livery man were the same man, both Stewart and Ellsworth had figured as much. He was probably the friendliest man in town and for this reason Stewart decided to strike up a conversation.

"Say, I don't believe me and my friend here got your name when we brought our horses in last night," Stewart said.

The man struck the shoe another time or two with the hammer he held in a gloved hand. "My names Jess Allen, I'll have Sadie good as new in an hour or so. I thought about trying to use that old shoe but whoever made it didn't do such a good job. I checked the other three and saw that they were made by someone other than whoever made this one. That shoe was lucky to last any time at all."

"I'm Jake Stewart and this is Raymond Ellsworth. You mind if we get another cup of that coffee, it's as good as any I've tasted lately."

"Help yourself; what are you two doing traveling this time of year in this kind of weather? I assume business."

The Pursuit

Stewart could tell the man liked to talk; probably not many people come to a smelly livery to strike up conversation. "We got some business but not here in Sweetwater. We were just traveling through and thought about getting that shoe fixed and maybe resting up a bit. That storm last night also had us looking for some place with a roof over it."

"Yeah, that storm was something but she was fast moving. Don't reckon she wanted to stay in Sweetwater, sort of like you two," Allen said.

"This seems to be a new town; I don't reckon any building on either side of the street looks more than a few years old. I've never visited any town where every building in it was built about the same time," Ellsworth said hoping to get a little history on Sweetwater.

"She's pretty new I guess. I think all the buildings were built about five years ago. Mister Fowler sent word that he would hire every carpenter around that wanted to come here and work. At its peak I think there were a hundred carpenters and another hundred laborers working here. This whole town was finished in less than a year," Allen said.

"You don't say, two hundred men sawing and nailing wood. I'll bet they were all sorry when they got finished. Not many places can work a man solid for a year driving nails," Stewart said as he winked at Ellsworth. The two were tag-teaming the blacksmith for information and so far it was working pretty well.

"Naw, no one lost their job when the town got finished. They all moved up on the hill and started that mansion Mister Fowler lives in. If anyone thought the town took a long time to build then they really must think the mansion was slow going. It took nearly two years for them to finally put the finishing touches on that structure."

Nathan Wright

"That's nearly three years of work for a crowd of men. Where did they all go when the mansion was completed? That many men that are handy with a saw and hammer would need to find gainful employment somewhere," Ellsworth said.

"They're still here. Most went to work building the sawmill that has the contract for the crossties. Others are working the silver mines on the other side of the mountain. A few were old enough that they stopped working, Mister Fowler still pays those men half wages which allows them to enjoy a decent retirement."

"That many men working full time would require some cash just to cover the payroll. Does this town really make that kind of money for Fowler?" Ellsworth asked.

"It does, and then some. Rumor has it the profits from the silver mine alone could keep the town going for years. That ain't counting the lucrative contract with the railroad to furnish timber for bridges and tunnels, not to mention all the crossties."

"Well, if the town is making its way now then what kept it going when it was first being built. The time spent building the town and the mansion was nearly three years and no money was being made then," Stewart said.

"Mister Fowler was a wealthy man when he came here. He had been buying up a lot of land around these parts; the money for that and the building projects he already had, and then some. I heard he was originally from back east, New York. He just got tired of the city and decided to head west to make his fortune. I reckon that would be his second fortune because he brought one with him when he came," Allen said with a chuckle.

"Why did he want to build a town this far north, looks like the easy money would have been to settle a little farther south, say close to Rapid City? There is already a substantial population there and the railroad services that town on a weekly basis," Stewart said.

"It's funny you asked. I always wondered that very same question. From what I gather, Mister Fowler doesn't like the territory any farther south than here. He won't allow a road to be built in that direction and pretty much forbids any of his companies to do business down that way. No sir, everything that can't be taken care of here must be directed north rather than south."

"Well, Ellsworth and myself have been invited to have lunch at that mansion in a few hours, anything we should know before we head that way?" Stewart asked.

Allen stopped working on the shoe and looked at the two men. Finally he said, "I can't say as I've ever known of anyone being invited to the mansion. You two must be of some importance to warrant such an invitation."

"That's kind of what we thought, but the two of us are really of no importance. Neither of us can figure out why we're invited or what the meeting is about," Ellsworth said.

"Maybe there isn't a reason other than Mister Fowler just found out there are a couple of strangers in town and he wants to meet you over lunch."

"Not likely, at least I wouldn't think so. Surely this Fowler doesn't want to meet every new face that comes to town," Ellsworth said.

The livery man turned back to his forge and added a little coal. As he stoked the fire he said, "I imagine you'll find out when you get there. I'll have Sadie good as new in a little while. If you two want to stop back by this afternoon for some more coffee then be my guest. I don't get much company around here other than horses, seems they never have much to say," Allen said with a laugh. Ellsworth and Stewart thought it was pretty funny too.

As the two men headed back toward the hotel Ellsworth asked, "Stewart, if there was one man you had to trust in this town, besides me of course, who would it be?"

Stewart didn't need to think long, "That livery man Allen I suppose. He seems to be the only person around here that wants to talk. Everyone else acts like they are either too good to talk to strangers or have some other reason that hasn't made itself evident yet."

"That's the same thing I was thinking. And if there is one man around here that doesn't fit in, who would that be, besides either of us of course."

It didn't take Stewart long before he answered, "Again it would be Allen, what are you getting at?"

"I really don't know but something tells me that we might be bringing bad luck to Jess Allen. Something about this town, and its people, that leads me to believe Allen is an outcast. He said himself that he don't have anyone to talk to during the day. I've never know a livery man that didn't have his regular friends stopping by every day to pass the time. You study on that a spell Stewart and see if you don't agree."

The marshal thought Ellsworth was right. Livery men always had someone around yacking up a storm. "Maybe me and you better not go there this afternoon for that coffee after all. If folks see us spending too much time there then they might assume something that ain't so."

As the two entered the foyer of the hotel both were met with the welcome warmth of stove warmed air. The storm might have blown over but it left some bitter temperatures behind. The same man from the previous night was at the counter where folks filled out the register and got their keys;

The Pursuit

he only glanced up at the two men and then looked back to his paperwork.

As the two men climbed the staircase Ellsworth whispered, "Not very friendly is he?"

"I reckon not, but in this town I'm starting to get used to it."

At the top of the stairs Stewart said he was going to take a short nap before heading back down to await the buggy. The marshal's room was first and as Ellsworth walked on down the hall Stewart unlocked his door and pushed it open. Sitting there in a chair was Gene Blair.

"Ellsworth!" Stewart said in a muffled voice he hoped would get the man's attention. When Ellsworth turned the marshal motioned him back.

Both men stepped into the room as Stewart closed and relocked the door. Blair had taken the covers off the marshal's bed and draped them around his shoulders. Even wrapped up the way he was and in a warm room he still shivered.

"Blair, you better have a good reason for cutting out in the middle of the night." As the marshal looked at the man he pulled his gun and demanded Blair show both his hands, which were hidden by the blankets.

Blair slowly parted the top blanket and revealed both hands, they looked nearly blue from cold but both were empty.

"I want to apologize to both of you for my actions. I knew the only way for me to ride out last night without both of you making a scene was to just excuse myself from the table and then leave. I went straight to my room and retrieved my saddlebags and then let myself into your room Marshal to get the canvas bag of gold coins."

Both men looked at each other and shook their heads. "You have only told us what we already know Blair. Now tell us why you headed out in the middle of the night like a common criminal, which is what I'm starting to believe you are?" Ellsworth said.

"Alright, I guess it's time I told you two the rest of the story. Most of what I've already said about the money is true. It was stolen from the folks that sold their land to the railroad. I came across this information because it was my job to purchase land on either side of the tracks that are going to be built in the near future.

"I approached each individual landowner and made an assessment of what their property was worth and then that information was sent to an organization called Five Oaks Development. The men who work for Five Oaks were then to take the offer to the landowner and close the deal.

"What I found out after the majority of the land had been surveyed, appraised, and a deal struck, was that Five Oaks was short-paying every deal by twenty-five percent. Now that may seem like a little thing that could easily be remedied. Well, it's not a little thing and the men who instigated the plan will never willingly make things right," Blair told the two.

"When you found out about the scheme what did you do?" Stewart asked.

"I had my suspicions all along. The amount offered was barely enough to compensate the landowners, but most accepted the deal anyway. I was told to let them know that if they didn't accept what was offered then the territorial government would intervene and the price would be far less. Most accepted out of fear they would receive the lower amount if they didn't.

"As I traveled through the region I began to hear grumblings that the land wasn't being paid for at the agreed upon price. When I looked at a couple of the new deeds that came along with the payments I found that each landowner was being paid exactly twenty-five percent less than the amount I had negotiated."

"Was there a reason given for the reduced price?" Ellsworth asked.

"There was, it was stated that there was a fifteen percent fee for clerical work at the government offices in Chicago. Another ten percent was withheld for taxes and transfer fees. It was explained that the twenty-five percent fees was the sole responsibility of the original landholders," Blair said as he rubbed his hands together.

"Were these fees discussed with the landowners before a deal was struck?" Stewart asked.

"No Marshal because there are no fees. I have dealt in survey and title work all my life and know for a fact that right-of-way purchases are never taxed. It is a perk the government gives the railroads to entice expansion. No fees are assessed to the roads in question and no fees are to be paid by the original landowners."

Stewart thought about what he had just heard and still couldn't figure out the reason why Blair had left town the way he did. "Let's just say that so far I believe you Blair. What happened yesterday to prompt your hasty exit from town last night?"

"I knew Five Oaks was headed by a man named Wilbur Westbrook who lived in Chicago. I also knew the Chicago branch of Five Oaks only controlled half of the company. In all my dealings with the landowners on behalf of Five Oaks, I was never told who out here in the Dakota Territory controlled the other half.

"When I found out last night that Norman Fowler had been asking for me then I figured out who the other party was.

When I heard he wanted to know if I had been around it hit me that he was the mysterious money man from these parts.

"Sure, I had heard of Fowler for the last two years or so, but never put two and two together so to speak. I even had the hundred and fifty thousand dollars hid right here in his bank in a safety deposit box."

Stewart thought Blair might have had things wrong and Fowler just wanted to talk to him about something totally unrelated. "What makes you so sure Fowler is the mystery man with all the money? All the man did was ask for you, just like he did for me and Ellsworth."

"Because Fowler doesn't know me and yet he was having his people ask around town for me by name. You say he asked for you, did he know you, or was he just trying to use you to get to me?"

Both Ellsworth and Stewart looked at each other. They knew the man named Patterson Hartman hadn't known their names but he did know Blair because he asked for him specifically. It was evident Blair was the one Hartman's boss really wanted to see.

"We were approached by a man this morning during breakfast by the name of Patterson Hartman; you know him or ever hear of him?"

Blair didn't need to think long, "Never heard of the man but I assume he works for Norman Fowler if he was asking around."

"Why did you come back to town if you think these men know you and mean you harm because you took some money," Ellsworth asked.

"I needed to hide the money, it wasn't safe to leave in the bank since I found out that Fowler is the mystery man. And I had to come back to warn the two of you," Blair said.

The Pursuit

"So you came back Blair. Now both you and the money are in the very town where you are most afraid to be?" Stewart said.

"The money isn't in town anymore. It's hidden about ten miles from here. The money is safe."

"Why did you hide it and not just keep going?" Ellsworth asked.

"Did you see the weather outside last night? It was all I could do just to make it to my hiding spot and get back here before I froze to death. Anyway, I had to come back here to warn both of you that you are probably in danger since they have now associated you two with me. I made it back no more than an hour ago and was thinking about going to the livery but didn't. Jess Allen is about the only man in Sweetwater I trust."

"One more question Blair. How did you get your hands on the money in the first place?" Stewart asked.

"The amount of land that was being purchased represented quite a few deeds. Money was transferred here once a month from Chicago. I simply met the train at the depot north of here and accepted the delivery. Everyone knew me and knew I worked for the men associated with Five Oaks. I signed for the money and then headed south. It was a bad plan because I was chased from the beginning but not before I deposited the majority of the money in the bank in a safety deposit box I had rented the previous week under a different name. The folks at the bank had never seen me before and I have only been in there three times, once to rent the box, once to hide the money in the box, and lastly to remove the money.

"With the money safe in the bank I thought I better lay low for a day or two. I spent two nights hiding in the livery until I was sure I could get out of town without being seen. Jess Allen will confirm this if you ask. That was a few weeks ago."

The last statement confirmed that the livery man was probably trustworthy. Ellsworth pulled out his pocket watch and looked at the time. "I suppose we better be heading down to the lobby. The buggy will be here in a few minutes."

Blair looked at the two as if someone had just walked over his grave. "You two aren't considering going up there are you?"

"We are, but I doubt if it would be wise for you to go, and you can't stay here. I suspect someone goes through the rooms when we are gone. So where will you go Blair while the marshal and myself are gone?"

"I plan on going back to the livery and hiding out there. I only came here to warn you. Allen has a room with a hidden door, well it's about as hidden as it can be I suppose. When you two come off the mountain you can look me up over there."

"You sure you can make it back to the livery without being spotted?" Stewart asked.

"I'll go back the same way I came. It's so cold outside there aren't many people on the street. I hid most of my face while out of doors today; most folks suspect I'm just shielding myself from the cold. Hell it ain't like anyone in Sweetwater looks directly at anyone anyway," Blair said.

"You better let us go first and then you can make your way back to the livery. How did you get through the lobby without being seen anyway Blair?" Ellsworth asked.

"I used the alley beside the hotel and then came up the back stairs. I might have broken the lock on your window Marshal, hope you don't mind," Blair said. Whoever designed the hotel had the forethought to build a narrow balcony along the entire rear of the building so if tragedy struck the occupants could escape. It had worked out really well for the slippery Blair.

Ellsworth and Stewart walked down the stairs into the lobby wondering if they were doing the right thing going to meet with Norman Fowler. With Blair reappearing like a magician it had changed the entire dynamic of the meeting. If what he said was true then the two men might be putting themselves in danger. Both accepted as much, they wanted to know what in hell was really going on and this might be the only way to find out. It might also be a good way for the two to get themselves shot.

At two minutes before noon a buggy pulled up out front. The driver was a man who looked to be in his late twenties, he wore a tied down gun. The buggy was a sturdy looking affair with a front seat for two and another in back that would also hold two. The entire rig was covered with a black canvas top that would shield the occupants, including the driver, from anything short of a blowing rain.

The driver stepped into the foyer and saw the two men he was to transport. "Ellsworth and Stewart I assume?"

"That would be us," Ellsworth said.

"I am here to take you to the meet with Mister Fowler. If you would climb onboard we can get started."

The three men exited the building and climbed into the buggy, Ellsworth in the back and Stewart in front beside the driver.

"I'm sorry, but only I am allowed in the front," the man said to Stewart.

"Not today, I believe I'll ride here to keep an eye on things if you don't mind." Stewart wasn't about to be lined up with Ellsworth where a well-placed bullet from a Winchester rifle could take out both men with one shot. With one man directly behind the driver and another beside it would present a problem for anyone trying to take advantage of an opportunity.

Stewart and the driver looked each other eye to eye and when it was apparent Stewart wasn't moving the driver released the brake and then tapped the right hand horse with a long pole. The trip to the mansion must have a substantial incline due to the fact that the buggy was pulled by a two horse team.

The buggy turned and headed in the general direction of the mill. This was good because it would offer a better view of what looked to be a large operation; at least it had looked that way from a distance.

As the road closed on the mill Stewart and Ellsworth took in the view. There were several two-mule teams pulling large ponderosa pine logs from the mountain. It seemed as if the teams stretched as far as the eye could see. It looked like the logs were trimmed smooth of any branches before beginning their long journey to the mill.

After the mule teams were unhitched they were turned and started back up the mountain via a different route than the one used to bring the logs down.

After the mules were released the logs were rolled by men with long lever poles onto a chain that ran continuously at a slow speed pulling them into one end of the mill. That was all that could be seen of the operation from the approach end but as the buggy came around the building the finished product of the mill could be seen exiting on the opposite side.

Another chain delivered the sawed lumber to this side of the mill where it was loaded onto flat-bed heavy wagons that were pulled by four stout horses to a staging area where they were stacked neatly by what looked to be a small army of laborers.

The Pursuit

The finished lumber looked to be of five different sizes. One size was undoubtedly crossties and the other four must have been what would be needed for either bridges or tunnels. The amount of wood stacked amounted to what looked like several months work for the mill. No doubt as the railroad made its way closer then this stock would be put to use. This operation wasn't that much different from the mill Stewart had seen at Elk Bend.

Once past the mill the driver headed up a narrow drive that looked to be well maintained. No more than two hundred feet from the main road there was a small structure which seemed to be a guard shack, but one of elaborate design and tasteful construction.

Before the buggy made it to the building two men stepped out, each carrying a double barreled Greener, these men could stop anyone trying to enter the property within a hundred feet of the shack. Stewart suspected there were probably long guns in the building in case someone was out of range of the Greeners.

"Looks like you've picked up a couple of passengers Lowell. Is the boss expecting these two?" one of the two guards asked.

"He is, check the log. I believe their names are in it," the man named Lowell said.

One of the two shotgun guards stepped back inside the building and immediately came back out holding a journal of some sort. He flipped a couple of pages and then looked at Stewart.

"State your name Mister."

The marshal didn't like being treated like a prisoner being transported to jail but felt if he wanted to get any answers then he needed to cooperate.

"Jake Stewart."

This seemed to satisfy the man so he turned his attention to Ellsworth, "And you?"

"Names Raymond Ellsworth."

"Well gentlemen, I'm going to need to disarm you. You'll be given your guns back when you leave," the guard said.

Now this startled Ellsworth and Stewart. If something was planned when they got to the mansion then they would both be defenseless. The two guards were both holding the shotguns at parade rest, meaning they were heavily armed but the weapons they carried were pointed away and downward from the two men they were going to disarm. Apparently these two had never had anyone disobey an order and weren't expecting any trouble now.

Stewart was sitting on the left hand side of the buggy and was closest to the two guards. He wasn't going to give up his gun under any circumstances.

Stewart looked at the man and gave him a reassuring smile as he said, "As long as we get our guns back when we..." Before he finished he quickly drew his Colt and pointed it at the guard who had done the talking. Ellsworth, in the back seat, had also drawn and was holding his Colt on the man named Lowell, the driver.

"Neither of you move a muscle. Now don't try any acts of bravery boys," Stewart said as he stepped from the buggy and disarmed the two. Ellsworth reached around and pulled the gun the driver carried.

"I was invited here for lunch and didn't realize I would be treated as a criminal. Either one of you want to explain why you wanted our guns?" Stewart said as he searched the two. Ellsworth did the same of Lowell.

The Pursuit

"Well, it looks like Lowell here is packing a hideaway," Ellsworth said as he held up a two shot Derringer nearly identical to the one Stewart carried.

Stewart sat the two Greeners in the back of the buggy along with the Colt Ellsworth had taken from Lowell. The two shot Derringer went into the front pocket of Ellsworth's vest. He had envied the way Stewart had gotten them out of trouble back in the Elk Bend jail and knew he would someday save up enough to buy one of his own. If everyone kept acting so unfriendly in Sweetwater then he might just decide to keep this one. He was sure, at the moment, that Lowell wouldn't mind.

As Ellsworth held the three at bay Stewart checked the guardhouse. Inside were two Winchester rifles, both with fancy scopes mounted on top. There was a shelf just inside the door that contained any number of boxes of ammunition in sizes to fit everything the guardhouse had in weapons.

Stewart stepped back out and looked over the landscape, he didn't like the way things were working out. "You two have enough ammunition in there to hold off a company of soldiers. Now why would your boss feel he needs that kind of protection?" he asked Lowell.

"I can't answer that Mister Stewart but you can ask my boss yourself when he gets here," Lowell said.

Now both Stewart and Ellsworth began looking around. The way Lowell had worded his statement they fully expected the man's boss to be within earshot, or maybe gunshot. As they looked over their surroundings there could be heard the rumblings of another buggy, it was coming around the hill where the road was hidden by trees and shrubbery.

The rig was not that much different than the one Lowell had used to pick the two up, although as it got closer it was evident this one was of much more elaborate construction.

Nathan Wright

There were only two men in the buggy, a driver and another man seated in the second seat. Both Ellsworth and Stewart wondered what would happen next.

The rig pulled beside the first one and the man in the back looked over the situation, he was smiling. "Gentlemen, I believe you and I are scheduled to have lunch shortly. I'm sorry if the welcome you received was less than friendly."

Stewart hadn't expected such cordiality from a man whose guards just had their teeth pulled. "We were just explaining to these men here that we didn't want to give up our guns and they seemed to think otherwise."

The man in the buggy looked at Lowell and the two guards, they seemed embarrassed that the very men they were supposed to disarm had managed to get the drop on them.

"Gentlemen, you must consider my situation, you are strangers in town and as far as I know you both might be highwaymen set on robbing me."

Stewart felt it was time for these people to know that he was a Deputy U. S. Marshal. Without taking his eyes off the man he reached into his right vest pocket and retrieved his marshal's badge. He promptly pinned it on his chest and then said, "The Marshal's Service typically doesn't rob folks."

The newcomer in the second buggy had the sudden look of a criminal who was about to be arrested. "Why would you be in the town of Sweetwater without wearing your badge? Are you investigating some sort of crime?" the man asked nervously.

"Before I answer that I would like to know who I'm talking to."

The man hesitated; this wasn't lost on either Stewart or Ellsworth.

"My name is Norman Fowler. I'm sure you are not in Sweetwater for me?"

The Pursuit

"Can't say that I am, but while I'm here I would like to ask you a few questions."

The man's expression took on the look of relief. "That would be fine Marshal. Maybe we can proceed to the house first and get out of this weather."

Stewart looked at the two men who monitored the drive from the guard shack. "I reckon your two shotguns and long rifles will be in the back of this buggy. We'll drop them off on the way back down the mountain when we've concluded our business with your boss." With that he picked up the two Winchesters and placed them in the back of the buggy beside the Greeners. He also tossed in a second Colt that was taken from the shack.

"I trust you two won't try anything now will you?" Stewart asked. Both men shook their heads. Stewart probably believed them because he would be only yards away from Fowler and if they misbehaved their boss might be taken prisoner or killed outright, at least that's what Stewart hoped the two would think.

Stewart turned his attention back to Fowler. "Promise me your men won't do something stupid."

Fowler looked at the two, "Marshal Stewart is to be allowed safe passage to and from the mansion, is that understood?" Both men indicated they did.

"Alright then, shall we proceed? I believe a hot meal will help each of us to get past this awkward introduction," Fowler said.

With that, both buggies proceeded up the mountain. As they travelled both Stewart and Ellsworth kept a vigilant eye out for any more trouble. Even though they had the word of Fowler it did little to soothe the two men's nerves. Out in the open, penned up in a buggy, they felt vulnerable.

Nathan Wright

The road they travelled was well maintained. It was landscaped back for a distance of at least twenty feet on either side. The road had no less than four switchbacks before finally opening up onto a large natural bench where the mansion stood.

If they had thought the house was large and elaborate from the base of the hill then now it looked no less than a palace, albeit one made of logs. The main door was covered by massive timbers which made an overhanging gable that kept the entrance dry. The building looked to be two full stories and dormers on the roof indicated a partial third.

Just under the gable, over the entrance, was a hand carved sign which read *Refahs*. As the buggies pulled to a stop the men dismounted. It was then that Stewart got his first good look at Norman Fowler.

The man was tall, exceptionally tall. In an era when most men measured an average of five-nine or five-ten, Fowler stood a few inches taller than six feet. He looked to be around forty years of age and was lean and fit.

When he stepped from the buggy though, he did so with extreme care. With both feet safely on the ground he turned and retrieved a walking cane from the buggy, Fowler was crippled. His left leg seemed to have been injured but whether the injury was recent or not couldn't be determined.

He turned to his two guests and said, "If we could proceed inside, the chill out here is hard on my leg."

Lowell stayed with the two buggies as the driver of Fowler's carriage quickly went to the front door and opened it for his boss.

"Excuse me Mister Fowler but this name *Refahs*, what does that mean?" Stewart asked.

The Pursuit

Fowler stopped and looked up at the name. "It is the name of my ancestors back in Scotland. I liked it so much that I named my home after it. I think it adds a bit of mystery to the mansion don't you agree?" Stewart and Ellsworth could only nod.

"Follow me gentlemen, let us go to the fire and warm while lunch is being prepared," Fowler said.

As the men entered the main door they were met, a few feet farther inside, by another much more regular sized door. It was apparent the double doors were meant to keep out the wind and cold.

Past the second door was a massive parlor with ceilings that were no less than twenty feet tall. To one side was a fireplace that a man could probably lie down in, it was at least eight feet wide. If was made of stone, no doubt mined from the mountain itself. Logs no less than a foot thick and four feet long were used for fuel. The heat that radiated seemed to fill the entire room with warmth that a dozen smaller fireplaces would have trouble matching.

The room was adorned with leather chairs and two leather couches. There were tables beside each chair and these were carved from single pieces of ponderosa pine. The tree that donated itself to the tables mush have been at least three feet thick.

The man who had driven the buggy for Fowler quickly grabbed his boss's coat and hat. He also took his gloves and then put each in a closet by the door. Ellsworth and Stewart grudgingly gave up their coats and hats when the man asked for them. It was probably a good thing because the house was warm and cozy; a coat would become uncomfortable real fast.

"Gentlemen, if you will follow me I'm sure lunch is ready," Fowler said.

Nathan Wright

Stewart could only imagine why such pomp and circumstance was being shown to a territory marshal and a trail bum. Just when it was starting to worry him he figured it out, Fowler lived like this and this was just another day for him. He was still curious why the man was so set on talking to two men he had never met before.

Forty feet farther into the house was the dining room. It was as elaborate as the front parlor. The table was truly a massive affair, it was surrounded by no less than twelve chairs and there was probably room for eight or ten more. Again it looked to have been hued from a massive tree. The top was no less than five feet wide and fifteen feet long. The most outstanding thing about the table was the top was carved from a single piece of wood. It was finely edged and the entire top was stained a dark walnut as were the chairs and cabinets that stood at the walls.

There were three chairs at the far end where place settings were arraigned. Fowler led the two men to that end of the table and took the seat at the head of the table for himself and motioned for Stewart and Ellsworth to take the two adjoining chairs.

No sooner had the men took their chairs than a door to the side opened and three women, each wearing clothing such as a kitchen staff might wear, came in, each carrying a plate of food. When the dishes were sat in front of the men Stewart and Ellsworth were both surprised to be looking at leafy greens and tomatoes.

"I can tell by your expressions that you aren't used to seeing such as this in October. I have been told that to live a long and healthy life a man must eat vegetables every day. Quite hard to do in the Dakota Territory this time of year. Two years ago I had enough plate glass shipped in to build a modest

192

greenhouse on the south facing side of the mountain. It will supply lettuce and tomatoes until mid-November. After that I'm afraid there isn't enough direct sunlight to grow them but once the railroad is built then I can have both fruit and vegetables shipped in using the new refrigerated railcars.

Ellsworth looked at the plate that sat before him and realized he hadn't eaten a vegetable, other than a potato of course, in months. There was a small container of sauce sitting beside the plate and Ellsworth knew it was for the leafy greens. He noticed both Stewart and Fowler pouring theirs onto the greens, he did the same.

There was little talking as the men enjoyed their food. Ellsworth was a man who took large bites and chewed sparingly. When he finished he noticed both Fowler and Stewart were only half way there. If he was embarrassed by this he never indicated it. He sat his fork down and wondered if this was all they were having. His question was soon answered when the three ladies came back in and took the plates away and soon brought out three more.

The second course consisted of lean steak and more vegetables but these seemed to have been steamed or possibly boiled. Ellsworth was a man accustomed to eating out of a skillet next to a campfire. Again Ellsworth jumped in paying little attention to Stewart and Fowler. Once more he was finished a good five minutes before the other two. As he sat he wondered if the meal was over, he was full but could continue eating if more food was offered. He was pleasantly surprised when a dessert was soon brought out, warm pumpkin pie with some sort of sweet thick cream drizzled on top.

Fowler noticed how the man ate and was appalled at his total lack of table manners, but it was expected. He was surprised though to see that Stewart ate with self-control and conducted himself as if he may have eaten in some of the fanciest eateries the west had to offer.

When the second course, and the dessert, was complete Fowler pushed his chair back and stood using the help of his cane. "If you like we can talk in the front parlor. I like to sit by the fire for a while after eating to allow my food to digest."

The three men went to the front room where Fowler took a chair that was apparently his favorite. He motioned and Stewart and Ellsworth both took chairs opposite. The three men now faced each other at a distance of ten feet.

"Gentlemen, I invited you here today so as to get acquainted. I had hoped the third man you are traveling with could also attend. The invitation was offered, did he decline?"

"No, he just never got the message. When your man Patterson Hartman talked to us at breakfast this morning he did extend the invitation but neither myself nor Ellsworth have seen Blair today."

Fowler listened; neither Stewart or Ellsworth could tell if the man believed what Stewart had just said.

"I suppose I can talk to the both of you in the absence of Blair. What this is about deals with my relationship with Blair and the railroad that is planning the expansion into the northern territory. You see Mister Blair answers to me and I in turn answer to the railroad."

As Fowler was talking, a lady dressed more like a house servant, came into the room carrying a tray. She held the tray in front of Fowler first and he selected a cigar from an assortment that numbered at least a dozen. She then went to the marshal and offered him a choice. He looked over the selection and chose a very dark cigar of average size. When Ellsworth was allowed his choice he immediately took the biggest cigar the tray held. It looked like a small club.

The Pursuit

The same woman then took the silver flint lighter from the center of the tray and went from man to man lighting the cigar each had chosen. There was a table between Ellsworth and Stewart and on this she sat a round glass ashtray. There was a floor stand ashtray sitting beside the chair Fowler occupied. It was apparent this man liked his cigars.

"I hope you gentlemen like my selection, I have them brought in once a month and stored in a humidor to maintain freshness. The one you have Mister Ellsworth is a variety from Cuba, it is one of my favorites; I hope you enjoy it."

Ellsworth leaned his head back as he blew a large cloud of smoke toward the ceiling. "Can't say I've ever tried any tobacco from anywhere other than Kentucky, but this is pretty good, I'll have to admit."

Stewart liked his choice but didn't want to talk about cigars, he wanted some answers, "You were saying something about the railroad and Blair."

Fowler turned his attention back to the discussion. "Yes, well it appears Mister Blair might not be the man I thought he was when I originally hired him. Some funds went missing a few weeks back and it's believed he may have had something to do with it," Fowler said as he took another puff and waited for a response.

Stewart also waited; he had nothing to say at this point. Fowler could see he was going to need to use a little more prompting if he was to get any information from the marshal.

"Anyway, I was hoping you might know something about the crime Marshal?"

Stewart took another puff before answering; he felt the pause might work to his favor. "That is interesting Fowler, this morning when you sent your invitation you didn't know I was a marshal. Now you say the meeting was to see if I, as a lawman, have any information about what you claim Blair did or didn't do."

Fowler could see he might have underestimated the marshal. This man not only carried a badge, he was smart. "You are correct; up until you pulled the badge from your pocket and pinned it on I was unaware of your position in the Marshal's Service. But that doesn't change the fact that a crime has been committed and I would like your help in bringing the guilty party to justice."

"If I do find something to arrest Blair for then he still won't be the guilty party you are looking for. He will only be arrested, the guilt will be determined by a judge and jury," Stewart said.

Fowler was growing impatient with this word game and saw he was dealing with someone that couldn't be reasoned with. Most men Fowler dealt with only said what he wanted to hear and he wasn't used to being talked back to.

"I see your point Marshal. When will the suspect Blair be arrested?"

"Without a warrant signed by a judge, or actually witnessing a crime myself, I can't arrest Blair. If you can convince a judge to sign an arrest warrant then it will be my job to act upon it. I believe the closest judge is down in Rapid City. His name is Thurman Preston."

Stewart knew of Fowler's aversion to doing business anywhere south of Sweetwater but wondered if this also extended to the legal system. He was paying close attention as he mentioned the judge down in Rapid City.

Fowler adjusted himself in his chair as he considered his answer. He was nervous when he said, "I didn't realize there was only one judge and he was in Rapid City."

The Pursuit

Both Stewart and Ellsworth noticed the tone and manner Fowler had assumed when he spoke of the judge in Rapid City. He was nervous.

Stewart thought he would press the question and see what happened. "Do you know Judge Thurman Preston?"

Without time to think his reply through, Fowler blurted, "I've never met the man but the rumors I hear indicate he is hardnosed and unfit for the bench," the tone was suddenly harsh and the words clipped.

Ellsworth and Stewart exchanged glances. Fowler had suddenly become defensive and accusing. Something about the name Thurman Preston had set the man off. Stewart thought he would keep digging. If one man that held a position of authority in the territory could bring about such a reaction then maybe he would try another.

"Tell you what Fowler, as soon as I make it back to Rapid City I will talk to my counterpart there about this Blair to see if maybe he has heard anything. His name is Pete Savage and he's worked that area much longer than I have. And by the way, he's a marshal also."

Fowler crushed out his cigar in the pedestal ashtray beside the chair and stood. "I think our discussions are over gentlemen. My driver will show you out." With that Fowler turned and went back through the house. As he left the room the same man that had driven the second buggy entered the sitting room as if on demand.

"I'll show you gentlemen to the door," the man said as he retrieved their coats and hats.

Once outside, and back in the cold, it was apparent it wasn't going to warm up any today. It was also apparent the two weren't going to be offered any transportation off the mountain. The driver had immediately closed the exterior door and as soon as it was shut the sound of a slide bolt could be heard engaging.

Both buggies were still sitting out front but the horses had already been unhitched and led away, they were nowhere to be seen.

"You don't suppose they leave these two fine carriages outside all night do you?" Ellsworth said.

"Doubtful, my guess is the horses are put away first and then the two buggies are rolled around back by a couple of men. My guess is also that we are going to be pretty frozen by the time we make it back to the hotel."

As the two pulled up their collars and started off the hill the marshal reached into the back of the buggy they had ridden and retrieved the two shotguns and the Colt. "You remember I promised the men at the guard shack that I would return their weapons when we came back off the mountain," Stewart said as he reached one of the Greeners to Ellsworth.

"You did at that Marshal, and you are a man of your word," Ellsworth said as he broke down the shotgun and checked that it was loaded. Stewart did the same and then both men started down the drive.

Once both were out of sight they cut out of the driveway and took a more direct route to town. "Say Marshal, how do you reckon Fowler knew there was trouble earlier at the guard shack? No sooner had we disarmed those three than he showed up."

"I've been thinking about that ever since it happened. My guess is he has a scope trained on that shack and was watching. As dense as the trees are around here he must have at least one small line of sight cleared. I don't recommend we go back by that shack. Something tells me Fowler has a way of communicating with his guards and for all we know they might

The Pursuit

try to stop us again," Stewart said as the two sprinted down the mountain.

No sooner had the marshal said this than there was the report of a Winchester and then the explosion of a section of bark on a nearby tree.

"Stay low and move fast Ellsworth."

"You don't need to tell me twice Marshal."

"We better stay to cover, I don't think I mentioned it but there were a pair of scoped Winchesters on a wall rack in the front sitting room of Fowler's mansion. A scope would allow a marksman to take both of us out at this distance," the marshal said.

Ellsworth and Stewart moved from tree to tree making sure to stay about five yards apart. It wasn't long before another shot rang out but the bullet went wide.

"I think that shot was just a guess," Ellsworth said.

"Maybe not, maybe they are trying to drive us into a kill zone," Stewart said. The thought of that made both men redouble their efforts to stay to cover while also staying low and moving fast.

When they finally made it to a spot near the bottom of the hill they were presented with a significant problem. It was at least two-hundred yards of open area between where they were and the road back to town.

"Looks like we are in a bit of a bind Marshal, we head across that open area and we are both dead men."

Stewart looked over the situation trying to find options. He finally spotted one. About three hundred feet to the left was the road used by the mule teams to bring the logs out of the forest. He and Ellsworth worked their way toward the logging road making sure to stay in the timber. Once there they each simply picked a team and ducked down on the opposite side.

"What in hell do you think you're doing," one of the teamsters that was driving the mules said to Stewart when he saw him running toward his team.

"Shut up and continue as if nothing has happened," Stewart roughly told the man. The man caught glimpse of the marshal's badge pinned to Stewart's coat and decided to obey whatever the man said.

Stewart looked behind him and was glad to see that Ellsworth had made it to the next team. Both men assumed they hadn't been seen. Even if one of the guards had saw the two a shot couldn't be taken without the possibility hitting a mule or the teamster leading it.

When the two mule teams made it to the mill both Stewart and Ellsworth darted inside and headed through the massive building. If any of the men working inside wanted to say anything to the two they probably decided against it once they saw the two Greeners the men carried. Funny how a shotgun will make most men mind their own business.

At the other end of the mill, the end where the finished product came out, the two stopped and caught their breath. It was bitterly cold and both had been running for their lives for the last ten minutes.

The large stacks of sawn lumber made excellent cover as the two worked their way toward town. The last quarter mile required they re-enter the tree line; it was safer than traveling out in the open. By four o'clock the two were in the center of town but decided at the last minute to head to the livery rather than the hotel.

They each took one last look to see if they had been noticed or followed and then darted in the side door. Both headed for the stove and coffee.

The Pursuit

"Glad to see you two. By the looks of things I take it that lunch was a bad idea?" Jess Allen said.

Neither Stewart nor Ellsworth answered; both were trying to get their hands thawed out.

"It's a good thing we didn't try to return fire Marshal. As cold as my fingers are I would have probably blown off my own foot," Ellsworth said.

The marshal was trying to pour some coffee into a tin cup but only managed to knock the cup to the ground.

"Here Stewart, let me pour that for you. Did I hear him just call you marshal?" Allen asked.

Stewart took the cup and only held it between his cold hands as he nodded down at the badge. "You guessed it, and I believe it just about got the two of us killed."

As the men talked a door could be heard opening toward the back. A few seconds later Gene Blair stepped into the center hall of the livery. He looked at the two and asked how the meeting went.

"Started out with handshakes and ended with gunfire," Ellsworth said.

"Gunfire, did anyone get hurt?"

"We were shot at but we never returned fire. We neither one knew where the shooter, or shooters, were. Plus we were too busy running and ducking," the marshal said.

"But you did get to meet with Fowler, so what did he say before everything deteriorated to attempted murder?" Blair asked.

"He had some not so pleasant things to say about you Blair. He wanted me to do his bidding and arrest you. When I mentioned he would need to have Judge Preston down in Rapid City issue a warrant he turned cold and left the room.

That's when we left and were shot at all the way down the mountain," Preston said.

Allen and Blair were quiet for a moment as they thought over what the marshal said. "Is this Judge Preston a friend of yours Marshal?" Allen asked.

"I really don't know the man that well, I would have to say he is fair and probably would help me if I ever needed it. Why do you ask?"

"I left here about an hour ago to get some food at the general store. I don't keep that much here and Blair and I decided we were getting hungry. While I was there I overheard two men talking, I was near the back and they didn't know I was there but I could hear them just the same. They mentioned the murder of a judge and a marshal in Rapid City," Allen said.

The news came as a shock to Stewart. "Are you sure Allen? I mean think hard."

Allen solemnly looked at the marshal. "I heard it that way, but I was a ways off and the two didn't talk loud, it was more in hushed tones but I did make out most of the words. I'm sorry Marshal."

Stewart mumbled to himself as he sat down on a hundred pound sack of feed, "Preston and Savage killed. I can't believe it."

Ellsworth knew both men and took the news nearly as hard as Stewart but tried to reason a different outcome than the one Allen might have heard.

"Maybe the two men were talking about an attempted murder. Or maybe they were just wishful thinking about a marshal and a judge they didn't like."

Stewart thought about what Ellsworth said and reasoned that maybe he had a point. It wouldn't be the first time someone heard something wrong and then repeated what they thought they heard. But in his heart he suspected that what Allen had said was more fact than fiction.

"What do we do now Marshal? You think we're safe as long as we are in town?" Ellsworth asked.

Stewart snapped out of his trance. If someone had really killed the marshal and the judge then he would make it his purpose to hunt down the perpetrators and bring them to justice. Right now he had to consider his own options while in town.

"I think me and you are safe as long as there are others around. A town in broad daylight is a hard place to commit a cold blooded murder and Fowler knows it. Night though would be a different story. If something is going to happen it will probably happen tonight," Stewart said.

"If we stay in our rooms at the hotel we might be safe but I don't like it. Folks will know exactly where we are and that puts us both at a disadvantage," Ellsworth said.

The marshal thought a minute as the feeling started coming back to his fingers. "Say Allen, you wouldn't have any twelve-gauge shotgun shells around here would you?"

"Got a full box of ten and maybe three or four more sitting over there on that shelf," the livery man said as he pointed.

Stewart walked over and retrieved the shells and then gave Ellsworth half. "We better carry these Greeners while we're in town. Shotgun is good in close quarters work."

As Ellsworth looked at the shiny Greener he asked the marshal, "We planning on giving these back when we leave town?" The tone of his voice, and the look on his face, indicated the man wanted to keep his.

"Oh hell no, we leave here we take these with us. I just confiscated these two weapons, and that goes for the Colt and Derringer you lifted off Lowell, the buggy driver. When a man takes a shot at me I figure if he didn't kill me then I take his weapons."

"I got a good Colt but I do appreciate the Greener and the Derringer," Ellsworth said. "We heading over to the hotel like everyone in town would expect us to do, or do you have something else in mind?"

Stewart wasn't going to stay at the hotel but he did want everyone to think that he was. "Oh we're staying at the hotel alright, for about ten minutes. We go right in the front door and straight to our rooms. Lock each of our doors and then prop a chair under the knob. After that we use Blair's escape route and come back here."

"I like it Marshal, let them think we are in our nice warm rooms. If anyone wants to cause us some mischief then all they'll find is empty mattresses. When do we head over?"

"It'll be getting dark soon. We wait here until about thirty minutes past dark and then head out. We go through the lobby and make sure we speak to that unfriendly man that waits the counter. A little after that we sneak out the back windows and head back here. As cold as it is outside hopefully everyone will be indoors at that hour," Stewart said.

"I'll make another trip to the store for food if you two are staying the night. What I got earlier was barely enough for me and Blair, he can really put it away," Allen said as he looked at Blair.

"That's no good; if you make two trips to the general store then someone will get suspicious. Tell you what, me and Ellsworth will head out now and purchase the food. We'll take it up to our room and no one will be the wiser. We can stuff what we get into our saddlebags so it won't slow us down on our race back here," the marshal said.

The Pursuit

"That's good, but how long are we planning on staying in Sweetwater Marshal?" Blair asked.

"I can't say but with this cold snap clamping down on the temperature I wouldn't want to head out until it passes. Maybe two days; if it's still frigid then we'll have no choice but to chance it. In the mean time I plan on asking a few questions. Like I said, we should be alright as long as we do most of our moving around in daylight."

About fifteen minutes past dark both the marshal and Ellsworth headed outside and up the boardwalk. They weren't trying to hide but they weren't trying to be noticed either, if such a thing were possible. The trip to the general store wasn't far but it was enough to chill the two men's bones.

The store was well lit when they entered and it was thankfully warm due to two potbellied stoves, one near the front door and the other farther toward the back. There was a man behind the counter reading a newspaper; he looked up when Stewart and Ellsworth entered.

"Say storekeep, where would you keep your tobacco?" Ellsworth asked.

The man behind the counter never smiled, he never even spoke. He just raised an arm and pointed to a shelf on the opposite wall. It was all Ellsworth could do to keep from jumping the counter and knocking the man on his ass. He felt, and was pretty sure, this was the most unfriendly town west of the Mississippi river.

As Ellsworth gathered a couple of pouches of chewing tobacco and the makings for cigarettes Stewart went to a shelf and pulled down four cans of tinned beef and a box of hardtack. The two men had already figured what could be put in their saddlebags and this was about it. As almost an afterthought Ellsworth grabbed a fistful of licorice sticks and laid them on the counter. Besides food the store had about anything a man might want, including numerous items that would fall under the category of hardware.

"That will about do us, how much do we owe you?" Stewart asked in a polite voice.

The man behind the counter tallied up the items on a scrap of paper and rather than telling Stewart how much he owed he just turned the paper around and slid it toward him. He didn't smile, he didn't grin, he didn't yawn or fart. He just looked at the two with a sour face.

Stewart smiled as he counted out the exact amount and laid it on the counter. The man picked the money up and put it in the register behind the counter. He then turned back toward the two, but instead of speaking, or just saying thank you, he went back to reading his paper.

Ellsworth and Stewart were shocked. They knew folks in Sweetwater acted standoffish but this was just too much.

"Pardon me mister," Stewart said in a low solemn voice.

It took a few seconds before the man behind the counter decided to look up at Stewart, the look on the man's face indicated he didn't appreciate being interrupted again.

Stewart looked the man in the eye and smiled. He then grabbed him by the collar and pulled him across the counter where they would be face to face.

"Listen to me you son of a bitch. I have just about had enough of you and your sorry attitude. You and everyone in this damn town are as unfriendly as I have ever seen and believe me I have seen a lot. Now you are going to answer a couple of questions for me and if you decide otherwise then I am going to whip your hardware selling ass right here and now, do we understand each other?"

The Pursuit

The man again didn't speak, he was too scared to. He did manage to nod.

Stewart realized he now had the man's attention. "Were you told to not speak to me and my friend here?"

The man shook his head yes.

"Were you told to report our movements to anyone?"

Again the man shook his head yes.

"This next one isn't a question, it's a demand. Who were you supposed to report to?"

Without hesitation the storekeep said, "Patterson Hartman."

"I thought so you sniveling little bastard. Well you can tell him this; the next time I see him snooping around I'm going to beat the living shit out of him. Now you tell him that, you tell him exactly what I said. Do you understand me?"

Again the man let out a weak reply, the reply was the one Stewart wanted to hear so he released the man's collar and then took his fingers and straightened the crumpled bow tie the man was wearing. "I've enjoyed our little talk. As you can see I'm wearing a marshal's badge so if you feel inclined to say I roughed you up, or threatened you, then I will have to agree because whatever you think I'm capable of right not ain't half what I'll do to you if I'm pushed. Again, do we understand each other?"

The response was predictable, a weak yes.

"It's been a pleasure doing business with you. If anyone wants to talk to me then you know where to find me," Stewart said as he turned to Ellsworth. He was pleased to see the man had been watching the street so no one could come from that direction and cause them any trouble.

Nathan Wright

The cold walk to the hotel was welcomed by the marshal. It allowed him to cool off and he really needed to cool off after the storekeep had made him lose his temper to such a degree.

"I really enjoy watching a man that knows his work," Ellsworth said with a laugh. When Stewart heard this he laughed too and the tension was immediately broken.

As they entered the hotel the same hotel clerk was behind the counter, it was as if he never left the place. He had probably been told by Hartman to keep an eye out for Stewart and Ellsworth just like the storekeep had. This time the marshal walked right up to the counter and said, "Excuse me."

The man slowly looked up but never said a word.

"I believe I would like to change my room tomorrow to a downstairs room, will that be a problem?"

The man never answered other than a nod.

"That's good; can I have my choice of any room I want?"

Again, the man just nodded.

"Well thanks, you have been very helpful. I'll come down in the morning and switch keys for the new room," Stewart said not waiting for a reply, he knew one would never come.

When the two men got to the top of the stairs Stewart motioned for Ellsworth to step inside his room so they could talk.

"Why did you lead that clerk to believe you wanted to change rooms tomorrow?" Ellsworth asked the marshal.

"When we checked in yesterday I noticed all the room keys were gone except four. When he gave me, you, and Blair, a key there was only one unrented room left in the entire building. When we walked in just now I noticed all the keys are there. Every key except for the three rooms we have."

The Pursuit

Ellsworth didn't need to think long, "Everyone has checked out but us. Why would folks be heading out in this kind of weather?"

"I suspect they were told to leave. It must have happened while we were up on the mountain enjoying lunch with that bastard Fowler. Someone came in here and told that hotel clerk to clear the hotel. Something is about to happen and I doubt it's anything good."

Ellsworth thought about the situation and what the marshal had figured out. "We better not dally here long. I say we get our stuff and head back to the livery. Blair and Allen are probably the only two men in this town that we can trust."

Ellsworth left the marshal's room and hurried to his own. He stuffed the tobacco and licorice into his saddle bags and then opened the window. The landing was maybe two feet wide and ran the length of the hotel toward one end where a narrow staircase led down to the street. As he was navigating the landing a window opened and the marshal stepped out.

"Good timing Marshal. Good thing this has a handrail or a man might step off and break his neck."

Stewart had to agree. The narrow walkway had a thin dusting of snow and it wouldn't take much for a man to get himself in trouble. "We better get a move on, being up here makes me feel like every Winchester in the territory is pointed at me right now," Stewart said. Ten minutes later and both men were back at the livery.

Wilbur Westbrook waited anxiously to hear from Pom and Eli. He knew the two should have arrived in Rapid City and would have met up with the Baldwin Felts men by now, which in fact they had.

His last conversation with the two was when they sent a wire one stop back from their final destination. The telegram simply stated when they expected to be in Rapid City.

Westbrook stood and walked to the window. It was a habit he was repeating more and more as time went by and his mind anticipated problems, both real and imagined. As he tried to collect his thoughts he was interrupted by a knock at the door.

"Come in," he said as he turned and headed back to his desk.

The woman who entered was his attractive secretary and she was holding a single sheet of paper.

"This just arrived. I thought you might be expecting it," she said as she reached the paper to Westbrook. He thanked her and she left the office.

The telegram was from Pom and Eli. It stated the two were now in a town called Langley. New information they had received there indicated they should head to a place called Sweetwater where their quarry was presently located. They promised to send more information on their progress as soon as they could.

Westbrook knew rail and wire service in the Dakota Territory was spotty at best and this made it difficult for him to control events taking place there. He now considered himself a spectator, something he was unaccustomed to.

He laid the paper on his desk and returned to the window. Hopefully things out west could be brought to a close before long. If not then he might be forced to concede the lucrative railroad contract to an adversary he hated almost as bad as the tainted cop he had beaten to death all those years ago.

The Pursuit

Eli and Pom, along with the remaining eleven Baldwin Felts men, had left out of Langley as soon as the telegram to Westbrook had been sent and verified. They set a course for Sweetwater using the shortest route possible. The route chosen was difficult to say the least. The storm that had blown through Sweetwater earlier was now interfering with Eli and Pom and their headlong rush to get there before Blair and his two companions left town.

At about the same time Ellsworth and Stewart were sneaking out the back of the hotel in Sweetwater one of Dietrich's scouts notified him that the lights of that same town could be seen just over the next rise.

Dietrich turned to Pom and Eli and told them what he had just learned. A smile broke out on the faces of the two hated Chicago men. Dietrich hoped that before this job was over he could arrange an untimely accident for the two.

"We must press ahead. I want to be in that town as soon as possible, "Eli told the leader of the Baldwin men. An hour later the group of thirteen riders entered Sweetwater.

"Which of your men knows this area the best?" Pom asked Dietrich.

"Jason Orwell has been here before, he is the most knowledgeable of the group," Dietrich said.

"Summon him forward. Eli and I will proceed to the mansion if Orwell knows the way. You and your men see to your horses and lodgings, and then canvas the town. If Blair and his friends are here I want them captured before morning," Pom said.

Eli must have been suffering from fatigue and the cold temperatures because no sooner had Pom spoken than he nearly repeated the same orders. "Once you've secured rooms at the hotel for your men and the horses are safely at the livery then get started. I want the town searched."

Both men figured if Blair and his two companions were around they wouldn't be leaving, at least not before morning. It wouldn't hurt to allow the men to see to their boarding and also care for the horses; it had been a grueling trip.

After Pom, Eli, and Orwell left, Dietrich split his men into two groups. He had five of the men take their gear to the hotel and secure rooms for the group. He and the remaining four headed toward the livery to stable the horses and see to their care. The animals had been driven hard getting to Sweetwater and needed to be rested and fed.

Something had happened earlier in the day to reinforce the Baldwin men's hatred of Eli and Pom. One of the pack horses had broken through the ice in a shallow stream only a foot or so deep, but in doing so had thrown a shoe and injured one of its front legs. When Dietrich stopped to investigate how badly the animal was injured Pom promptly pulled his Colt and shot the poor horse right there in the stream.

"We don't have the luxury of time gentlemen, we proceed at once," Pom told the group after he killed the animal.

Dietrich wasn't a man to injure an animal and surely not kill one if it could be saved. When Pom pulled his gun and shot the horse it was all Dietrich could do to not kill the man. Again he told himself he would see both Pom and Eli dead before this job was over.

After the five grabbed the saddlebags and long guns from the horses they headed toward the hotel. When they got to the building and entered they found no one stationed at the front desk. By the looks of things there were only three rooms rented, this was evident by the fact that all the other keys were hanging on the numbered board behind the counter. All the keys accept three.

The informal boss of this group in the hotel was a man by the name of McGinnis. After waiting a minute he shouted but it soon became apparent that the clerk must have stepped out.

"We take six of the rooms downstairs. If the clerk comes back we can square things then but for now grab a key and let's get this gear stowed," McGinnis told the other four men.

As it worked out Orwell knew Sweetwater well enough to know where the driveway was that would lead the three to the mansion of Norman Fowler. He also knew there was a guard house that was manned twenty-four hours a day. He used caution as the three approached.

"Hello the guard shack," Orwell shouted.

"Step forward and be recognized," came the reply.

When the three stepped their horses forward they were met by two men holding Winchester rifles. Stewart and Ellsworth had relieved them of their Greeners and scoped Winchesters earlier in the day.

The three men stepped their horses cautiously toward the two guards. The three were tired and cold and wanted nothing more than to make it to the mansion where they hoped to be invited in and possibly given hot coffee or even better, a stiff shot of brandy or bourbon.

"We are here to see your boss, his name is Norman Fowler," Pom said.

"We know who our boss is friend, now who are you?" one of the guards demanded. After being disarmed earlier in the day the two were in no mood to be disarmed again.

"My name is Patrick O'Malley and this is Eli Dobbs, we are from Chicago and I believe your boss is expecting us."

The guard looked at the third man and asked his name as well.

"I'm Jason Orwell; I work for Baldwin-Felts Detective Agency."

The three were allowed to pass with instructions to follow the drive to the mansion where they would be questioned again before being allowed entrance to the house.

When Fowler was notified that two gentlemen from Chicago were at the door he quickly limped to the front sitting room and gave word for the two to be allowed in.

"Gentlemen, I've been expecting you," Fowler said as the men's coats and hats were gathered by two of the women that helped maintain the house.

Fowler looked at the third man, "I was told to expect only two."

"My name is Jason Orwell; I work for Baldwin-Felts. Knowing the town the way I do I was asked to escort these gentlemen here."

"Are you the head of the detachment of Baldwin men Mister Orwell?" Fowler asked.

"No sir; that is a man by the name of Elon Dietrich. He and the remaining men are seeing to the horses and taking rooms at the hotel."

When Orwell mentioned the hotel Fowler flinched but hoped it wasn't noticed. "How many men do you have in Sweetwater?" Fowler asked.

"Ten besides me, Dietrich probably has five seeing to the horses and the others are securing the rooms we will need."

Five men Fowler thought. There would still be five if worse came to worse. The proper thing to do was to sound an alarm

The Pursuit

but that would implicate himself in what was about to happen. Fowler could handle the guilt; he had done far worse in the past.

"Gentlemen, follow me into my study if you don't mind. We can talk and catch up on your progress," Fowler said as he directed two of his servants to bring drinks.

The study Fowler mentioned wasn't a room that Ellsworth and Stewart had been in earlier that day. He thought about inviting them but didn't want the two trail bums to contaminate his office. It was bad enough to have them eating at his table and sitting in the front parlor.

He felt Eli and Pom might be impressed with his office and gladly invited them in. Once the four were seated he motioned for one of his servants to bring a selection of cigars. Kentucky Bourbon and Cuban cigars was offered and the guests gladly accepted.

"After we finish our drinks I would like Mister Orwell to wait in the sitting room out front while we conduct our talks," Fowler said.

This didn't go over well with the three. Eli and Pom would have liked to have Orwell in attendance, if for nothing else than to be a witness to what was discussed. It was Fowler's home and the three men would obey his wishes, for the moment anyway.

Once the drinks were finished and Orwell was escorted to the front parlor the three remaining men got down to business. Eli and Pom thought of Fowler as nothing more than a cripple who had managed to insert himself into the affairs of their boss, Wilbur Westbrook. They were going to get what information was available from Fowler and then sever their partnership. It wouldn't be done with pen and paper but rather a gun.

"I see five men coming down the street, each leading a horse," Blair said.

He had been stationed at the door where he could monitor the happenings outside. His field of view was no more than he could see through a small hole drilled in the front wall by the door. As the happenings in Sweetwater had become more mysterious Allen had come up with the idea of drilling a few holes here and there where he could see what might be going on out in the street without being seen. He could look out but no one could look in. He had hung old harnesses and other junk on the outside to make it impossible for anyone to press their face against the wall to look inside.

Allen looked at the marshal. "You three head back to that farthest stall. Keep your ears peeled and if you see I'm in trouble you can come out and back me up."

Stewart thought this was a pretty good plan. If this was part of the group searching for Blair then some information might be gained. He, Ellsworth, and Blair, ran toward the back and scurried through a tight fitting door in the side of the farthermost back stall. Once inside Stewart was surprised to find a room at least six feet wide and twelve feet long. There appeared to be another door in the back of that room but it was anybody's guess where it led.

When Dietrich and his men split up from the five that were heading to the hotel he immediately grabbed the reins of two horses and headed in the direction Orwell had said the livery was located. Ten minutes later he was there. Not seeing a walk door in front he stepped to the side and banged on a door there.

After a minute the door swung open and Jess Allen looked out. "Evening men, can I help you?"

Dietrich was cold, tired, and hungry, and was in no mood to be nice. "Open up, we got horses that need tending to."

"How many horses you got?" Allen asked.

Dietrich pushed the man aside and went in. He unfastened the front door and as he pushed it open he said, "We got what we got, what do you care? I expect these horses to be fed and watered, I ain't talking just hay neither; you'll give each some grain or oats."

Allen didn't like this man but didn't want to cause trouble that might bring attention to the men hiding in the back. When he saw how many horses were outside, there were at least a dozen along with a pack horse or two, he protested. "I ain't got that kind of room. There are already four horses stabled here tonight." He had the three from Stewart's group along with his own horse.

Dietrich turned to Allen and said, "If you ain't got the room then put the four horses you've already got outside. My horses are staying inside."

In the back Stewart heard everything and assumed the man forcing Allen's hand was part of the group sent to apprehend Blair. He didn't like the way the conversation was going, he picked up his Greener from where he had placed it against a wall and prepared to barge out and assist Allen if the situation got too far out of hand. Ellsworth did the same and even Blair pulled the worn out Colt he had been given a few days back. Blair might not be a fighter but he was willing to do his part.

Allen decided to agree with this son of a bitch and once he was gone he could see how Stewart wanted to handle it. "Sure thing Mister, your horses will be seen to. If I can't fit them all inside then I'll just have to put the four I've already got outside. As far as the feed goes I got grain sweetened with molasses. Horses love it and I ain't heard a complaint yet."

This must have satisfied the man because he stepped aside as his men brought their horses in. They were all lined down the center hallway; it looked like the livery was going to be able to handle the extra business after all. Dietrich didn't know it but Allen had no intention of putting any of the horses outside that were already there, it wasn't the right thing to do. If all the horses hadn't fit he would have dealt with that problem when it showed up.

"Alright Mister, they are all yours and I meant what I said. I find one of these horses of mine outside I'll make sure you regret it." With that Dietrich and his men started out the door. As soon as Dietrich, and the four men with him, were outside Allen slid the door shut and locked it.

As Dietrich and his men started toward the hotel to get the rest of the men and begin the search of the town there was an explosion. It had apparently come from the direction of the hotel. Dietrich looked at his men and then they all took off at a sprint. He could only imagine what might have happened.

When Stewart heard Allen close the big sliding door he and the other two men came from their hiding spot and walked up front. The center hall was crowded with the horses Dietrich had brought in.

"Can you believe that guy Marshal? I've been a livery man nearly all my life and this is the first time anyone ever ordered me to put horses outside because of a lack of room. Last horse, or horses, always stay outside, not the ones already here," Allen said.

"Did he even offer to pay you for stabling this bunch?" Stewart asked but before Allen could answer they heard the explosion.

As Fowler sat opposite Eli and Pom he quizzed the two for information but suspected what he was being told wasn't actually fact but a version of truth mixed in with tidbits of fiction. Already he had heard two explanations that he knew were far from true.

What he needed was timelines of the events that had already transpired and timetables of events to come. If these two Chicago ruffians thought they, along with Wilbur Westbrook, had a handle on all things west of the Mississippi then they were mistaken.

The network of business acquaintances Westbrook employed in the Dakota Territory might have seemed extensive to the Chicagoan but Fowler had his own network that he had built over many years. His information was better than Westbrook's and it was also more current.

Fowler had also managed to have his own informant installed in Chicago. This unknown person had managed to insert himself in the same suite of offices that Westbrook and his associates used. Information gathered couldn't be trusted to the telegraph for fear that Westbrook might have some of the telegraphers on his payroll. Everything gathered was mailed to an address south of Chicago. The letters were delivered a mere twenty four hours from the time they were sent. The information was then sent from this southern location westward and was in Fowler's hands two hours from the time it was first sent by wire. The two hours being due to a transfer between several telegraph offices along the way.

It was believed by Fowler that at times he got the news before it could be written up and hand delivered between the myriad of offices Westbrook possessed.

The greatest advantage Fowler had was that the town of Sweetwater never possessed a telegraph office. The wires to that town ran directly to Fowlers mansion and no one other than Fowler used it. It wasn't even obvious any wires ran to the mansion. A mile from the house the wires were ran underground using newly invented insulated transmitting wires. A ditch had been dug and the wires then buried.

Anyone noticing the wires running toward Sweetwater was simply told the wires were started but the company in charge of this region of the telegraph network simple stopped construction without finishing the job. Fowler had his own telegrapher hired and he lived at the mansion.

The conversation taking place in the study was lopsided to say the least. Fowler knew more than he was letting on and the information he was hearing could be easily categorized in his mind in three different groups. First were the lies, second was the information he knew to be true and already had, third was the facts that filled in the pieces of the puzzle, the pieces that he needed.

"Well Mister Fowler, you seem to have lots of questions but you have failed to answer anything we have put forth. Is there a reason for your silence?" Eli asked.

Fowler thought a second and realized he had heard everything he needed to hear. He was in a situation now where he didn't need the Chicago men or what they had to offer. It was now as simple as letting these two go on their way.

The Pursuit

"I believe we are finished here. You say you have problems with one of your operatives, a man by the name of Gene Blair. My operations here are not dependent upon, or associated with, Mister Blair. Thanks for your help and I wish you both luck with your attempts in finding Mister Blair," Fowler said.

What the two didn't know was that their troubles with Blair had all been orchestrated by Fowler. When word got out, Westbrook, and these two associates of his, would probably go to prison, compliments of Norman Fowler.

Eli and Pom sat there not believing what was happening. They had come here to find out what they could from Fowler and ended up not learning anything. They had even divulged a few trinkets of valuable information in hopes of loosening Fowler's tongue, it didn't work. As far as what they had told Fowler, it wasn't going to be a problem, because they never intended for him to live long enough to put their advice to work.

Pom and Eli knew they had been played. Fowler had promised information; at least this was what his telegrams to Chicago had indicated. The two men knew it was time to silence forever one half of Five Oaks Development.

Both Pom and Eli looked back at Fowler and as they did each pulled a two shot Derringer from a breast pocket on their jackets. Fowler could only look on in stunned disbelief. He had always suspected the Chicago half of the company to be ruthless but he never suspected they would stoop to this. The only thing he could think of was to try and reason his way out of whatever these two had in mind.

"Gentlemen, surely our dealings haven't fallen to a level where gunplay is warranted," Fowler said.

"I'm afraid it has Mister Fowler. But if you think it was something you said that has cost you your life you are mistaken. We had orders to eliminate you after we learned a few things. You denied us the information we needed but either way we were ordered to kill you.

"Most of my dealings with murder, thus far, were outright, never have I had the opportunity to actually talk about what is going to happen with the victim himself. I am curious to know what goes through a man's mind when he knows he is about to die and there isn't a thing he can do to prevent it," Pom said with a smile. He truly relished the opportunity to speak to a dead man.

Fowler knew he was in a bad way. He was unarmed and there was no one in the house that could rescue him. Sure there were several men patrolling the grounds but they were of no use to him out there. His only hope was to do as he was told and look for an opening where he could either talk his way out of this or try to escape. With his crippled left leg the hope of an escape seemed out of the question.

"Please stand up and let's get this over with," Pom said.

Fowler slowly stood, his mind racing. What could he do now but accept the inevitable. This was going to be the day he died and there wasn't a damn thing he could do about it. Once standing he reached for his cane.

"I'm afraid you are going to have to make do without the cane. I would hate for you to take a swing at myself or Eli. If you did then I would be forced to kill you where you stand. Now move to the door and lead us to the front entrance," Pom said.

Fowler did as he was told; he now understood what they were going to do. He would be led through the front parlor door but not the heavy exterior door. They planned to shoot him there where the noise of a gunshot would be muffled between two doors.

The Pursuit

As the men moved through the large sitting room they were met by Jason Orwell who had been requested to sit there while the other two men met in Fowler's office. The look on Orwell's face told that he was aware of the plan from the beginning.

As Fowler moved toward the foyer he knew this was it, he was going to be murdered in his own house. He also knew the heavy ponderosa pine timbers the house was made of, and the robust thickness of the two doors, would muffle the sound of the shots that would soon end his life. The men would make their escape before his body was found.

Orwell opened the door allowing Eli and Pom to enter the foyer to await their victim. Orwell held the door with an outstretched arm as he smiled at the slowly moving Fowler.

"Come now Fowler, no need to put off the inevitable," Pom said with a smile.

Just as Fowler made it to the door and was ready to step inside the foyer an explosion could be heard in the town below. It wasn't expected by Eli, Pom, or Orwell, and the three instantly turned toward the outer door thinking it was a gunshot. It was the break Fowler needed.

With the speed and strength that comes from a man who was expecting to die, Fowler shoved the unsuspecting Orwell into the foyer and slammed the heavy door shut. He slid the locking bolt home and hoped the heavy door would be able to take a tremendous amount of punishment before it gave way. It was very strong and should hold longer than he actually needed.

Fowler, once sure the inner door was secure, turned and hurried back to his study. He stepped into a small closet just inside the door and took down his gun belt. When he buckled it on he was amazed at how good the feeling was. It had been more than a few years since he had felt the need to wear it.

With the confidence only a Colt can give a man he went back to the front and unlocked the inner door. His intention was to yank the heavy door open and kill all three men where they stood. In years past Fowler had killed men, some in fair fights and some not so fair. He had practiced diligently and knew his abilities. Even now, after so many years, he felt the ability to kill still ran through his veins.

Fowler pulled the Colt and forced the door open, both in one smooth move. The foyer was empty. He opened the other door and stepped outside. As he stood looking over his surroundings one of the guards ran up the driveway.

He was out of breath when he made it to where Fowler stood, or at least that is what it first looked like. When the man made it to where his boss stood he collapsed face down right there in front of Fowler. He had been shot. Fowler knelt beside the man and turned him onto his side knowing if he placed him on his back it might cause the man to choke. Fowler knew the man, his name was Robert Tuttle and he had worked at the guard shack for a few years.

"Bob, what happened?"

Tuttle opened his eyes and looked at Fowler but probably didn't see him; there was no focus in the stare. The man had just died right there in front of Fowler.

Fowler stood and headed down the drive. He had completely forgotten about his cane, and the pain in his left leg and ankle. He was consumed by hatred for the three men that had tried to kill him and did kill at least one of his faithful employees.

As Fowler made his way down the drive he was joined by two of the other men that patrolled the grounds. When he told of how Tuttle had died the two guards, both carrying Greeners, cocked both hammers of their weapons, they had business to finish.

As the three came into view of the guard shack they saw the second guard lying face down beside the building. Fowler suspected the three assailants approached the guard shack under the guise of having concluded their business at the mansion and once they had lured the two guards into thinking all was well, they shot both. It was a miracle that Tuttle, having been delivered a mortal blow, had managed to make it to the mansion trying to warn Fowler.

"Get the other men together. Post two men here at the guard house and have the rest meet me at the mansion. We are going on a hunting trip tonight," Fowler said before turning and heading back up the drive.

Eli, Pom, and Orwell, were totally caught off guard when the explosion at the hotel had happened. In that split second when the mind is caught between what it had been doing and what had just happened, Fowler had managed to push Orwell through the door and secure it from the inside. All three men tried to push it open but it was useless, the door wouldn't budge.

The three knew Fowler would sound the alarm and guards would soon swarm the grounds to try and capture them. They weren't going to allow that to happen. The horses the three had ridden up the hill were still tied out front where they had left them. All three mounted up and headed off the mountain, not at a full gallop but at a normal pace that would indicate to anyone seeing the three that all was well. They knew it was the only way to fool the two men at the guardhouse.

As they approached the guardhouse they were met by the same two men as before. When one tried to speak Eli drew his gun and shot him.

The second man began to raise his Winchester but Pom had already drawn his derringer. The shot caught this man in the forehead and he fell, he was dead before he hit the ground.

As the three spurred their horses into action Eli saw the man he had shot get to his feet and start up the mountain, he was unarmed, having dropped the Winchester when he had been shot. Eli had no problem shooting an unarmed man. The man was facing away and heading up the drive as fast as he could. Eli also had no problem shooting a man in the back. He raised his gun and fired once more striking the man in his right shoulder, he continued moving. The two shot derringer was now empty and would need to be reloaded soon in case it was needed again.

As the three rode away Pom looked at Eli, "Is that the best you can do? You shot that man twice and he was still heading up the drive."

"I was shooting from a moving horse and shooting from behind. If you like you can follow him back to the mansion and finish the job," Eli said.

Pom only laughed. "We get back to Chicago I think you need to spend a little more time at the firing range."

The laughter the three enjoyed was soon replaced with doubt and apprehension. As they rode away from the guard shack they could see flames rising above a building in town. When they made it to the street where the hotel was located they found confusion and death.

Eli spotted Dietrich on the opposite boardwalk with several other men. They appeared to be giving aid to someone lying beside the street. When the three men rode up they quickly dismounted and rushed to where Dietrich stood.

"What happened here, it looks like a bomb has gone off?" Pom asked.

It was a true statement, what remained of the hotel was scattered and burning with debris littering every square foot of the street. It looked like the front wall had been blown outward and then the rest of the roof and upstairs had partially collapsed onto itself. Flames were starting to spread as men pushed the town's firefighting wagon to the front of the building. Other men were carrying water in buckets and tossing what they could onto the burning remains. The explosion had started a number of lesser fires but when the building collapsed it extinguished most of the flames.

"We were just coming from the livery and heard an explosion. When I got here I found McGinnis lying in the street, he hasn't come to yet but I suspect he can shed some light on what's happened once he does," Dietrich said and then added, "He doesn't appear to be that badly hurt."

"Was anyone else in the building when it blew?" Orwell asked. He knew Dietrich and a few of the other Baldwin men were going to secure rooms at the hotel and by the looks of things if anyone was in the building there was no way they could have survived.

Dietrich stood and looked at the hotel. "The rest of you men, lend a hand with the firefighting detail. We need to extinguish the flames to preserve the evidence. Work fast; there might be others still alive and trapped under the rubble."

Fifteen minutes later and the few flames that had survived the collapse had been extinguished. Several of the townsfolk had volunteered in the search for survivors. It was later determined that the five Baldwin men were the only occupants of the building when the explosives went off.

Of the five, McGinnis was the least injured. He was standing near the door when the explosion occurred and the blast knocked him into the street. He was banged up a little with some minor cuts here and there. He came to as the men were putting out the last of the flames.

"Where are the others? I got four men in that building," McGinnis said as his head cleared and he realized what had happened.

Two of the Baldwin men were dead, it appeared the two were nearest the spot where the explosion occurred, they never knew what hit them. Two other men were nearer the front door and were knocked into the first landing of the staircase. That was the most fortunate event of the evening. The heavy steps and first landing had shielded the two when the upstairs fell. There was just enough space to keep the two from being crushed.

One of these two had a broken arm and lesser cuts and bruises; he would be fine in a few weeks other than letting the broken arm mend.

The other man was pretty much in the same shape as McGinnis. He had been knocked around a bit but nothing was broken. Considering three men had survived an explosion that had otherwise leveled a two story structure was nothing short of miraculous. As the men were pulling the others from the rubble Jason Orwell and his two companions looked over the situation.

"Where is the man that works the front counter?" Pom asked.

McGinnis was now standing when he was asked the question. "When we entered there wasn't anybody at the check-in counter. I had the boys grab a few keys and stow our gear. As we were leaving the damn building blew up," McGinnis said.

"The man must have known something was going to happen, why else would he have left? We need to find the son of a bitch that was supposed to be working the hotel tonight. We find him, we find some answers," Eli said.

"Weren't there any other folks staying at the hotel? In this kind of weather I would suspect there would have been more than a few rooms rented," Orwell said.

"Only three rooms were rented, there were three keys missing from the key rack," McGinnis said.

Orwell knew his job, in the years he had worked for Baldwin Felts he had developed a tactical way of looking at things. "If three rooms were rented then we have to assume the explosion was meant for the people that rented those rooms. No one knew we were coming here tonight so it goes to believe that this wasn't meant for us. We are also looking for three men, Blair and his two friends. I would hazard to guess that someone knows Blair is in town and was looking to silence him."

Pom and Eli considered the evidence Orwell had just speculated upon. They both knew who wanted Blair dead, besides themselves of course. Norman Fowler had said Blair was their problem now and if he was dead then he couldn't refute the accusations Fowler was making against the man. Wilbur Westbrook stood the most to lose from this and Norman Fowler had the most to gain.

"Find the clerk that works the hotel and bring him to me. Also, we need to find somewhere defensible to spend the night. I suspect Fowler is putting together a squad of men to come into town and finish the job we tried to pull on him, kill us off, along with anyone else he feels is in the way," Eli said.

Dietrich had made it to where the men stood and heard the conversation. "Counting you, we have eleven men and three of them are injured, one with a broken arm. We can't just take the injured men to the doctor in town; Fowler will kill them for sure."

Eli thought for only a second before answering, "We find someplace suitable to hole up for the night and then bring the doctor to where we are. We get the two men that are most injured patched up as best as we can and then we ride out of here. We ride out at first light. There are eleven of us and we are heavily armed, I doubt anyone will try anything in broad daylight."

Dietrich didn't like the two Chicago men but had to admit the plan they had was probably what he would have come up with. "We best stay at the livery; I wouldn't want to leave our horses unattended during the night in a town full of folks we can't trust."

Stewart ran to the front wall when he heard the explosion. He could make out some flames and a lot of confusion in the street.

"Allen, is there a back way out of this place?" Stewart asked.

"Got a door right back there in that hidden room you were just in."

"That won't work, we need to get out of here and take our horses with us."

"That won't be a problem. There is a door at the end of the center hall of the livery, it ain't obvious but it's there just the

The Pursuit

same. Come on back and I'll show you," Allen said as he made his way back through the center hall of the livery.

"You see this wooden pin and that one up near the top. We pop out these and the door will swing outward. It's wide and tall enough for a man to lead his horse out."

Stewart looked over the door, it really looked like just part of the wall. He saw how it was built and knew it would work. "This is just what we need. What prompted you to put a door back here that no one would see unless they knew what they were looking for?"

"The way this town has been going, I just figured someday I might need to sneak off in the middle of the night without being seen. In my spare time I came up with this and built it while no one was looking."

"Well it's just what we need. Looks like the three of us will be the first to use it," Ellsworth said.

"Not just you three, I'm going along too," Allen said.

"You're part of this town Allen. You leave now then you won't have anything left to come back too, "Blair said.

"I don't leave now then I'm a dead man anyway. I figure it won't take long for them to find out I helped you three. It's time for me to leave. This town has changed for the worse and it makes me feel like an outsider. Fowler can have his livery back and then good riddance to Sweetwater," Allen said.

"We best be getting our horses saddled and out that door before someone comes. If that happens we might have us a shootout right here at the livery. Grab whatever we can fit on the horses; stuff that will see us through to Rapid City. Load up whatever food we got here, along with some grain for the four horses. We need to be out of here in the next fifteen minutes," Stewart said as the four men went to work. Fifteen minutes later and all four horses were saddled and trotted out the back door.

Just as Allen was pushing the door back to wedge it into place Stewart stopped him. "We better do something to slow down them bastards in case they want to give chase tonight."

Allen looked at the horses, "What have you got in mind Marshal?"

"How about we cut the stirrups off their saddles, I figure a man can't get far without stirrups."

The horses Dietrich had brought in earlier were still saddled; it didn't take long before every saddle had been relieved of the stirrups on each side. "That's good thinking Marshal, it would take a few hours for someone to repair the kind of damage we just done," Allen said.

"Alright, let's get this door shut and get out of here. Allen, you got a plan on which way we head?" Stewart asked.

"I do Marshal. The livery is backed up against the side of the river, but she's running low this time of year. We ride down and pick up the gravel bank on this side and go upstream for about three miles where she grows wide and shallow. We cross there and stay in the timber for about six or seven miles. There's a spot or two where the ground turns to rock and we stay to that. We'll be hard to track after we leave the river, shouldn't be a problem."

Stewart thought about the route Allen suggested. He knew the horses would leave a trail a blind man could follow but once they made it to the rock Allen mentioned it would help hide their trail. As the night progressed and the temperature continued to fall the ground would become frozen and hopefully the horses wouldn't leave any tracks.

The four men moved out after securing the false door in the back of the livery. The lay of the river bank was just the way Allen described it and no more than an hour later they made it across and into the timber. The horses had waded in water up to their bellies and for this reason the men kept moving until they dried a bit. The temperature was cold, well below freezing, but the water didn't freeze on the horses due to their exertion and movement.

"Where are you leading us Allen? I reckon this ain't anywhere near the trail we used to get here," Ellsworth said.

"About thirty more miles is a place I know pretty well. It's an old dugout the buffalo hunters used to use. I've actually stayed there a time or two myself over the last few years. You might say I took a few trips laying out an escape route just in case I ever needed to get out of Sweetwater in the middle of the night, you know like tonight," Allen said as he laughed.

"You seem awful lighthearted for a man that just turned his back on his business. I figure that livery was worth a lot of money and you just ran out on it," Blair said. He was a man that always looked at the value of property, what it would cost or what it would bring.

"I never ran out on anything. I reckon when Fowler allowed me to take possession of that livery it was nothing more than a loan. I never got a deed, never even got a promise. I was just told to run the place as I saw fit. He owned the land and the building, I just ran the business and called it mine but I never owned a thing."

"Now why would any man agree to an arrangement like that? You weren't nothing more than a squatter. You tend the business and see to its needs and then that Fowler feller just comes in the front door and says leave. I find that to be as crazy a thing as I've ever heard," Ellsworth said.

"Maybe it is but it's better than not knowing where your next meal is coming from or where you're going to go when you hear thunder in the distance. Nearly everyone in town has an agreement like that. They behave and do as they're told and they are allowed to live a pretty good life in a town that has everything they need. Some would say that is a pretty good bargain," Allen said.

Ellsworth looked over at the marshal, "So that's why everyone in town was treating us the way they did. Everyone does as they are told or they get tossed out into the street. No wonder the whole town was refusing to speak to us, or even look our way for that matter."

"What time you figure we'll make it to that dugout Allen?" Blair asked.

"I figure at the pace we're traveling we should be there around three tomorrow afternoon. The lay of the land is rough between here and there so we can't make any speed. We can rest the horses and catch a little sleep at the dugout. First though, we'll take a two hour break just before first light this morning to rest the horses and make a pot of coffee. Darkness will hide the smoke from our fire."

"This place got anything like a corral for the horses Allen?" Stewart asked.

"It does, last time I was there was about two months ago. I always go there and do a little work to keep the place livable and do a little hunting. There's also a good trout stream running not more than fifty yards from the front door."

"I love trout, baked or fried. Too bad we ain't got us any fishing line and hooks," Blair said.

"Oh we got that, I do a little trout fishing and always leave my stuff there. I can catch six or eight in a couple of hours, and I ain't talking little fish neither. That is one of the best trout streams I've ever come across. I often wondered if the buffalo hunters built that dugout where it was because of the buffalo or because of the trout."

This was music to Blair's ears, he had mentioned when they rode into Sweetwater how much he enjoyed trout and now it looked like he was going to get his wish.

Norman Fowler made it back to the mansion without the use of his cane. He was so grateful for the timing of the blast; it had saved his life when there was no other way to save it. He instructed one of his servants to make coffee and bring it to his study. He told her to make enough for at least a dozen men.

When Fowler rode into Sweetwater in a couple of hours looking for Eli and Pom he fully intended to kill both men, possibly even Jason Orwell, the Baldwin man. He hadn't fully figured that out yet but at the moment, and in the mood he was in, he was leaning more toward killing the man.

Even though coffee was being prepared he decided to forgo the hot drink for something a little stronger. He pulled a bottle of bourbon from a drawer and filled a glass nearly to the top. He was just now beginning to feel the pain in his leg and needed a brace of whiskey to numb the pain. It would also help fight off the chill he experienced when he descended the mountain and then climbed back up to the mansion.

As he sat and sipped his bourbon he wondered how he had been so badly fooled by the intentions of the three men that had nearly taken his life. He would most likely see all three dead by morning. He also had to contend with the Baldwin men that might have survived the explosion at the hotel.

If there was any good news the evening had brought it was the explosion and subsequent deaths of Blair and the two men he had met with earlier in the day, Ellsworth and Marshal

Stewart. Stewart especially, a lawman had seen his face and that was something that just couldn't be swept under the proverbial rug.

What terrified Fowler so much about lawmen was the secret he carried ever since he came to the backwater little town of Sweetwater, and then built it into the town it is today.

Fowler had a secret; it was a terrible secret that, if discovered, would land him not in jail but at the end of a rope. He had already seen that rope and the scaffold it hung from. He had stood trial and been found guilty, his sentence was death by hanging. He had been less than twelve hours away from experiencing that briefest moment of weightlessness that happens between the time the trap door opens and the noose stops your fall.

Fowler was now a very rich man, before his trial he had been just a rich man. His money and family had managed to purchase his escape and for this he would always be grateful. Not only had he managed to escape the noose but he had also staged his own death.

The horse that was supplied to Fowler was strong and fast and was selected for this reason. It was planned for him to race out of town after his escape and five miles away, at a spot where the river was fast and deep, he was to abandon the horse and then make his getaway with the help of two of his operatives on a spare horse which would be waiting with the two men.

There was a man there who wouldn't be leaving with Fowler and the other two men. He was going to be the witness. The story was that a man on a fast horse had attempted to cross the swollen river but no more than twenty feet from the bank the horse became skittish and Fowler was swept away in the ragging current. A search would be made but no body

The Pursuit

would be found. With an eyewitness it would be assumed Fowler, in his panic, had tried to ford the river but never made it across. Before Fowler and the two men with him left they would make sure to lead the horse a few feet into the water and then wet her down with a bucket.

When the posse made it to the spot a few minutes later all they would find was a soaking wet horse and a man sitting there stunned that he had just witnessed the drowning of a man.

The scheme went off just as Fowler had planned. The search was conducted for the next few days, but it turned up nothing. This all happened in the town of Rapid City and was the reason Fowler would never travel to that part of the territory again. He rarely ever left the safety of his mansion. Anyone that met him was first screened by Patterson Hartman. If there was ever a fear that Fowler had been recognized then an accident was planned for whoever might have seen the man and associated him with the escapee that supposedly drowned in the river.

In the few short years since his sentencing, and subsequent escape and death, Fowler had changed his appearance as much as possible. His hair had been tinted gray using some of the best colorings available. He had grown a mustache and side-whiskers. Age itself was also helping; it was turning his hair gray and soon he hoped to not need the weekly hair treatments. He had even lost a substantial amount of weight. The man who represented himself as Norman Fowler looked nothing like the man who had escaped and drowned in the river all those years ago.

Plus the name he had taken, that of Norman Fowler was not to lead anyone to his original self. The name had been taken from a steelworker that had fallen to his death in New

York. One of the men who helped devise the escape and drowning gave Fowler's old self a list of five new names to choose from and he chose Norman Fowler. He felt the name was distinct enough but didn't stand out in a way that might bring unwanted questions.

The man Norman Fowler had once been was now hidden from view from the rest of the world. Though there was no body, the river had never given up a body; there was still a marker in the paupers section of the cemetery in Rapid City. The marker was intentionally left blank. Judge Thurman Preston, the man who had sentenced Fowler to death, felt all men deserved something after they passed, this blank headstone was it.

As Fowler thought of how close he had come to dying all those years ago, and again tonight at the hands of the hated Chicago men, one of the ladies came in and announced the guards were at the door and asked if they were to be allowed in.

"Yes, have them come to my office immediately." Fowler relished the thought of the revenge he was about to take on Eli and Pom.

The same lady soon came back followed by twelve men, all heavily armed. They were led by Patterson Hartman. Anyone that thought of Hartman as just an errand boy for Mister Fowler would be thinking wrong.

Fowler had recruited Hartman from his home state of New York. He was offered a sum of money that almost guaranteed his acceptance although that wasn't really the reason he accepted the job. Hartman was a Shootist, but in the sense of the word had never managed to actually kill a man. Fowler not only offered the money to get Hartman here but guaranteed the man he would be able to quench his thirst, a thirst that could only be satisfied by killing another man. This could very well be Hartman's day.

"I have eleven men with me Mister Fowler. There will still be enough left here on the property to adequately guard the mansion," Hartman said.

Each of the men was given hot coffee and told to wait outside in the parlor while Fowler had a word with Hartman.

"There are three men in Sweetwater that have earned my attention this evening. Their names are Patrick O'Malley, Eli Dobbs, and Jason Orwell. These are the three men that tried to kill me earlier this evening. There are a number of Baldwin Felts men in town and they are to either be warned off or killed outright if they can't be reasoned with. What has been done of what we talked of earlier?" Fowler asked.

"The clerk at the hotel has been disposed of; no one will be asking any questions of that man. As you know the hotel was destroyed but so far I can't verify if Blair and the two men he rode in with were inside. I have men there now continuing to sift through the debris. If they are there then I will be notified at once. From what I gather there are nine Baldwin men in town plus the two from Chicago but three Baldwin men are injured," Hartman said.

"And, what of our attempts to persuade the Baldwin men to step aside?" Fowler asked.

"I have a dependable man talking to the head of the Baldwin men that remain. The problem is to speak with him without raising the suspicions of the two men you know as Eli and Pom. From what we have been able to gather, since the men rode in earlier, the two from Chicago are suspected of killing the original leader of the group, a man by the name of Dorian Matus. There is no love lost between the Baldwin men and the Chicago men. A sum of money will be offered if the

Baldwin men simply step aside and let us deal with Eli and Pom on our own terms."

Fowler sat and listened before he asked, "And if the Baldwin men don't step aside?"

"Then we will kill each of them, it's as simple as that."

"Gather your men, it's time we paid a visit to the town of Sweetwater," Fowler said.

Dietrich had his men assist the wounded as they headed for the livery. Two men were sent to find the town's doctor and bring him to the livery also. Two more were sent to the general store with orders to take everything they would need to see them through the night and possibly for the next few days. They still possessed supplies on the two remaining pack horses but these were getting thin.

With four men going to find the doctor and take what supplies they would need, the remaining seven started for the livery. One was sent running ahead to let the livery man, Allen, know they were coming. As they walked Dietrich considered the offer he had been made. He was promised a substantial sum of money and safe passage out of Sweetwater if he and his men would simply step aside and allow the two Chicago men to be dealt with. If not he was guaranteed that none of his men would survive.

As much as Dietrich hated Eli and Pom he still had to consider the effect their deaths would have on the working relationship between Baldwin Felts and Wilbur Westbrook. On the other hand, if he and his men were the only ones to return from this little adventure then who was to say that they hadn't fought valiantly alongside Pom and Eli but in the end the two were killed.

The Pursuit

While he considered his options the man that was sent on ahead to the livery came running back to the group. Dietrich hoped Allen had turned the four original horses out and was going to allow his business to be turned into a hotel for the night. If not then he would be persuaded physically.

"The livery man is nowhere to be found and the four horses that were there earlier are gone," the man said.

Dietrich wondered what more could happen tonight. "Are our horses okay?"

The man had only noticed what he had already shared with his boss; he hadn't noticed the sabotage to the saddles. "Looks like our horses are fine boss. What do you want me to do?"

"Head back over and make sure no one enters the livery before we get there." Dietrich was slowed by the three injured men but would be at the livery in ten minutes or so.

"Who were the four men that had horses at the livery? And if they have left do you think it is because we are here in Sweetwater looking for them?" Pom asked.

Dietrich looked at the man, "How do I know, all I do know is there were four horses at the livery when we left our horses there and the four are now gone. We were only looking for three men so I wouldn't think that would be the case."

"But maybe there were four men, Blair and three others. All we know is that he has been helped by a couple of strangers, maybe it was three strangers and our information was faulty," Eli said.

Dietrich was ready to explode. He just had two men killed and these two idiots from Chicago could only talk about some men and horses that weren't at the livery. "I would like a little time to think without any more incessant questions from you two."

Eli looked at Pom and then, without the least indication, struck Dietrich on the side of the jaw with all his might. It was a cheap shot but nevertheless had the effect of knocking Dietrich to the ground. He shook it off and then got back to his feet. "Why you son of a bitch," Dietrich said as he swung a vicious right at Eli. It was easy enough for him to simply duck a little to the left and all Dietrich hit was air. The man's momentum was enough for him to land face down on the hard packed street.

Dietrich sat there in the middle of the street as he tried to gather his thoughts. He thought about pulling his gun and killing both men but suddenly another thought came to mind. He already had an offer to receive, what to him, was a substantial amount of money and in doing so someone else would kill these two Chicagoans. If the Baldwin man had been on the fence about accepting the offer then this little street fight that he had just lost was all it took to make up his mine.

Dietrich slowly stood and looked at both Pom and Eli. "I'm sorry if I was out of line, it won't happen again."

Pom and Eli just considered it the caving of a man that had just had his ass handed to him in the middle of the street. If there was one thing the streets of Chicago had taught the two, it was how to fight.

"Your apology is accepted Mister Dietrich. Now if you don't mind I would like to make it to the livery and get out of this cold," Eli said.

If Eli and Pom thought the livery was going to be warm they were sadly mistaken. The only difference between the inside of the livery and the outside was there was no breeze. At least that made it feel slightly warmer. Once the men entered they found the other Baldwin man there inspecting the saddles.

The Pursuit

"Why these have been tampered with. Every stirrup on every saddle has been severed. We won't be using these anytime soon," the man said.

Dietrich walked over and picked up one of the stirrups from the floor of the livery, he and his men were now trapped here until the saddles could be repaired. If his mind hadn't been made up before it was surely made up now. He would accept the offer if for no other reason than to save the lives of his men.

"I'm afraid I need to leave you men for a while. It's necessary for me to seek someone that can repair our saddles before morning or we will be trapped here in Sweetwater. The longer we stay the more time Fowler has to plan our deaths. You saw what happened at the hotel. It's my guess he was the man that ordered the building blown up and he will soon do the same thing to the livery. When the doc gets here have him patch up the wounded." With that Dietrich turned and left the livery.

Pom and Eli watched the man leave and then Pom whispered, "That was rather strange. Why would he walk the streets of a town he has never been in before, knowing there will soon be a group of men coming into town with the intent of doing us in?"

"I agree, I don't credit Dietrich with that much backbone to walk out of here alone and try to seek assistance. Something else is up."

Pom and Eli had dealt with crooked men all their lives and felt they were dealing with one now. They had both heard the grumblings from the Baldwin men and knew they would both need to stay sharp or be betrayed by the very men they employed.

"Pom, you know horses and their riggings better than I, is there a way to repair two of the saddles so you and I can leave before it's too late?"

"I can rig a set of rope stirrups to get us through for the moment. We can take the severed stirrups with us and at the next town have them repaired properly."

"I suspect we better do it and get out of here before Dietrich comes back. Something tells me he won't be coming back alone. Allow me enough time to clear the livery so our intentions of leaving won't be suspect," Eli said.

Eli turned to the six Baldwin men that presently occupied the livery with them. The two that were injured the least, along with the three uninjured men were sent out and up the street to guard against an assault that was sure to come from Fowler. Once the five were gone Eli picked up a length of wood and struck the remaining Baldwin man in the head, knocking him out cold.

"Alright Pom, let's get to it before anyone comes back." Ten minutes later Pom had the two saddles on their horses repaired.

"You intend on opening that front door and us riding out that way," Pom asked.

"That's the only way out of here, first let me take a look up the street to make sure the coast is clear," Eli said as he walked to the sliding livery door and peered through a crack. What he saw wasn't good.

"Dietrich and some men are at the end of the street, it looks like some strangers with him that we haven't met before," Eli said.

Pom stepped to the door and saw the same thing; the men would be at the livery in minutes.

The Pursuit

"Let's check out the back of the building and see if there's any other way of getting out. If not then we might have to stand and fight," Eli said.

Both men ran to the back of the livery and took a look. The wall back there was of planks that were nailed to cross members. Pom raised a foot and kicked, hoping he could knock enough boards loose so they could escape. On his third hard kick one of the wooden pins that kept the hidden door closed popped out. A quick look revealed the second pin, which was promptly removed.

Pom and Eli quickly led their horses out and then re-closed the door. Pom had picked up the two pins before exiting and that was when he noticed they could be removed or reinserted from either inside or outside the livery by way of a gap in one of the planks.

"So this is how they got the four horses out of town without being noticed. This livery man has a secret of his own, why else would he have gone to the trouble of building a door that looked like any other part of the wall?" Pom wondered out loud.

The two headed down the back of the small slope toward the river below. Once there they had a decision to make. Head downstream and by the bulk of the town, and the sawmill, or head upstream and away from the glow of the town of Sweetwater. They headed upstream.

Dietrich headed toward the end of town where he assumed the drive to the mansion was and before long he ran into the very men he sought.

As Dietrich was heading through town Fowler and his men were headed down from the mansion. Fowler never had any intention of actually going into Sweetwater; he would wait at the guard shack as his men searched for Pom and Eli. When they got to the foot of the hill they saw a man heading in their direction, it was Dietrich.

With all that had gone on this evening the men weren't going to take any chances. Hartman stepped to the front of his men and had them spread out as he did. He intended to see who this man was and what his intentions were.

"Stop and be recognized Mister. Fair warning though, we have no less than a dozen guns pointed in your direction."

Dietrich saw the group of men and when he was told to stop and identify himself he recognized the voice as that of Fowler's head man, Patterson Hartman.

"Hartman, is that you?"

Hartman also recognized the voice; he had spoken to Dietrich just after the explosion at the hotel. Once that was accomplished Hartman had headed back to the mansion not knowing that Eli and Pom had just tried to kill his boss.

"It's me Dietrich, approach with your hands in the air if you don't mind."

Dietrich did as he was told and was soon standing face to face with Hartman and the rest of the guards. Fowler hadn't met Dietrich and didn't want to. He could never be sure if a man might be able to recognize him from a long ago wanted poster, especially a man that worked for the hated Baldwin Felts Detective Agency. Fowler would just stay at the guard shack with the two men now guarding the entrance to the driveway.

"Dietrich, I hadn't expected to hear from you so soon. I hope you have considered my offer and came to a conclusion that will see your men all safely away from Sweetwater," Hartman said.

The Pursuit

"I have, but there is more to it than just my men's safety. There was the mention of a reward," Dietrich said. With so many men around that he didn't know Dietrich had phrased the word, *reward,* into the sentence rather than the much more unpleasant word, *bribe.*

"The reward I spoke of earlier is still in effect Mr. Dietrich. There is the matter of one of your men that accompanied Pom and Eli to the mansion a short time ago. His name is Jason Orwell."

"Orwell is attempting to find medical help for some of my men. I lost two good men when the hotel blew up. Three more are injured but will most likely pull through. I believe the accident at the hotel was not an accident at all but an attempt to kill the three men we followed here. If there is a question of me allowing Orwell to be associated with anything Eli and Pom tried at the mansion then I'm afraid I will call the whole thing off and let the chips fall where they may," Dietrich said.

He had already been told by Orwell of what the two Chicagoans had tried to do earlier. Orwell claimed he was sitting out in the parlor when the two came out leading Fowler. He was going to intervene but the explosion at the hotel had changed the need for that.

Hartman considered what Dietrich had just said. If he did hold Orwell accountable and therefore couldn't strike a deal with Dietrich then many men would die. Sure they had the Baldwin men outnumbered but it was doubtful any of them would just give up. The Baldwin men would fight ferociously knowing it was a fight to the death. Hartman would accept the new terms and then try and convince Fowler that Orwell had only been caught up in the unfortunate incident.

Hartman stepped forward and stuck out a hand. "Agreed, I will guarantee you and your men safe passage as long as you don't interfere with the business my boss has with Eli and Pom."

"And the reward?" Dietrich asked.

"The reward will be paid upon the business being concluded with the two men from Chicago." Both men shook.

Pom and Eli, both glad to have made their escape from the livery, rode up stream for nearly half an hour when they came to a spot were the river was wide and slow moving. They knew they would need to make it to the far bank because the river was starting to crowd them against the base of the mountain. At this rate they would run out of navigable ground very soon.

"The river has widened. Do you think this is a suitable spot to cross?" Eli asked.

"Possibly, if it gets deeper than the flanks of the horses though I recommend we turn back. Deep water, especially as cold as it is, might cause the horses to seize up. If that happens they will drown and so will we. If they can walk across without needing to swim I think they will be alright," Pom told him.

Both men stepped their mounts into the water and slowly marched them across. They were helped immensely by moonlight that leaked through broken clouds. The path the two followed was identical to the one Stewart and his three companions had used not more than an hour earlier. If the two groups had any idea they were this close then both would have used more caution. As it was the six riders rode on, oblivious to each other.

Dietrich led the men from the guard shack back into Sweetwater. Once near the street that would lead them to the livery he cautioned them, "I've got eight men there; probably the doctor is there as well tending to the wounded. If we just march in then Eli and Pom will fight like cornered rats, which is exactly what they are. Let me go and see how things are in there. I'll have my men arrest the two before they know what happened and then we will gladly turn them over to you."

Hartman thought the offer over. If he and his men stormed the livery then Pom and Eli would surely fight and probably the other Baldwin men as well. That wasn't going to work. Fowler had given him instructions to try and take the two Chicago men alive and then bring them to the mansion. Hartman knew his boss could be sinister and no doubt had some plans on how he wanted to kill the two.

"Alright, but if you are not back out here in ten minutes then we open fire on the livery. I'll see to it that every man and beast in there is killed. Do you understand me?"

Dietrich found the ultimatum to be harsh but had no other choice. "I'll be outside in less than ten minutes; you just make sure none of your men open fire." With that Dietrich turned and headed for the livery.

When he got to the door he heard men talking inside. "This is Dietrich, I'm coming in."

He opened the side door and stepped inside. Several of his men had drawn their weapons but once they saw it was their boss they relaxed. The doctor was there and he was working on the most injured of the three from the hotel. As he scanned the room looking for Eli and Pom he noticed there was an opening in the main back wall.

"What happened here Orwell?" was all he asked.

"I don't know other than when we got back from finding the doc Eli and Pom had managed to take down part of that back wall and head out on their horses. They sent the men out into the street to stand watch and while they were outside they clobbered Red, damn near killed him too. The doc says he has a concussion, whatever that is," Orwell said.

"Get the doc out of here so I can talk," Dietrich said.

"Two of the Baldwin men roughly got the doctor to his feet and pushed him out the door, Baldwin men were not known for their finesse. Once the grumbling doctor was outside, the men gathered around Dietrich.

"I have maybe ten or twelve Fowler men waiting outside. They want Eli and Pom, either we turn them over or they will open fire on the livery."

At this a couple of the men turned toward the door and prepared to defend themselves. The Baldwin men weren't cowards in any sense of the word.

"Hang on a minute before anyone starts shooting. I have arranged a deal where we step aside and allow Fowler's men to go after the two. If we go along then we will be guaranteed safe passage. There is also some money in it for anyone that agrees. The way I see it we were sent out here searching for a man named Blair and have landed right in the middle of a war between Norman Fowler and Wilbur Westbrook. Now I'll leave it up to the majority, we fight or we step aside, and in the process each of us will walk away with at least a full year's pay. The Baldwin higher ups will never know about the money and I suspect they probably didn't think any of us were going to survive this job anyway. Now what will it be?"

None of the men knew exactly what they were up against outside but assumed it was enough to lose if things devolved into a gun battle. One by one they agreed to go along with the plan Dietrich presented to them but each said under no circumstances would they be disarmed.

The Pursuit

"Alright then, I'll go back outside and let them know what we have agreed on. I can't say with any level of certainty they still won't open fire once they find out Pom and Eli have escaped. If they shoot me then you men do the best you can. Fight as long as you have a chance and if it looks like you will be overrun then take out that back way on foot." With that Dietrich turned and went back outside.

"Look sharp, here comes Dietrich," Hartman told his men.

Once he was close enough Hartman asked, "So what will it be?"

Dietrich looked at the men and wondered what the response would be once they found out the Chicago men had escaped.

"I'm afraid both Eli and Pom are gone. They knocked out one of the injured men and then busted out the back wall of the livery while my other men were guarding outside. I doubt they could have gotten far."

Hartman stood there looking in the direction of the livery wondering how inept these Baldwin men really were. "If you allowed them to escape then what are your plans?"

This wasn't the response Dietrich expected. "We didn't allow them to escape, they just escaped. How was I to know they would turn tail and run?"

"You traveled with the two for the last few days and you didn't know their ways? I thought you Baldwin-Felts men were professionals," Hartman said hoping to provoke the man.

Dietrich smiled as he looked over the men arrayed against him. Each seemed to be wearing a smirk. If it were only himself to worry about he would draw his gun and kill as many of these men as he could before he was killed himself, he was that mad. But it wasn't just him, he had eight more men back at the livery and knew in this town not a one would make it out alive.

251

Dietrich decided the best response at the moment was no response at all. He would let Hartman determine what would happen next.

If Hartman thought his statement was something that might set off the Baldwin man then he was mistaken. Dietrich only stood there looking at him and his men. And then an idea came to mind. What if Dietrich could be persuaded to take on another job, a job that involved a killing or two in exchange for his men's safety?

"I tell you what, since you and your men managed to allow Eli and Pom to escape then our original deal is off the table. But I am willing to offer you another job, if you agree to take it then our original agreement stands, except I will double the money, five thousand dollars."

This grabbed the attention of Dietrich, what kind of job would be worth that kind of money. "I'm listening," was all he said.

"Three days ride from here in Rapid City is a couple of men that Mister Fowler would like taken care of. We already have men on the payroll that have offered to take the job but both myself and Mister Fowler think it might be best if outside help is used. Would you be interested?"

Dietrich didn't hesitate, "I would, what are the specifics of the job?"

"There is a judge and a marshal down there that have made it their life's work to try and destroy Mister Fowler. He has tried reasoning with the two but these men don't understand reason. It's an easy job. I assume no one in Rapid City knows you or your men. You ride in; keep an eye on the town for a day or two to find the best way to do the job. Then you take care of the two and ride out. I can guarantee that once you get back to Sweetwater you will be in the good graces of

The Pursuit

Mister Fowler and there might be steady work for you in the future."

"What of my men? Are they still guaranteed safe passage, the ones that might not want to take on this job?"

"Now that presents a problem. Once you tell your men the details then there is no turning back. If any refuse then we will have no choice but to kill them. Once the cat is out of the bag then it can't be put back in. And if you haven't figured it out yet, you are already aware of our problem in Rapid City so you are already committed."

"If me and my men agree then how do you know we won't just ride out and never come back?" Dietrich knew he was asking a dangerous question but he felt Hartman was holding all the cards and also had all the answers.

"As of now we have one volunteer which is you. You will pick three other men you can rely on and then head out at first light. I will keep the other men here as a guarantee that you won't double-cross us. Now pick out the three you intend to take so my men can march the other five up the hill where they can be watched."

"You said the men had a choice?" Dietrich said.

"They do, take this job or be killed."

"Not much of a choice. Do I get to go back in there and explain the way things are going to be?"

"No, give a shout and have your men step out one at a time," Hartman said.

Now Dietrich had a problem, his men wouldn't allow anyone to disarm them. They would go down fighting first. "That won't work. Let me go in there and get the three I think will take the job and we will come back out. After that you can take the others."

"Done and done, you have five minutes," Hartman said.

Dietrich figured as much, Hartman had this figured out from the beginning. Dietrich headed back to the livery and a couple of minutes later he stepped back out with three men behind him.

"Alright Hartman, you have a deal but I want your guarantee that the four men in the livery will be treated fairly until we do the job and return."

"Did you say four men in the livery? There are five I believe."

"There were five, the one that was clubbed died a few minutes ago."

Hartman wasn't without a conscious. "I am sorry to hear that, I believe you said Eli and Pom did this?"

"They did. Since me and my men are now working for you what are your plans for those two Chicago bastards?" Dietrich asked.

"Since you and your men are taking care of the problem in Rapid City that frees up my men to go on the hunt for the two. There is also the matter of Gene Blair and his friends, my men will also deal with that problem. All you have to worry about is taking care of the matter in Rapid City."

"It'll be done. If we are expected to leave at first light then we're going to need supplies and also someone that can repair saddles," Dietrich said.

"I'll have a man sent over to work on your gear and two more men will be here an hour before first light with the supplies you'll need to get you to Rapid City." With that Hartman turned and walked away.

Dietrich and his three volunteers went back to the livery and told the four men the new plan. They reluctantly agreed, two were injured and would use the time to heal, the other two would have gone along with Dietrich but they weren't needed.

The Pursuit

They drew the short straws and were relegated to stay with the other two.

About an hour before first light Stewart and the men stopped near a clear stream in order to rest the horses and make some coffee. After a two hour rest, and then a few hours travel, they hoped to be at the dugout where a full night's rest was anticipated.

"Did you manage to pack anything to eat before we scurried out the back of the livery?" Blair asked.

Allen untied one of the saddlebags and pulled out a paper sack. In it was the dried pork and hardtack he had purchased the previous evening at the general store. "This is all we got other than coffee and tobacco."

"And how many days is it to Rapid City," Blair asked.

"Two more good days after this one, that is if my calculations are correct. I figure if the trout are biting we can eat tonight and that's it until we make town," Allen told him.

"What if we kill some game?" Blair asked.

Stewart just looked at the man before answering, "Me and you done had this conversation Blair. You go shooting off a gun then anyone within ten miles of us will know where we are. I don't care if a deer jumps from cover and starts attacking you there'll be no shots fired."

Blair did remember that little conversation from a few days back but hoped it might not apply now. He liked to eat as well as the next man but decided to put on a tough face. "Well, if you three can stand a little hunger then so can I." He might have said it, and his ears might have heard it, but his stomach was going to take some convincing.

Nathan Wright

The horses were allowed to drink and then picketed in some prairie grass. Coffee was made using the smallest of fires. The men sat and nibbled on their meager provisions and considered where they were and how far it was to the dugout.

"Marshal, I believe we should go a few miles out of our way and retrieve the hundred and fifty thousand dollars. If we are to end up in Rapid City then I hope to turn it over to the judge there, I believe you said his name is Thurman Preston," Blair said.

Allen was unaware of any hidden money and immediately wanted to know the story. "Best if you don't try to figure out that little matter Allen. I've been around Blair for the better part of ten days and damn if I understand it. We'll just turn it over to the judge and let Blair try to explain it to him."

Blair looked at Allen and only smiled. He was glad he didn't have to go over that story again, he was kind of tired of hearing himself tell it.

During the two hour break each of the men managed to sleep for at least an hour. Once they pulled out the horses were a little more fresh but the men were a little more tired. A man running on no sleep will usually find that one hour only makes things worse.

Both Pom and Eli had stopped during the night. Their stay was a little more than two hours, city boys needed their sleep. Once the two climbed back in the saddle a full four hours had elapsed. The difference between the group Stewart led and the two Chicago men was coffee and food. Stewart and his men had a little while Pom and Eli had none.

"You remember the trail we used to get here from Langley Pom," Eli asked.

The Pursuit

"Pretty much, we can find our way back if we head due south and slightly west. We will cross the railroad somewhere and that will lead us to Rapid City."

"I believe our mission here was a failure Pom. We have nothing to show for our efforts. Our only problem now is to book passage on the first train east."

"To the contrary Eli, our mission was a resounding success. We discovered Norman Fowler to be a liar and a cheat. Westbrook can dissolve Five Oaks Development and then install himself as the sole representative for the railroads. By eliminating Fowler we have essentially doubled the profits we were previously taking in."

Eli looked at Pom. "But we didn't eliminate Fowler. He is still in Sweetwater. He is also closest to the actual operations and will have sway over the work being done here in the territory."

After a moment's thought Eli added, "He may be closer to the excavations for the railroads but Westbrook is closer to the corporate offices of the two roads in question. We know now that Fowler is a man operating under a fictitious name and this can be used to steer the roads away from him."

"But we don't know the true identity of Fowler. We know he won't travel south of Sweetwater and that is the extent of our knowledge."

"You haven't figured it out yet Pom? If Fowler won't go to Rapid City then we have to assume there is someone there that knows his previous identity. All we need to do is find out if anyone was either driven out of town or left in the middle of the night and we will have our man."

"I'm sure several men from a town the size of Rapid City may have left in the middle of the night, how will we know which one?" Pom asked.

"You are correct in your reasoning, many men may have left on the sly but the one we seek was a man of substantial wealth. I doubt there are many that fit that description."

Pom might have been the better man when it came to horses and street fighting but Eli had proven once again he had the better tactical mind.

An hour before first light two men with supplies knocked on the livery door. Dietrich and the three men with him pulled their guns before opening the door. Hartman was good to his word. Two men stood outside and each carried a feed sack and in each was the supplies that would see the four men through to Rapid City. The man that worked the leather had been there earlier and had the four saddles as good as new by the time the Fowler men knocked.

Before leaving, one of Hartman's men reached into a pocket and pulled out a thousand dollars cash. "Our boss said to give this to you, said you might need some walking around money. You finish the job and there'll be four times that waiting on you when you return."

After the two left Dietrich looked at the other three men. "You know, working on this side of the law might be a bit more lucrative."

The other three men agreed. It was apparent it was going to be hard for any of them to continue working for Baldwin Felts. The remaining men felt like they had been misled from the get-go on this trip and it was as much Baldwin's fault for the deaths of the others as it was Fowler's.

"Let's get this stuff into our saddlebags and head out. It'll be light in less than an hour and we got some traveling to do," Dietrich said.

The Pursuit

The four men headed out the back, the same way Eli and Pom had gone the night before. With light fast approaching it was easy enough to see where the horses had traveled. The only thing was there were more than two sets of tracks; it looked like the other four houses that were in the livery when Dietrich and his men first arrived must have left out before Pom and Eli. The trail could be followed by a blind fool.

Dietrich and his men followed the trail to the spot where the six horses had crossed the river. They crossed and then rode hard. As they traveled the trail became harder to spot due to the hardness of the terrain and also the fact that the previous horses were now traveling over frozen earth leaving little sign.

Four hours after first light Pom and Eli came to the spot where Stewart and his men had built the fire and rested their horses earlier.

"I believe this was used by Blair and his companions," Eli said.

Pom checked the spot where the fire had been. Someone had carried water to extinguish the flames but the ground was still warm. "They were here no more than three or four hours ago. Do we really want to continue on this trail? If we meet up remember, there are four of them and only two of us."

Eli considered the question and then took into consideration their options. "Our original instructions were to find Blair and eliminate him as a possible witness, but I believe things have changed. With what we learned from Fowler I think he has much more to lose if Blair is allowed to live and then goes to the authorities. As far as Five Oaks and Wilbur Westbrook are concerned I think they are in the clear, which also means we are in the clear. If we find Blair and kill him then we will be putting ourselves at risk. We are deep into the Dakota Territory and we might have difficulty getting back to Chicago if we are implicated in a killing. I doubt if Westbrook's contacts out here, at the present, are powerful enough to assist us in a defense if we are arrested on a suspicion of murder"

"It sounds like a proper course of action concerning Blair, but we still need to get to a depot and book passage back east. You know Fowler has put together a posse by now and is probably in pursuit of us as we speak. If four against two sounds bad then try eight or ten against two. I agree, we allow Blair to go unharmed and then he will be Fowler's problem. In the meantime we need to be moving," Pom said.

"I agree. The nearest train depot is in a town called Langley. We make it there and buy passage on the first available train heading anywhere that puts some miles between us and this place. We will pay board for a week at a livery there and leave the horses in the livery man's care. When the week is up and he can't find us he will confiscate the horses and saddles as his own and that will be that," Eli said.

"If we book passage in Langley do we stop at Rapid City and ask around about Fowler? We need to know who he really is," Pom said.

"No, once past Rapid City we will telegram Westbrook at the next town that has wires. He can use some of his sources to find out who Fowler really is. Also, I am going to advise Westbrook that our relationship with Baldwin Felts be terminated at once. I believe those men can be bought and if so they can do harm to our plans." Eli had just made a statement that was truer than he or Pom could have imagined.

Both men turned farther west from the trail Stewart and his men used in order to bypass the four. The plan the two came up with was solid. They had successfully disengaged themselves from the troubles of the region, troubles they had helped engineer.

Hartman led the four Baldwin men, or prisoners, up to the mansion after leaving the livery. Accommodations had been made in the bunkhouse used by the guards that patrolled Fowlers estate. Although the men had said they wouldn't allow themselves to be disarmed they now carried no weapons. Once Dietrich and Hartman had come to terms the remaining three agreed to being disarmed. They were promised to be well cared for and any medical needs that remained would be seen to.

Hartman went inside to Fowler's study after the four prisoners were situated. "What do you plan to do about the men we now hold hostage? Do you really plan on doing them harm if Dietrich doesn't hold up his end of the deal?"

Fowler rubbed his side whiskers and then his chin as he thought. "Not at all, two days from now I want the four escorted north to the rail depot there and booked passage back east. They are each to be given five-hundred dollars if they will sign a document stating they were simply caught trespassing and by leaving town no charges will be filed. Once they have signed let them know if they ever set foot back in Sweetwater they will be arrested.

"I think to be heading eastward with that much money in their pockets will convince them to sign. To be a free man heading east is far better than being held here with their futures dependent on the outcome of Dietrich's trip to Rapid City."

"I like that plan. If Dietrich is caught or if the four we release say anything, or accuse anyone in Sweetwater, then it is simply a matter of whether they are believed. If anyone tries to investigate here they will find no one to talk to. I also warn you not to visit the bunkhouse until the four have been delivered north to the depot," Hartman said. The number of people in Sweetwater who had ever actually seen Fowler could be counted on one hand. It was as if the man were a ghost, or phantom, that could be heard from time to time but never visibly seen.

"Don't worry, if any of the three see my face then I will be forced to kill them. At this stage of my life the last thing I want is to be recognized," Fowler said.

"I'll see to it they are confined to the bunkhouse. Now there is still the matter of Blair, Pom, and Eli."

"How many men can we spare if we split the operation, some to find and eliminate Blair and others to do the same to Eli and Pom?" Fowler asked.

"Twelve in all, I believe either possess an equal risk. Pom and Eli have proven themselves to be ruthless but they are only two men. Blair now travels with three men we don't know but I doubt those four are as dangerous as the other two. I say we split our forces equally with six going after each group. I will also be going along with the men chasing Blair."

"Sounds about right, but I prefer Eli and Pom be captured alive if possible and brought back here. Blair and his group can simply be killed when found. Before you kill Blair have him give up the whereabouts of the funds he took, it is substantial and would be lost forever if the location of the hidden money isn't revealed," Fowler said with a smile.

The Pursuit

At around four that afternoon Stewart and his companions came within sight of the dugout. Stewart had expected something not much better than a hog lot and that was pretty much what he now saw from a distance. There was a crude corral beside the monstrosity, it looked to be attached.

There was one thing he liked about it though; it was nearly hidden from view. Unless you knew where to go and where to look you might ride right by the place without knowing it was there. It was only visible from the front and even from that direction it was well hidden by the lay of the land and the trees and scrub brush that grew right up to the front door. This was the position Stewart was looking from now and it was apparent Allen must always come to this spot to make sure everything was alright before he rode on in.

As the men drew closer it looked like the roof of the dugout extended a few feet over one side of the corral. It was apparent that was intended to give partial shelter to any horses penned in by the fence.

"Did you say you come up here from time to time and do a little work on this place Allen?" Stewart asked.

"I do, that's why it's in such good shape. Well, what do you think?"

"I think if the inside looks anything like the outside I might just sleep with the horses," Stewart said.

"Don't let the outward appearance fool you Marshal. I made sure to keep the dugout as ratty looking as possible so maybe anyone that spotted this place would be tempted to just ride on by. The work I spoke of was to the inside, plus making sure the roof would keep the rain and snow out," Allen said, still smiling.

The men rode up to the front door and dismounted. The outside was truly a picture of dilapidation and decay. The corral though looked sound so at least the horses could be turned loose for the night instead of being tied to a tree stump or ground hitched. Water wouldn't be a problem either due to the slow moving stream that ran past the front of the dugout.

Blair stepped from his horse and walked to the stream, it wasn't more than fifteen feet wide with pools here and there that looked to be eight or ten feet deep. It was in these pools that trout could be seen lying near the bottom. Allen hadn't been exaggerating when he said the water here teemed with fish. The cold clear water held a bounty; one that Blair hoped would soon provide supper.

Let's get these horses into the corral and see about catching a few of those fish," Blair said as he quickly slid the gate poles to the side.

As Blair and Ellsworth tended to the horses Stewart stepped inside the dugout, followed by Allen. As he walked through the door, it wasn't really a door in any sense of the word but a canvas tarp nailed to the uppermost log that made up the front of the structure, he expected to see a mud floor and a hammock. The inside was far better than he expected.

The floor was dirt but looked to be level and packed solid. The front and side walls were of six inch pine logs which also made up the supports for the roof. The back wall was actually the edge of the hill the building was built into. The most pleasant find was a stone fireplace against the back wall with a grate and cast iron kettle. The chimney went up through the roof, not just some crude metal pipe but stone, all the way out the top. On either side of the fireplace was a double bunk built one over the other. In the center of the room was a rough looking table with two benches built of the same logs as the walls and roof. The room was extremely cold and damp, something the fireplace would remedy as soon as it got dark. No smoke could be chanced during daylight hours.

A beaming Allen looked at Stewart and asked, "Well, what do you think Marshal?"

"Not bad Allen, but why are you so proud of this place if you only found it and have made a few repairs. The way you speak of this dugout a man might think you own it."

"I do own it. Once I discovered it I checked and found the property in this area belongs to no one. When I made the trip to Rapid City to check the maps and titles I made up my mind that I needed the dugout as a place to hide if I ever found the need to leave Sweetwater. I paid the fees and for the sum of two-hundred dollars I now own the tract, which consists of a hundred and twenty-five acres. I didn't mention the dugout when I paid, I doubted it had any value and I also wanted anyone looking in the title room to think the land wasn't being lived on."

"So you had intentions all along of leaving Sweetwater. I suspect there is more to that town than I've figured out or been made aware of," Stewart said.

Allen was still admiring his dugout when he said, "I doubt anyone will ever figure out how that town came into being. The sawmill and the silver mine makes the town a prosperous place to live and work but the townsfolk walk around as if they are in some sort of trance, afraid to look anyone in the eye or speak for fear of someone hearing something they don't like. I made up my mind a year ago to leave and I guess you and Blair happening into town was the prodding I needed to get out of there and start over."

"Okay then, let's see to the horses, that trough needs to be filled with water and then we can break open that sack of grain. Unless you catch a trout or two the horses are going to be eating way better than any of us," Stewart said.

Allen went to a shelf nailed to the wall and took down a pole. "Won't take me no time to catch a couple if you can see to the needs of the horses?"

Thirty minutes later and the horses were stripped of saddles and gear and the water trough was filled. Stewart told Ellsworth to use a third of the grain which would allow enough for two more days if needed.

True to his word Allen began catching trout almost as soon as he threw a line in the water. Within an hour he had caught five of decent size which Blair immediately cleaned. The most maddening thing for Blair was that a fire couldn't be built for at least another hour. The man just stood there looking at the fish fillets. The other men were afraid he was going to try and eat one raw but he managed to wait.

By the time it got dark Ellsworth had a fire going with the skillet sitting on the grate and three trout fillets sizzling inside. The men didn't have any cornmeal or flour but it didn't matter, as hungry as they were the fish would taste good without batter or seasoning.

When Allen came in about thirty minutes after dark he had another five fish ready for Blair to clean. "We can put these back outside and let them freeze. If I can't catch anymore in the morning then this will be our supper tomorrow night," Allen told the others.

One whole trout apiece did little to satisfy the men's hunger but it helped. "If I can catch a few more in the morning then at least we can eat twice tomorrow. After we leave here in the morning I figure it's two more days to Rapid City. Whatever fish we got, either in our stomachs or frozen for tomorrow night, is all we're getting," Allen said.

The Pursuit

"We better get some sleep; I want to be out of here early tomorrow morning, before daylight would be best. We got a ways to go and we probably got men searching for us. Allen, how do you intend to catch any fish if we leave before first light?" Stewart asked.

"I plan on using my time during guard duty to see if those trout can see in the dark. You won't need to worry about me falling asleep during my watch, I love to fish and that will keep me entertained while you three get your beauty sleep."

All right then, Blair and Ellsworth can take first watch, four hours. I'll take the middle watch and that will leave Allen to the early morning watch and his fishing. Let's get at it," Stewart told the men.

The night went off without any trouble. The fire was kept going while the men slept and the inside of the dugout was pleasant, not hot and certainly not cold, just pleasant.

Allen managed to catch six trout in the four hours he was outside. Blair was put to cleaning fish, breakfast was the same as supper, fried fish and coffee, no one complained. Just as the sky began to grow orange to the east the four men pulled out leaving the nice warm dugout behind.

Eli and Pom had traveled until dark without trying to find a suitable campsite. It was agreed to forgo a fire but by midnight the two men were nearly frozen to death, neither had bedrolls. Finally it was decided to build a fire and if anyone found them then so be it. They would tackle that problem if it showed up. Both men only managed to nap during the remainder of the night. It could very well have been the worst night either of the two had ever experienced.

Nathan Wright

An hour before first light they extinguished the fire and pulled out of camp. They would ride all day and all the next night if it meant making it to Langley. They were cold and hungry; Langley would have food and a depot. All other concerns were abandoned as the two made their way toward warmth and food. Little did they know their path would take them in the same direction as that of Stewart and his three companions.

"Got a couple of riders to the east Marshal," Ellsworth said.

The four men had been riding for nearly five hours since leaving the dugout that morning. Stewart stopped his horse and looked in the direction Ellsworth was pointing. In the distance, at a range of nearly a mile could be seen two men on horseback, they were moving in the same general direction as Stewart and his men.

"You think they've seen us yet?" Stewart asked.

"I just spotted them myself. We just came out of the timber when I noticed the two. I don't think they know we are here but it won't be long before they do," Ellsworth said.

Let's head west a little further and stay out of sight. I want to try and get ahead of those two and surprise them. They are either hunting us or someone is hunting them. Let's go, stay in cover and move fast," the marshal said.

The men moved slightly right for another half mile and increased their pace. Almost an hour later they found a spot where they could keep an eye on the two unsuspecting riders as they approached.

"Spread out, each man at least ten yards from the next. When they get here you three stay put and let me do the talking," Stewart said.

The Pursuit

Eli and Pom had ridden with the mechanical movements of men that are exhausted and cold. Both had their minds on other things and neither had paid much attention to the trail they rode. All they wanted was to get to Langley and off these horses. The two could handle themselves in a city like Chicago, or even in a town the size of Sweetwater, but on the open range they were out of their element.

"Stop right there and hold your hands up, I got four guns trained on each of you," Stewart demanded as he stepped from cover.

The cold and hunger the two had felt only a moment earlier was now replaced by the shock of what they had just heard. Both stopped their horses and raised their hands, what else could they do.

"Are you two traveling alone or are there others following behind," Stewart asked. He already knew the answer but knew a question was the best way to keep the two men's minds focused on him rather than trying to think of a plan of action.

"We're alone mister, what gives you the right to stop us out here and hold a rifle pointed our way?" Pom asked as he tried to think of his options.

Stewart heard what the man asked, by the accent and diction he knew he wasn't from the west. "Where do you hail from Mister?" Stewart asked.

Pom kept quiet so Eli could answer. "Down Rapid City way, we were heading there now until you decided to bushwhack us." Eli decided to try and provoke the man, he felt a man that was angry was a man he had an advantage over. He was wrong about Stewart.

"I've rode these parts for years and that includes the town of Rapid City. Don't ever recall seeing you two before."

Both Pom and Eli doubted they knew enough about the area to prove they had spent more than five minutes in Rapid City. "Why have you stopped us Mister? As far as I can tell you're alone, now who are you and what business is of yours where we're from," Pom asked in a tone that would indicate he was holding the gun and not the other way around.

"Ellsworth, how about you step out here and cover me while I pull the teeth on these two? The rest of you stay behind cover."

Eli and Pom waited to see if this man holding a gun on them was lying about not being alone. Both knew they were in a fix when a tall unkempt man stepped from the brush carrying a Winchester. "Go ahead Marshal, take their guns while I keep this rifle trained on em, I doubt either wants me to shoot at this range."

Stewart put down his rifle and pulled his Colt. He walked up to the two cautiously. It was easy enough to take each man's holstered gun but he was going to need to search each to make sure neither carried a hideaway.

Stewart pointed his gun at Eli and said, "Step down real easy so I can search you."

"That man just called you a marshal, is it true?" Eli asked.

Stewart didn't answer, he just reached into a vest pocket and pulled out his badge and pinned it on using one hand.

"If you are truly a marshal then why would you carry your badge in your pocket?" Eli asked.

"Let's just say I don't like to advertise who I am until I know who I'm dealing with, now step down from that horse." Stewart and Ellsworth had already noticed the crude rope stirrups someone had attached to the saddles. They both knew where these two riders came from.

Eli slowly swung a leg over and as he stepped to the ground he looked at Pom for some sort of sign that the man knew what to do, he didn't.

"Keep both hands on the saddle while I check you for any weapons," Stewart said.

Ten seconds later the marshal stuck a hand inside Eli's vest pocket and pulled out a two shot derringer. It wasn't that much different than the ones he and Ellsworth carried.

"Is this all you got on you Mister or is there anything else I need to be worried about?" Stewart asked.

"No, I reckon you got everything," Eli said dejectedly.

"Allen, do you mind stepping out here and giving Ellsworth a hand?" Stewart said.

Eli and Pom now saw a third man step from the brush, no doubt there was a forth. Stewart looked up at Pom, "Alright, why don't you step down nice and slow just like your friend."

Again the marshal found a two shot derringer hidden in a vest pocket. "Step over there by your friend so I can ask you two a few questions." Stewart did have a question or two but that wasn't the reason he had the two step away from where he stood. He wanted to let Ellsworth and Allen know that for the next few hours they were not to call Blair by name. He suspected these two were part of the group of men searching for Blair.

Pom and Eli felt comfortable telling the marshal their real names, neither had committed a crime, at least one that could be pinned on them. Eli, being the more tactical of the two decided to spin the truth to make it look like he and Pom were being chased rather than the other way around.

"Marshal, I believe we should be moving, I doubt it's safe here out in the open," Eli said.

"Why would that be?"

"We were in Sweetwater a day or so back and got into a scuffle with some locals. We cut out and made it this far when you stopped us. We've committed no crimes and demand to be released at once," Eli said.

Stewart really didn't know if the two were running from the law but he was confident the two were running from something. Why else would they have lit out of Sweetwater using saddles with rope stirrups.

"Which way are you two headed?"

"Langley, we're going to Langley to catch a train," Eli said.

"Which way are you heading once you board the train?"

"East, anywhere to get us away from Sweetwater. There's some dangerous men in that town, men that will kill you if the notion hits them," Pom said.

Now Stewart had a problem. He couldn't just let these two go free and he was in no mood to take them along with him. As far as he knew they might not have committed a crime, but then again maybe they had. Maybe with both unarmed he could allow them to ride along until they got to Rapid City and then let Marshal Savage and Judge Preston see what should be done. If Preston said to let them go then who was he to complain?

"Alright you two, step back up on your horses and come along with us. Before they do Ellsworth, how about checking in those two saddlebags to make sure nothing is in there that might cause us trouble."

Pom and Eli looked at each other and let out a collective sigh of relief. They were glad they were going to get moving,

The Pursuit

both men expected to see a group of Fowler's men come barreling over the next rise any minute.

"Alright, this is what we're gonna do. Two of us will ride up front, you two in the middle, Ellsworth and myself will bring up the rear. If you two are telling the truth then you have nothing to worry about from the four of us. If you try anything then I will be forced to kill you both and leave you out here for the coyotes and wolves. Do we understand each other?" Stewart asked the two. Both shook their heads yes.

As the six riders headed out Stewart decided to run a couple of things past Ellsworth. "You know, if what those two are saying is true then we might not be that far ahead of anyone that might be looking for these two. And not just that, the same people are probably looking for Blair."

"I think you got it figured about right Marshal. I doubt it would be wise to stop before we get to Rapid City. We better try and spread the distance a little, just in case."

Stewart was thinking the same thing, "Alright here's what we'll do. We ride all day, stopping only to allow the horses to drink. Hopefully by then we will be near the wagon road that runs from Langley to Rapid City. If we can find the road then we follow it all the way without stopping," Stewart said.

"Where do you think we'll be when we find that road?"

"My best guess is somewhere east of Fort Clemons. If that's the case then we can be in Rapid City five or six hours after that if we can see the road well enough after dark and can move at a trot."

"That would put us in Rapid City somewhere after midnight, probably two or three hours after midnight," Ellsworth said.

"That's about what I figure if all goes right. The horses will be worn out before that so we'll need to slow our pace

273

considerably. Still though, I think it's our only hope. We get caught out here then some of us are going to die; against the number of men chasing us we all may die," Stewart said.

"You know Marshal, if that rumor we heard about someone already killing the judge and the marshal, or going to kill the two is true, then we need to get there as fast as we can. If they ain't already been killed then we might be able to save their lives. If the deed has already been done then we can go after the culprits," Ellsworth said.

Stewart liked the grit Ellsworth had. He wasn't a lawman but was more than willing to hunt down anybody that committed such a heinous crime as killing a judge and a marshal.

"You know Ellsworth, you might be right. At any rate we need to be getting there as soon as possible," the marshal said.

Stewart and Ellsworth knew some men were probably chasing them and they also figured more men were in Rapid City to try and kill Judge Preston and Marshal Savage, that was if they weren't already dead.

What they didn't know was the number of men arrayed against them was substantial. The group heading toward Rapid City with orders to kill the judge and the marshal consisted of Dietrich and three more. Blair was being chased by Hartman and six more of Fowler's men. Pom and Eli were being hunted by another six men. Fowler now had a total of seventeen men heading toward the town of Rapid City.

Hartman gathered the twelve men together and decided who would be going with him in search of Blair. "You six are to find Eli and Pom and when you do find them our boss has instructed me to try and take the two alive if possible. They are to be brought back here. If they pose too much of a danger then kill them. I will be leading the rest of you in search of a man by the name of Gene Blair. He travels with three other men that are of no concern to us unless they get in the way.

"We follow the two groups until they are either captured or dead. If we are unsuccessful in our attempts to find the men we search for then we will all meet up in Rapid City. It would normally be a four day ride to that town but time is something we don't have an abundance of. If either of our groups hasn't found our quarry then we will all meet up in Rapid City on the evening of our third day of pursuit.

"I'm almost positive we will find the men we search for there and when we do I expect each of you to do his part. We won't leave that town until every last one of them is dead," Hartman said.

The man in charge of the six chasing Eli and Pom, a man by the name of Ralph Porter, needed one more question answered. "What of this Eli and Pom, from what I gather they are dangerous men and pose a serious threat to my men."

Hartman smiled, he had no real wish to capture Pom and Eli. "I know I mentioned that the two are to be captured if possible, that is the wishes of Mister Fowler. I promised him I would pass along that piece of information, and I have done so. With that said what I really want is to bring back their bodies. Does that make my intentions any clearer?" Hartman said.

"It does, we will kill the two," Porter said. "And if it comes to that it will be because there wasn't any other way." Hartman knew by Porter's response he would see to it that Pom and Eli were both brought back dead.

Stewart and Ellsworth kept a close eye on their two new trail partners. Neither wanted the two men in their group but what else could they do. They knew the two had just come from Sweetwater and couldn't know for sure which side of the law they rode on. Time would tell.

The group of six riders rode the entire day with only brief stops to allow the horses to drink and for the men to refill their canteens. Just after dark it was decided to stop long enough to fry up the remainder of the trout Allen had caught the night before. There wasn't that much but what they did have was shared with Eli and Pom who ate as if it was the best meal the two had ever experienced, funny how hunger makes food taste better.

As Ellsworth put out the fire and stowed the skillet, he wondered out loud how far it was to the road that connected the towns of Rapid City, Fort Clemons, and Langley. Stewart had been noticing the lay of the land for the last hour or two before dark and figured they were close, maybe an hour away, maybe less.

As the marshal and Ellsworth were talking they assumed Allen and Blair were keeping a close watch on Eli and Pom, they weren't.

Eli had been keeping notice of the other four men and was hoping an opportunity would present itself. As everyone was preparing to mount up the four had inadvertently allowed Eli and Pom to get close to the two horses they rode. Just when Stewart and Ellsworth bent by the stream to refill their canteens, Pom grabbed the reins of his horse and swung into the saddle. He had already untied his and Eli's horses and while doing that he also untied Stewart and Ellsworth's horses.

When Eli made it into the saddle Pom swatted the two horses he had untied just as he and Eli headed off into the darkness hoping the two horses they rode could see well enough in the dark to avoid danger. Stewart heard the commotion and raced to where the horses had been tied out, all he found were the two mounts Allen and Blair rode in on.

As he looked around he knew what had happened. When Blair and Ellsworth came running up they both got the wrath of the marshal.

"You two were to look after our horses and the two bastards that just lit out of here. What in hell were you thinking?" It was then that Stewart noticed Allen was unsteady on his feet.

Allen looked at the marshal and said, "Sorry Marshal." He then promptly fell to the ground.

Ellsworth bent and checked the man out, there was blood running from a nasty knot on the back of the man's head. "Looks like someone cracked Allen a good one," he said.

"What in hell happened Blair," Stewart asked.

"I don't know Marshal. Allen was watching the two men and the next thing I know I heard horses heading out at a full run. As I ran this way Allen was getting up and that's all I know."

"Looks like Allen got clobbered with something. Why didn't you stay with him while he was watching Eli and Pom?" Ellsworth said as he continued checking the back of Allen's head.

"He said we were about to leave and asked me if I would refill his canteen when I filled mine. No sooner had I started toward the steam than I heard the sound of the horses," Blair said. "I'm sorry, I really am."

Stewart cursed some more and then said, "We better go find mine and Ellsworth's horses. I just hope they didn't get far or this is going to be a long night. Check Allen's saddlebags and see if the four guns we took off them bastards are still there. If they are armed then we might be in a bad way."

Ellsworth checked and found both Colts and both derringers still there; at least they wouldn't need to worry about Pom and Eli shooting them as they rode away in the darkness.

The horses Stewart and Ellsworth rode were quickly gathered up and the four men pulled out of camp. Allen hadn't really passed out when he was hit earlier but it was enough to daze the man. He was going to have a bad headache for the next day or so.

After mounting up and racing out of camp Pom and Eli rode as hard as they dared trying to put some distance between themselves and Stewart. No more than twenty minutes later they came to the stage and wagon road that led to town but rather than heading toward Rapid City they chose to turn toward Langley.

"We make it to Langley and then book passage on the first train east," Pom said.

"There might still be a problem with that; any train from Langley must go through Rapid City. What do we do if Stewart and his men intercept us there?" Eli asked.

"My guess is they will be too busy dealing with Fowler's men. With any luck they will arrive in town about the same time and that should keep them busy. I doubt they will be expecting us on the train from Langley anyway," Pom said.

"Maybe I've underestimated you Pom. That is some brilliant thinking on your part. From now on try and speak up more; my brilliant plans have damn sure got us in one hell of a predicament this time."

The Pursuit

Pom only rolled his eyes at the suggestion. "Let's ride; I want to get to Langley as soon as possible. We can eat and get warm there. Depending on when the train leaves we might have time to purchase a couple of pairs of gloves too, my hands are nearly frozen." The two men might have been disarmed but both had cash, neither traveled with less than four-hundred dollars and were glad the marshal was only checking for guns and not searching for anything else. He only patted them down and the two wads of cash each carried weren't found.

"Too bad we had to leave all our belongings back in Sweetwater. I guess it was a small price to pay; the larger price could have been our lives," Eli said as he scanned the road ahead.

"I believe you are correct. Next time Westbrook has a job out west I believe he should go, might do him some good," Pom said with a laugh.

Both men could barely see the outline of the road as they turned their horses toward Langley. It would be another three hours before they made it to that little town.

When they arrived the town was dark, other than a few kerosene street lamps here and there. They found the livery and left both horses with a man they roused from sleep and paid a week's board for the two.

The livery man took the money and then looked over the two men that stood in front of him. "You two don't look like you're from around these parts."

"We are not, this I believe is the first time I've visited your quaint little town," Pom said. He and Eli had passed through with the Baldwin men a few days prior but didn't want to be associated with that group any longer.

The livery man looked at the two saddles and then at Pom and Eli. "Looks like someone wrecked your saddles," he said.

"Yes, we were set upon by some highway bandits and they took most of our belongings. Lucky for us they didn't find all our money," Eli told the man.

"Why didn't they take your horses and saddles and leave you both afoot?"

Pom and Eli didn't have another lie handy and wondered why this man was being so persistent in his questioning. "I guess they figured the crime of robbery was not as bad as the crime of horse stealing," Eli said.

The livery man must have been satisfied with this answer. "I believe that might be right. You take a man's money and you get a year in jail if you're caught. You take a man's horse and you get hung."

Eli was quite proud of himself. He only made up the story on the spur of the moment and now he found his lie could actually be explained. "Well we must be on our way. Take good care of the horses." With that the two headed for the depot to see if someone there could sell them a ticket.

The depot for the town of Langley housed not only the ticket booth but also the telegraph office. It had been less than two months since it was determined that Langley had grown enough to warrant a full time working telegraph. Three different men took shifts that guaranteed the office would be open twenty-four hours a day.

Langley was the most westerly town in this part of the territory so its telegraph office became a crucial part of the growth and development of the area.

Eli and Pom walked up to the building fully expecting it to be locked up tight but to their pleasant surprise the door wasn't locked. They entered to find a chilly main room that was used for anyone waiting for the next train. To the right was another door and above it were the words, 'Telegraph Office, Langley.'

The two entered to find the room much warmer than the main room. They also found a man sound asleep on a cot in the middle of the floor. When the man heard the door close he opened his eyes to see two tall men looking at him.

"Good morning gentlemen, can I help you?" the man asked as he sat up and stretched.

"Maybe, could you tell me the time the ticket office opens?" Eli said.

The man pulled a watch from his pocket and opened the face. "In two more hours, it opens at five sharp."

"That will be fine, also is there a place in town where a man might find breakfast, along with hot coffee?"

"Sorry, not at three in the morning but you are welcome to have a cup from the stove over there. I made it fresh last evening," the man said as he stretched back out on his cot. "You're both welcome to wait out in the main room if you like. The restaurant opens at five, same as the ticket office. First train leaves at seven so you two ought to have time to get your tickets and then head over to the Iron Skillet for something to eat," the telegraph man said.

Eli knew he and Pom were going to get chilled sitting out in the depot's main room but it was still better than sitting on the back of a horse traveling the unknowns of the Dakota Territory.

"Pardon me, but did you say the restaurant is named the Iron Skillet," Pom asked.

"It is, there are a few others in town but the Iron Skillet opens the earliest and the food is good. I think you'll enjoy their cooking, I know I sure do," the man said as he closed his eyes and got comfortable on his cot. It was apparent he wasn't going to say much else so Pom and Eli quickly filled two coffee cups and went back to the main room.

About the same time Eli and Pom were riding into Langley Stewart and his men came into view of the lights of Rapid City. Stewart guessed it was somewhere between three and four in the morning.

"Let's make our way to the sheriff's office. Hopefully one of the deputies will be there and we can fill him in on what's about to happen." Stewart didn't like to think that someone had already ridden into town and killed the judge and the marshal. Until he heard otherwise he was going on the assumption that both men were still alive.

As the four riders rounded a corner and went down the main street of Rapid City they kept a close eye on their surroundings. With everything that had happened in the last few days each suspected a Winchester was pointed in their direction.

"That's the jail up ahead on the left. Let's see if anyone is there before we head over to the livery," Stewart said.

When the four pulled up out front a light could be seen through the front window. Ellsworth jumped down and twisted the knob to the door. "It's locked Marshal," he said as he knocked.

A few seconds later the door opened and there stood a deputy holding a Colt. "Can I help you mister," the deputy asked.

Stewart recognized the voice but couldn't see the face, "Is that you Cecil?"

The Pursuit

Cecil stuck his head out the door and looked at the marshal. "Well howdy Stewart, why don't you all come in and warm yourselves by the fire?"

The men tied their horses to the hitch rail and hurried inside. The room was chilly but warm compared to the temperature outside. There was a big coffee pot on top of the stove and Stewart went straight to it, it was empty.

"Anyway we can get some coffee going Cecil, damn if the four of us ain't about froze to death," Stewart said.

"Why I reckon so Marshal. I was just about to fix a fresh pot when I heard the knock at the door. Say, what's got you out at this time of the morning anyway?" Cecil asked as he looked at the other three men standing behind the marshal.

"When is the last time you saw either Judge Preston or Marshal Savage?" Stewart asked.

"Saw them both last evening. Why do you ask?"

"I need to get word to both that there's some men bent on doing each of them harm."

Cecil filled the coffee pot and sat it back on the stove. "Hell you say. Who are these men?"

"You ever hear of a town called Sweetwater?" Stewart asked.

"I've heard of it. Nothing more than a mud hole beside the road I reckon."

"Well it might have been a mud hole a few years ago but now it would rival Rapid City in size and population. We just came from there and probably got some men that might be after us," Stewart said.

As the marshal spoke Cecil got a good look at the three men he was with. He didn't know two of them but he recognized the third. "Gene Blair, I figured you had lit out of the territory by now."

Blair looked at the deputy. "Not yet Cecil but now that you mention it I wish I had. Since the last time we spoke I've been chased through half the territory."

"Well, I think Judge Preston thought you might have ran into some trouble because he expected you back a couple weeks ago," Cecil said as he got a bag of Arbuckle coffee off a shelf.

"That's where I'll go as soon as he makes it to the courthouse. In the meantime I might just stay here," Blair said as he looked at the warm potbellied stove.

Cecil looked at the man suspiciously, "You said you been chased. Now who would be chasing you Blair?"

"You remember when I was here a month or so ago. Preston knew who I worked for; at least he knew the name of the company I worked for. Someone involved with that company is of interest to the judge so he wanted me to do a little scouting around on my next trip out. I did and it damn near got me killed," Blair told the deputy.

"When will Sheriff Coleman be in Cecil? I need to talk to him about the trouble that's coming this way," Stewart said.

"He should be here about mid-day. He went to Fort Clemons day before yesterday. Marshal Savage and Bill went along too. They were serving some warrants on a few men for Judge Preston. From what Coleman said they should have gotten finished late yesterday and were going to head out first thing this morning. They should be here sometime after noon today."

Stewart looked at Ellsworth, "We might be in a bad way. That just leaves the four of us and Cecil here."

Cecil could tell by the marshal's tone that whatever he was referring to was serious. "Did you say the four of you and me? What on earth are you talking about Marshal?"

The Pursuit

"We've got some trouble heading this way from Sweetwater. I believe it will be here before Coleman and Savage get back. Right now I think we need to go wake up the judge and fill him in," Stewart said.

"You think we got time to have a cup of coffee first Marshal?" Blair asked.

"Make it fast; I believe we could all use a cup. It might thaw out my shooting hand," Stewart said as he poured himself a tin cup. The coffee wasn't exactly hot yet but anything above freezing was a bonus.

At a quarter till five Judge Thurman Preston was roused from a sound sleep by a knock at the door. He must have slept through the first series of knocks because the one that finally woke him was vicious.

Preston went to the door in his stocking feet holding a candle in one hand and a loaded thirty-eight in the other. He yanked the door open with every intention of giving someone a good cussing until he saw it was Cecil.

"Cecil Spriggs, what on earth are you doing out at this time of night?" Preston asked.

"It ain't night Judge, it's morning. I got Marshal Stewart with me and he needs to talk to you, says it's urgent."

Preston stuck his head out the door and saw at least four other men standing on his front porch. "Why come on in gentlemen," Preston said as he stepped back to allow the men in."

The judge led the five to his study where he told each to take a seat. Stewart was amazed that there were enough chairs for the five men, there were still a couple more that weren't needed. Preston quickly stoked the fire in the study and then added a couple of pieces of wood. He then went around the room lighting numerous kerosene lamps. When he was finished the room was nearly as well-lit as if it was noon and the sun was shining. The judge found that as the years began to pile up he needed more light in order to enjoy his favorite pastime, reading. When finished he took a chair himself and looked at Stewart.

"Well Marshal, what is it you want to talk about?"

"Judge, me and these men here just came from a town up north called Sweetwater, you ever hear of it?"

Preston took on a serious look. "I have, as a matter of fact Mister Blair sitting there has been gathering information for me for some time now. I suspect you believe something in Sweetwater isn't as it would seem?"

"That's exactly what I wanted to tell you, among other things. I didn't realize you and Blair knew each other though," Stewart said as he looked at Blair.

"We do, as a matter of fact I've known Gene for a number of years. His path and mine have crossed on numerous occasions. As you know, he is a surveyor and does title work in the territory. He came to me a few months ago and outlined some activities in the area that deal with the transfer of land from honest hardworking men and women to two different railroads that are planning expansions in the area," Preston said as he rubbed his hands together, his study was cold.

"Would those expansions also include theft of proceeds that should be going to the original landowners?" Stewart asked.

"That's part of it. There is also the matter of an old crime that has reared its ugly head again. Did you ever hear of a man by the name of Lloyd Shafer?" Preston asked.

Stewart took his eyes off the flames dancing in the fireplace and looked at the judge. "The man that was sentenced to die a few years back, I believe it was for the murder of a number of men, and something to do with a land scheme." Stewart had arrived in the territory after that little episode and wasn't familiar with all the particulars.

"That's right. I held his trial here in Rapid City; he was found guilty by twelve honest jurors from right here in the city. Shortly before his execution was to be carried out he managed to escape with the help of some hired guns. I lost two of my bailiffs to those men.

"We decided to keep Shafer in the basement of the courthouse rather than the regular jail. The basement was the original jail for Rapid City before we built the new one Sheriff Coleman uses now. It's a solid affair and we felt, due to the notoriety of the crime, he would be safer in the courthouse than in the town jail. Anyway, he was busted out by at least six men and in doing so they killed the two bailiff's we had guarding him that night. He hasn't been seen or heard from since," Preston told the marshal.

After a moment's thought Stewart thought of something that might be relevant to the discussion, "The person that runs Sweetwater is a man by the name of Norman Fowler. He lives in a mansion on the hill directly above the town with a commanding view of the area. Ellsworth and I were invited there for a meal and got to meet with Fowler."

This information intrigued the judge. "You got to meet him. I have been aware of this man named Fowler but could never get any information on what he looks like or what type of fellow he is. Tell me what you know Marshal," Preston said.

"Well, he is above average height, a few inches over six feet I would imagine. He seems to be a powerfully built man and would be, I believe, a capable adversary if not for his handicap."

Preston's eyes lit up. "Handicap, what sort of handicap?"

"Well, he is crippled to a degree. His left leg was crippled in some sort of accident he told us."

Preston leaned forward in his chair. "Was the injury above the knee or below? Think hard Marshal, this information is crucial."

"Below the knee I believe. There is no way of really knowing but the way he carried himself I think either his left foot or his left ankle are damaged to a degree. It could even be both. What's your opinion Ellsworth?"

Ellsworth looked to be deep in thought, he was thinking of the meal and the conversation afterward that the two had experienced at the mansion. "It would be below the knee. As the marshal said, it was probably either the foot or the ankle of the left leg."

Preston was deep in though when Stewart spoke up. "Judge, the reason I needed to speak to you at such an early hour is to warn you that your life may be in danger. The four of us just came from Sweetwater, as I just mentioned, and while there we heard some men might be on their way here to do you and Marshal Savage harm. We ourselves barely escaped with our lives and I feel the threat against you and the marshal is credible."

Preston got up and went to a cabinet and pulled out a bottle of whiskey. He placed it on his substantial desk and then from the same cabinet grabbed six glasses. As the judge poured a liberal amount into each glass he said, "I think the six of us can finish this bottle off before we go for breakfast. I hope you like Old Grand-Dad, it's my favorite."

As he reached a glass to Cecil he said, "I reckon you're on duty Cecil. Consider this a brace against the cold outside and let's just keep this one glass of bourbon to ourselves. The last thing I need is a tongue lashing from Sheriff Coleman about giving one of his deputies a drink."

Cecil gladly took the drink and told the judge, "Thank you kindly Judge and you can count on me to keep my mouth shut."

The men each took a sip; Preston smacked his lips in satisfaction while the other men thought their tongues were going to catch on fire. Old Grand-Dad was a powerful drink that the judge had grown accustomed to, the other men not so much.

As they sat and sipped their drinks the big grandfather clock Preston had in his front parlor sounded quarter till six. "I believe the Lolli Pop opens at six-thirty. You men sit here while I go shave and get dressed. The six of us are then going to go and have us a good breakfast. If assassins are about then we will put up the good fight if our stomachs are full."

Cecil looked uncomfortable at the suggestion of breakfast at the Lolli Pop and this didn't go unnoticed by the judge. "Cecil, I believe this meal will be my treat, how does that sound?"

Cecil broke into a big smile. Preston knew the two deputies for the town of Rapid City didn't make much money and anytime he could he bought the two a meal.

Thirty minutes later the judge was clean shaven and dressed. Just before heading out the door he put on his hat and a heavy coat. The walk to the Lolli Pop was a little over fifteen minutes and they got there shortly after the place had opened. The inside was well lit and cheery, it was also warm.

The judge led the five men to the biggest table in the room, it was round and was circled by eight chairs of which only six were needed. No sooner had the men got seated than a lady approached carrying a tray that held cups and a coffeepot.

"Morning Judge, you are out early this morning. Would any of you gentlemen like coffee this morning?"

All six men indicated they did. The lady quickly filled six cups from the oversized pot and then asked, "What will it be?"

"Just bring us six of your breakfast specials Marsha. I believe another pot of coffee is in order too," Preston told her. "We got some business to attend to this morning, will the special take very long?"

"The special is the fastest thing we've got so I'll have it out in a few minutes," Marsha said as she headed for the kitchen.

Everyone at the table took a sip of their coffee, everyone except Preston. He grabbed the container that held the sugar and put two heaping spoonfuls in his cup. He then picked up a small white porcelain pot that sat in the center of the table and finished filling his cup to the top with cream. Stewart noticed Marsha had filled everyone's cups nearly to the top but she had only filled the judge's cup halfway. It was evident Marsha knew the judge liked a little coffee with his cream and sugar.

As the men sipped their coffee Marsha and another woman came from the back carrying plates of steaming food. Five minutes later and each man sat facing a platter of scrambled eggs and country sausage. Each also had biscuits and gravy. Cecil didn't wait for a blessing to be said; he just lit right in as if he hadn't eaten in a week. Preston watched as the other four men also ate as if they were famished.

"Sorry Judge, but me and the boys here ain't had anything in the last two days but a few trout fillets and creek water. I don't remember when I've ever been this hungry," Stewart said.

Preston laughed, "That's perfectly alright Marshal. You men get your fill while you finish telling me the story about

The Pursuit

Sweetwater. In particular anything you remember about this Norman Fowler."

"Well Judge, there ain't much more to tell other than after we talked a bit he pretty much threw us out of his house. We were brought there in a buggy but weren't offered the same courtesy on the way back down, we had to walk to town, dodging bullets the entire way. Oh, and one more thing, this Fowler must have liked his mansion a lot because he gave it a name," Stewart said.

"I've known a few men to name their spreads but I don't ever recall anyone naming their house, what was it called?" Preston asked.

"That's the thing Judge, it was a crazy sounding name, he called it *Refahs*," Stewart told the judge.

"That is odd, how was it spelled?"

"*R e f a h s* Judge, I can't ever remember hearing that name before."

As the men ate Preston put down his fork and thought about what he was just told. He pulled a pencil and paper from his pocket and placed them on the table. Stewart could see the judge carried the two so he could write down notes as they came to mind.

Preston wrote the name on the paper and sat there looking at the letters. The more he looked the more he thought the name should make sense in some way. Finally, he picked up the paper and walked to a small picture that was actually just a mirror with flowers etched into the glass. Preston held the paper up as he looked at the reflection in the mirror.

Preston stood there looking at the mirror as a look of surprise came upon his face. "Marshal come here, hurry."

Stewart got up and hurried to where the judge stood. "Look in the mirror Marshal and tell me what you see."

Stewart turned his gaze to the glass and looked at the reflection. The paper Preston held up had a name that was now recognizable.

"Shafer, it spells Shafer," Stewart said.

Preston walked back to the table in deep thought. "You say men are on their way to Rapid City with the intent of doing harm to me and Marshal Savage. At first I couldn't figure out who hated me and the marshal bad enough to send that many men more than a hundred miles to kill the two of us. Sure, I have sentenced men to prison over the years and I believe there are a number of them that would wish me ill fortune.

"If the man you met was truly Lloyd Shafer, and I now have no reason to doubt you, then he is probably the only man that possesses both the hate and the money to try and pull something like this off."

Stewart sat down and looked at the men around the table, most were nearly finished with their meals. "Judge, this man is Raymond Ellsworth and I would like you to authorize him to be deputized. I have only known the man a few days but in that time he has proven himself to be reputable and also brave. I don't think we have much time and I believe we could use his help."

Preston looked at Ellsworth and said, "If the marshal speaks that highly of you then that is all I need to know."

Preston looked at Allen and then asked the marshal, "What about this fellow?"

"His name is Jess Allen; I don't know that much about him. So far he has been a great help in getting us out of Sweetwater and here in one piece. I wouldn't be opposed to having him wearing a badge for the time being either," Stewart said.

There was no one else in the restaurant, probably due to the early hour and the cold temperatures so Preston decided to do a swearing in right there over plates of biscuits and scrambled eggs. He had both men raise their right hands and swear to uphold the law as to the best of their abilities. They both agreed, he then announced them deputies for the city and the territory.

"Ellsworth, head over to that front window and keep an eye on the street. You know what to look for. Cecil, do you have any extra guns and ammunition at the sheriff's office," Stewart asked.

"I sure do Marshal. Sheriff Coleman has got anything you need over there under lock and key. After the troubles from a few years back the town gave him pretty much anything he asked for."

"Alright then, Judge I believe you need to stay close to me and these men here. We'll head over and see what kind of weapons the sheriff has and arm everyone. I doubt this is going to be a job for Colts, I think Greeners and Winchesters are what's needed," Stewart said.

Preston stepped to the door that led to the kitchen and saw Marsha. "I'm sorry dear but me and these men must leave. Have a bill tallied up and I'll stop back by and settle up this afternoon," After a little thought he decided if men were out to kill him he might never make it back. "On second thought Marsha, put the meals down to the sheriff's account. I'll mention it to him this afternoon."

Ellsworth looked from the window, "Marshal, we got six riders coming down the street."

Stewart and Cecil ran to the window and peered out. Six men, each bundled against the cold, were coming down Main Street, each was heavily armed.

"Everyone step back from the windows and let them pass. Once they're gone we make our way to the jail," Stewart said.

Judge Preston stepped to the window and peered out, he wanted to see what the men looked like. "You might want to step back Judge. We don't know if this is some of the men from Sweetwater or not," Ellsworth said. Stewart was impressed that the man wasn't intimidated by the fact that he had just given orders to a judge.

"As soon as they round the end of the street we'll head over to the sheriff's office," Stewart said.

Preston instinctively patted his shoulder, the same shoulder where he usually carried his hidden holster and the thirty-eight Smith and Wesson he'd purchased a few years back.

"I really wish I had brought my gun with me this morning," Preston said.

"You got a gun Judge? I figured you did most of your threatening with a gavel," Cecil said as he stepped back to the window.

"Sure I got a gun Cecil, don't you remember? It's the one I had pointed at your nose when you were pounding hell out of my front door this morning."

Cecil sniggered, "You do know which end the bullet comes out of don't you Judge?"

Preston just snorted. Stewart figured the two had a history and weren't above some good natured ribbing. Funny how men that are looking down the wrong end of trouble can kid each other at a time like this.

"All right, it looks like they are out of sight. The jail is across the street and two doors down. When I say move we all head that way at a run. I don't like being on the street with just a Colt. After we get some long rifles then we can return fire with confidence," Stewart said.

The Pursuit

Stewart gave the street one more look and then ordered the men to move. One minute later and all six were in the sheriff's office. Cecil pulled a key from his vest pocket and unlocked the big gun case that sat behind the sheriff's desk.

Five minutes after they entered the office all the men were armed to the teeth. Even Blair was given a scattergun. He was offered a Winchester but said his eyesight was more suited to a Greener.

"What do you plan on doing Marshal? We don't know if those men were the ones from Sweetwater or not," Preston said.

Stewart had a problem. The men couldn't just wander the streets knowing men were about that wanted trouble. They couldn't just stay holed up in the jail all day either.

"Preston, I think you and Blair should stay here and keep the door locked. Don't open it to anyone, not even if you know em. I think me and the deputies here are going to go and have a little talk with the six strangers that just rode in."

"Where do you think they were heading?" Blair asked.

"The last we saw of them they were headed in the general direction of the livery. We got four horses tied up out front and they need to be stabled and fed. We'll lead the four horses in that direction. I'd feel better on foot if I needed to use my gun anyway. Horse just throws off my aim.

"Remember the both of you, don't open this door. Keep your eyes and ears open for any sign of trouble," Stewart told Blair and Preston.

"Don't you worry about me and Blair, this jail is built like a fort," Preston said as he filled the coffeepot. "The both of us will be nice and warm in here sipping hot coffee. By the way Cecil, where does the sheriff keep the sugar?"

Nathan Wright

"Cecil, does the sheriff have any extra badges lying around?" Stewart asked.

Cecil went back to the gun case and grabbed two tin stars; he tossed one each to Ellsworth and Allen.

"Alright, lets each grab the reins of a horse and head to the livery. Keep your eyes open and don't bunch up. We spread out five yards apart. I'll take the lead and Cecil you bring up the rear," Stewart said.

Ten minutes later and the four men were within sight of the livery. There were six horses tied out front but there was no sign of the riders.

"Listen up, I got a new plan. Let's tie these horses to that hitch rail over there. Cecil, you stay back and make sure no one slips up behind us. The rest of us are going to ease up to Fitch's and see what we can see." Stewart was more comfortable with Cecil watching the men's back than the other two. He still didn't know how Allen, or Ellsworth, would react if bullets started flying. He knew Cecil was experienced and that was why he always had him bring up the rear.

With the horses secure and Cecil positioned to cover the others Stewart eased toward the livery using the utmost caution. They were on a street that didn't go directly in front of the livery and this allowed the three to make it there without being seen from either the big open door or the tiny window that faced the front street from the office.

"Ellsworth, you and Allen stay here and keep me covered until I can see if they're in the livery or not," Stewart told the two.

With three men now watching his back the marshal could concentrate on what was going on in the livery. As he got closer he could hear men talking, they were actually shouting.

The Pursuit

When he got to the edge of the big front door he could hear the conversation and it didn't sound good.

"I'll explain it to you one more time liveryman. We got horses outside and we want them brought in and stabled, and I don't mean later I mean now," one of the men in the stable said.

Stewart assumed the six wanted their horses brought in off the street and out of sight. The man doing the talking was using words and a tone that meant he probably was accustomed to giving orders and getting his way.

"Now before you start with the horses I need some information and this ain't to be shared with anyone that's not in this building right now, do you understand me liveryman?"

"I understand you mister, I also understand you can take them damn horses of yours and shove them up your bossy ass. Naw, on second thought, I wouldn't do a horse that way," the man said. No doubt it was Lester Fitch.

Stewart knew things were getting ready to spiral out of hand. He turned and motioned for the other three men to hurry on over.

"Well that is real funny liveryman. Before I beat the living hell out of you I need some information. Where would I find two men by the name of Thurman Preston and Pete Savage?"

This was all Stewart needed to hear. These men were from Sweetwater and they were looking for the judge and the marshal.

"Alright, when I give the signal we'll step from cover and challenge the men in the livery. There are six of them but we have the advantage of surprise on our side," Stewart whispered.

Just as the man doing all the talking demanded to know where the judge and the marshal could be found a second time Stewart gave the signal and all four men stepped across the front opening of the livery. The six men were all facing toward the inside of the building and didn't see Stewart and his men until it was too late.

"Say liveryman, you got room for another horse?" Stewart asked matter of factly. His voice was calm and what a man might use if he didn't realize there was trouble about.

Each of the six men in the livery turned to see four men wearing badges and holding Winchester rifles and Greener shotguns on them. Not one of the six spoke, the marshal had the drop on them and there wasn't a damn thing they could do about it.

Stewart stepped into the livery. "Put your hands in the air, anyone reaches for a gun won't live long enough to clear leather."

The six reluctantly put their hands in the air.

"Allen, how about you taking their guns while I ask a few questions," Stewart said.

"Be my sincere pleasure Marshal," Allen replied.

Allen searched each man; He removed six Colts and four derringers. The last man he checked had a five shot Smith tucked away in one of those rare shoulder rigs that kept the gun close at hand but well hidden.

"Got em all Marshal," Allen said as he placed the last of the guns on a side table in the livery's office.

"You men follow me to the jail, I don't intend for this to take all day so step it up," the marshal said.

"Now hold on there Marshal. I don't believe you can arrest us, we ain't broken no laws in this town."

"Didn't say I was arresting you, I said to follow me to the jail. Now move your ass before my hand slips off this Greener." Stewart didn't have the shotgun cocked but the way he held his hand the men might have thought so.

The Pursuit

There wasn't any more talking as the ten men walked to the jail. Before leaving Stewart told Lester Fitch, the livery's owner, to stable his four horses and also the six the other men just rode in on.

"Looks like Stewart has got all the men that rode in earlier heading this way Judge. I believe they're all under arrest, looks like each has an empty holster," Blair said.

Preston looked out the window and sure enough the six riders were heading toward the jail, followed by Stewart and the three deputies.

"Better open the door when they get here Blair. And keep your gun trained on them as they walk in. I won't trust these strangers until they are locked up nice and safe in the back," Preston said.

When Stewart got to the front door Blair swung it open, he was holding a Colt and gave the six men a once over as they walked in. He was trying to see if he recognized any of the men. He recognized two from his survey days working out in the territory. The two men recognized Blair and knew he was one of the men their boss wanted found and eliminated.

"Put them in the back, two to a cell," Stewart said as he grabbed the ring of keys from behind the sheriff's desk and tossed them to Cecil.

As the six were being led to the back Stewart grabbed one of the men and told him to wait. It was the one that was being so unruly to Lester Fitch.

After the other five were in the back and Cecil was determining which cells he wanted each man to occupy, Stewart closed the door that separated the cells from the sheriff's office. He went to the coffee pot and poured a cup. He then pointed to a chair opposite the desk and told the man to sit down as he reached him the coffee.

"This might warm you a little while I ask you a couple of questions," Stewart said.

The man sat and took the coffee. "What do you intend to do with us Marshal? As I said we ain't broke any laws in this town," the man said.

"I believe I told you I was going to ask the questions, not you, now shut up and listen. You and the five men you rode in with, what is your business in Rapid City?"

"I don't have to tell you that. What's our business is just that, our business."

Stewart nodded at Ellsworth who was standing right behind the man. Ellsworth stepped in front of the man and reached for his coffee cup, the man gave it to him. Ellsworth gently sat the cup on the edge of the desk and without any warning he balled a fist and knocked the man backwards out of the chair. Blair and Preston helped him to his feet and put him back in the chair. Ellsworth picked up the coffee cup and reached it back to the man.

Stewart then repeated himself in the same tone he used before. "You and the five men you rode in with, what is your business in Rapid City?"

The man held the cup in a shaky hand. He eased it to his busted lips and slowly took a sip. "I work for a man up north of here, his name is Norman Fowler. He sent us here to get some information on a few people." The man slowly took another sip of his coffee.

"Is information all you were supposed to gather while in town or were you to act on the information once you got it?" Stewart asked.

"If I help you will this mean you are going to use what I tell you against me? I mean, I know what is supposed to happen but if I say anything then I'm just cutting my own throat."

The Pursuit

Stewart nodded at Ellsworth again. Ellsworth stepped in front of the chair again and reached for the coffee cup. The man held up a hand, "Don't hit me again mister. I'm trying to help but if I do then what guarantee do I have that I'm not shooting myself in the foot."

Ellsworth just looked at the man. "Cutting your own throat or shooting yourself in the foot might not be necessary because I will gladly do it for you."

The man took his eyes off Ellsworth and looked at Stewart. "My name is McCaga Nolen. I've been working for Mister Fowler for a couple of years now. If you can help me stay out of jail then I can tell you a lot about what is going to happen here."

Stewart nodded to Ellsworth again and again he balled a fist and knocked the man out of his chair. This time though, he didn't ask for the coffee cup. Nolen hit the floor for the second time but with the added bonus of hot coffee splattering him from head to toe.

Blair and Preston stepped over and righted the chair and then helped Nolen up again. As they sat Nolen back down he looked at Ellsworth and said, "I'd appreciate it if you wouldn't hit me again."

"Then you tell the marshal everything you know about what you and your friends are doing in Rapid City."

Nolen wiped coffee from his face with the sleeve of his coat. His lip bled and the left side of his jaw was swelling, the man had had enough. Stewart now felt Nolen had been softened up enough to possibly make a deal.

"Tell you what Nolen, if you tell me everything you know and I find that what you're telling me is honest and sincere then I will talk to the judge and see what kind of deal he might make with you for your cooperation," Stewart said.

"Alright, but how do I know after I tell you what you want to know you won't double-cross me and not tell the judge?" Nolen asked the marshal.

"Because the judge is standing right behind you Nolen, he's one of the men that put you back in your seat."

Nolen twisted in his chair and looked at the man Stewart pointed at. "So you're Thurman Preston?"

"That's right, now tell the marshal what he needs to know and tell him quick. Somehow I feel that time ain't exactly on our side right now."

Nolen turned back to the marshal. "What do you want to know Marshal?"

"First of all, why were you asking about Judge Preston and Marshal Savage?"

Nolen looked down at his shoes as he said, "Me and the five you got locked up in the back were sent in search of two men by the name of Patrick O'Malley, who goes by Pom, and Eli Dobbs. They are both extremely dangerous men. It's believed they killed a man by the name of Dorian Matus a few weeks back."

Preston stepped in front of where the man sat and asked, "I know of this Dorian Matus death but it was ruled accidental. I believe he worked for a detective agency."

"He did at that, Fowler has information that would implicate Eli and Pom in the death of Matus, at least that's what he told me. We were told to hunt the two down and return them to Sweetwater."

"If that is the case then explain why the five of you were asking about Preston and Savage," Stewart demanded.

"In our attempts to find Eli and Pom I regret to say that we have failed. If we couldn't find the two we were instructed to

The Pursuit

go to Rapid City and assist the four men sent here looking for the judge and the marshal."

"What were you to do when you found Judge Preston and Marshal Savage?" Stewart asked.

"Verify they are both in town and monitor their activities until the other four men got here. That's all we were supposed to do Marshal, I swear."

Stewart doubted the six men were in town to follow a judge and a marshal around just so they could report back to another group of men when they arrived. "What was to happen when these other men arrived and you gave them the information you obtained?"

"We were to continue our search for Eli and Pom. If we were unsuccessful in our attempts to find them we were to head back to Sweetwater in a few days."

"I guess that explains why you are here but it doesn't tell us what the four men are to do once you tell them what you know," Stewart said.

"I don't know what the four were to do after we left town," Nolen said to the marshal. It was a lie; he knew Preston and Savage were to be killed.

Preston got in the man's face, "Is that all you know because if I find out there's more and you withheld the information then I can guarantee you will spend the better part of your remaining days on this earth behind bars. Now think real hard because my patience is growing thin."

Nolen looked at the judge and then the marshal and decided he better mention one more thing. "There are seven other men from Sweetwater heading this way. They are led by a man by the name of Patterson Hartman. Hartman is Fowler's right hand man, so to speak. They are looking for a man by the name of Gene Blair."

Stewart and Preston didn't look at Blair directly not wanting to draw attention to the man. It was apparent Nolen didn't recognize Blair.

"Why are they looking for Blair and what are they going to do when they find him," Preston asked.

Nolen knew Blair was to be killed but not before he gave up the information pertaining to the hidden hundred and fifty thousand dollars, there was no way he was going to admit to that.

"I was never made aware of their plans, only that he was to be found," Nolen had just told his second lie in less than a minute.

Preston walked to the window and looked out onto the street. "Sounds like we got eleven more men heading this way Marshal, that makes a total of seventeen men sent to Rapid City and this son of a bitch says they are all coming here just to talk. Lock this bastard up and let's figure out what our next move is going to be."

"Now wait a minute Judge, me and you had us a deal," Nolen shouted.

Stewart nodded at Ellsworth again. What took place next surprised Nolen even more than the two times he had been struck in the face. Ellsworth stepped up behind the sitting man and wrapped his arm around the man's throat. He then manhandled him out of the chair and pulled him backwards toward the jail room door. Cecil yanked the heavy door open and then quickly unlocked one of the cells in the back. Ellsworth kept Nolen off balance the entire way back and once he was at the open cell door he shoved him inside. Cecil slammed the door shut and then locked it.

"You lying sack of shit. If I hear another word from you then I'll finish what I started out front," Ellsworth said as he pointed at the man. Nolen knew his efforts to hide the attempted murders had failed to convince anyone.

Cecil and Ellsworth walked back out front and sat down. Ellsworth was mad as hell and couldn't hide it from anyone. He knew a lot of men were headed toward Rapid City and probably couldn't be dealt with as luckily as the six now locked up in the back.

Marshal Pete Savage trotted his horse along as he scanned the four riders in the distance. With him were Sheriff Avery Coleman and Deputy Bill Adkins. "What do you make of those riders Marshal?" Bill asked.

"Looks like they're hunting someone, each have a Winchester across their saddles," Savage said.

"That's the same way I see it Marshal. It looks like they are heading the same way we are, toward Rapid City," Coleman said.

"Where you reckon they're from, looks like they're riding out of the north? I don't believe there's a town in that direction for over a hundred miles," Bill said.

"You're right Deputy. Ain't nothing between here and the badlands except a mud hole by the name of Sweetwater," Savage said.

The three rode on in silence as they eyed the group of riders. The distance between the two groups was diminishing. "It looks like they're heading this way Marshal," Bill said.

"Better pull our long guns. I don't like the idea of facing a group of riders that have Winchesters in their laps," Savage said.

The four riders Savage had spotted were Dietrich and the three Baldwin men that had agreed to ride to Rapid City and kill the judge and the marshal down there. Little did they realize they were now within a thousand yards of one of the men they were searching for.

"Stay sharp men. We don't want to get caught off guard out here. It looks like the one on the right is wearing a marshal's badge, I believe him to be Savage." Dietrich said as he peered through his collapsible pocket scope. He had been given a good description of the marshal by Hartman. Around fifty years old wearing a cross draw holster and has the look of a hunter. The man Dietrich was looking at through the scope looked more like a predator than a hunter.

When the two groups were no more than fifteen yards apart, Dietrich stopped his men and shouted, "Stop where you are."

Dietrich continued to study the three riders, "That man on the right with the fancy holster rig is Savage. I'll shoot the marshal while you three take out the other two but only when I give the signal," he whispered.

Savage stopped and looked the four men over. No one had raised a rifle to fire yet but he knew that could change quickly. "We better step our horses apart a few feet. Be ready for anything, I don't reckon these four are going to be rolling out any welcome mats."

Dietrich looked hard at the three riders, the man on the left was definitely Savage. "Fire," Dietrich shouted as he brought his rifle up.

The Pursuit

The three lawmen might have been suspecting trouble but didn't think it would escalate to gunplay without at least exchanging a few words.

Savage, Bill, and Coleman, each tapped their horses as they raised their rifles. Each lawman had learned a long time ago that a moving horse in a situation like this was better than one standing still. The movement would probably throw off their aim but it would also affect the aim of the four men that were shooting at them.

Dietrich and his men managed to fire first, their shots hit both Savage and Coleman. Savage was struck in the left hip, the bullet mostly tearing a hole in his trousers but doing little damage. Coleman was struck in the shoulder, the shot taking him out of the saddle. If the horses the men rode hadn't been prompted to move then all three would have suffered serious wounds. As it was Savage and Bill managed to return fire.

The man to the left of Dietrich was hit in the chest by Bill's shot. Dietrich, the man that had commanded the three lawmen to stop and had also shouted the order to fire got the full attention of Savage. The marshal would have wanted a head shot but knew he better go for the chest of the man. His rule of thumb was to always shoot a man six inches under the chin and that is exactly where the bullet hit, it didn't stay there very long though. It exited Dietrich's back, severing his spine in the process. Dietrich hit the ground and didn't move after that, he was dead.

Of the four Baldwin men, two were now dead. The other two quickly ratcheted another round into the breach and fired, both shots missed but only by inches.

Savage and Bill also returned fire; Savage's shot a complete miss, probably due to the fact that he himself had been shot. Bill again found the mark and struck the man he fired at in the side knocking him out of the saddle. The remaining Baldwin man dropped his rifle to the ground and raised his hands.

"Don't shoot, I've had enough," the Baldwin man said as he looked at his three companions lying on the ground near him, only one was still moving.

"Keep your Winchester on that last feller Bill while I check on the sheriff," Savage said as he slid to the ground.

The marshal felt his hip as he headed to where Coleman lay. He could tell the bullet hadn't hit any bone, which was good. There was some blood but by the amount he figured he had just been grazed rather than the much worse entrance and exit wound a direct hit would have caused.

Coleman was trying to get up when Savage made it to where he lay. "Stay down Sheriff, let me take a look at you before you tear something loose. Where did he get you?" There wasn't any visible blood but that didn't mean the man wasn't out of danger.

"In the shoulder, damn if it don't hurt like hell."

Savage had known Coleman for years and this was the first time he remembered hearing the man swear. "Hold on there Sheriff while I look at that wound."

Savage helped Coleman sit up and then eased the jacket from the wounded man. When he unbuttoned the shirt he could see a nice clean hole in the front of the shoulder. When he looked at the back he could see the exit wound.

"Looks like the bullet found a way out Sheriff; can you move your arm at all?"

Coleman lifted his left arm and the look on his face indicated the amount of pain it caused him. "Did it hit bone Savage or can you tell?"

Savage felt around but couldn't tell if what he was feeling was the movement of muscle or bone. The amount of blood wasn't great but any blood loss this far from town could prove bad real quick. "I don't think it hit bone but we best be getting you to town sooner rather than later. If you can stand the cold for a minute I can bandage it up but I'm going to need your shirt to do it. If I can get the bleeding stopped then you can pull your coat back on over the bandage."

"I can stand the cold Marshal, let's make this fast though before anyone else shows up and decides to pull the trigger on us. Say, how did we do anyway, other than me getting shot out of the saddle?"

"I'd say we came out better than we had any right to. We shot three, I don't know how badly. After I get you patched up I'll go check things out."

"How about Bill, did he get hit?" Coleman asked. Bill had been a deputy in Rapid City, and the territory, for a bunch of years and the sheriff would take it hard if he had been shot.

"Didn't get a scratch, he's keeping the four covered while I patch you up. Of the four I believe only one managed to not get shot but I'll know as soon as I get there."

It didn't take the marshal more than five minutes to get Coleman bandaged and his coat back on. "I think your shoulder is going to be okay but I doubt if that shirt is going to make it," Savage said. Coleman chuckled.

When the marshal got back to where Bill stood he slapped the deputy on the back. "What do you say we head over and check things out? Coleman and me believe we best be getting out of here pretty quick. Anyone can sit a horse we'll allow it and if they are injured to badly or dead then we got no choice but to tie them to a saddle," Savage said.

Now that Savage was up and about Bill took his eyes off the four and looked around. "I think getting to Rapid City as soon as possible is about the best idea I've heard ever since these four complete strangers tried to kill me."

Bill and the marshal walked over to where the men lay. After a quick check it was determined two were dead and one was badly injured. The one that hadn't been shot was looking at the three lying on the ground, only one was still breathing.

"Why did you four challenge us Mister?" Savage asked as he scanned the surrounding area.

The man only looked at the marshal. He knew he was in a lot of trouble and didn't know what he should say or shouldn't say for that matter.

Savage limped over to the man and punched him in the ribs with the barrel of his Winchester. "I asked you a question and I want an answer right now."

"We were on our way to Rapid City. My boss, that's him over there lying face down, well, he ordered us to fire on you."

Savage figured he wasn't going to get much from this man, out here in the middle of nothing was probably the wrong place to be questioning anyone anyway.

"Were you four traveling alone or are there more of you out here that might take a shot at us?" Savage asked.

The man looked around, this was all Savage needed to know. He knew if the four had been traveling alone then the man would probably have said so but he didn't. He cast his eyes over the terrain and this told the marshal more men were out there, probably men that would shoot first and talk later.

"Alright mister, you keep your answers to yourself. When we get to town you might feel more talkative but right now I need you to help get these dead men loaded onto their horses. Bill, gather up the mounts and let's get these bodies loaded," Savage said. As Bill and the only survivor headed after the four horses the marshal gathered the dead men's weapons.

The Pursuit

By the time the deputy rounded up the horses the third man had died. It didn't take long to tie the bodies over their saddles and then pull out.

Coleman was helped onto the back of his horse as gently as possible. To the sheriff it felt like they had picked him up and tossed him on.

"How does that shoulder feel Sheriff?" Savage asked.

"It'll feel a lot better after I get a shot or two of whiskey in me."

Bill looked at his boss, "I reckon you earned a shot or two Sheriff. Just don't get all sloppy drunk or Cecil might lock you up in your own jail."

"Bill, you and the sheriff take the lead. The four horses strung together with the dead men and the one that ain't, will follow you while I keep watch on our back trail." Savage looked at the man that had survived, "Let me explain something to you Mister, if you try anything just remember, I would just as soon bring in four dead men as three."

The men moved out and headed for Rapid City. It was getting late and they knew it would be after dark by the time they made it, assuming no more riders started shooting at them.

Stewart and the others had spent the day in the sheriff's office cleaning their guns and inventorying the ammunition. When it began to get dark Ellsworth started worrying about their chances. A straight up fight in daylight was what he preferred. He now wondered if the eleven men heading into town might try to do their mischief in the dark.

"When were you expecting the sheriff back Cecil?"

"After noon was my guess but now I ain't so sure. With what happened here I wonder if the three might have run into a little trouble of their own out there."

Ellsworth walked to the window and peered out as he rolled a smoke in his left hand. Outside it was at least five degrees below freezing, maybe ten. It looked to be a clear night with a nearly full moon; it was going to get colder.

When Ellsworth finished with the tobacco he struck a match on the window sill. No sooner had the match caught than there was a gunshot. Ellsworth was knocked backward, nearly knocking over the potbellied stove in the process. Stewart and Cecil ducked for cover, both drawing their Colts. Cecil crawled to a lamp and extinguished it, the room was mostly dark now other than the little beams of light that leaked from the joints of the stove.

"Check on Ellsworth while I see what's going on," Stewart said.

Allen, Blair, and Judge Preston, were in the back interrogating the six prisoners when they heard the shot. Preston drew the Smith from his shoulder holster as he eased the door open and looked into the front office.

"What happened our there Marshal?" Preston asked.

"Ellsworth's been shot, I don't know how badly he's hit but Cecil is checking. You and Blair better keep your heads down until I can figure out what's going on. Have Allen keep an eye on that back door."

Stewart was at the broken front window and as he eased his head up a shot nearly took his hat off. "You men stay down. Cecil, can you and the judge get Ellsworth to the back where you can check him out. I'll stay out here and return fire once I see who's shooting at us."

The Pursuit

Ellsworth hadn't moved from the time he had been shot. Stewart wondered if the man was dead. Preston and Cecil half carried, half pulled the wounded man through the door that led to the cell room. Once inside Cecil closed the door and looked at the prisoners.

"That's probably some of your friends out there, they shot Ellsworth, might have even killed him. Judge, you and Blair do what you can for him if he's still alive. That cabinet on the back wall has the jail's doctoring supplies. I gotta get back out front and help the marshal." Cecil eased the door open and crawled back out front on his hands and knees.

"You see anything yet Marshal?" No sooner had Cecil asked the question than a thunderous roar of gunfire filled the street. Bullets came through the window and struck the back wall. As both Cecil and Stewart hunkered down both men noticed the door, it was taking most of the shots.

"They're hammering the hell out of that front door Marshal."

"Looks that way, what do you suppose is going on?"

Just as the marshal asked that question one of the iron joints of the door popped loose. "They're trying to break it loose from the hinges," Cecil said.

"If that door fails then we won't have any cover, they can angle a shot in here from either direction," Stewart said as he looked around the room.

"Help me turn that desk on its side. Let's ease around behind it and once we tip it over we can scoot it against the door. That might buy us some time," Stewart said.

It took the two nearly ten minutes to get the desk slid against the front door. No sooner had the door been secured than the last of the hinges popped loose. The amount of punishment the door had taken was impressive.

"Do you figure they were planning to make a run at that door once it fell?" Cecil asked.

"I believe that's exactly what they planned. After they shot that door off its hinges I believe they would have charged in here and killed both of us before heading to the back to release their friends."

"Well, they still might do that because that desk is being chopped to pieces," Cecil said. It was true, the men outside must have had an abundance of ammunition because they continued to hammer away at the door. It was splintered from top to bottom and the desk was now starting to buck with each shot.

Back in the cell room Preston and Blair were tending to Ellsworth while Allen guarded the back door. The bullet looked to have only grazed his head, any more to the left and he would have had a third nostril. They managed to slow the bleeding with some bandages and then put him in an empty cell. "I think he'll be alright, that is if we don't get overrun and killed," Blair said.

Preston didn't like being back here when the fight was taking place out front. He eased the door open and looked around the front room; it looked like a war had taken place. Everything in the room seemed to be splintered by either a bullet or a ricochet.

"Better get back Judge," Cecil said.

Preston tried to make out the two men in the darkness, he finally spotted Stewart and the deputy crouched against the front wall. Every now and then one would fire a shot out the window but didn't dare raise up to do it. Preston knew there wasn't anything he could do out front so he eased back inside the cell room.

The Pursuit

No sooner had the judge got back to safety than the door at the back of the building took a massive hit from something outside. A couple of minutes later and the door shook again.

"What are they trying to do Judge, break down the door," Blair asked.

"That'd be my guess," Preston said as he ran to the back. Just when he got there the door was hit for the third time, the blow knocked the top of the door inward at least six inches. Preston caught a glimpse of what the men were using. It looked like a heavy timber had been placed in a wagon and this was what they were using to batter down the back door.

Just when the wagon was being pushed by four men back at the door Preston fired two shots with his Smith. One of the four yelped and fell to the ground. The other three dropped behind the wagon for cover as Preston loosed another round.

"Ease that front door open and see if Cecil can slide us a Winchester back here," Allen told Blair.

Cecil quickly informed Blair that all the weapons in the gun cabinet had been shot to pieces. As luck would have it the gun case was on a wall directly opposite the front window. All the Winchesters and Greeners looked to have been damaged by rifle fire.

"I figure if we got men in front and back then it's only a matter of time before this building is overtaken. They get in here we're done for," Cecil told the marshal.

No sooner had Cecil spoken than the front of the building took another barrage from the gunman outside. It was apparent they were loading their rifles and then firing them empty.

The top of the front door had now ceased to exist; it was nothing more than splinters. The front wall of the building was made of stone but this offered little help to the men inside.

Shots were coming through both the window and the door giving the two men inside little in the way of cover.

"Cecil, I doubt we can hold out much longer. You head to the back and try to fight your way out along with Preston, Allen, and Blair, while I hold them off out here."

Cecil gave the marshal a sour look. "I believe I'll stay right here. You won't last a minute when those varmints barge in here. Me and you together might be able to make the price they pay a steep one."

"Well I can't fault you for staying Deputy; chances are we won't need to worry about breakfast the way things are looking."

Savage and his men were approaching Rapid City when they heard gunfire. The sound was enough to bring the sheriff around, he had held to his saddle as best as he could, his injured shoulder had managed to sap his energy.

"Is that gunfire Marshal?" the sheriff asked.

"It is, and by the sound it must be some kind of battle." Savage turned his horse and headed back to the prisoner. Once he was beside the other man's horse he pulled his Colt and clubbed the man in the head. He fell from the saddle and didn't move.

"We better head into town and see what's going on. Coleman, I didn't want to leave you here with that bad shoulder of yours to guard that man by yourself. I thought it best to knock the son of a bitch out, he won't cause you any trouble until we get back," Savage said.

Coleman straightened in his saddle and pulled his Colt. "He ain't going to give me no trouble because I'm going with you.

The Pursuit

Three of us riding into trouble is a sight better than two. We better hurry."

Bill and the marshal admired the sheriff's spunk but wondered how he would hold out in a fight. As the three approached Main Street they could tell the fight was at the sheriff's office.

"We better tie up and walk the rest of the way, pull your Winchesters," Savage said.

Coleman eased down and reached the reins to Bill. Savage tied his horse, Biscuit, to a hitch rail and then grabbed the reins of the other two horses from Bill.

"You two head across the street and I'll take this side. We move together until we can see who's doing all the shooting," Savage said.

The desk supporting what was left of the heavy front door to the sheriff's office had finally collapsed, the remnants of the door falling on top. "Get ready Cecil, I believe this is it," Stewart said.

Both men had used the time to reload their Colts and then prepared to defend themselves. Neither believed they would live very long now that the front of the building was wide open.

"We got six shots apiece so make every shot count. After that all we can do is use our fists. We won't have time to reload," Cecil said.

Coleman eased down the left boardwalk followed by Bill. Both men could see Savage on the opposite side of the street thanks to the town's kerosene street lamps. Within minutes they could see the sheriff's office, or at least what was left of it.

The front window and the frame it sat in was splintered and gone. Parts of the stone face around the window opening had begun to crumble. The door was nothing but a pile of kindling.

Men could be seen on the other side of the street, the same side Savage was on, shooting long guns from behind hastily built barricades. Savage sprinted across the street to where Bill and Coleman stood.

"Looks like five or six men with Winchesters are blasting the hell out of the sheriff's office. Whoever is inside is either out of ammunition or dead because I haven't heard any return fire. We better step in and help. I'll head back across the street. When I get there we give em hell, and by the way, shoot to kill." With that Savage was gone.

Once he made it across the street safely he took a position behind a porch post and steadied his Winchester, Bill and Coleman did the same.

As soon as Savage lined up a shot he pulled the trigger and then ratcheted shell after shell, pulling the trigger each time. Coleman and Bill did the same. Three fully loaded Winchesters fired over and over from a flanking position ended the battle for the front of the jail within seconds.

Cecil and Stewart heard the shots from up the street and first thought someone had taken an angle to try to clear the front room of jail. When they noticed none of the bullets were hitting the building they both eased up to get a look at what was happening. Across the street Cecil saw one of the attackers rise up to shoot at someone, he used the opportunity to shoot the man. Soon another did the same and Stewart shot him. Seconds later and the street grew quiet.

"I see three men walking down the street Marshal, I believe it's the sheriff," Cecil said.

The Pursuit

Stewart and Cecil couldn't get through the door because of all the debris so they simply stepped through the window opening. Both eased across the street as the three other lawmen advanced down the two boardwalks. What they found opposite the jail was five men, all dead.

"Sheriff, am I glad to see you," Cecil said.

Coleman nodded and then promptly collapsed. His wound, and the exertion and excitement of the gun battle, had finally taken their toll, he had passed out.

"Bill, go get the doc," Savage said.

Stewart and Cecil looked back at the jail, it was a mess. "There's some other men trying to batter down the back door; my guess is when they heard all the shooting out front they lit out. We better head back there and check it out," Cecil said.

As Cecil and Stewart went back through the front of the jail Savage stomped around the side as he reloaded his Winchester. He was in a killing mood.

All they found out back was a single man lying against a water trough, he was wounded and unconscious. The wagon was still there along with the timber the men used to try and batter down the back door.

"Get this man inside, we'll have the doc look him over after he sees to the sheriff," Savage said. He was disappointed there was no one out back he could shoot; it would have helped his disposition.

As the town began to realize the battle was over some of the men came out to see if they could lend a hand. Although it was nearly midnight men began grabbing brooms and shovels to clean up the mess. Two men were sent to each end of the street to provide cover in case anyone else decided to cause any more trouble tonight.

Nathan Wright

Coleman was carried on a stretcher to the doctor's house by four of the stoutest men in the crowd. He would be there for a few days where he could be looked after and made comfortable. Bill made sure the wounded sheriff got the two drinks of whiskey he'd mentioned earlier.

The wounded man behind the jail wasn't afforded such luxury. He was carried in and placed in one of the few remaining cells. His wound had stopped bleeding and he had come to. Cecil assured him the doctor would be over as soon as he saw to the town's sheriff.

Ellsworth regained consciousness shortly after the last of the gunfire had ended. His head was heavily bandaged and he was disoriented; there was one thing he could really use at a time like this. "Would someone please bring me a bottle of whiskey, just the bottle, I won't need a glass." he hollered. He wanted to get drunk and pass out, hopefully not to sober up until the pain had gone away.

After the doctor had cleaned and dressed Coleman's wound he headed over to the jail.

A couple of lanterns had been hung out on the boardwalk and along with the streetlamps the extent of the damage could now be seen. It looked like something from back in the days of the war.

At least ten men were helping load the five bodies onto a wagon. The man that did the burying for the town of Rapid City was there and he wasn't happy, he didn't want the job of undertaker but had inherited it from his father. Now he was looking at more death than he had ever seen at one time.

The front window couldn't be replaced until a new pane of glass was delivered so the next best thing was used to seal the opening, wood. Three men that were handy with tools quickly built a makeshift door and stood it in place. Two rusty hinges

The Pursuit

were brought from the blacksmith's shop and before long the front room of the jail was again warm and the smell of hot coffee filled the air.

Cecil and Bill had been sent to bring in the three dead men and the lone survivor Savage had knocked out earlier. It was looking like the jail and the cemetery were doing a booming business tonight.

The wounded man from the gun battle out back of the jail was seen by the doctor. Once his wounds were cleaned and patched up Stewart went to work on the man.

"We got five dead men across the street. That makes six men counting you that attacked us a little while ago. How many more are there?"

The man looked up from the cot in the cell he occupied and thought about whether he should answer or not. Savage had listened in and decided he needed information sooner rather than later. He stepped into the cell.

The marshal put his boot on the man's chest and pressed down. With each second the marshal pressed harder. The prisoner's eyes grew wide as he looked at the scariest man he had ever seen in his life. Finally when he couldn't take in another breath he held up a feeble hand. Savage took his foot off the man's chest.

"Answer the question before I crush every rib you've got."

The man took in a deep breath and stuttered, "Only one more, he escaped when the men across the street got killed."

Preston looked at the man and wanted to put his own boot to work. "That's a lie; I saw at least four of you out there trying to push that wagon into the back door."

"Not a lie, there were four but after I got wounded two decided to head back across the street with the others." This satisfied the judge.

"What's the man's name," Savage asked.

"Patterson Hartman," the man said through clenched teeth.

Stewart knew the name. "Do you know which way he was heading?"

"Sweetwater, he was going back to Sweetwater," the man said just before he passed out.

Savage slammed the cell door and walked back to the front office. The temperature had gone from twenty degrees to comfortable once the door and window were patched up. By the time everyone filled a tin coffee cup the pot was empty. Preston added his usual half cup of sugar before taking a sip.

"Savage, there are a few things you need to be caught up on. Number one is we think we know who is behind these attacks," Preston said.

Savage was cold and tired and in no mood for any guessing games. "I trust it's someone we know personally by the way you worded that statement Judge."

"It is; all indications point to Lloyd Shafer and we believe he is in a town up north called Sweetwater."

Savage nearly choked on his coffee, "The hell you say. How soon can we head that way?"

Preston knew Savage hated Shafer nearly as much as he did and wanted nothing more than to bring the outlaw to justice. "We need to give it a few days. Once Coleman and Ellsworth are able to keep law and order in Rapid City we leave. Cecil, Bill, and Marshal Stewart, along with you and me, head north and capture the son of a bitch."

"Why are you going Judge? It's a hard trip, at least four days on horseback," Savage said.

Preston smiled. "When we capture him I plan to hold court and carry out the sentence that was handed down all those

The Pursuit

years ago. We'll hang the son of a bitch in the town he's been hiding in."

Savage knew the judge was right. Shafer had managed to escape justice twice before. The outlaw wasn't a man to be trifled with, find him and hang him was the only way.

Five riders headed up the main street of Sweetwater. The weather had gone full winter in less than twenty-four hours; the men were tired and cold. It had taken nearly five days to make the trip from Rapid City but every frozen mile was going to be worth it.

"See that house on the hill, it's the mansion named *Refahs*," Stewart said. "I believe the man I met there has a complete view of Sweetwater. He apparently knows what goes on in town at any given time. My guess is there's a scope of some sort up there that allows him to keep watch, he's probably looking at us now."

Savage looked the town over; no one was on the boardwalks, no one was outside at all. "I believe everyone is hiding. Let's get straight to it, we'll head to the drive and disarm the two guards you say are there before we approach the mansion."

Savage and the others unsheathed their Winchesters. As they approached the guard shack they were stopped by two men, one held a Greener, the other a Winchester.

Savage announced who he was and why he was there. The two guards might have been impressed with the fact that Savage was a marshal. What really put fear in the two was his appearance and voice. Both men laid down their weapons and started walking back to town.

"Looks like the coast is clear, let's head on up and arrest Mister Norman Fowler, also known as Lloyd Shafer," Preston said.

As the five riders topped the driveway and came into full view of the house they noticed several women running out the front and side doors. Moments later a slight puff of smoke could be seen coming out one of the front windows. The five men stepped from their horses and approached one of the women.

"What's going on in there?" Preston asked.

"There's a fire, I don't know what happened. One moment everything was alright and the next we smelled smoke. The below ground floor is completely aflame," the terrified woman said.

In the few minutes that had gone by the ground level floor became completely engulfed as fire shot from the windows.

"Is everyone out or are there people inside, "Savage asked.

One of the women that came out had been busy counting the survivors. There were now five women and three men, all stood and watched the home that represented their job going up in flames. Savage approached one of the men and asked again if everyone had made it out.

"All the house staff made it out but Mister Fowler is still inside. He is in his upstairs bedroom. I doubt if he can make it out, he's crippled and also suffering from many other ailments. When we noticed the fire I tried to climb the stairs but smoke made it impossible," the man said. He and the other staff were consumed by grief at the tragedy that was taking place right in front of their eyes.

As the fire grew the men knew no one was escaping from the house. Within thirty minutes flames were escaping the roof and already the heavy timbers that held the porch over the front door had collapsed.

Preston and the four lawmen found rooms for the night at a newly opened boarding house. They stabled their horses in the same livery Jess Allen had abandoned only a few short weeks before. It appeared the new owner was an amiable sort that loved to talk. It seemed everyone in Sweetwater now found the need to get out and visit with their neighbors, the cold temperatures notwithstanding.

The next morning it was learned that a single body had been discovered in the burned remains of *Refahs*. No one had a doubt who the body belonged to. Lloyd Shafer, or Norman Fowler as the rest of the town knew him, had finally received the death sentence that had been handed down by Judge Preston years before.

At a little before noon the five men gathered their horses and prepared for the long journey back to Rapid City. Each of the men now felt a measure of relief knowing the notorious outlaw Lloyd Shafer was finally dead, never to haunt the Dakota Territory again.

The noon stage heading for the northern railroad siding was at that time preparing to leave Sweetwater. Today it would carry two men and one woman north to the depot. Just as it was ready to pull out a solitary passenger emerged from the ticket office and hurried to the stage. The driver held the horses as the man, bundled from head to toe against the wind and cold, made his way. It took a little longer than normal for this last passenger to make his way to the waiting carriage, he walked with a noticeable limp.

The End

Made in the USA
Middletown, DE
20 August 2022

71835680R00186